MISSOURI GUNS

LARRY NAMES

EAGAN HILL PUBLISHERS

USA

MISSOURI GUNS
By LARRY NAMES

ISBN-10: 0-910937-58-3
ISBN-13: 978-0-910937-58-0

www.larrynames.com

up here won't be treated so courteously. Now get!"

Creed mounted up and rode away without saying another word, but he was filled with wonder at what Quade had done to upset the old gent. He decided to stop in at the dry-goods store and ask a few questions.

The sign above the porch stated that the establishment was owned by one Josiah Ewing, Esquire. A team of horses hitched to a freight wagon were tied up at the rail out front.

Creed rode up to the store, dismounted, wrapped Nimbus's reins around the rail, stepped up onto the porch, and went inside. He halted just inside the door, allowing his eyes to adjust to the dimmer light, while he unbuttoned his coat because the air inside was stifling.

A woman in her mid-thirties, wearing a heavy coat and a man's hat that was pulled down over her ears, waited at the counter. A man who was about the same age as the lady customer scurried back and forth retrieving canned goods from the shelves. The woman gave Creed a cursory scanning, then resumed watching the clerk fill her order. The clerk also noted Creed's presence with a quick glance.

Creed saw a bar in the rear of the store and started in its direction. As he walked past the woman, he tipped his plainsman to her, nodded, and said, "Good morning, rna'am."

She glanced sideways at him and returned the greeting, although not with the same spirit in which Creed had offered his.

Creed moved on to the bar, put his foot on the rail, and leaned against the bar in such a way that he became quite aware of the Colt's beneath his coat. He bided his time while the clerk finished filling the lady's order.

"Be right with you, sir," said the clerk. "No hurry," said Creed.

The clerk was bald with dark auburn sidewalls and matching mustache, aquiline nose, and eyes that looked like a pair of hazel-nuts set in deep sockets. He was average height, and his belly was beginning to show signs of a middle-age pouch. He wore a leather apron and maroon garter sleeves over a white woolen shirt and black woolen trousers.

"That's everything on your list, Mrs. Bums," said the clerk, placing the last can in a basket on the counter. "Will there be anything else today?"

"No, Mr. Ewing, thank you," said Mrs. Bums. She put her arm through the handle of the basket and started for the door. "Good day, Mr. Ewing."

"Good day, Mrs. Burns," said Ewing. He watched her leave, then put her list in a box beneath the counter where he kept other such lists. He would total up her charges at a later time and add them to her running bill. "Now, sir," he said as he looked up at Creed and started toward the bar, "what may I do for you today?"

Creed put a silver dollar on the bar and said, "You wouldn't happen to have some sweet cider, would you, sir?"

"Absolutely, sir," said Ewing. He took a glass from a rack beneath the bar, set it in front of Creed, then pulled the cork on the cider jug and filled the glass. "That'll be five cents, sir," he said, replacing the cork in the jug.

Creed pushed the cartwheel toward Ewing and said, "Take it out of here."

Ewing made the change from the cash box below the dry-goods counter and put it down in front of Creed. "Saw you over at the post office a little bit ago," he said. "Are you looking for someone?"

"As a matter of fact, I am," said Creed. "I was looking for the Perkins residence."

"Didn't Sam over to the post office tell you where it was?"

"Yes, he did, and I went there."

"Wasn't anybody to home?" asked Ewing.

"Oh, there was someone at home all right," said Creed with a chortle. "An old gentleman came to the door and said he was Mr. Perkins, but he rudely sent me packing at the end of a shotgun."

Ewing laughed and said, "That's Cornelius Perkins all right. Cantankerous old fart, isn't he?"

"You might say that," said Creed with a smile.

"What did you want to see Corny about?" asked Ewing. "If you don't mind me asking, that is."

"I'm looking for some fellows I know. Old friends. One of them is named Marsh Quade. Mr. Perkins said Quade wasn't here, but he refused to tell me where he'd gone."

Ewing laughed again and said, "I don't doubt that. Your friend Quade married Corny's youngest daughter this past fall."

Creed noted the humor in Ewing's tone and said, "I take it they got married without Mr. Perkins's approval."

"You might say that," said Ewing. "You see, Quade and some of his friends got into some trouble with the Yankees last summer. It

To
William
and
E'Lisa
Clay

.

Special Thanks

The author wishes to express special thanks to Sophie Murphey at the Clay County Savings Association Museum in Liberty, Missouri; Frieda Waters of the Clay County Archives in Liberty; Betty Stone of the Kearney, Missouri, Public Library; and Jack Wymore of Liberty who is the world's leading expert on the Liberty Bank Robbery. All of these people made considerable contributions toward the historical accuracy of this book.

Real History

The first peacetime, daylight robbery of a bank in the United States took place on February 13, 1866, when a group of outlaws dressed in Union Army overcoats robbed the Clay County Savings Association in Liberty, Missouri. That notorious event is depicted in this chapter of the life of Slate Creed with as much accuracy as the best authorities on the subject have been able to reveal.

Of course, Jesse and Frank James and all their relatives mentioned in this book were historic persons, as were all the men included herein as gang members. Nearly all of the other people described within these pages were also real people, especially those men who were connected with the Knights of the Golden Circle.

All of the places - the towns, the businesses, the rivers, creeks, valleys, etc., mentioned herein existed at the time of the story. Most important of all, the conditions of life in Missouri during and after the War Between the States are as accurately portrayed as possible. It was not a good time for the brave people of that war-ravaged state.

Prologue

Creed was riding the Louisville & Nashville Rail Road, heading south to Nashville. His left arm was in a sling, which made finding a comfortable sitting position difficult at best. He squirmed in his seat, making the letter from Texada that. he had received that morning crinkle in his coat pocket. He twisted in his seat again and felt the comer of Texada's letter dig into his chest. Heaving a sigh, he took it out and read it for the fifth time that day.

My dearest darling Clete,

I hope this letter finds you in good health and good spirits. I miss you, my darling, and I love you always.

Granny made it through Christmas and the New Year, but she died on the second instant. I know we expected it to happen at any time, but I still cried like a baby. She was the only real parent that I ever knew, Clete. I will miss her terribly. Nearly everybody in Lavaca county came to her funeral. Malinda and Colonel Markham were there, too. She sends her love.

Harlan was the Delchen that you killed in Indianola. Everybody around here was sad to hear that Kent and Clark Reeves had been murdered, but we were just as glad to hear that you killed Harlan in return. Jim Kindred and Farley Delchen brought his body back here to Hallettsville for burial. They testified before a grand jury in Indianola that you shot Harlan in cold blood, and now you are wanted for murder down there. Of course, no charge was made against Kindred or Farley for murdering Kent and Clark because Kindred and Farley claimed that the brothers were resisting arrest and drew down on them first.

Kindred went to Markham and told him that you had gone to New Orleans on a boat, so Markham telegraphed the Army in New Orleans to arrest you when you landed there. I am glad you got away from them there. When Markham heard that you had escaped again, he threw a fit and sent Kindred to New Orleans to hunt for you. Malinda tells me that Markham got a letter from Kindred today saying that he was heading up the Mississippi to look for you because he had heard about a Texan who was running a horse racing meet up in Kentucky.

Please be on the lookout for Kindred, Clete. He is a federal marshal now, and he can go anywhere to arrest you. I hope you finish your business in Kentucky real soon, if you have not already, and that you will continue to pursue Blackburn and the others in Tennessee and that you find them and make them confess the truth about their crime, so you can clear your name.

Jake says all the boys wish you were here because they are not sure what they should do with Double Star Ranch.

It belongs to Jess Tate's brother Matt, if he is still alive. Of course, you know that already. Should they keep working it? Or should they leave it to the state to handle? They want to know.

Please write soon, my darling. I miss you and love you, and I wish you were here with me now. You are all I have now. I love you, my darling. May the good Lord keep you safe until the day when we can be together again.

Your ever loving,

Texada

Creed refolded the letter carefully and replaced it in his coat pocket. He looked wistfully out the window and saw the outskirts of Nashville ahead. He heaved a sigh and thought, Blackburn and the others. I've got to find them, so I can go home once and for all.

1

Jim Kindred had no friends, and he didn't care that he had none. He was a lawman, and that made him somebody special. At least, he thought it did. He was wrong.

Being short made Kindred a man with a chip on his shoulder. Only his chip was the tin badge of a United States deputy marshal. He wore it not with pride, but with arrogance and disdain for anybody with less authority than he had, and that included just about everybody outside of government officials and other federal lawmen. Even to them, he wasn't one to show any proper respect for their positions in the order of things.

The amazing thing about Kindred was how unsuccessful he was at enforcing the law. Ever since the days when he was the Enrollment Officer for the Confederacy in Lavaca County, Texas, he had failed to carry out his duties properly or even completely. He hardly ever caught a draft-dodger, and when he did round up one or two, it was always with lots of help from the county sheriff and the Home Guards, who were sometimes called Heel Flies because they were such pests to just about everybody in the county, especially to the men they were trying to force into joining an army that was fighting a war that they had no desire to fight. The only thing that had separated the draft-dodgers and the deserters from Kindred and the Home Guards when it came to taking a stand on the war was their courage. The dodgers and the deserters had the grit to take a stand, while most of the Guards had joined the local militia to avoid the real fighting. Kindred fit right in with the Heel Flies. He had been one of the first to raise the Confederate flag when Texas seceded from the Union in '61, and as soon as the war was apparently lost, he left the service of the Confederacy and got himself an appointment as a deputy sheriff of Lavaca County.

As the county enrolling officer, Kindred learned that more money could be made under the table than above it. He accepted bribes from those men who were just as eager as he was to stay out of the fighting, but he never seemed to be able to save any of that gold for the future. As a deputy sheriff, collecting the county's taxes, he found the pickings a bit slimmer, so he turned to robbery-highway robbery. He put together a band of outlaws, and he led them in raids on freight wagon trains in neighboring counties. Finally, he was recognized and arrested. He lost his badge, but he was released on bail.

Robbing a few freight wagons wasn't Kindred's worst crime, however. While free on bond, he tried his hand at rustling with the aid of two of Lavaca County's worst menaces, the Detchen brothers, Farley and Harlan, the foster sons of the county's most notorious female, Sophia Campbell.

Kindred and his gang tried to steal a mixed herd that was being driven from Lavaca County to New Orleans. Denton Slater, the young owner of Glengarry Plantation, ramrodded the drive with the help of his older brother, Clete. Jess Tate, the owner of Double Star Ranch and Clete. Slater's best friend, provided all but two of the drovers for the task. The exceptions were Harlan and Farley Detchen. On the trail to Louisiana, the Detchens murdered Jess Tate, threw his body into the Sabine River, then tried to make it look like Tate had met with an accident and had been swept down the river. While Clete Slater was off looking for Tate, the Detchens slipped away from the trail crew and joined Kindred and the rest of the gang. They set up an ambush in Louisiana. Clete Slater returned in time to foil Kindred's raid, but he was too late to save his brother who was fatally wounded by an outlaw bullet.

The murders of his best friend and his brother put Clete Slater on a blood trail. He swore that he wouldn't let their deaths go unavenged. He started his vendetta by hanging the two outlaws that he and the Double Star hands had captured in Louisiana and by hanging another one that they caught up with in Lavaca County. Knowing that Slater was gunning for them, the Detchens hid behind their foster mother's skirts on her ranch. Kindred and his gang thought to escape Slater's wrath by running off to Mexico. Before he could wreak complete vengeance on the Detchens, Kindred, and the other outlaws, Slater was falsely accused and convicted of a crime against the Union army-robbing supply wagons. He was sentenced to hang, but he escaped and rode off to Mexico in pursuit of Kindred and his gang. His own name blackened, Slater assumed a new identity, calling himself Slate Creed.

True to form, Kindred chose the wrong side in the Mexican Civil War, joining the Monarchist forces in Matamoras. Every man in his gang was killed in the fighting. Kindred escaped the Juaristas and found his way back to Lavaca County, where the charges against him for robbing a freight caravan had been dropped.

Colonel Markham, the Federal military commander for the area, wanted to see Clete Slater at the end of a rope, but his hands were tied somewhat because he was married to Slater's sister, Malinda. He needed someone else to do his dirty work. He found the perfect man in Kindred.

Markham arranged to have Kindred appointed a deputy marshal, working for the Army. His assignment was to catch Clete Slater, alias Slate Creed, and see that he became dead.

Kindred relished the task because now he was the hunter instead of the prey. He hired the Detchen brothers to help him find and kill Creed. They learned that Creed had been in Victoria, but that he had left there for Indianola where he Was to take a ship to New Orleans. The three crooked lawmen hurried to the port town, but they were too late. Creed's ship was already churning up the water, headed for the open sea. Angry that he had' gotten away from them, the Detchens murdered his two friends, Kent and Clark Reeves, who were on the dock to see him off. Creed saw his friends die. He ran to his cabin and fetched his rifle. Although the steamer was moving away from his target, he shot and killed Harlan Detchen.

Kindred and Farley Detchen testified before a grand jury that Creed had murdered Harlan Detchen in cold blood and that the Reeves brothers had been resisting arrest when they were shot. Not having any other valid testimony, the grand jury ordered a warrant for Creed's arrest.

Having failed to catch Creed in Texas, Kindred was sent to New Orleans to bring him back, but by the time he arrived in the Crescent City, Creed was long gone, and no one knew where. Kindred wanted to give up the chase then and there, but news that a Texan was getting up a horse-racing meet at a place called Mammoth Cave, Kentucky, dissuaded him from returning to Texas just yet. The lawman learned that Creed had met and befriended a young Kentuckian on the boat to New Orleans and that the youth had been in Texas retrieving his Thoroughbred colt. Kindred added this up and figured that Creed had gone to Kentucky. For once, he was right.

Kindred took the train from New Orleans to Bowling Green, Kentucky. He arrived there on the last day of January, 1866, and while he was waiting to change trains for Glasgow Junction, the terminus for Mammoth Cave, the stationmaster told him that the horse-racing meet had already been held up to Mammoth Cave in Edmondson County on the previous Saturday and Sunday; he was two days late for it.

"I don't give a shit about the races," he said. "I'm looking for a man who might be up there."

Seeing Kindred's badge, the stationmaster said, "Does it have to do with the trouble they had up there on Sunday?"

"What trouble is that?" asked Kindred, curious about the man's question.

"It seems that one of the gamblers was involved in some shooting, and was killed in the Mammoth Cave by the Texan who was running the whole thing."

"Is, that right?" asked Kindred, eyebrows twitching up his forehead. This was good news as far as he was concerned. If Creed was the Texan who had shot the gambler, then it only followed that he was probably in jail right this moment. "Have they got the killer in jail now?"

"I don't know," said the stationmaster. "If he is, he'd be in the jail up to Brownsville. I heard that the Texan was hurt, too. Seems the gambler got him with a knife before he was killed."

"You don't say?" An evil smile spread across Kindred's face.

Creed hurt? This was better news. If the Texan was Creed, that is. There was only one way to make sure. "Where would I find this place, this Brownsville, you mentioned?"

The stationmaster told him how to get there, and before the sun set that afternoon, Kindred was sitting atop a newly bought horse and riding toward Brownsville.

2

Creed didn't tell anyone in Brownsville where he was going when he left Edmondson County. He did tell the Houchin family that he was planning to resume his search for Jack Blackburn and the other men who had implicated him in their robbery of Army supply wagons. Young Scott Houchin guessed that Creed would be heading for Tennessee.

On his previous brief visits to Nashville, Creed hadn't had the opportunity to get to know the city. As far as he knew it was a strategic military location because it was the munitions manufacturing center for the South. Beyond that, his knowledge of the Tennessee capital was limited to the railroad depots.

Creed stepped down from the Louisville & Nashville train and immediately went to the express car in which his horse had made the short trip from Glasgow Junction. Kentucky. He paid a porter to saddle Nimbus in the car, then the railroad worker off-loaded the Appaloosa by walking him down a freight ramp. With great difficulty, Creed swung himself atop the stallion, thanked the man for his help, and rode off toward the center of town to look for a hotel.

Like all the other major cities of the former Confederate States of America, Nashville was an occupied city. Unlike the others, the Tennessee capital had been under Federal control since February, 1862, when Union General Don Carlos Buell marched into the city with 50,000 soldiers, many of whom he garrisoned in the Maxwell House, Nashville's newest hotel. A large part of those original forces were still billeted in the Maxwell and other hostelries throughout the city, making rooms scarce at best.

Riding through the city, Creed couldn't help experiencing an episode of Deja vu. Although on a much larger scale, Nashville reminded him of Victoria, Texas, where he had spent several days just a few months earlier. Soldiers, many of them former slaves, seemed to be on every street comer, standing guard over their former oppressors. Creed wondered whether these negro Yankees were having less trouble with the local populace than the ones in Victoria had. He hoped so.

Creed had no luck finding lodging at any of the hotels, but he was able to locate and rent a room above the Odd Fellows Hall on South Cherry Street. He settled into it, then looked for a stable where he could board Nimbus for the night. He found a livery and smithy in the next block. After seeing that the Appaloosa would be properly tended, he sought a place to eat supper, finding a saloon that served free sandwiches to its drinking customers. Although Creed wasn't much of an imbiber, he did like to whet his appetite with a foamy mug of lager.

Kendrick's Barrel House was beginning to fill up with its regular clientele when Creed entered it. From the looks of the men, most of them were factory workers, and a few were attired like clerks. None of them paid him much attention as he strolled up to the bar.

The bartender was a tall fellow with a bushy black mustache, a balding pate that was covered with wisps of black hair, a long, narrow nose, and dark eyes that were set close together. He served Creed a beer, scooped up the silver dollar that Creed had put down on the bar, and went to get change from a cash box on a lower shelf of the back bar. Turning back to Creed, he put ninety-five cents on the counter. Pointing at the sling around Creed's left arm, he asked, "Is it broken?"

Creed finished his first swallow of beer and said, "No, knife wound."

That raised the bartender's eyebrows. "Knife wound?" he repeated loud enough for several others to hear. "How did it happen?" "Fight," said Creed calmly, noting that the other drinkers near him had inched closer.

"Really?" queried the bartender. "Around here?"

"No," said Creed. He took another pull on his beer, then set the glass down. Glancing around him, he noted how many conversations had ceased and how most ears in the establishment were straining to hear him. "Up in Kentucky," he said finally.

"What was the fight about?" asked the bartender.

"Cheating," said Creed. Realizing that these men seemed starved for a bit of exciting news, he decided not to relate the true tale of how his shoulder came to be injured, choosing instead to make up a story. "The other fellow was a gambler. I caught him cheating at cards and called him on it. He pulled a knife and stuck me with it. I pulled my Colt's and sent him to Hell where he belonged." The only details that rang true were the first and last - Percy McGrath bad been a gambler, and Creed had shot him dead.

But he hadn't done it over a card game. His reasons for killing McGrath were much more complicated than that, but he saw no reason to explain them to this group of strangers.

"Law go after you?" asked a man dressed like a factory hand. "No, it was clearly self-defense," said Creed. "The county sheriff let me go on my way."

"Are you from Kentucky," asked another fellow.

"No, I was just up there on business." said Creed "I'm from Texas."

"What brings you to Nashville?" asked the bartender.

"I'm looking for some old friends of mine who came up here after the war." said Creed.

"Are they Texans, too?" asked the bartender.

"That's right," said Creed. Figuring that there was no time like the present to start his search for the cowards who had blamed him for their crime, he said, "Their names are Jack Blackburn, Dick Spencer, Jasper Johnson, Jonas Burr, Dick Barth, and Marsh Quade. Anybody here know them? "

"Can't say that I do," replied the bartender.

Every other man in the place had the same reaction, which was as much as Creed expected. Nashville was a city of fair size, and unless the men he sought had achieved some notoriety in the area, it was unlikely that they were known to the general populace.

"What business are you in?" asked the factory hand.

"Cattle," said Creed without giving the question any thought.

"Buying or selling?" asked the same fellow.

"I run a spread down in Lavaca County, Texas," said Creed. "When I'm there, that is. It's called the Double Star Ranch." He took another pull on his beer, then asked, "Mind if I help myself to one of those sandwiches?" He nodded at the covered plate of sandwiches on the back bar.

The bartender turned, picked up the plate, removed its glass cover, and offered the food to Creed. "Take two," he said.

And Creed did. He finished the beer, then took a bite of a ham and cheese sandwich.

"You own that ranch down in Texas?" asked the factory hand.

Creed shook his head, swallowed, then said, "No. It belonged to my closest friend until he was murdered last summer while we were driving a herd to New Orleans."

"Murdered, you say? How?" asked the bartender.

Creed hadn't thought about Jess Tate's murder for almost a day now. As the memory of that tragedy passed, the murder of his brother Dent also flashed through his mind. He lowered his eyes and said softly, "If you don't mind, gents, I'd rather leave it at that."

"Sure, mister," said the factory hand.

"Nobody meant to pry," said the bartender.

"It's all right," said Creed. He pulled out another silver dollar, put it down on the bar, and said, "Why don't you set them up for every man in the house, Mr. Bartender?"

"Yes, sir," said the bartender.

Several drinkers saluted Creed as they were served their beers, and he acknowledged each of them with a friendly nod as he finished his two sandwiches. He washed down the last crust of bread with another beer, then headed for the door.

"Say, mister," said the bartender.

Creed stopped as he reached the doorway, turned, and said, "Keep the change."

"That's not it," said barkeeper. "Those friends of yours?"

"Yes, what about them?"

"You might go down to the newspapers and ask about them there," said the saloonkeeper. "Those reporters have a way of keeping tabs on folks around here."

"Thanks," said Creed. "I think that's what I'll do. First thing in the morning."

3

Bob Hazelip didn't like late arrivals at his hotel in
Brownsville. He was already a fairly surly fellow, but he
became more so when some fool carne ringing his bell after
dark, like Jim Kindred did on that last day of January, 1866.

"Something I can do for you, stranger?" asked Hazelip. His thin,
brown eyebrows pinched together over his angular nose as he looked
down on the much shorter man.

Kindred looked Hazelip straight in the eye with a dullness that
disguised his true feelings. He didn't like Hazelip simply because the
innkeeper was taller than he was. He would have disliked the
hotelman if he were only an inch taller than he was, but Hazelip's
height, which allowed him to look down on the top of Kindred's
head, made the slight Texan's instant dislike for Hazelip mutate into a
morbid, psychopathic hatred. He could deal with that, though; he had
a badge, and he didn't mind flashing it, either.

"Cold out," said the deputy evenly as he began unbuttoning his
blue wool coat, starting with the collar and working down.

"Usually is about this time of the year," said Hazelip with every bit
of sarcasm that he could muster.

Kindred finished with his coat, spread the lapels, and revealed his
deputy marshal's shield pinned to his black corduroy vest. He puffed
up his chest, smiled, and said, "Yep, you're right about that. That's
why I came in here. To get out of the cold night and into a warm
bed. You have one, of course."

The badge hardly impressed Hazelip. He frowned and said, "Of
course, I got beds here, Mr. Law Man. The sign outside says this is a
hotel, don't it?"

"Yes, I suppose it does," said Kindred. He glanced around the sparsely furnished room.' Ain't exactly luxurious, is it?"

"You want luxury, mister," snarled Hazelip, "you can go to Louisville or New Orleans or some other place. I provide my customers with clean rooms, clean beds that ain't ticky, and good food that sticks to your ribs, and if you're of a mind to have a drink or two, I got some of the best home-stilled whiskey in these parts." He spun the registration book around for Kindred and added, "Now if that's good enough for you, then you can sign the book, and I'll get you a key." He took a pencil from behind his ear and placed it in the alley of the open book.

"How much?" asked Kindred.

Hazelip jabbed a thumb over his shoulder at a white wooden sign that had the hotel's rates painted on it in red letters. "Just like it says up there," he said. ""Fifty cents a night and ten cents a meal."

Kindred glanced up at the sign, nodded, then looked back at Hazelip and said, "It'll do." He picked up the pencil from the valley of the registry and signed his name and address on the first available line. Replacing the pencil, he said, "In advance, I suppose."

"You suppose right, friend," said Hazelip, taking a little friendlier tone now that he was certain that this diminutive fellow was a real customer. He turned the book around again and read aloud, "James Kindred, Hallettsville, Texas." The innkeeper twisted up his mouth and took a closer look at Kindred's shield. "Deputy marshal, too. Hmm. If you came for the races, you're too late, Mr. Kindred. They were over this past Sunday."

"I don't give a shit about any goddamn races," said Kindred, annoyed with Hazelip. He dug into his pocket and pulled out a silver dollar. He slapped it on the counter and said, "I suppose it's too late to get a hot meal around here."

"Hot, yes," said Hazelip, picking up the cartwheel. "But if you're real hungry, I can make you a sandwich, if you like."

"Sounds good enough to me," said Kindred.

Hazelip retrieved a key for the guest and gave him his change. "Dining room is right through there," he said, pointing to a doorway. "You can have your sandwich in there, or you can have it in the saloon over yonder." He pointed to another doorway. "You tell me."

"I'll have it in the saloon," said Kindred. "I got a horse outside. "He'll need tending. You got a boy to do that for me?"

"Stable's around to the back," said Hazelip. "I'll have your horse looked after for you. Two bits for feeding and boarding him for the night." He picked up a quarter from the change before Kindred could pocket the coins. "Your room is up those stairs over there." He nodded in the direction of the staircase that ran up the wall to the second floor. ·

Kindred picked up his little carpetbag and headed for the steps. At the landing, he stopped, turned back to Hazelip, and said, "I heard there was a fellow Texan running these races you just had up here. Is that true?"

"Could be," said Hazelip.

"Uh-huh," grunted Kindred, his head bobbing as he kept a steady eye on Hazelip and took the innkeeper's noncommittal reply as a yes. "His name wouldn't have been Slate Creed, would it?"

"Could've been," said Hazelip. "Why? Is he a friend of yours?"

Kindred snickered and said, "Not hardly. Slate Creed is an outlaw, and I've come to take him back to Texas to hang."

"You don't say?" said Hazelip, although he was really thinking, *Little shit like you ain't about to take the Slate Creed I know back to Texas.*

Kindred ignored Hazelip's attitude. "I'll be back down in a minute," he said. "Have my sandwich and a beer ready for me in the saloon." He turned and started up the stairs.

While he watched the deputy marshal ascend the steps, Hazelip couldn't help thinking that Kindred was a bossy little bastard who needed setting down. And he just might get it right here in Brownsville, he thought.

4

With the fall of Fort Donelson on February 16, 1862, the publication of all newspapers in Nashville ceased. Not too many people cared, though, because everybody was more concerned with preserving their lives. No man thought of much more than his own safety and how that should best be secured. The members of the press, a huge majority of whom were firm advocates of secession and the Confederacy, were particularly anxious in this respect. They figured, if those damn Yankees were planning to seek vengeance against any class of people, it would surely be the members of the fourth estate. Or so they all thought when they abandoned their offices with forms in all stages of preparation from paper wet and ready for the press to manuscripts half set upon the cases.

The first paper to publish after the occupation of the city by the Union army was the *Nashville Times*, but it failed to last more than three months because its owners, the former employees of the *Nashville Union and American*, lacked the proper financial backing to succeed. Seven more tabloids started up in the next two years, but only three of these survived the war intact.

Of these, Creed chose to visit the offices of the revived *Nashville Union and American*, located on the northeast corner of Church and Cherty Streets, as the place to begin his search for Blackburn and the others. Upon entering the building, he immediately saw a familiar face in the lobby and approached the gentleman who owned it.

"Colonel Burch?" inquired Creed.

"Yes?" replied the balding, full-bearded Burch. He looked expectantly at Creed with bright blue eyes that said he didn't recognize Creed but intended to be friendly just the same.

"Colonel Burch, you don't know me," said Creed, extending his hand in friendship, «but I served with Colonel Morgan during the war."

"John Hunt Morgan?" queried Burch cautiously.

Creed smiled and said, "Yes, sir. My name is, uh, Slate Creed, Colonel."

Burch accepted the handshake carefully and said, "I'm sorry, sir, but I don't recall the name. You see, I didn't serve with Colonel Morgan."

"Yes, sir, I know," said Creed. "When I met you, you were on General Nathan Forrest's staff. Of course, you wouldn't remember me. I was only a third lieutenant then."

"You know, you do look familiar," said Burch. He pinched his lower lip between the index finger and thumb of his right hand and squinted at Creed. "Yes, I recall the face but not the name."

Creed looked nervously around the busy room and noticed that several other men were watching them. With eyes downcast, he said softly, "My name was Clete Slater then, Colonel."

Burch glanced around the room, noted the prying eyes set on them, then took command of their conversation. "Yes, of course," he said with the booming voice of the thespian. "Now I remember. Lieutenant Creed of Morgan's brigade. Yes, how are you, sir?" He took Creed's hand and began pumping it vigorously. "It's wonderful to see an old comrade-in-arms. I'm glad to see that you survived the war." Then noting Creed's arm in the sling, he added, "This isn't a result of some battle, is it?"

"No, sir," said Creed, a bit confused by Burch's sudden change of deportment.

"It's a recent injury. Sustained a few days ago in Kentucky."

"In Kentucky? Were you up there for the races?"

"Why, yes, I was," said Creed, rather surprised.

"Wish I'd been there," said Burch enthusiastically. "Come. You must tell me all about it." He led Creed through the lobby to a stairway. "My private office is upstairs," he explained.

As they ascended the steps, Burch continued to speak animatedly to Creed, but he said little of nothing, choosing to make idle chatter about the weather. Once they were upstairs, he lowered, his voice and directed Creed toward a frosted-glass door that had gilt-edged black lettering reading: John C. Burch, Editor. Burch opened the door for Creed to enter the room first, then followed the Texan inside and closed the door behind them.

"Please have a seat, Lieutenant Slater," said Burch, now being like the military man that he had once been, as he stepped around the large desk that dominated the office. He pointed casually toward a straight back wooden chair in front of Creed and sat down himself.

Creed hesitated, unsure of what to make of Burch's display of hospitality and congeniality.

"Is something wrong, Lieutenant?" asked Burch, who was now perplexed by Creed's attitude.

Creed smiled and said, "Well, sir, I'm not sure what to make of this."

"To make of what?" queried Burch.

"Well, being here in this office," said Creed.

"You did come to see me, didn't you?"

"Not exactly, Colonel."

"But you said downstairs that your name is no longer Slater, that you're going by the name of Creed now. Isn't that so?"

"Yes, sir, but that isn't why I came here."

It was Burch's turn to be perplexed. "Then tell me. Why did you come here?"

"Well, sir, I came here looking for some help," said Creed.

"Precisely," said Burch, nodding as if he knew the answer before it was given, "and you came to me."

"Well, no, sir, not you specifically. I came to the newspaper. I had no idea that you are the editor here."

"But I'm not the editor here," said Burch. "But the door has your name on it."

"That's left over from before the war when I was the editor here," explained Burch. "Now I'm a lawyer, and I use this office out of the good graces of the owners of this building, who happen to be my former employers."

"I see," said Creed, a bit embarrassed but not really willing to show it.

"So how did you want the *Union and American* to help you, Lieutenant?" asked Burch, trying to move the conversation ahead. Creed sat down and explained his purpose for being there, that he was trying to locate six men who were last known to be in the vicinity of Nashville.

Burch replied as expected, asking, "Why do you wish to find these men?"

"They took part in a raid on a train of Federal freight wagons down in Mississippi last May," said Creed, "and when they were caught a few months later, they told the Yankees that I led them on that raid."

"Did you?"

"No, sir, I didn't," said Creed, looking Burch straight in the eyes.

"But the Yankees believe these other fellows and not you," said Burch. "Is that it, Lieutenant?"

"It's worse than that, Colonel." said Creed, and with his next breath he began explaining how he had been tried, convicted, and sentenced to hang for the crime that he had not committed.

"And you're just now getting around to looking for these men, Lieutenant?"

Creed burped a laugh and said, "No, sir, not exactly." He then proceeded to relate how his best friend and brother had been murdered and how he had gone to Mexico to find their killers and avenge their deaths before starting out on his search for the men who had framed him. From there, he told Burch how he had been delayed by certain events in Victoria, Texas, and how he had wound up in Kentucky conducting a horse-racing meet in late January. "And now I'm here," he said in conclusion, "looking for Blackburn and the others."

Burch had listened patiently, occasionally nodding, but never speaking while Creed narrated the last nine months of his life's story. Now it was his turn to speak.

"Lieutenant, do you remember what I said downstairs a few minutes ago about seeing old comrades-in-arms?"

"Yes, sir, I do," said Creed.

"That wasn't meant to be taken lightly, Lieutenant."

"Please, Colonel, would you mind not calling me that, uh, lieutenant anymore? I'd prefer that you call me Creed or Slate, if you please?"

"Yes, of course," said Burch, smiling apologetically, "We aren't in the Army any longer, are we?"

Creed crooked his neck and stared at Burch, then said, "I'm not, Colonel, but something tells me that you are."

"Not exactly," said Burch. "Allow me to explain. We lost the war, Slate, and now the Yankees are our masters. I haven't met one yet who would help a former Confederate officer. That is why we must help each other when we can, Slate. That is what I meant when I said it's always good to see an old comrade-in-arms. It seems that we only see each other when we need each other's help. Of course, our meeting this morning is only chance, but even so, you need my help, and I am prepared to give it to you as best as I can." He stood up and added, "Come. We'll have to go over to the *Daily Dispatch*."

Creed didn't understand why they were going to a different newspaper, but he went along just the same.

The *Nashville Daily Dispatch* was located on College Street. During their walk through town, Butch explained that the *Union and American* had only been in business again since December 5, but that the *Daily Dispatch* had been the second newspaper to start up-and-survive after the Yankees possessed the city in '62.

If Blackburn or any of the others had been caught near Nashville, then the event would certainly have been newsworthy enough to make the pages of the local newspapers, meaning they would have to look for the article in past copies of the *Dispatch*.

The morgue of the *Dispatch* contained issues of every number that the newspaper had published. A clerk, recognizing Burch, aided them in their search.

The first article was dated May 20, 1865, and it detailed the raid on the army freighters, reporting how a band of former Confederates had attacked the wagon train, had killed all but three of the soldiers and teamsters, and had stolen $14,000 in gold and silver. One of-the survivors identified the bandits as Texans because they bragged that they would be rich men when they got back to their home state of Texas.

Dated June 26, 1865, the second article detailed the capture of Marsh Quade, Dick Barth, and Jonas Burr. Barth had gotten drunk at a saloon in a little place called Wrencoe and was boasting of becoming a rich man. To support his contention, he produced a bag of silver and gold coins. The cloth sack was plainly marked "Paymaster U.S.A." One of the onlookers was the district constable, a former Confederate like Barth, who put his duty before old loyalties. He reported the incident to the sheriff, a Yankee appointee, who, in turn, told the local military commander. Barth was arrested at a farmhouse near Wrencoe along with Quade and Burr. The three of them were then sent to New Orleans to stand trial.

The *Dispatch* failed to report anything more about the trio of outlaws or their trial.

"From the way it was told to me at my trial," said Creed, "they made a bargain with the Yankees for their lives. They told the Yankees who the others in the raid were in exchange for a pardon and the return of their share of the stolen money. General Canby accepted this deal, and they named Blackburn, Spencer, Johnson, and a few others as having taken part in the raid. They were caught and brought to New Orleans, too. When General Canby saw them, he recognized Blackburn and Spencer as two of the men who had been with me when he personally paroled me in New Orleans. You see, I had led Blackburn and the others into the city to surrender ourselves at the end of the war. I told the general that there were others like us scattered all over who were afraid to come into the city to surrender because of the terrible things they'd heard about what the Yankees would do to them if they surrendered. I volunteered to go into the countryside and lead these boys into the city to surrender. I did this for a week or so, then the general let me go about my business. At my trial, the Yankees said Blackburn named me as the leader of the raid and had sworn out an affidavit to that effect, and the others backed him up."

"And, of course, they were lying," said Burch.

"That's right, Colonel. I was on my way back to Texas when they raided those wagons, but the only way I'm going to prove that is to find Blackburn and the others and make them tell the truth."

"It's not as easy as that, Slate," said Burch. "The Yankees will most likely hang you first before they'll listen to you."

"That's a risk that I'll have to take."

"Not necessarily so. There are other ways of approaching this problem." Burch smiled. "I am a lawyer, Slate, and I think I can help you here. If you want me to help you, that is."

"What did you have in mind, Colonel?"

5

After eating a breakfast of fried eggs, grits, biscuits, and gravy at the Bob Hazelip Hotel, Jim Kindred wandered across the street to the county courthouse to look for Sheriff Mason Morris. The sheriff was in.

"I've been expecting you," said Morris after Kindred identified himself. The sheriff remained relaxed in his chair with his feet up on the desk and his hands behind his head.

"You have?" queried Kindred.

Morris chuckled behind his full brown beard, although there was no mirth in his blue eyes. "Well, not you specifically," he said. "I meant I was expecting some lawman from Texas. Exactly who, I had no idea."

"Then you must know why I'm here," said Kindred.

"I got me a pretty good idea of that," said Morris. "You're looking for Slate Creed."

"Precisely, Sheriff," said Kindred, producing a warrant for the arrest of Clete Slater, alias Slate Creed. "Do you know where I can find him?"

"Nope," said Morris, ignoring the paper that Kindred held out to him.

"No?"

"Nope," repeated Morris, still refusing to acknowledge the existence of the habeas.

"Are you telling me you don't know where he is?" asked Kindred, replacing the warrant in his pocket. "Or are you refusing to tell me where he is?"

"Which do you think, Marshall?"

Kindred ignored the sheriff's question and said, "I thought Creed was in this county running some sort of horse-racing meet. Is that true?"

"Oh, that's true enough," said Morris quite convincingly.

"Then, where is he?" asked Kindred.

"I don't know," answered Morris honestly. "Is he still in this county?" asked Kindred.

"No, I don't think so," said Morris.

"You don't think so," repeated Kindred. "I see." He shook his head, then made eye contact with Morris. "Sheriff, I think you need to be reminded that I am a federal officer and that I have the power to put you under arrest for obstructing justice."

That brought Morris to his feet. He shook a finger at Kindred and said, "Listen to me, you little piss ant! This is my county. Edmondson County. And we were all loyal to the Union during the war. I fought for the Union, and so did the judge and just about every other man around here who was fighting age. We defended our state and our country, and we're proud of it. We were loyal Unionists then, and we're loyal now. We didn't tolerate the Confederates coming in here and telling us which side we should fight on, and we won't tolerate a galvanized Yankee like you coming in here telling us we're obstructing justice. Just who the hell do you think you are?"

Kindred was unabashed. He stuck a thumb under his badge, pushed it out from his chest, and said, "I'm a deputy marshal of these here United States. That's who I am. And if you don't start cooperating with me pretty damn fast, Sheriff, I'll go find me a federal judge and have him issue a writ against you so fast that it'll make you dizzy."

"Well, you just go ahead and do that," said Morris calmly.

"Is that your final word?" asked Kindred.

"You heard me, Marshal. Go ahead and get your writ. I'll be right here when you get back with it." He sat down again. "Yes, sir. Right here "

Kindred stared at Morris for a second, then turned and started for the door. He stopped at the doorway with his hand on the latch and turned back to Morris. "Now I see it, Sheriff. I know Creed was hurt by some gambler that he killed up at some place called Mammoth Cave. I'm thinking that he's laying up somewhere in this county until he can ride again, and you're hoping I'll leave to get that writ. You want me to leave so you can warn Creed that I'm here and he can have enough time to get away. Well, it won't work, Sheriff. I'm going to stick around here until I find out where Creed is."

"You do that, Marshal," said Morris. "Personally, I don't care what you do." He leaned back in his chair and put his feet up again.

Kindred shook his head and said, "You dumb ass. You call yourself a loyal Union man, and still you let an outlaw like Creed run free through your county. Creed fought for the Confederacy, only then his name was Clete Slater. He killed lots of you Yanks, and he killed more of you Yanks after the war was over and he'd been paroled. And now you protect him. How can you do that and still call yourself a loyal Union man? You can't do it, Sheriff. You called me a galvanized Yankee because I'm a Texan wearing the badge of a deputy marshal of the United States. Well, maybe I am, but at least I'm doing my job. What the hell are you doing, Sheriff?"

Morris was had, and he knew it. Kindred was right. He was protecting a convicted man, and that was against his own moral code-to some extent. On the other hand, he was protecting a man who had helped the people of his county enjoy some much needed prosperity, fleeting though it was. Even so, he had his duty to do.

"All right, Marshall," said Morris. "You've made your point."

He put his feet down again and leaned forward on the desk. "I'll tell you as much as I know." He slid forward in his chair before continuing. "I believe Creed has left the county, but I don't know where he's gone. He didn't tell me where he was heading, and I didn't ask him. The last I saw of him was up to the Mammoth Cave Hotel this past Sunday. He said then that he would leave as soon as he could, and I figured that would be the next day or so because he was only hurt in his left shoulder. If it suits you, Marshal, I'll ride up to the hotel with you to see if he's still around."

"That suits me just fine, Sheriff," said Kindred. "I'd like to leave as soon as possible."

Morris glanced at the clock on the wall, saw that it was almost a quarter past nine, and said, "I'll meet you out front of the courthouse at ten."

Kindred nodded and left.

Damn, thought Morris, I sure hope Creed has moved on.

6

Colonel Burch explained to Creed that Wrencoe was a crossroads community straddling the Nolensville Pike where it crossed Mill Creek nine miles southeast of Nashville.

"Nolensville Pike is Fourth Avenue here in the city,". Said Burch. He and Creed were standing on the street corner outside the Nashville Dispatch. "Just follow it out of town, and you'll come to Wrencoe. According to the newspaper article, the farmhouse near Wrencoe where Barth, Quade, and Burr were captured was owned by Cornelius and Mary Perkins. You'll have to ask someone there how to find the Perkins farm. It's a rather long walk, I'm afraid."

"I have my horse," said Creed.

"Good. Then you can ride out there this morning and be back this afternoon. By then, I will have drafted the letter to General Canby."

"Do you think it will work?" asked Creed.

"It can't hurt," said Burch. "He thinks you're guilty now. That is the bottom, my friend. You have no place to go but up. At the very least, we might be able to get you a fair trial in another court."

Creed shrugged and- said, "Well, I suppose I don't have anything to lose."

"Of course, you don't. Now you ride out to Wrencoe and see what you can learn there about these blackguards who pointed their crooked fingers at you, and when you've finished there, hurry back to my office."

Creed agreed to do just that. He left Burch at the *Dispatch* and walked to the stable where Nimbus had been boarded for the night. Remembering his Grandfather Hawk McConnell's words about being prepared for whatever might come his way, he made certain that his

24

two revolvers were loaded and that their nipples were properly capped. He put one back in the saddlebag from which he had removed it, and he stuck the other Colt's inside his belt to the left of the buckle so that his coat would cover it. It was a warm day, making him want to leave the coat open, but he knew that to do so would risk exposing the butt of the pistol, which he was chary to do in view of the times and the locality. He wished that he had a strap sewn to the inside of his coat, one that he could hook over the butt of the revolver to hold his coat in place when it was unbuttoned. He made a mental note to see a tailor about this possibility as soon as the opportunity presented itself.

Wrencoe wasn't much of a village. It had a smithy, a dry-goods store, and a post office; the three businesses being surrounded by several homes, a few of which were farmhouses. At the post office, Creed was directed to a two-story clapboard frame house on the hill overlooking the village. This was the residence of the Perkins family.

Creed had ridden through Wrencoe during the war, but he had never stopped there. As he walked up to the Perkins's front door, he tried to recall whether Blackburn or any of the others had ever mentioned Wrencoe, and for the life of him, he couldn't remember hearing any of them saying anything about the place.

He did recollect that Quade was sparking a girl named Perkins, but that was down in Murfreesboro. Or was it? He couldn't be certain about that either. He knocked on the door and waited.

The door opened to reveal an elderly man in a collarless shirt, suspenders, brown trousers, and shoes-attire that had seen its best days. His lips were hidden behind a long white beard, and the sun behind Creed reflected off his bald head. He had hazel eyes that pinpointed a stare at Creed. "Yes?" he queried.

Creed removed his hat politely and queried, "Mr. Perkins?"

"Yes?"

"Good morning, sir," said Creed. "I am Slate Creed of Lavaca County, Texas and I-"

"He ain't here," interrupted Perkins, and he started to close the door.

"Beg your pardon, sir?" asked Creed, completely baffled by the old man" s response.

The old man stopped closing the door and said, "Are you deaf, boy? I said he ain't here."

"I'm sorry, sir," said Creed with a smile, "but I don't understand."

Perkins squinted at Creed and said. "Didn't you just say that you're from Texas?"

"Yes, sir, that's right."

"Lavaca County, correct?"

"Yes, sir that's right."

"Well, then he ain't here." And again, the old man started to close the door.

"Who isn't here, sir?" asked Creed.

"Why, Marsh, of course," said Perkins, stopping once again.

"Marsh?" queried Creed. "Marshall Quade?"

"You got more than one fellow named Marshall down there in Lavaca County, Texas?"

"Well, no, sir," said Creed a bit sheepishly. "Not that I know about."

"All right then. He ain't here. Good-bye."

Creed stuck his foot in the door and said, "Beg pardon, sir, but could you tell me where he is?"

"I could," said the old man, looking down at Creed's foot, "but I won't."

Creed noted the anger in the elderly man's voice and eyes and quickly withdrew his foot. "Look, sir, I need to find Marsh Quade and talk to him. Would you please tell me where I might find him?"

"No." And he shut the door in Creed's face.

Out of frustration, Creed replaced his hat on his head and banged his fist on the door. When it opened again, he said, "Look, sir, I've come a long-" He stopped in midsentence when he saw the business end of a shotgun glaring at him. Without giving it a second thought, he raised his hands in surrender.

"Now lookey here, you," said the old man with real venom. "I said he ain't here, and that means he ain't here. And I said I ain't going to tell you where he went, and that means I ain't going to tell you where he went. Now you just get off my property and don't come back. You hear me?"

"Yes, sir," said Creed, backing away. He backed all the way to the hitching post where he'd tied Nimbus. He walked backward because the old man followed him all the way, waving the shotgun at him.

"Now get on that horse and get away from here," said Perkins. "I've just about had my fill of you Texans. The next one who shows

seems that they took part in a raid on a bunch of Federal supply wagons down in Mississippi after the war was over. Damn fools came up here then, and Quade and these other two fellows came in here one day, got themselves all pissed up, and started bragging about how they were going to be rich once they got back to Texas. One of them went so far as to show off all the money he had on him. Only trouble was he showed it to the wrong fellow. Henry Curran, our local constable, happened to be in here that day. He saw the Army money bag this fellow had his money in, and he told the county sheriff about it. The sheriff told the Army about it, and they came down here from Nashville and arrested Quade and the other two fellows and hauled them off to jail. We didn't see Quade around here again for a couple of months. When he got back, he said he and the other fellows had returned the money they'd stolen, and the Federals pardoned them."

"Why did he come back here?" asked Creed.

"Love," said Ewing with a wink. "He was sparking Corny's youngest daughter, Sal. Sal isn't her real name though. Her real name is Sidney Ann Linn Perkins. Or I should say, Sidney Ann Linn Quade now. When she was a little girl, she made up that name of Sal from her initials. S. A. L. Sal. Not Sally, she used to say. Just Sal. Well, she married Quade against her father's wishes. Old Corny pissed and moaned that Quade was no good, that he was a wild-ass Texan who would never amount to a hill of beans. When the old man refused to bless their union, they ran off to Murfreesboro and got married anyway."

"Is that where they're living now?" asked Creed.

"Nope," said Ewing. "Last I heard they were going up to Logan County, Kentucky, to see my cousin George Washington Ewing." "Your cousin?" queried Creed with wrinkled brow.

"Yes," said Ewing. "You see, Sal is my niece. Her mother is my sister."

"I see," said Creed.

"You said Quade is a friend of yours or something?"

"We served in the war together," said Creed. "I am Slate Creed from Lavaca County, Texas." He offered his hand to Ewing who accepted the handshake and introduced himself. "I last saw Quade down in New Orleans last spring. We had just gotten our paroles along with five other friends from back home. He and the other boys decided to come back up here to see some girls they had sparked during the war when we were fighting around here. I went home to Texas."

"So why are you looking for them now?" asked Ewing.

Creed was leery of the question and decided to give him an evasive answer. "Their families are curious about them," said Creed obliquely.

"Are you related to Quade or something?"

"No, I'm not, and I'm not related to any of the others either," said Creed, anticipating Ewing's next question.

"What are those other boys' names?" asked Ewing.

"Jack Blackburn, Jonas Burr, Jasper Johnson, Dick Barth, and Dick Spencer."

Ewing gave the names some thought before he said, "I believe the two fellows that were with Quade when the Army took him were named Barth and Burr. I recollect that because they sounded like a law firm to me." He laughed at his remark.

"You don't know what happened to them, do you?" asked Creed.

Before Ewing could answer, an older woman entered the store.

She wore a heavy blue cape over her shoulders, and a matching bonnet was tied tightly over her ears.

Creed turned to see the lady coming toward and absently, he allowed his coat to open wide, exposing the butt of his Colt's. He failed to notice this miscue of his because he was surprised to see that the woman bore a striking resemblance to the storekeeper.

Ewing caught sight of the gun, and it gave him food for thought.

In the first place, he wondered why this stranger - or any man in this area - should be armed. The war was over, and the only men who carried weapons were soldiers, lawmen, and outlaws.

Peaceful citizens had no need to arm themselves. And this fellow was asking a lot of questions. Maybe he was telling the truth about who he was and what he was doing here. Maybe he wasn't. Maybe Henry Curran should talk to this fellow. Or maybe the sheriff.

"Hello, Mary," said Ewing to the lady.

"Hello, Josiah," she replied, although she was looking at Creed when she said it. "How do you do, sir?" She held out her hand to Creed. "I am Mrs. Perkins. I believe you are owed an apology, sir, for my husband's rudeness."

Creed accepted Mrs. Perkins's greeting with one hand and removed his hat" with the other. "How do you do, ma'am? I am Slate

Creed of Lavaca County, Texas."

"Yes, sir, I know," she said, "I am so sorry for the rude greeting my husband gave you, Mr. Creed. He gets very upset whenever someone mentions Texas to him. It reminds him of our son-in-law, Marshall Quade, and that really upsets him."

"Yes, ma'am, I know," said Creed with a smile.

"I was just telling Mr. Creed about Marsh and Sal," said Ewing. "How they ran off and got married and all."

Mrs. Perkins ignored her brother and said, "I understand you are looking for Marshall, Mr. Creed."

"Yes, ma'am, I am. As I was telling Mr. Ewing, his family is worried about him."

The lady's brown eyes pinched together as a frown darkened her face. "His family?" she queried.

"Yes, ma'am."

"What family, Mr. Creed?" she asked. "Marshall said he was all alone in the world."

Creed was caught in the lie, and he knew it. He could hear his Grandpa Hawk telling him how lying was evil and only weak men lied. "Well, ma'am, I didn't mean Quade's family. I meant the families of the other men who were with him. You see, rna'am, I was with Marsh and five other fellows when the war ended. We received our paroles together, and they came up here, while I went back to Texas. The families of the other boys are worried about them."

"I see," said Mrs. Perkins. "So, they sent you to find them? Is that it, Mr. Creed?"

Creed looked the lady straight in her chestnut eyes and said, "Not exactly, ma'am."

"Then why do you wish to find them?" she asked firmly.

Time for beating around the brush is over, thought Creed. He replaced his hat on his head, and when he did, the butt of his Colt's stuck out from beneath his coat flap for a brief second that was long enough for Mrs. Perkins to catch a glimpse of the weapon. Again, he looked her straight in the eyes and said, "Mr. Ewing mentioned that Quade and some other fellows had taken part in a raid on a Yankee supply train. I suppose you know about that, ma'am."

"Yes, I do. What of it?"

"Did Marsh tell you how they got their pardons for that raid?" asked Creed.

"He said they returned the money and the Yankees let them go," said Mrs. Perkins.

"Is that all he said?"

"Yes, that's all. Why?"

"Because that's only half the truth, rna'am. The other half is Quade and the others swore oaths that I led that raid."

Mrs. Perkins studied Creed's face for a moment, then said, "I take it you weren't the leader."

"Mrs. Perkins, I wasn't even there," said Creed. "I was on my way to Texas at the time of the raid. Quade and the others swore that I led them, so the Yankees arrested me and court-martialed me for their crime. They were going to hang me for it, but I escaped. And now I'm trying to find Quade and the others, so I can make them tell the truth and I can be a free man again. Do you understand, rna'am?"

Her view fell on his left hip where the Colt's hid behind his coat. "Yes, I do," she said.

"Then will you tell me where I can find Marsh Quade?"

When Mrs. Perkins hesitated to reply, Ewing said, "Mary, I told Mr. Creed that Marsh and Sal went up to Kentucky to see our Cousin George."

"Yes, that's right," said Mrs. Perkins. "They went to visit Cousin George up in Logan County."

"How long ago was this, ma'am?" asked Creed.

"Right after Christmas," she said.

"Do you expect them to come home soon?"

"Yes, I do. Very soon. In fact, they've stayed too long up there. I should think that Cousin George would have tired of them by now and sent them packing." She feigned a smile.

"Yes, that's right," said Ewing nervously. "Cousin George doesn't have much patience for young folks. Why, they're probably on their way home right now. Don't you think so, Mary?"

"Yes, of course, they probably are on their way home right now," said Mrs. Perkins.

Creed perused the lady's face, then studied her brother for a second. He had the feeling that they were lying, or they weren't telling him everything, but if he pursued the matter much further with them, they might clam up on him. He couldn't allow this. Slowly, he spread open his coat and deliberately showed them the Colt's inside his waistband. "Mr. Ewing, Mrs. Perkins, I don't think you folks understand the situation here," he said methodically. "My life is the one that hangs in the balance. I don't think you folks appreciate this fact."

"I don't believe you," said Mrs. Perkins. "If you were a law-abiding man, you wouldn't be carrying that gun."

Creed drew his revolver and said, "It's because I am a law-abiding man that I carry this gun." He pointed it at Ewing. "I think this will help you see things my way."

"There's no need for violence," said Ewing, his eyes wide with fright.

"That's up to you," said Creed. He aimed the Colt's at Ewing's face.

"What do you think you're doing, Mr. Creed?" demanded Mrs. Perkins angrily.

"Mrs. Perkins, I've already been condemned to hang," said Creed. "I have nothing to lose by putting the barrel of this six-shooter up your brother's nose and blowing the top of his head to kingdom come."

"You can't shoot me," said Ewing fearfully.

"Yes, I can," said Creed. He pushed the gun toward Ewing's nose and cocked the hammer. "I'm from Texas, Mr. Ewing, and I can shoot you dead in the wink of an eye. And I will, if you don't tell me where I can find Marshall Quade."

"Why should we tell you?" demanded Mrs. Perkins. "So, you can shoot Marshall dead and make my daughter a widow?"

"I don't want to shoot Quade, Mrs. Perkins," said Creed with a bit of exasperation in his voice. "I told you. I want to find him and make him tell the truth about that raid in Mississippi."

"I don't believe you," said the lady.

"Have it your way, ma'am." He turned to Ewing. "He's your brother."

"We've already told you," said Ewing, paling before the muzzle of Creed's revolver. "He and Sal went to Kentucky to visit Cousin George."

"But you said they were due to return here soon," said Creed. "Is that true?"

"No, it's not," said Ewing.

"Quiet, Josiah!" snapped his sister.

Creed shoved the barrel of the Colt's against Ewing's nose.

"Where's Quade, Mr. Ewing?"

"They're still in Kentucky," said Mrs. Perkins.

"No, they're not," said Ewing more than anxiously. "They've gone to Colorado."

"Josiah!"

"Colorado?" queried Creed.

"Yes, that's right," said Ewing rapidly. "Sal wrote that Marsh was talking about removing to a place called Denver."

The Texan looked at the man's eyes to see if he could detect any sign of deceit. When he saw none, he pulled back the revolver and said, "All right, Mr. Ewing, I believe you." He eased the hammer back to its safety position, then turned his view on Mrs. Perkins and said, "I'm sorry that I had to threaten your brother, ma'am, but if you folks had told me the truth in the first place -."

Mrs. Perkins wasn't listening to Creed. Her anger was now aimed in another direction. "Damn you, Josiah!" she swore. "Why did you tell him they went to Colorado? Why? Damn your hide!" Creed tipped his hat to Mrs. Perkins, nodded at Ewing, and started for the door. As he closed it behind him, he could still hear the lady ranting at her brother. While mounting Nimbus, it struck him that Cornelius and Mary Perkins were a match made in heaven. Well, maybe not in heaven.

7

Creed returned to Nashville that afternoon and went straight to Colonel Burch's office at the Union and American. "Any luck," inquired Burch as soon as Creed entered the room.

He motioned toward a chair in front of his desk.

"I'm not sure," said Creed, sitting down.

"I take it none of the three men were in Wrencoe," said Burch.

"No, sir, they weren't, but I did learn something about Marsh Quade."

"Oh?"

Creed reviewed his experience in Wrencoe for Burch, finishing the tale by remarking how he thought Ewing and Mrs. Perkins might have still been lying.

"Do you really think so?" asked Burch.

"I can't be certain one way or the other," said Creed. "I do know that Ewing told me before Mrs. Perkins entered the store that Quade and his wife had gone to Logan County, Kentucky. That makes me think that at least that part of their story is true."

"You said Quade and his wife went to visit George Ewing up there" said Burch.

"Yes, that's right. Why? Do you know him?"

"Yes, I do," said Burch. "Well, I know of him. He was a Kentucky congressman in the Confederacy. I should think that your next move would be to call on Mr. Ewing in Kentucky."

"Yes, I suppose that's what I should do," said Creed. "Do you know Logan County?" asked Burch.

"Somewhat," said Creed. "My company was posted there when we

35

first came north." He smiled as he remembered those earlier days. "We were there for some time before we saw our first action. It was so easy then. We were going to whip the Yankees in a few weeks, and then go back to Texas as heroes. It didn't quite work out that way, did it, Colonel?"

"No, it didn't," said the lawyer wistfully. He sighed, then seemed to gather strength as he asserted, "We may have lost the war, but we haven't lost our spirit or our love of freedom." He winked at Creed and added, "We'll still defeat those damn Black Republicans and their nigger pawns. Won't we?"

Creed forced a smile but said nothing to indicate any agreement with Burch's statement. As far as he was concerned, the war was over, and he intended to let it rest in memory. If others - either North or South - wished to continue fighting, that was their choice, but they could leave him out of it.

When his guest failed to respond to his question, Burch said, "Well, we can discuss politics some other time. For now, I think I should write you a letter of introduction to Mr. Ewing up in Kentucky." He pulled a blank sheet of paper from a drawer and took up his pen. He opened an inkwell, dipped the tip of the pen in the ink, inscribed a salutation, then looked up at Creed. "To a total stranger, Mr. Ewing might be as difficult as his cousins in Wrencoe. A letter from me will make him co-operate with you fully."

"It will?"

Burch winked and said, "He's one of us, Slate."

Creed wasn't exactly sure what Burch meant by that, but he didn't question the colonel about it. He waited patiently while Burch composed the missive.

"You give Mr. Ewing this letter," Said Burch as he folded the paper in thirds. He handed it over to Creed and added, "I've already sent the other letter to General Canby in New Orleans. I told him that you are innocent of the crime for which you were convicted in Texas and that all you need is the proper opportunity to prove your innocence. I asked him to give you a new trial in New Orleans in which you could be properly represented by legal counsel such as myself. I also asked him to have the men who swore oaths against you arrested and brought to the trial so that you may face your accusers as the Constitution guarantees every citizen."

"Do you think that will do any good?" asked Creed. "I mean,

we're Confederates. Or we were. Do you think General Canby will listen to either one of us?"

"You tell me," said Burch. "You've met the man. I haven't. I don't know anything about him except what you've told me."

"I don't know him that well either," said Creed. "For a Yankee, he seemed like a decent sort. He treated me with respect and fairness when I was in New Orleans last year. He never once questioned my honor."

"Well, let us hope that he still has some of that respect for you," said Burch, "and that he's willing to be fair about this matter. It's probably all we can expect from him."

Creed looked at the letter of introduction for a second, then put it in an inside coat pocket. "What if the general isn't willing to give me a chance to prove my innocence?" he asked.

"Then we'll try other legal routes," said Burch. "I will send other letters appealing your case. If I have to, I will write the President and ask him to intervene for you. Mr. Johnson may have been a Unionist, but he was a Tennessean before he was a Yankee-lover. In the meantime, I suggest that you leave for Kentucky immediately. I have the feeling that Mr. Ewing and Mrs. Perkins in Wrencoe might send word to their cousin that could negate my letter. You can still catch the late train for Edgefield where you can make the connection for Kentucky."

"Yes, I suppose I should be on my way," said Creed.

"Keep me informed of your movements, Slate, so I can keep in touch with you at all times."

"Yes, sir." said Creed; rising from the chair. He extended his hand in farewell, and as he shook hands with Burch, he said, "Thank you, Colonel. You'll be hearing from me. If there is anything that I can ever do for you, just say the word."

"I'll keep your offer in mind," said Burch. "As I said before, we old comrades-in-arms should help each other, especially in these troubled times."

"Yes, sir," said Creed, and he departed Burch's office.

Before dark settled over Nashville that evening, Creed was on his way to Kentucky.

8

Sheriff Morris accompanied Jim Kindred to the Mammoth Cave Hotel, the hostelry that Creed had made his headquarters during most of his stay in Edmondson County. Mr. Proctor, the inn's manager, met the lawmen in the lobby, then invited them into his office where they sat in cushioned chairs in front of Proctor's desk.

"Now, sir," said Proctor as soon as he was seated in his high-backed leather armchair, "what can I do for you?"

"I'm looking for a man that you might know as Slate Creed," said Kindred, coming straight to the point.

"He's not here," said Proctor curtly.

"Where did he go?" asked Kindred.

Proctor's charcoal eyes shifted askance toward Morris.

"Don't look at him!" snapped Kindred. "I'm asking the questions here. Now tell me where Creed went."

"I don't know for certain," said Proctor coldly.

"Mr. Proctor, Creed is a condemned man," said Kindred. "He's a traitor to our country. He's going to swing for his crimes against the Anny and the state of Texas. Unless you want to swing with him, I suggest you answer my questions truthfully and completely. Do you understand me, sir?"

"You've made yourself quite clear, Mr. Kindred," said Proctor. He was unruffled by this squawking sparrow, but he felt it would be best to throw him a few crumbs of co-operation.

"Fine," said Kindred. "Now, where did Creed go from here?"

"He went down to Glasgow Junction," said Proctor evenly. "What's that?" asked Kindred.

"A railroad junction," volunteered Morris. "It's about nine miles southeast of here. The Louisville & Nashville Rail Road goes through there."

Kindred nodded and said, "I see. So, Creed went down there to catch a train. Is that it?"

"I suppose so," said Proctor. "He didn't say really."

"Uh-huh," said Kindred. "When did he leave here?"

"Yesterday, " said Proctor. "Right after breakfast."

"Did he say where he was going?" asked Kindred. "Besides this Glasgow Junction, I mean."

"Nope," said Proctor.

"He didn't say anything about going to Nashville or some other place in Tennessee?"

"No, sir," said Proctor. "Not to me, anyway."

Kindred looked at Morris and said, "Did he say anything to you about Nashville or some other place in Tennessee?"

"We talked about a lot of things," said Morris. "He mentioned Nashville a few times when we talked about the war. He talked about a lot of other places, too."

"Any of them in Tennessee?" asked Kindred.

"Some," said Morris. "Some in other states. He rode with Morgan, you know."

"No, I didn't know," said Kindred, "and I don't give a shit either. I'm only interested in where Creed is riding now. What places in Tennessee did he mention?"

"Murfreesboro, Chattanooga, Gallatin, Sparta, Knoxville, Shiloh," said Morris. "Morgan and his men got around a lot. I should know," he added with a smirk. "My outfit chased them all over Kentucky enough."

"What about you, Mr. Proctor?" asked Kindred, ignoring Morris's reference to the war. "Did Creed ever mention any places in Tennessee to you?"

"He might have," said Proctor, "but I don't recall any. We never talked that much about anything except the horse races and the attendant business."

Kindred nodded and said, "All right, Mr. Proctor. You've been very helpful. Come on, Sheriff. I want to go down to this railroad junction now."

Morris thought of protesting but didn't, knowing it would avail him nothing except another threatening lecture from Kindred. Instead, he said, "I'd like to eat some lunch here before we go."

Kindred agreed to the sheriff's request, then they rode down to Bell's Tavern at Glasgow Junction that afternoon.

Tall, lanky, pale, balding Josiah Wilson was the proprietor of Bell's. He was alone at the inn when Kindred and Moms entered the premises. "Sheriff Morris," he said with a long-toothed smile, "what brings you down here again? You chasing another desperado or something?" He laughed, remembering the last time the Edmondson County sheriff had come to his tavern.

On his last visit, Morris had been accompanied by Constable Jethro Otter, and they were looking for Creed with loaded guns. When they found him, instead of shooting it out, Morris and Creed struck up a friendship, much to Otter's chagrin and Wilson's surprise and relief.

"As a matter of fact," said Morris, "we are looking for Creed again."

Wilson's beady eyes shifted toward Kindred and figured him rightly for some sort of lawman. So, what if he was? This was his place, and he'd behave any way he pleased. Even so, it might be wise to act and speak with caution "Is that a fact?" asked Wilson. "Don't tell me Brother Locke has changed his mind about him again."

"No, that's not it," said Morris.

"Who's this Brother Locke?" asked Kindred.

My God! What a nosy little bastard he is! thought Morris of Kindred. He found himself wishing to be rid of this wart on humanity's bum.

"He's a minister at Elko," said the sheriff.

"Elko," queried Kindred. "You mean that little crossroads place we went through this morning?"

"That's the place," said Morris.

"Why didn't you tell me about this Brother Locke then?" asked Kindred. "Were you trying to hide something from me?"

"Of course not," said Morris, totally exasperated with Kindred. "It just didn't cross my mind, is all."

"Yeah, I'll bet," said Kindred. He turned to Wilson and introduced himself, making certain that the innkeeper understood who was in - charge here. "I'm looking for Clete Slater. You know him as Slate Creed. I understand he spent some time here recently. Is this true? "

Naturally distrustful of authority, especially when it was represented by outsiders, Wilson looked to Morris for guidance in this situation.

"Go ahead and tell him, Mr. Wilson," said Morris. "Something tells me Creed would want you to anyway."

Kindred glared at Morris and said, "And what the hell is that supposed to mean, Sheriff?"

Finally getting his fill of Kindred, Morris spat out, "It means that I'd sure love to be there when you do catch up with Creed. Something tells me he'll put two or three big holes in your hide with one of those big Colt pistols he carries, and that will be the end of you once and for all."

Kindred blanched, shuddered, then turned red with rage. He reached for the Remington .44-caliber revolver sheathed inside the left side of his waistband, and as he did, he swore, "You sonofabitch! I've had about enough of you! I'm going to fix you permanent, you sonofabitch!" He drew but was unable to bring the gun to bear.

Morris grabbed the wrist of Kindred's gun hand with his left and shouted back, "The hell, you say, you little bastard!" And he promptly smashed his right fist into the marshal's chin, reeling Kindred but not knocking him down. The sheriff drew back his fist and slugged the shorter man again, crashing his knuckles solidly into Kindred's left cheek, staggering him backward against the wall. Morris lost his grip on Kindred's arm but didn't bother trying to regain it. His victim collapsed in a heap without discharging his weapon.

Wilson carne over the bar prepared to enter the fray with a bung starter in his hand, but when he saw Kindred fall to the floor unconscious, he held back from using the mallet.

"Now I've gone and done it," said Morris, panting heavily. "Damn! Now what do I do?"

"Creed took the train to Nashville," said Wilson calmly. "It seems to me that Mr. Kindred here should go the other way."

Morris peered at Wilson as if worms were crawling on the innkeeper's face. "What are you saying, Mr. Wilson?"

"I'm saying the northbound train is due within the hour," said Wilson smiling. "It would be a shame if Mr. Kindred missed his connection."

"Are you saying we should put him on the train to Louisville?" asked Morris.

"Something like that," said Wilson.

The sheriff shook his head and said, "I can't do that. I'm an officer of the law. That would be obstructing justice, and I'm sworn to carry out the law, not get in the way."

"Yes, sir, I understand perfectly," said Wilson. "And I am the postmaster here in Glasgow Junction, and it's my duty to see that the mail gets where it's supposed to go. It's the law. And like you said, it's your duty to uphold the law. With that in mind, Sheriff, I'd appreciate your help in seeing that this piece of mail here gets where it's supposed to go."

"Piece of mail?" queried Morris, not following Wilson's line of thought. "What piece of mail?"

"Well, he don't exactly look like a piece of mail right now," said Wilson, indicating Kindred, "but after I stamp him good and proper and get him into a mail bag, he'll be first-class mail on its way to..." He paused in thought, then said, "Now where could this piece of mail be headed? Louisville? How about Cincinnati? What do you think, Sheriff? Cincinnati?"

Morris finally understood what Wilson had in mind. He snorted a laugh and said, "Hell, why not? This little bastard deserves it. Where's that mail bag?"

9

When he was posted in Kentucky during the war, Creed learned that Logan County was named after one of the state's earliest settlers, Benjamin Logan, and that Russellville, the county seat, was named for Revolutionary War Hero General William Russell. Later on, when he was riding under Colonel John Hunt Morgan's command, he picked up more facts about the locale, all instructed to him by a trio of soldiers from Logan County; brothers Bill and Ben Whittaker and George Morgan.

As he stared into the evening darkness beyond the windows of the Nashville & Louisville train, Creed reminisced on the Whittakers. Bill and Ben had been captured in separate engagements and sent north to Union prison camps. Creed remembered them as being good fellows who were only fair soldiers. He hoped that they had survived the ordeal of being imprisoned by the Yankees.

Recalling the Whittakers also conjured up memories of their sister, Mattie. As her image became focused in his mind, he recalled those early days of the war and the first time he saw Mattie back when he was still Clete Slater.

When the Confederate army occupied Kentucky in the late summer of 1861, the 8th Texas Cavalry was assigned to patrol an area that covered Logan, Warren, Edmondson, Hart, and Barren counties. Their job was to watch out for any encroachment of Union forces coming south from Louisville with Bowling Green as their strategic goal. The Texas companies were placed under the command of local generals, and to make them more effective, they were paired with Kentucky units.

Creed's outfit, Company F, had the duty of protecting the western reaches of Logan County. During the day, they scouted the two roads that went west out of Russellville to Elkton and to Tightsville over in Todd County; at night, they posted pickets in the outlying areas, while the majority of the men bivouacked west of Russellville near Walnut Grove. At every opportunity afforded them, the troopers rode into town to go "skirt hunting" or drinking, should their pursuit of the fairer sex prove unsuccessful. It was during one of these excursions that Creed met Mattie.

Autumn leaves were still falling from the trees when Creed rode into Russellville with a half dozen other Texas boys. They had heard that Russellville Collegiate Institute at Seventh and Summer streets was attended by some of the prettiest, smartest, and above-all friendliest girls in Kentucky. They thought they'd have a look for themselves to see if this statement should prove true or false.

The Texans rode up to the school, and from the street, several of them called out to the girls in the dormitory built onto the brick classroom building. Giggling and laughing, some of the young ladies opened their windows and leaned out to talk to these gallant young men from faraway Texas. One girl stood silently at her window, glaring out at the boisterous soldiers. Of the three adjectives that they had heard applied to the Russellville girls, she appeared to fit only one: smart. She was rather plain, with curly dishwater blonde hair, glasses, pale skin, and a straight-lipped mouth.

"That one's for you, Slater," said Jack Blackburn, pointing to the girl behind the closed window.

"Is that so?" shot back Creed. Then a thought occurred to him.

"Tell you what, Blackburn. I'll bet you a dollar that I can get her to smile before you can talk one of those gigglypusses into coming out here to meet you close up."

"Too easy, Slater," said Blackburn. "Make her open her window and talk to you and smile, and then you've got a bet."

Creed thought about it for a second, then said, "You've got a bet, Blackburn." And with that, he kicked Nimbus in the ribs, gave out a Texas yell, and charged up the lawn to the building.

The girl's window was on the second floor, near the corner of the dormitory, and the rain ·pipe ran right by it. Creed climbed up on his horse's back, stood on the saddle, then pulled himself up the rain pipe until he was beside the girl's window.

"What are you doing out there?" she shouted through the glass.

Creed held onto the pipe with one hand and cupped his ear with the other, pretending to be unable to hear her. "What?" he shouted back.

"What are you doing out there?" she repeated. "Are you insane?"

Creed continued to feign his inability to understand her. "What's that you say?" he shouted.

Exasperated, she unlatched her window and threw it open. "I said, what are ·you doing out there? Are you insane?"

"No, ma'am, I'm not insane," said Creed with as straight a face as he could muster. "If I was, I wouldn't think you're the prettiest thing I've seen yet in this here Kentucky town."

The girl gasped, covered her mouth with her hand, and backed away from the window.

"My name is Clete Slater, rna'am." He tipped his hat with one hand, while maintaining a precarious grip on the rain pipe with the other. He replaced the hat, then said, "I hail from Lavaca County, Texas, ma'am, and I'm in the Army, as you can plainly see by my uniform. Dandy, ain't it?" When she made no reply, he continued, saying, "I was just passing by and-"

Creed was unable to finish the sentence because the rain pipe came loose from the gutter at the top just then. He held on for dear life as the pipe bent away from the wall, leaving him dangling high off the ground.

The girl gasped again and rushed forward to the window. "Oh, sir," she said, "are you all right?"

"Not to worry, ma'am," he said, holding tightly to the pipe. "It's all right. Just watch." He gave out a piercing whistle that his horse recognized as a summons.'

The Appaloosa moved beneath him as if he had done this sort of thing on several occasions.

With perfect nonchalance, Creed dropped into the saddle, grabbed the reins, kicked Nimbus into a gallop, and rode off, swinging his hat over his head and screaming like a Comanche. As soon as he reached the street comer, he tugged on the reins, halting the stallion and replacing his hat on his head, then he turned the animal around and raced back to the dormitory. As Nimbus galloped past the building, Creed leaped off the horse but held onto the saddle. When his feet hit the ground, he bounced up and over the horse's back, landing on the other side, and again he bounced up and over the horse's back. He repeated this trick twice more before regaining his posture in the saddle. When horse and rider reached the other street corner, he halted Nimbus again and rode back to accept the applause of all the girls in the dormitory except the one he wanted to smile. Chagrined, he rode up to her window again. He looked up at her blank stare and said, "I must be insane after all, ma'am."

"Why is that?" she asked evenly.

"A sane man wouldn't do what I just did just because he wanted to see a girl smile."

"Is that why you did that? To impress me?"

"Didn't I say you were the prettiest girl in Russellville?"

"That proves you're insane, sir."

"No, ma'am, it only proves the poet's words," said Creed.

Her brow wiggled a bit in curiosity. 'The poet's words, sir?" she queried.

"Yes, ma'am. The ones about beauty being in the eyes of the beholder. In my case, my Grandpa Hawk always taught me to see with my heart and not just with my eyes. That's why I say you're the prettiest girl I've seen in this Kentucky town."

A smile came over the girl's lips, and a sparkle danced in her blue eyes. She leaned through the window and said, "Please stop addressing me as ma'am. It makes me feel old. My name is Matilda Whittaker, but I'd rather you called me Mattie."

Creed took another look at Mattie. A more serious view. And he recollected his grandfather Hawk McConnell telling him that everything is not always as it seems on first sight. That old Choctaw-Scots warrior was right. Especially in this case. Mattie was really quite pretty when she smiled. Creed felt a flutter in his heart as he removed his hat again and said, "I'm pleased to make your acquaintance, Miss Whittaker."

"No, please," she said, "call me Mattie."

Blackburn rode up and said, "All right, Slater, you win. I owe you a dollar."

Mattie's smile vanished. She frowned at Blackburn.

"No, you don't," said Creed.

"Sure, I do," said Blackburn. "You got this girl to open her window and talk to you, and she smiled. You win the bet."

"What's this all about, Mr. Slater?" demanded Mattie.

"Never mind that now, Jack," said Creed.

"No, sir," said Blackburn. 'A bet is a bet, and I am not a man to cheat on a bet."

Now Mattie understood, and she was furious. "You made a wager that you could entice me to open my window and that 1 would speak with you and I would smile at you?" she gasped. "Well, I never!"

"Yes, it's true," said Creed with all the honesty that his two grandfathers had taught him since childhood, "but that was before you spoke to me, Mattie Whittaker."

"What's this, Slater?" asked Blackburn in mocking disbelief. "Don't tell me you're taken with this homely crone, Slater. I ain't believing that, boy."

Creed reached over and grabbed the reins to Blackburn's horse. He gave them a quick jerk that forced the animal off balance, causing it to stumble and fall sideways, throwing Blackburn to the ground.

Blackburn rolled onto his back, propped himself onto one elbow, and said angrily, "What the hell was that for?"

"I believe you owe Miss Whittaker an apology, Jack," said Creed evenly.

Blackburn snickered and said, "The hell, you say. I ain't agonna do it. You want to apologize to her, you go right ahead, but I sure as hell don't intend to." He started to get up.

Creed leaped from the saddle and landed on Blackburn's back, sprawling him on the ground again. Creed scrambled to gain the upper hand, straddling Blackburn and forcing his face into the grass with one hand while his other put pressure on Blackburn's neck. Blackburn tried to buck Creed off his back, but as soon as he tried this maneuver, he paid for it. Creed grabbed his hair and slammed his face into the ground.

"No, sir," said Creed through clenched teeth. "I said you were to apologize to the lady."

"Mr. Slater, please," pleaded Mattie.

"No, ma'am," said Creed over his shoulder. "He had no call to say that about you, and he's going to apologize for it." He jerked Blackburn's head up and said, "Aren't you, Jack?"

Blackburn gasped for air, and when he caught his breath, he swore, "Goddamn you, Clete Slater! You'll pay for this!"

Without waiting for another word, Creed made a fist and

slammed it into Blackburn's spine at the base of his neck. The force of the blow snapped Blackburn's head face first into the grass, leaving Creed with a handful of greasy hair. Feeling Blackburn's form go limp beneath him, Creed realized that he had knocked him unconscious. To make certain that Blackburn was out cold, Creed turned Blackburn's head sideways and lifted an eyelid to see if his eyes were rolled up; they were. Creed stood up, looked down at Blackburn, then remembered Mattie Whittaker. He shifted his view to her.

"I'm really sorry about that, Miss Whittaker," he said. "He had no call to say what he did."

"He isn't dead, is he?" asked Mattie.

The other soldiers rode up now.

"No, he's just got his lamp put out is all," said Creed. "He'll have a good headache tomorrow, but he'll live."

"You best not be around when he comes to," advised Marsh Quade. "He won't soon forget this, Clete."

Creed glared at Quade and said, "Why don't you just shut up, Marsh, and get Jack on his horse and take him back to camp?"

"What are you going to do, Clete?" asked Quade.

Creed looked up at Mattie and said, "Now that all depends, don't it?"

Quade understood. He dismounted, and with the help of the other soldiers, he placed Blackburn over his saddle and took him back to camp.

Creed stuck around to explain things to Mattie, but she said no explanation was necessary. His actions had said all that she wanted to know. He asked for permission to call on her, and she gave it readily. He said he would be calling soon, then rode off to join the other soldiers.

Back at camp, Blackburn confronted Creed about the beating he had taken. "You sonofabitch!" he swore. "You'll pay for what you did to me!" He pulled a knife and started toward Creed. Creed simply drew his Colt's, cocked it, and took aim at Blackburn's upper lip. "One more step, Jack," he said calmly, "and I'll make it a lot easier for you to breathe through your nose." Blackburn made the wise decision to stop where he was. With his voice full of poison, he said, "Just you wait Slater. I'll make you pay for this."

"No, Jack, you won't," said Creed. "You were rude to Miss

Whittaker and that's no way for a Texan to behave in the presence of a lady. Now you've paid for that, but if you can't accept a proper whipping like a man, then I guess we'll have to take this thing up the ladder a bit, won't we?"

Blackburn stared at the black hole at the end of Creed's Colt's and saw death in its depths. "No, I guess not," he said. "This ain't the sort of thing worth killing for." He slipped his knife back into its sheath and turned away.

That was the last time Creed had trouble with Jack Blackburn until Creed learned that Blackburn was one of the men who had blamed him for their crime.

Creed romanced Mattie all the time that he was posted in Logan County. He thought he was in love with her, although he never told her that he was. When his company was sent south, he wrote her letters, and she wrote back. This went on until he -was captured at Shiloh. After that, he was too busy fighting the war to find the time for courtship of any kind, whether in person or through the mails. Mattie might have continued to write to him, but he never knew for certain because he never received another letter from her.

Over the ensuing years, Creed thought about Mattie on several occasions, but he made no effort to contact her, figuring it would do no good for either of them. She might get his letter, he reckoned, but he most likely would never receive hers because his unit was always on the run, never staying in one place long enough to receive any mail. Writing letters and never getting any would be too woeful for him, so he refrained from picking up a pen. When Blackburn and the others wanted to return north after obtaining their paroles in New Orleans, he almost went with them just so he could see Mattie again. But he didn't go with them. He rode home to Texas where he fell in love with Texada Ballard, the tomboy brat of his childhood who had matured into the beautiful, wonderful, desirable woman of his dreams.

Now he was returning to Russellville. He wondered if he would see Mattie. Would she even be living there yet? Maybe she bad forgotten him and had married a local. Most likely, even if she had told him and written him that she would never love another man, especially since they had known each other in a Biblical sense. But what if she had been like Texada and had made a vow that she would never wed and hadn't? What would she do when she saw him? What would he do when he saw her? These were thoughts that hadn't occurred to him before this moment. He found them troubling, plaguing his mind still as the train pulled into Russellville.

10

No one in Russellville recognized Creed the evening that he arrived in town and checked into Gray's Hotel for the night. He wasn't that lucky the next morning.

Creed ate his breakfast at the hotel, which was located on the north side of the town square. Then he headed over to the post office to inquire after George Washington Ewing. He entered the small building and introduced himself to the postmaster, Mr. Elias Porter, a tall man with long red sideburns and a thick, square red mustache.

"I was wondering if you could tell me where I might find Mr. George Washington Ewing," said Creed.

"You won't find him around here," said Porter. "He lives down near Adairville."

"Adairville? That's south of here, right?"

"That's right," said Porter. "You just take the Adairville Road out of town and keep going south until you come to the Riverside Mills on the north fork of the Red River. You cross the river there and keep going south for another half mile or so where you'll come to a road that leads off to the east. Go past that one until you come to the next road that leads off to the west." He paused and stared hard at Creed, then said, "You getting all this, son?"

Creed scratched the back of his neck and said sheepishly, "Not exactly, sir."

"Thought so." Porter produced a piece of paper and a pencil. "Here. I better draw you a map." He started making lines on the paper as he repeated the directions that he'd already given Creed. "Then you go that road," he said, picking up where he left off, "this one here that goes to the west. You go up that road until you come to another road that leads off to the south. Take that one. A short ways along you'll come to a house on the right. That ain't his. A little further down the road you'll see a big place up on a hill to your left. That's the one that belongs to George Ewing. "

He should be there. If he ain't, someone there can tell you where to find him." He handed the crude map to Creed. "You shouldn't have any trouble finding it with this. If you do, just stop at any house down that way and someone will set you on the right road real quick like."

"Thank you," said Creed, accepting the written directions. He started to leave, but another thought stopped him. "You wouldn't know if there's a Mr. and Mrs. Marshall Quade visiting Mr. Ewing, would you?"

"Seems to me that he did have someone visiting him recently," said Porter. "Folks from Tennessee?"

"That would probably be them," said Creed. "Marshall Quade rode with me during the war."

"Union?" queried Porter.

Creed looked the postmaster straight in the eye and said, "No, sir. Confederate."

Porter nodded and said, "Well, I guess it don't make no difference now, does it?"

"That's the way I see it," said Creed. He tipped his hat and added, "Thank you again, Mr. Porter."

"Don't mention it," said Porter.

Creed departed the post office and started off toward the livery stable where he had boarded Nimbus the night before. As he walked down the street, he saw a quartet of familiar faces ahead of him. Riding along Main Street and stopping in front of the Nimrod Long and Company Bank were Alex James, Jim White, and George and Oll Shepherd, four men that he had met at the races the week before at Mammoth Cave. Oddly, they were all dressed in long overcoats, the kind that Union soldiers had worn during the war. Creed picked up his pace as he watched them dismount and take a look around the town. George Shepherd and James started to go into the bank, while Oll Shepherd and White held onto their horses, which was another oddity.

"Hello, there!" called out Creed.

James and Shepherd stopped at the bank door. Fear was all over their faces, and their right hands disappeared inside their coats as they looked to see who was hailing them. Once they saw Creed they seemed to relax and moved away from the bank entrance. "Alex James, isn't it?" queried Creed.

"Yes, that's right," said James a bit nervously. He held out his hand and said, "How are you, Mr. Creed?" He pointed to Creed's left shoulder. "How's the arm?"

Creed shook hands with James and said, "Still pretty sore, but I'll live." He turned to George Shepherd and said, "How are you, Mr. Shepherd? I hope you don't mind the formality, but I'm embarrassed to admit that I don't recollect which of you is George and which is Oll." He looked at Oll.

"I'm George," said Shepherd, taking his turn at shaking hands with Creed.

"And I'm Oll" He shifted the reins in his right hand to his left, so he could shake with Creed.

"And you're Jim White," said Creed, greeting the fourth man with a firm grip.

"Yes, sir, that's right," said White.

"I'd forgotten that you boys were from over here," said Creed.

"It's nice to see familiar faces in a strange town."

"What brings you to Russellville." asked James.

"I'm looking for a fellow I rode with during the war," said Creed. "His name is Marshall Quade. You boys wouldn't happen to know him, would you?"

"I seem to recall something about a Marshall Quade a few weeks back," said Oll Shepherd. "Seems he was visiting with some folks in these parts. Yes, that's right. He had a new bride, and they were visiting some cousin of hers or something."

"That would be Mr. George Ewing," said Creed.

"Yes, that's right," said Shepherd. "And it seems that they weren't staying long but were planning on visiting some other folks before heading west to California or some place."

Creed nodded gloomily and said, "I was a afraid of that. I'd really like to find Quade soon." Brightening again, he said, "But never mind about that. What are you boys up to? A little banking business?"

James smiled nervously and glanced at George Shepherd before saying, "Yes, some banking business. We were just going inside to get a bill changed."

"Do you plan on being around town long?" asked Creed. "I'd like to buy you boys a drink later on, if you're going to be here, that is."

"Sure, we'll be around," said George Shepherd. "We'd be honored to drink with you, Mr. Creed. Wouldn't we, boys?"

The others voiced their agreement.

"Good," said Creed. "I'm staying over to Gray's Hotel. I've got to ride down to Adairville and see a Mr. Ewing about my old friend. It seems that Marsh married his niece or cousin or something, and he might know where they are now. I should be back before dark. How about meeting me at sundown at the hotel?"

"Sounds good to me," said Shepherd. "All right with everybody?"

The others agreed instantly, and the appointment was set.

"Well, I'll see you then," said Creed, and he resumed his walk to the livery stable. Fifteen minutes later he was atop his Appaloosa stallion, riding through the town square.

"Clete? Clete Slater?"

The female voice calling his real name sounded vaguely familiar to Creed. He looked around him but didn't rein in his horse. "Clete Slater, it is you," said a young woman hurrying along the boardwalk toward Creed.

Creed halted Nimbus and studied the lady's face. Brown hair, brown eyes, rather thin, a little prudish, but always neat, clean, and fresh in appearance and fragrance. He knew her, and he was pleased to see her again. "Ginny? Ginny Rapp?" A smile broke out on his face. He jumped down from the saddle, removed his hat, and met Ginny at the edge of the sidewalk. "Ginny Rapp. How are you, Ginny?"

"I'm fine, Clete," she said. "How are you?"

"Doing just fine, thank you," he said happily, his eyes beaming with delight.

"I never thought I'd ever see you around here again."

"Neither did I," said Creed. "I mean, I never expected to come here ever again."

"Yes, I'll bet you didn't," said Ginny with a touch of anger. "Well, why'd you come back here, Clete?"

His smile faded. "I'm here on some personal business," he said casually, although he was curious as to why she should make such a remark to him in that tone.

"Personal?" she queried. "How personal?"

Her question surprised him, and he was beginning to feel an irritation at her attitude. Even so, he thought it best to be polite and answer her. He forced a smile. "I'm looking for some fellows I rode with during the war," he said slowly. "Maybe you remember them? Jack Blackburn, Marshall Quade, Dick Barth, Jonas Burr, Jasper Johnson, and Dick Spencer."

"Jack Blackburn, I remember him," said Ginny, "but I haven't seen him since you were last here."

"Well, they're why I'm here."

"Oh?" It was her turn to be surprised. "Then you're not here to see Mattie?"

"Mattie? Mattie Whittaker, you mean?" queried Creed.

"Yes, of course, Mattie Whittaker. You didn't come back here to see Mattie, did you?"

"Well, no," said Creed hesitantly. "Why do you ask?"

"I thought not, Clete Slater," she said angrily. "You men are all alike. Especially you Texans."

"What does that mean?" asked a baffled Creed.

"You know perfectly well what it means," said Ginny.

"No, I don't, Ginny," said Creed with complete honesty. "Why are you so angry with me?"

She studied him for a brief moment, then said, "You really don't know, do you?"

"No, I don't," said Creed. "Just what are you talking about, Ginny?"

"I'm talking about what you did to Mattie."

"What I did to Mattie?" Now Creed was really curious. Did Ginny know the real truth about Mattie and him? Hell, did he know the real truth about Mattie and him? "I don't understand what you're getting at, Ginny. Is something wrong with Mattie?"

"Do you mean to tell me that you don't know how you broke her heart'?"

"I broke her heart?"

"Don't play so coy with me, Mr. Clete Slater. You know perfectly well that Mattie was in love with you from the first time she ever laid eyes on you."

"Well, I suppose she did care some about me," said Creed meekly and modestly.

"Care about you?" Ginny was incredulous. "She was so madly in love with you that she would have done anything to have you love her half as much."

"I loved Mattie," said Creed defensively, although with some difficulty.

"Did you, Clete? Did you love her so much that you quit writing to her less than two months after you left here?"

Creed bowed his head and feebly said, "I was captured at Shiloh, Ginny."

Ginny waited for him to add something to that statement, but when he didn't, she said simply, "And then what happened to you?"

"I escaped and joined up with Colonel Morgan," he said.

"Yes, I know," said Ginny.

Creed looked up at her and saw that she was telling him the truth. She did know. "You know?" he asked. "How could you know that?"

"How do you think I know, Clete?" she retorted as if he'd asked a stupid question.

Creed thought about it for a second, then realized how she knew that he had ridden with Morgan. "Bill and Ben, right?"

"That's right," said Ginny. They wrote home that you were in their regiment."

"I didn't see much of them in those days," said Creed as memories of those days flashed through his mind. "They were captured soon after I joined the regiment."

"Yes, I know that, too."

Frustration was beginning to take control of Creed. Very evenly, he said, "If you know so much, Ginny, why are you asking me all these questions and making all these accusations that I don't really understand at all?"

"Mattie Whittaker was my best friend, and you broke her heart, Clete Slater. Now she's gone."

"She's gone?" asked Creed, fearing the worst but hoping that he was wrong. "Do you mean she died?"

Ginny peered at him queerly, then said, "No, she's not dead. She's gone. She left Russellville a few months after she heard that you were in the same regiment with Bill and Ben and she figured out that you didn't really love her. Because if you did, you would have written her and told her that you were alive and well at least." She paused to let that much sink in before she asked, "Why didn't you at least do that much, Clete?"

Creed didn't know what to say, but he muttered, "I don't know. I guess I figured that she'd be better off not writing to me anymore. I remember thinking that I wouldn't make it through the war and that she'd be better off if she forgot about me. I suppose that's how it was, Ginny."

Ginny searched his eyes for the truth, found it, but still didn't like it. "Well, you figured wrong, Clete Slater," she said. "Mattie loved you more than life itself. She said that she'd always love you."

This conversation was beginning to hurt, and Creed had no desire for any more pain than he was already feeling over women in his life. "Where did she go, Ginny?" asked Creed for no particular reason.

Ginny was incredulous. "Are you kidding me, Clete Slater? After four years of never giving Mattie a second thought, you want to know where she is? Is that it, Clete?"

"Where did she go, Ginny?" demanded Creed, suddenly feeling a little anger himself.

"I'll never tell you," said Ginny. "I won't be the one to give you another chance to break her heart again. No, sir. Not Virginia Rapp. You'll have to find out where she is from someone else. I will never tell you."

Creed studied her face for a moment and came to the conclusion that she was adamant, that she meant exactly what she said. She wasn't about to tell him where Mattie had gone.

"All right, Ginny," said Creed. He nodded and added, "Have it your way. I'll find out from her family where she went. I know where they live."

"They won't tell you either," said Ginny.

Creed replaced his hat and swung up into the saddle. "I wouldn't be so sure about that, Ginny."

"I would!"

He tipped his hat and said, "It was nice seeing you again, Ginny. I hope you fare well with your life." And he rode away toward the Adairville Road.

11

As he rode south toward **Adairville, Creed's** thoughts turned to the conversation he'd had that morning with Virginia Rapp. More so, he thought about the subject of their talk, Mattie Whittaker, and memories of those days with her floated through his mind like a warm dream.

While attending the Russellville Collegiate Institute, Mattie Whittaker boarded at the school. Her family lived at Whittaker's Grove south of Russellville on Orndorff Mill Road. Although he met her at the college and saw her there often during November and early December, Creed didn't begin to court Mattie seriously until she invited him to her parents' house for Christmas dinner that first year of the war. He accepted gladly and joined the Whittakers for the holiday meal. Bill and Ben Whittaker were home on furlough, so the whole family was present.

Mr. Whittaker questioned Creed extensively about Texas, longhorn cattle, and the Plains, while Mrs. Whittaker centered her interest around his people: where did they come from before they moved to Texas? who were his antecedents? and the like. Mattie's brothers discussed the war with him, and Mattie just listened and watched and allowed her love for him to grow beyond sensible limits.

That evening as the crisp day faded into cold night Mattie and Creed went for a walk through the walnut grove, and it was during this stroll that Creed kissed her for the first time. It was a quick kiss, not much more than a peck, but it was still a kiss with all the intent of love behind it. Backing away from her for a second, he wondered if he'd done the right thing or if he'd done it the right way. "I'm sorry," he said, "but I just had to kiss you, Mattie."

She blushed, lowered her eyes, smiled reflexively, and said, "No, don't be sorry. It was me. I've never been kissed by a young man before, you see."

Creed appreciated her candor and said, "I've never kissed anyone like you before, Mattie." He removed his hat and dropped it on the ground beside them. He took her arms in his hands and pulled her toward him. She was hesitant, and this made him want to hold her all the more. Her eyes met his for an instant, and he read everything in them. Fear, love, insecurity, desire, no, yes, now, forever. He bent down a little and brought his lips to hers. He felt a quiver run through her, and he pulled her closer and pressed his mouth bard against hers. In the next second, her arms were around his neck, and he was embracing her, holding her as tightly as he could without hurting her. The kiss seemed to last for an eternity, and at the same time it was finished all too quickly. Parting their lips but not their embrace, he whispered in her ear, "Oh, Mattie, I've wanted to do that for such a long time."

"And I've wanted you to kiss me for such a long time," she whispered back to him.

He kissed her again, and suddenly, the night was not so cold, as the warmth of love braced them against the chill air. At that moment, they were both deeply in love with each other.

Creed called on Mattie twice more at her parents' home during the holidays, then she went back to school and he became busy with the war again.

As he rode up the lane to the Whittaker home four years later, Creed wondered what sort of reception he would receive this time, considering the way Virginia Rapp had treated him in town that morning. He knew of only one way to find out:

The Whittaker house didn't appear to be as prosperous as the last time he had seen it. The paint was peeling, a shutter hung by one hinge, the steps were bare wood and cracked from the weather. The war had evidently taken a toll here, too.

Creed knocked at the front door, and when it opened, he was surprised to See Mrs. Whittaker looking so much older than he remembered her. "Yes?" she said, not recognizing him.

"Good morning, Mrs. Whittaker," said Creed, removing his hat.

He smiled and said, "I don't believe you remember me."

Before he could say anything more, her tired gray eyes grew wide with surprise first, then became dark with anger and disgust.

"You are wrong, sir," she said coldly. "I do recollect you. You are that Texan who spoiled my daughter. If I were a man, sir, I would take the snake to you like an overseer does to a lazy nigger."

"Who is it, Martha?" called Mr. Whittaker from behind her. The senior Whittaker appeared beside his wife. "May I help you, sir?" he asked. Then he, too, recognized Creed as Clete Slater. "You!" He nudged Mrs. Whittaker aside as he moved past her through the doorway at Creed. He shook his fist at the Texan and swore, "Damn you! Damn you! You sonofabitch! Damn your soul to hell for all eternity!" He continued to move toward Creed.

This was a reception for which Creed was totally unprepared. He backed away unsteadily and stumbled down the porch steps, falling to the dirt walkway.

"Damn you, you sonofabitch!" Mr. Whittaker continued to curse him from the top step. "If I had my gun, I'd shoot you down like the dirty dog that you are! Get off of my property!" He turned to his wife and said, "Martha, get my rifle. I'll show this sonofabitch that he can't spoil a girl like our Mattie and live to boast about it. Hurry, dear, before he rides away."

Creed got up awkwardly. "Mr. Whittaker, I don't understand," he said. "What are you talking about? Spoil your daughter? I don't understand."

"Liar!" yelled the old man. "You deflowered my daughter, and you deny it. Liar! I'll send you to Hell for that foulest of deeds, you sonofabitch!"

Omigod! thought Creed. They found out! Now he knew what Ginny Rapp had been talking about. Without another thought, he turned and ran for his horse.

"Run, you cowardly sonofabitch!" screamed Whittaker. "Go on and get out of here while you can, and if I ever set my eye on you again, I'll shoot you dead. I swear by the Almighty, I will. Go on! Get!"

Creed wasted no time leaping atop Nimbus and riding away as fast as he could toward Adairville.

They found out, he thought as soon as he felt he was safely away from the Whittaker farm. But how? Then he recalled his last night with Mattie.

Rumors had come down to the troops that with the fall of Fort

Henry on the Tennessee River in early February that General Albert Sidney Johnston was planning to withdraw all Confederate forces from Kentucky and set up a defensive line from Memphis to Nashville. Creed's unit heard that they were to cover the evacuation of Bowling Green, then ride to the aid of the men that were soon expected to come under Siege at Fort Donelson on the Cumberland River.

Like most of the other soldiers who had found sweethearts in the area, Creed mounted up and rode into Russellville for one last kiss and to say good-bye to the girl he was leaving behind. He found Mattie at the college, waiting for him inside the front door.

"We're going to pull out tomorrow," said Creed. "Maybe tonight. I don't know for sure when yet."

"I know," said Mattie softly. "We heard already."

"I came to see you one more time," said Creed. "I wish we didn't have to go. I wish those Yankees would go back north of the Ohio River and leave us alone down here."

"If it wasn't for the war," said Mattie, "we would have never met."

Creed peered at her quizzically and said, "I suppose that's one way of looking at it, but you are the only good thing that's come out of this war so far for me."

"I'm frightened that I'll never see you again, Clete," said Mattie anxiously. "Isn't there any possible way that you could stay here?"

"No, Mattie, there isn't. I have to go with my company. There's lots of other fellows who want to stay here as badly as I do, but if we all stayed, who would be left to fight the Yankees? No, Mattie, I have to go."

She looked around the foyer at the other couples there. "Come on," she said. "We can't say farewell properly here." She led him through the building to the door to her room. "Wait here while I get my wrap." She left for a brief minute, then returned wearing a long brown cape. Taking his hand, she said, "Come on," and she led him out the back door of the school.

The winter night was cold, crisp, and clear. As Mattie led Creed across the rear yard, the young lovers could see their heavy breaths steaming in the air in front of them. They crossed the street and walked between two houses to a bam in the rear of one. Mattie scanned the darkness to make certain that they hadn't been seen, then she quietly opened the door and took Creed inside. After closing the door behind them, she took his hand again and led him to the ladder that went up to the loft. They climbed in silence until they reached the hay mow. Mattie found the right spot and pulled Creed down beside her. She lay back, untied the string of her cape, and spread it out on the hay.

"Now, Clete Slater, I want you to give me a proper farewell," she whispered.

At first, Creed was unsure of what she meant, but after a few wet kisses, he knew. He wasn't inexperienced in lovemaking, having had the frivolous pleasure of enjoying the promiscuous May sisters, Lucy and Marcella, more than once each, although not at the same time. Both being full of experience, they had taken the time to teach Creed what a woman wanted from a man when she was in the throes of passion. And now Mattie was giving him the opportunity to use that carnal knowledge. They made love several times through the night until the cocks began crowing just before dawn.

"Come on," said Creed. "We have to get back."

"I don't want to go," said Mattie. "I want this night to last forever."

A rooster reminded Creed that daylight was breaking. "I wish it would go on forever, too," he said, "but the world stops for no one. Or so I've heard. We must go, Mattie."

She pulled him to her one more time and said, "Give me one last kiss, then you may go, Clete." He kissed her long and hard hen broke away. He refused to look back and see the tears streaming down her cheeks. He slipped out of the barn and was soon on the way back to his company's camp.

As he continued to ride along toward Adairville, Creed recalled the months after leaving Mattie in Russellville. She wrote to him. He wrote to her until he was captured at Shiloh. He tried to remember their letters, but his memory failed him as he couldn't recollect anything in them to indicate that there was any reason for him to suspect that she had told her parents about their night of love making in the barn. Then he thought about Mattie's brothers.

In the few short months that he served with them in Morgan's regiment, both of them were as friendly as they had been that Christmas day at their parents' home, and neither of them said anything about their parents being distressed about his relationship with Mattie. In fact, Bill and Ben said that they were hoping he would marry their sister after the war.

Possibly, he thought, Mattie had told Ginny Rapp about their night in the barn. Girls did that sort of thing, he reasoned. Then, possibly, in a fit of anger, Ginny told the Whittakers. Yes, that was possible, but that still didn't explain why Mattie had left Russellville. Only shame would have driven her from her home. Possibly Ginny had told the whole town. No, neither of those propositions was likely. Ginny wasn't that sort of person.

Then how did the Whittakers learn about his night with Mattie? They knew. Ginny knew. Who else knew? He wasn't sure he wanted to find out.

12

Creed found George Washington Ewing's house with little trouble; the directions on the map given to him by Elias Porter being perfect. He rode up the hill to the Ewing house, tied Nimbus to the hitching post, and climbed the porch steps to the door where an older man, coming outside, met him.

"May I help you, sir?" asked the gentleman dressed in a tan planter's suit.

"Yes, sir," said Creed. "I am Slate Creed of Lavaca County, Texas. I am looking for the Honorable George Washington Ewing. I have a letter of introduction for him from Colonel John C. Burch of Nashville."

The older man smiled and said, "Colonel Burch. How is he these days, Mr. Creed?"

"Colonel Burch is fine," said Creed. "I take it, sir, that you are Mr. Ewing."

"Yes, I am," said Ewing. He held out his hand and added, "May I see the letter please?"

Creed reached inside his coat, pulled out the letter, and handed it over to Ewing.

The older man broke the seal and read the missive quickly, then refolded the paper and squinted at Creed. "Colonel Burch says you rode with Morgan. I thought you just said that you're from Texas."

"Yes, sir, I am, but I was captured at Shiloh, escaped, and when I couldn't locate my own regiment again, I joined Colonel Morgan's brigade. I rode with him until he was captured."

"I see," said Ewing, looking a little distant. "One of our bravest and most gallant leaders in the late war, Colonel Morgan was. A great son of Kentucky. A few more like him and the Yankees would have quit the war instead of us."

"Yes, sir," said Creed, patronizing Ewing, although trying not to show it.

Ewing cleared his throat and said, "Well, enough of that. I'm pleased to make your acquaintance. Mr. Creed." He offered his hand in friendship, and Creed shook it. "Come into my house, Mr. Creed, and tell me what I can do for you." He opened the door and went inside.

Creed followed Ewing into the house, and they went into the parlor where Creed sat on a sofa and his host eased himself into a high-backed cushioned chair. Mrs. Ewing came in and was introduced to Creed. Like the good Southern lady that she was, she asked her husband whether Mr. Creed would be staying for dinner, which was close at hand. Ewing then extended the invitation to Creed, and being a good guest, the Texan accepted, saying he'd be honored to sit at Mrs. Ewing's table. The lady then left the men to talk about whatever it was that men talked about on these occasions.

"Now what may I do for you, Mr. Creed?" asked Ewing.

"Sir, I am looking for Marshall Quade," said Creed, coming straight to the point. "I was told by a kinsman of yours, Mr. Josiah Ewing of Wrencoe, Tennessee, and his sister, Mrs. Mary Perkins, also of Wrencoe, that Marshall Quade and his bride, Mrs. Perkins's daughter Sal, came here to visit you recently. I was told in Russellville that they are no longer here, that they have moved on west."

"Yes?" queried Ewing noncommittally.

"Well, sir, I need to find Marsh Quade," said Creed.

"What sort of business do you have with him?" asked Ewing.

Very quickly, Creed related the tale of how Quade was one of the men who bad raided the Federal wagons down in Mississippi and how Quade and the others had lied, after they were caught, about Creed participating in the robbery. Without going into detail, he continued the story by telling Ewing that he needed to find Quade and the others, so he could get affidavits or some other form of sworn testimony from them declaring him to be innocent of their crime.

Ewing nodded rhythmically as he listened and studied Creed for any sign of deception. Seeing none, he said, "Marsh and Sal were here, just as you were told in Russellville, but they're gone now. They carne here hoping that I could help them, meaning Marsh was looking for work and hoping that I could provide him with employment. As you can see, Mr. Creed, I am not a wealthy man, especially since the fortunes of war turned against me back in '62. Of course, I don't have to tell you about that. You were here fighting, weren't you, when matters became critical in this locality?"

"Yes, sir, I was," said Creed. Then he succinctly told Ewing about his war experience in this part of Kentucky.

"Well, as I was saying, sir," said Ewing, "I couldn't offer Marsh any employment, so I suggested that he and Sal move west. I gave them a small sum of money to help them along, and I said that they might try my cousin James Berry in Lexington, Missouri. He's a newspaper publisher there, and newspaper publishers are always in need of help. Besides, James is one of us."

"Is that where they went?" asked Creed, ignoring Ewing's last statement. "Lexington, Missouri, I mean."

"That's where they said they were going when they left here last month," said Ewing.

"Last month?" queried Creed. "I was under the impression that they only left here a few days ago."

"More like a few weeks ago," said Ewing. "They came right after Christmas, then they departed from here…hmm…let me see now. Yes, it must have been a week ago this past Monday. Yes, that's it. A week ago, this past Monday. That would have been the twenty-third instant, I believe."

"How were they traveling?" asked Creed.

"I took them to the railroad depot in Russellville," said Ewing.

"They caught the morning train for Memphis. From there, they were going to book passage on a packet boat to St. Louis, where they would catch another train for Lexington, if the railroad stretches that far, that is."

"Well, this is better news than I expected," said Creed.

"Oh? How so, Mr. Creed?"

"Your cousin Josiah said that they had written Mrs. Perkins that they were going to Colorado. A place called Denver."

"They did discuss such a move with me," said Ewing, "but I argued against it. I told the young people to try Missouri first, and if there were no opportunities for them there, then they could go to

Colorado and seek their fortune. Will you be going to Lexington to look for Marshall and Sal there, Mr. Creed?"

"Yes, sir, I'll probably do that."

"Then you'll need this letter from Colonel Burch, and I'll give you one from me for my cousin. You know, we can't be too careful these days."

"No, sir, we can't be too careful these days," said Creed, although he wasn't quite certain exactly what Ewing meant by that last statement.

Mrs. Ewing came into the room and said that dinner was ready. Creed ate with the Ewing's and enjoyed a pleasant meal, then headed back to Russellville that afternoon, now with two letters of introduction in his pocket.

13

Upon returning to Gray's Hotel later that afternoon, Creed was met in the lobby by the owner; George Gray, a middle-aged man of average height, weight, and build with a bland face, brown eyes, salt-and-pepper hair and beard, and horn-rimmed spectacles. The proprietor had Creed's few belongings in a pile on the counter.

"Mr. Creed," said Gray quite nervously, "I would like you to leave my hotel at once. Here is the return of your money for tonight's lodging." He handed Creed a fifty-cent piece.

"I don't understand, Mr. Gray," said Creed, peering at the innkeeper quizzically. "Is something wrong?"

"Yes, something is very wrong, Mr. Creed," said Gray, glancing over Creed's shoulder.

"Well, what is it?" asked Creed impatiently.

"It's the Whittakers," said Gray, heaving a sigh.

"The Whittakers?"

"Yes, Ben and Bill," said Gray. "They were in here earlier looking for you. The word around town is that they intend to take you out somewhere and take the whip to you or worse."

Creed frowned and turned toward the front door in reaction to Gray's statement. So now it was Ben and Bill though of course, he couldn't blame them. If someone had deflowered his sister, he'd be mad as hell, too.

"They aim to do you harm, Mr. Creed," said Gray, "and I don't want it to happen in my hotel."

"No, of course, you don't," said Creed. "I understand your feelings in this matter. I'll move along right away."

"If I were you, Mr. Creed, I'd leave town immediately."

"I just might do that," said Creed. "Thank you, Mr. Gray, for the warning. You've got a nice hotel here. I enjoyed my stay." He tipped his hat, picked up his belongings, and left.

Creed went outside and started putting his saddlebags and bed roll on the Appaloosa's back. As he tied on the blanket and slicker, he heard a familiar voice call his name behind him and turned to see Alex James coming toward him.

"Are you leaving town?" asked James.

"Yes, I am," said Creed, "but not before finding you and your friends first."

James smiled and said, "Well, that's good. Come on. Jim and the Shepherds are waiting for us over to the saloon."

They headed down the street for the drinking establishment that James had mentioned. They were almost there when the crack of a whip halted their progress.

"Hold it right there Slater!"

Creed knew that voice, too, and he recognized its owner as Bill Whittaker. He turned to see Bill standing in the middle of the street. Ben was about twenty feet to his left. Each of them held a nasty blacksnake coiled in their right hands. They were both about Creed's height and weight with sandy blond hair, blue eyes, and a slight sneer to their lips. Each sported a thick mustache and long sideburns.

"I heard you boys were looking for me," said Creed, trying to be friendly. "I'd hoped to see you while I was here and we could talk some about old times, but from the looks of those snakes you're carrying, I guess that's out of the question now."

"How could you even think of talking to us after what you did to our sister?" demanded Bill.

"What happened between Mattie and me was our business," said Creed frankly.

"A decent man would have married her," said Ben.

"Don't think that thought didn't cross my mind more than a few times," said Creed, "but I figured I wouldn't live through the war, so why bother?"

"Why bother?" queried Bill. He was incredulous at Creed's cavalier attitude. "Did you hear that, Ben? Why bother? Can you believe that?"

"I heard it," said Ben. "But I don't believe it."

"I'll show you why you should have bothered, Clete Slater," said Bill. He unlimbered his whip and came at Creed with it. Without hesitating, Creed drew his Colt's and took aim at Bill's face. "No, sir!" he growled. "You will not use that whip on me."

Whittaker hesitated, remembering that Creed was a dead shot with any kind of gun. His brother must have forgotten because he stretched out his snake and snapped it at Creed's gun hand. The leather viper wrapped itself around the Texan's forearm, and the younger Whittaker gave it a good jerk causing Creed to pull the trigger. The bullet missed Bill and shattered a window across the street.

Creed held on to his gun as he freed himself from Ben's whip, but by then, Bill had his lash in motion, striking Creed's other arm with it. Before Creed could defend himself, Ben had his cracker in action again, knocking Creed's hat off his head. Both brothers were attacking him furiously now, and Creed could do nothing except back away and protect his face with his arms and hope that they would give him an opening somewhere and he could use the Colt's that he continued to hold firmly.

James didn't know exactly why the Whittakers were whipping Creed, but he felt that he should intervene because the Texan was a former Confederate. He drew his Remington .44, cocked it, took careful aim at Ben Whittaker's right foot, and fired.

Whittaker felt the impact of the ball before he heard the explosion from the gun. The heel of his boot disintegrated as his right foot was kicked out from under him. He lost his balance and fell to the ground.

Bill heard the gunshot, then saw his brother writhing in the dirt and holding his injured foot.

"Sonofabitch shot me in the foot!" swore Ben.

James bent up his arm to let the cap fall from his revolver, then he cocked the gun again and took aim at Bill's face. "Now I don't know what this is all about, mister," he said, "but you're whipping my good friend here, and I think you ought to stop it."

"Your friend?" queried Whittaker.

"Damn, Bill!" whined Ben. "He shot me in the foot."

"Shut up, Ben!" snapped Bill. "You ain't dying."

"No, but you will be if you go to whipping Mr. Creed again," said James.

"Mr. Creed?" queried Whittaker, staring at Creed. "Your name is Clete Slater."

"It was," said Creed evenly. "I changed it."

"Why? So you could hide the shameful thing you did to Mattie?" demanded Bill.

As a crowd began to gather around them, Creed picked up his hat and said, "What happened between Mattie and me is no one's business but hers and mine. That means you, your brother, and your whole family can just butt out, Bill."

"You sonofabitch!" swore Bill. He started to raise his whip again but was stopped by the sight of Creed raising his Colt's and taking aim.

"I can understand your feeling the way you do," said Creed, cocking the pistol, "and that's the only reason why I'm willing to let you live, Bill. But if you call me that one more time, I will shoot you dead and not regret it one bit. The same goes for you, Ben."

The brothers stared at Creed for a second, then at each other.

Bill scanned the growing group of spectators and decided further violence would be unwise. He rolled up his whip and said, "I believe you would, Slater or Creed, or whatever it is you call yourself now." He moved to his brother and knelt down beside him. "Let me see your foot, Ben."

Reluctantly, Ben showed him the foot, and both of them realized that James had only shot the heel off the boot. "All right, so there ain't no blood," said Ben. "It sure as hell hurts a lot."

"You'll live, Ben," said Bill. He looked back at Creed and James who had moved next to the Texan. "Lucky for the two of you that he's all right."

Creed pulled back his coat, replaced his gun, then stepped up to them and said, "Bill, I'd like to know where Mattie is."

"Don't tell him, Bill," said Ben.

"Haven't you shamed her enough already?" demanded Bill, ignoring his brother.

Creed perused Bill's face, then Ben's. He realized that he would get nothing from either of them except their hatred. "Have it your way," said Creed, "but remember this. I loved your sister, and she loved me. The last thing I ever wanted to do to her was hurt her. She knew that, and she was willing too."

"Willing?" shouted Bill. "Liar! My sister would never give herself to a man without a parson having said the words first."

Creed grabbed Bill by his coat lapels and jerked him to his feet. He shook Whittaker violently, then threw him down on the cold, hard ground. In the next instant, he was moving toward Bill, but before he could deliver a solid kick to Whittaker's ribs, Ben grabbed him around the legs and wrestled him to the ground. Creed rolled onto his back just in time to see Bill get to his feet and come over to stomp him in the dirt. He jerked one leg free from Ben and kicked him with it. Bill raised his foot over Creed's face, but the Texan grabbed it, twisted it, and spilled Whittaker to the ground again.

Shooting either of the Whittakers was a little too drastic, even for a former guerrilla like James, but giving Bill a boot in the face wasn't beneath him. He put his six-gun away, swung his foot forward, and caught Whittaker on his right cheek with the toe. Bill's head snapped to the side, and Whittaker, who had crawled to his hands and knees, dropped like a brick, totally senseless.

Creed was able to free himself from Ben and get to his feet. He grabbed Whittaker by his coat and jerked him upright. He made a fist and smashed Ben in the jaw, drew back, and repeated the blow. When his victim went limp. Creed held off hitting him a third time and let him fall unconscious to the street.

With heaving breath, Creed stood over the brothers and stared down at them. "When they wake up," he said to anyone who was listening, "tell them that I don't blame them for hating me, but if they ever come near me again with the idea of doing me harm, I will forget that we once rode together, and I will kill them both." He looked up at the crowd around them, shifting his view from face to face. "Did everybody hear that?" To the first fellow who nodded affirmatively, he added, "Be sure you tell them exactly what I said."

"Yes, sir," said the nervous little man.

"Come on, Alex," said Creed. "I'll have that drink with you and your friends, and then I'll be on my way."

14

As soon as he arrived in Nashville by train, Jim Kindred went straight to City Marshal James H. Brantley's office and presented his credentials to the local lawman.

"And what brings you to Nashville, Marshal Kindred?" asked Brantley as he leaned back in his desk chair. The Nashville marshal was an elected official, and Brantley had the look of a politician about him. He was dressed dapperly in a suit and vest, and his dark brown hair and mustache were properly brilliantined.

"I'm on the trail of a fugitive named Clete Slater," said Kindred.

"He also goes by the name of Slate Creed."

"What's he wanted for?" asked Brantley.

Quickly, Kindred explained the case against Creed, then said, "I was misled by friends of his up in Kentucky that he went to Louisville. That was several days ago. I discovered that he wasn't in Louisville but had come here to Nashville."

"Nashville is a large city, Marshal Kindred," said Brantley. "A man doesn't have to try too hard to hide here."

"Yes, I can see that," said Kindred. "That's why I came directly to you. I figured your office would be the perfect place to begin looking for Slater."

Brantley smiled sardonically, and with a twinkle in his blue eyes, he said, "I assure you, sir, that he's not in this office."

Kindred laughed politely and said, "Very good, Marshal Brantley. A good joke, sir."

"Thank you, sir. Yes, of course, this office would be more than glad to aid you in your search for this man." He rocked forward and came to his feet. "I have the perfect man to help you." He went to the door, opened it, poked his head out, and said to the desk sergeant, "Get Cavitt for me, McCracken." He closed the door, returned to his seat, and resumed his conversation with Kindred. "Ransome Cavitt is our chief detective, Marshal Kindred. If your fugitive is here in Nashville, Cavitt will find him."

"And if he isn't here?" queried Kindred.

"Then Cavitt will find out where he went from here - if he was ever here, that is." There was a knock at the door. "Come in," said Brantley.

The door opened, and Ransome Cavitt entered the room. Nashville's chief detective was a rather nondescript fellow, being average in height, a little thick about the middle, with a bland face, reddish brown hair and mustache, and chestnut eyes that appeared dull and lackadaisical. His attire was plain, too. A navy blue suit with worn cuffs and lapels and a yellowed white shirt and collar with a maroon tie that had food stains on it. He stepped to the end of Brantley's desk and said, "You wanted to see me, Jim?"

"Yes, Ransome, I did," said Brantley. He introduced Kindred and explained the marshal's reason for being in his office.

"I see," said Cavitt. "Well, I'm at your disposal, Marshal Kindred, if you would like my help in finding this fugitive."

"I would like nothing better," said Kindred.

"Well, sir, if you will come to my office and tell me everything you know about this man," said Cavitt, "we can begin looking for him immediately." He turned to Brantley and said, "If you'll pardon us, Jim?"

"Certainly, Ransome," said Brantley. "Keep me informed about your progress in this case, won't you?"

"Yes, sir."

Brantley held out his hand to Kindred and said, "It was a pleasure to meet you, Marshal Kindred. As I said before, if your man is here in Nashville, Ransome will find him for you."

"Thank you, Marshal Brantley," said Kindred, shaking hands with the local lawman. He left the room with Cavitt.

As soon as Kindred and the detective were gone, Brantley looked hard at the hand that had just been gripped by Kindred, and he immediately took a handkerchief and wiped it clean as if it were soiled with grime. Dissatisfied with that, he went to the pitcher and basin that he kept on the stand in the comer, poured water over his hands, and washed them thoroughly. At last happy that his hands were clean again, he donned his plug hat and left the office.

"I'm going over to the *Union and American* building, McCracken," said Brantley as he passed by the desk sergeant. "Don't bother me there unless someone important gets killed."

A few minutes later Brantley was sitting in Colonel John Burch's office. "You say this fellow is a federal marshal, Jim?" asked Burch casually.

"He's got papers to prove it," said Brantley.

"I sort of expected something like this," said Burch.

"Colonel, you didn't tell me this client of yours was a fugitive from the Army."

"You didn't ask," said Burch with a friendly smile.

"Well, I know now," said Brantley.

"And what do you plan on doing about it, Jim?"

"I'm going to help this Kindred fellow as much as I can," said the city marshal. Then he looked down at his feet and said, "Although for the life of me, I don't know why." He looked up at Burch again. "There's something about him that I don't like, Colonel. Kindred, I mean. When I shook hands with him, it was like getting hold of a dead fish. You know what I mean?"

"From what I learned from my client. this Kindred fellow isn't one of us, Jim. He was an enrollment officer down in Texas during the war. You know the kind. Rally 'round the Stars and Bars, boy, until the Yankees come, then rally 'round the Stars and Stripes."

"Yes, I know the kind, Colonel. Even so, I have to help him look for your client."

"You don't have to look too hard, do you, Jim?"

"Are you suggesting I do anything less?"

"Of course not," said Burch. "I'm an officer of the court, the same as you are. I would never think of aiding and abetting a fugitive from the Federals."

Brantley studied Burch, then said, "Why don't I believe you, Colonel?"

Burch merely shrugged

.

75

15

Creed had his drink with Alex James, Oll and George Shepherd, and Jim White, and he told them that he was leaving town immediately. When they asked him where he was going, he didn't hesitate to say that his destination was Lexington, Missouri.

"Lexington, you say?" asked James. What takes you to Lexington, Mr. Creed?"

"One of the fellows I'm looking for," said Creed. "I understand that he and his new bride went there recently."

"Well, I'm from Clay County, Missouri," said James, "and that's not too far from Lexington. Clay County is just a few counties away from Lafayette County. That's the county that Lexington is in. Lexington's the county town for Lafayette County. I spent a little time there during the war. So did you boys, didn't you, Oll?"

"That's right," said Oll, "Lot of nice folks in Lexington. Our kind of people, Mr. Creed."

"I wish you boys would quit calling me Mr. Creed. Slate will do nicely."

"All right, Slate," said James. "As I was going to say, I'm from Clay County, and I was thinking about going home soon for a visit. I've just about worn out my welcome here with my Uncle George, and Oll's wife is tired of feeding me, too."

"No, she ain't," said Oll.

James slapped Shepherd on the back and said, "I know she isn't, Oll. I was just joshing you a bit. Anyway, my brother Jesse is still ailin' from his war wound, and I'd like to see him again before anything bad happens to him, Lord forbid."

"Amen, Buck," said George. "Dingus was a good soldier."
"Dingus?" queried Creed.

George chuckled and said, "Oh, that's what we called Buck's brother Jesse. You see, we were riding along this one day soon after Dingus joined up with our outfit, when he got his balls caught between his pistol and his saddle."

Creed winced at the thought of how much pain that could cause a man.

George and the others chuckled at Creed's reaction, then George continued with telling the tale. "Well, sir, it sure did smart that boy in his man's parts, but the best swear word he could come up with was dingus. 'Dingus, that hurts!' he yelled out. Well, it was funny enough that he got his balls caught like that, but when all he could do was yell dingus - Well, sir, it was all we could do to contain ourselves from laughing so hard that we almost fell off our horses. We had us a good laugh about it for several days, and we all started calling him Dingus from then on. He always took it pretty good. Like I said, he was a good soldier. It wasn't right what them Yankees did to him when he tried to surrender himself."

"Wisconsin company, wasn't it?" said Oll.

"That's right," said George. "We came back from Texas last spring and found out General Lee had surrendered in Virginia and General Johnston had quit in Carolina. We took a vote, and most of us decided that it'd be best that we surrendered, too. Of course, not everybody was in favor of calling it quits because we wasn't sure how we'd be treated since we was guerrillas and all, so even them that was in favor of surrendering didn't want to surrender to any Redlegs or Home Guards or Militia. So Dave Pool said we ought to give ourselves up at Lexington because our people had been in control there most of the war and regular Union army soldiers was occupying the town then. Dave took forty men and rode into Lexington and gave himself up to this Yankee officer named Harding. When they was treated fairly by the Yankees, Dave rode out and brought in some more. Dingus wasn't among them, though. I heard tell he was sticking with Arch Clement and Jim Anderson who was afraid to give up because he was Bloody Bill's brother and he figured they might hang him for what his brother done during the war. Well then, I guess Dingus had a change of heart and came in to surrender, but those Wisconsin Yankees was drunk on duty, I heard, and they started shooting at him and the other boys who was with Dingus. Poor kid took a bullet in the lung, but he made it to the woods and got away."

"He got home from there," said James, "but no one was there. Damn Militia forced Ma and the family to move to Nebraska late in the war, but some Yankee named Rogers found them all right and sent Jesse to them. Last Ma wrote was they all went back to Missouri because Jesse didn't want to die in a Yankee state. They went to stay with my Uncle John in Harlem. Jesse was still alive at Christmas, but Ma said he still wasn't good."

"He'll make it, Buck," said George. "Dingus is a pretty tough kid."

"I hope you're right, George," said James. "Anyway, I'd like to see him again, just in case the Lord has other plans for him. So, I was wondering, Slate, if you'd mind if I rode along with you to Lexington."

"No, I wouldn't mind at all," said Creed. "As a matter of fact, I was hoping that was what you were getting at."

"You leaving right away with him, Buck?" asked Oll. "If Slate's leaving right away, then I am, too," said James.

"Why do you ask?"

"Well, I thought we had some unfinished business here in Russellville," said Oll.

"I ain't exactly interested any longer," said James. "You boys can handle that deal without me. You and Jim got lots of old friends around here who'd like to deal with that bank as much as you do. You can get one of them to take my place."

George and Oil looked glumly at each other, but neither said a word of what was on their minds. Jim White said it for them. "It wouldn't be the same without you, Buck."

"Well, there's banks in Missouri," said James. "We can do some business with one of them, if you like."

The Shepherds brightened at the suggestion, and Oll said, "Sounds like a reasonable idea to me, George. What do you say? Should we try a bank in Missouri?"

"Sounds good to me," said George with a big grin.

"Me, too," said White eagerly.

Creed chuckled and said, "Sounds good to me, too. From what I've heard about matters in Missouri, I think I'd prefer to ride in a group than alone."

Oll poured whiskey into everyone's glass, then picked up his glass and said, "To Missouri then." The others joined him in the toast.

That settled it. Creed had four companions for his journey to Lexington

.

16

Detective Ransome Cavitt took a stubby pencil and a little note- book that he kept for such purposes in his inside coat pocket and wrote down all the information that Kindred could give him about Creed. He asked questions that the short Texan had never thought of asking anyone else, such as a description of Creed, to which Kindred responded immediately: "Tall fellow."

"How tall?" asked Cavitt, thinking that just about every other man in the world had to be taller than Kindred.

"Probably six foot," said Kindred. "Maybe a little taller than that."

"What color is his hair?"

"Kind of red but not quite red. More like straw colored. No, that's too yellow. It's darker than that."

"I see," said Cavitt, writing. "How about his eyes? What color are they?"

"Color of his eyes? Hell, I don't know. What difference does it make what color his eyes are?"

"It makes it easier for me to find him, Marshal Kindred," said Cavitt patiently. "When I make inquiries, I can describe the person I'm looking for to people and they can tell me whether they've seen a person of that description."

Kindred nodded gravely as understanding set in. "I see," he said. "Well, I guess his eyes are blue."

Cavitt put down his pencil and said, "I can't go on guesses, Marshal Kindred. I must have precise details."

"Well, he's got light-colored eyes," said Kindred. "I know that for certain. His eyes are definitely not brown. They're either blue or gray or maybe even green."

Cavitt picked up his pencil again and wrote while he said, "Blue or gray or green." Then he looked up at Kindred again. "Anything else about him that you can recall, Marshal? Is he a heavy man? A lean man? Does he have any scars that can be seen clearly? Things of that nature."

"He's not heavy," said Kindred, "and he's not lean either. I'd say he's somewhere in between."

"Medium build," said Cavitt as he wrote the words in the pocket-sized notebook.

"And he doesn't have any scars that I know about," said Kindred. A thought crossed his mind. "He had a mustache the first time I saw him, but he didn't have one the last time I saw him. He could have a mustache again. It was a real chestnut color. His mustache, I mean. And it drooped down around the corners of his mouth. Leastways, that's what it looked like back then. Last spring it was, down in Texas."

"I see," said Cavitt, still writing.

"One thing that might be a dead giveaway to Creed could be his horse. He rode a gray Appaloosa down home. From what I was able to learn up in Kentucky, he was still riding it."

"What kind of horse did you say it was?" asked Cavitt. "An Appaloosa," said Kindred. "Gray one."

"Never heard of the breed," said Cavitt. "What do they look like?"

"About the only real difference in an Appaloosa and other horses is the spots."

"The spots?"

"Yes, sir. The hind quarters are usually white or a lighter color than the front half of the horse, and they're spotted with black and white spots of all different sizes. Sometimes there's lots of spots. Sometimes only a few."

"A horse like that should be rare around here," said Cavitt. He closed his notebook and said, "Well, I guess that's enough for me to go on for now, Marshal Kindred. As soon as I learn something, I'll let you know."

"Let me know?" queried Kindred.

"I'm going with you." Cavitt frowned and said, "I work alone, Marshal. Besides, most of the folks I'll be talking to won't take kindly to me having a stranger along, especially a federal lawman."

"I don't give a shit what these local yahoos think about me," said Kindred. "I'm going with you."

Cavitt was exasperated. He sighed, then said, "Marshal, do you want to find this man or not?"

"Of course, I do," said Kindred.

"Then let me find him for you," pleaded Cavitt. "My way. I promise you results, Marshal."

Kindred considered Cavitt's request for a moment, then said, "I'd rather go with. you, Mr. Cavitt, but if you insist on doing this alone, I suppose I should stand aside for now, but I expect results immediately."

"Don't worry, sir," said Cavitt, relieved that Kindred had backed off, "I will have them in no time at all. Just tell me where you are staying, and I'll be around with a report as soon as I have something."

"I haven't bothered to find a hotel room yet," said Kindred.

"And most likely you won't find one either," said Cavitt. "The Army has quartered their soldiers in nearly every available hotel room in the city." He gave it some thought, then said, "Maybe you'd better come with me after all. The first place I was going to start looking for this fugitive of yours was at the hotels and boarding houses. We might as well find you a room while we're asking around."

Cavitt and Kindred began making the rounds of the hotels, asking three questions at each establishment: Did the hotel have a guest named Creed? Did the hotel have a guest named Creed who had checked out recently? Did the hotel have a room available for Marshal Kindred? The answers - No, No, and No - were the same at every hostelry, until they came to the Odd Fellows Hall on South Cherry Street.

"Yes, we had a man staying here last week by that name," said the clerk, Mr. Bunch, a square-headed fellow with short-cropped black hair. "Came in one evening and checked out the next. He didn't say where he was going, though."

"Do you know what this Creed was doing here in Nashville?" asked Cavitt as he wrote down Bunch's previous statement in his notebook.

"He said he was looking for some friends of his," said Bunch.

"He gave me their names, but I couldn't help him any. I hadn't heard of any of them."

"Do you know of any other place that he might have gone while he was here in Nashville?" asked Cavitt.

"Only that he boarded his horse down the street at Blacksmith Deaton's Livery and Stable, and I think he took his supper at Kendrick's Barrel House. Other than those two places, I don't know what he did or where he went in Nashville."

"Thank you," said Cavitt, putting his notebook away. "Would you happen to have a vacancy now? Marshal Kindred here is in need of lodging."

The clerk scanned Kindred and asked, "Did you say Marshall Kindred, Mr. Cavitt?"

"What if he did?" asked Kindred, ready to pounce.

"Well, I was just wondering what kind of marshal, was all," said Bunch.

"United States Deputy Marshal James Kindred," said Kindred, showing the man his badge. "I'm looking for Creed. He's an escaped criminal with a price on his head. There's a hanging rope waiting for him down in Texas."

"What did he do?" asked Bunch.

"He killed some soldiers while he and a bunch of other no-goods were robbing some Army supply wagons down in Mississippi last spring," said Kindred.

"Before or after the war ended?" asked the clerk.

This put a ripple in Kindred's hackles. "What difference do that make?" he demanded.

"None, I suppose, unless they did it before surrendering," said Bunch. "Then I suppose it would make a difference if they were in the regular Confederate army or whether they were guerrillas like those boys over in Missouri."

"They did the deed after Lee surrendered," said Kindred. "That makes what they did a crime instead of a victory for the Confederacy, and that's why I'm taking Creed back to Texas to hang."

"What about the room?" asked Cavitt.

"Sorry," said the clerk. "We've got nothing available at this time."

"You're lying mister," said Kindred angrily. "You've got plenty of empty rooms."

"And what makes you think that, Marshal Kindred?" asked the clerk calmly.

"All them keys hanging up there," said Kindred, pointing to the key rack on the wall behind Bunch. "Those are keys to vacant rooms, ain't they?"

"Yes, they are," said Bunch.

"Then I'll take one of them for the night," said Kindred.

"Marshal, I said that we have nothing available."

Kindred was a little slow, but he caught Bunch's drift quick enough. "I see," he said. He reached inside his coat and drew out his gun. Leveling the Remington at the clerk, he said, "Mr. Bunch, you are under arrest for aiding and abetting an escaped criminal."

Bunch glared at Kindred and said defiantly, "You can't arrest me."

"Oh, yes, he can," said Cavitt. "He's got the right."

"He does?" queried Bunch, who was quite agitated now.

"Yes, sir, he does," said Cavitt.

Bunch stared at Cavitt with disbelief, then looked down at Kindred's six-gun. Both sights convinced him that he should reconsider his position that the lodge had no rooms available at that time. "I beg your pardon, Marshal Kindred," he said. "Perhaps I was a bit premature with my announcement that we have nothing available this evening." He turned and took a key from the rack, then turned back to Kindred. "This room is very clean and spacious, sir. I'm certain that you'll find it to your liking. I'd be more than happy to show it to you."

"That won't be necessary," said Kindred as he took the key.

He replaced his gun inside his waistband. "Just send a boy down to the city police offices to fetch my bag back here before I return this evening."

"Yes, sir," said Bunch. "I'd be delighted to do that, sir."

"I'll bet you will," said Kindred with an evil smile. "That won't change nothing, you know. You're still under arrest."

Bunch's jaw dropped, but before he could make any sort of protest, the lawmen left the Odd Fellows Hall. They called on Blacksmith Deaton who confirmed Bunch's story about Creed having boarded his horse with him a and that Creed had left the next day without saying where he was going, although he did recall that the Texan had mentioned something about going for a ride out of town, but exactly where to, Deaton couldn't say.

From Deaton's Livery and Stable, the lawmen walked around to Kendrick's Barrel House where they questioned Horace Kendrick, the bartender, about Creed.

"Sure, there was a fellow like that in here one night last week," said the bartender who was familiar with Cavitt. "He bought a round for the boys and had himself a couple of sandwiches. What about it?"

With his notebook in hand, Cavitt quickly explained the purpose of their investigation, then he asked, "Did he say anything to anyone?"

"He talked to a couple of the boys," said Kendrick as he watched Cavitt write in his notebook. "I didn't hear it all, but I heard him say that he was from Texas. Stockman, I think he said. He was looking for some friends of his. He said their names, but I couldn't tell you what they were. Not now."

"Did he say anything about where he was going after he left here?" asked the detective.

"Nope, nothing." Then the bartender recalled advising Creed on how he might look for his friends. "He could have gone down to the newspapers and asked around about his friends."

"What makes you think that?" asked Cavitt.

"That's what I told him he should do," said Kendrick, "and he said he might do that."

"Sounds like a reasonable thing to do," said Cavitt. "Of course, I would have started with the police, but seeing who he is, I suppose I would have done it his way. Thank you, Horace. I'll see you around."

"Glad to help, Mr. Cavitt," said the bartender.

Outside on the street, Cavitt checked his pocket watch, then said to Kindred, "It's too late to go down to the newspaper offices now. Besides, there's more than one to call on, so I'll start with them first thing in the morning."

"What time should I meet you at the police office, Mr. Cavitt?" asked Kindred.

The detective replaced his watch in his vest pocket and said, "I thought we had this discussion earlier, Marshal Kindred. I work alone."

"Have I been any trouble to you, Mr. Cavitt?"

Cavitt was tired and didn't feel like arguing with this runt from Texas. "Come around to the office at eight," he said. "We'll start with the *Union and American*."

17

Josiah Ewing and Mary Perkins lodged a complaint with Constable Henry Curran, charging Creed with threatening them with a handgun. Curran noted the depth and intensity of their anger and reported the incident to his superior, Davidson County Sheriff Jacob Demmer, but the sheriff failed to act on the complaint because neither Ewing nor Mrs. Perkins was hurt. As far as he was concerned, the matter was finished. He was wrong.

After ridding himself of Jim Kindred, Detective Ransome Cavitt returned to the Nashville Police Department to report his findings to City Marshal Jim Brantley. In a few quick sentences, he told Brantley where he and Kindred had gone and what they had learned that day.

"Very good, Rance," said Brantley. "Stay on the case and report to me every day on your progress."

"Report to you every day, sir?" queried Cavitt, himself curious about Brantley's interest in the matter. "Is there something special about this case?"

Brantley was surprised by Cavitt's question, but he recovered quickly. "Yes, you might say that, Rance," he said. "It's this federal lawman, this deputy marshal, ah - what was his name again?"

"Kindred, sir."

"Yes, Kindred. I don't like him, and I take it you don't think too highly of him."

Cavitt wasn't humorless. He smiled and said wryly, "Well, he is the short one, sir."

Brantley laughed and said, "I didn't realize I was making a pun there, Rance. He is a runt, isn't he?"

"Yes, sir."

"Well, I don't dislike him because he's a runt. There's just something disgusting about him. He makes me think of white trash. Don't you agree?"

"Yes, sir, I do," said Cavitt, "but he is a U.S. deputy marshal, and it's our duty to co-operate with him."

"You don't need to remind me of that, Rance," said Brantley, a bit annoyed by Cavitt's remark. "Well, let's go ahead and co-operate with him and get him on his way back to Texas as soon as possible. And if we can't get him going back to Texas, let's at least get him out of Nashville."

"Yes, sir," said Cavitt. "Will that be all, sir?"

"Yes, Rance, thank you."

Cavitt returned to his own office, thinking that Brantley hadn't quite told him the truth about his concern over this case. City marshals didn't usually take an interest in much of anything except their share of the payoffs from the bawdy houses, saloons, gambling dens, and other such businesses that often crossed the line of legality in dealing with their customers. This explanation - that he didn't like Kindred because he seemed like white trash - was just so much smoke. The detective wondered what Brantley's real concern was with this case. Was it this fugitive Slate Creed, or Clete Slater, that had Brantley so concerned? Was it really Kindred, but for some other reason? Whatever it was, he would have to find out, if for no other reason than to satisfy his own natural curiosity about questions that seemed to need answering, no matter what.

But that would have to wait. Right now Cavitt had a hunch to play. He recalled that Blacksmith Deaton had told him that Creed had mentioned going for a ride out of the city. Where had the fugitive gone on this little jaunt? Had anyone seen him? Maybe one of the county constables on rounds had noticed a stranger on a gray horse, an Appaloosa as Kindred had called it in his area. The only way to check that was to pay a visit to Sheriff Jake Demmer.

Cavitt walked over to the. Davidson County Courthouse and went directly to Demmer's office. He knocked on the office door and waited to be invited inside. The sheriff was in.

Black-bearded, balding Jake Demmer was sitting behind his desk, writing a letter, when Cavitt entered the room. He looked up at the detective and greeted him with happy blue eyes and a friendly smile. "Rance, how are you?"

"I'm doing fine, Jake," said Cavitt. "How are you doing today?"

"Just trying to get some of my correspondence done," said Demmer. He put the pen down on the desk. "But it can wait. What brings you over here at this time of the day?"

"Nothing much, Jake." Cavitt pulled up a chair and sat down opposite the sheriff. "I'm working on a fugitive case and was wondering if maybe one of your constables might have seen the fellow I'm looking for."

Demmer chuckled and said, "That's what I like about you, Rance. You come straight to the point. No beating around the bush for Rance Cavitt. No, sir." He chuckled again, then asked, "Who is this fugitive you're looking for."

"His name is Clete Slater, but he's going by the name of Slate Creed. He's wanted down in Texas by the Federal Army for killing some soldiers during a raid on a bunch of supply wagons down in Mississippi last year."

"I remember that raid," said Demmer. "Seems to me that we caught a few of those fellows up here last year and turned them over to the Yankees. I didn't hear much about them after that, except that most of them were let off for testifying against some of the others and for returning their share of the stolen money."

"That's what happened all right," said Cavitt. "It's seems that they pointed the finger at this fellow Slater as being their leader, and the Army tried him and sentenced him to hang, but he escaped. Now there's this U.S. deputy marshal here in town who's looking to take him back to Texas to hang. I think he came here looking for some of the men who put the blame on him. I think this Slater is out to kill them."

"Well, if he is, I hope he picks some other place to do his killing," said Demmer. "We've got enough trouble around here with all these nigger soldiers. We don't need any more problems from outsiders."

"No, I guess not," said Cavitt rather noncommittally. Unlike many other policemen and white Tennesseans in general, Cavitt had no racial bigotry distorting his view of the world. As far as he was concerned, good and evil came in all colors, races, and nationalities.

"Well, this Slater was here all right," he continued, "but now it seems that he's moved on. He spent a night at the Odd Fellows Hall last week, then left the next evening without giving a forwarding address. It seems that he went for a ride outside of town, but I don't know where he went. I was wondering if maybe one of your constables might have seen a stranger riding a spotted gray horse." He took his notebook from the inside pocket of his coat and flipped it open. "An Appaloosa is what it's called."

"You know, I just might be able to help you there, Rance," said Demmer. "Hank Curran came in last week with a complaint from Josiah Ewing and Cornelius Perkins's wife Mary down to Wrencoe that a fellow riding a horse like you described was down their way last week and threatened them with a big horse pistol."

Cavitt sat up straight and dug into his coat pocket for his pencil. "What were those names again?" he asked.

"Josiah Ewing and Mrs. Mary Perkins. Down to Wrencoe. Josiah owns the general store down there. They told Hank that this fellow rode into town looking for Mrs. Perkins's son-in-law." Two thoughts made a connection in Demmer's brain. "You know, if I recollect rightly, her son-in-law was one of those fellows we arrested and turned over to the Army for that raid down in Mississippi last year. I don't recall his name right off, but I can look up the arrest records."

"That won't be necessary, Jake," said Cavitt "I'll just go down to Wrencoe and talk to these people myself." He sprung from his chair and headed for the door. Over his shoulder, he said, "Thanks, Jake, for your help."

As he walked back to his own office at the police department, Cavitt asked himself another one of those questions that seemed to need answering, no matter what. What pointed this Creed or Slater fellow to Josiah Ewing and Mary Perkins down in Wrencoe? Maybe it wasn't a what but a who. The detective was more determined than ever to find out which.

18

Josiah Ewing and Mary Perkins were very talkative when Ransome Cavitt called on them the next morning. They spared no adjectives as they described how Creed had threatened to kill Ewing if he didn't tell the Texan where Marsh Quade had gone, and they dramatized the incident so greatly that a casual listener might have gotten the impression that Creed was some sort of lunatic on the loose from the county asylum instead of a man forced by two very stubborn people to employ desperate measures.

Cavitt took their editorializing and embellishments with a grain of salt and only made notes of the pertinent information that they imparted to him. Much to his relief, they gave him one detail that he was very glad to hear: they had told Creed that Marsh Quade and his bride had gone to Kentucky and were probably on their way to Colorado now. The detective surmised that Creed had probably left Nashville immediately after returning to the city. If Creed had left Nashville, then Cavitt would soon be rid of Kindred. But maybe Creed hadn't left yet. Then what? The detective would have to continue to look for the fugitive. But if Creed had left Nashville, where did he go and what did he do between the time he left Wrencoe and the time he departed Nashville? How long a time was that anyway? And how did he leave? Did he ride away on his horse? Did he take a train? Maybe a steamboat. So many more questions that needed answering.

Cavitt returned to Nashville before noon and found Jim Kindred cooling his heels at the police department office. He hadn't forgotten about the deputy marshal; instead, he had chosen to exclude him from the interrogation in Wrencoe. He didn't like the little Texan anyway, and the less he saw of him, the better.

"I thought we had an appointment at eight this morning," said Kindred, his tone expressing annoyance at being, made to wait for more than three hours for Cavitt to return.

"Something came up that had to be attended to first thing this morning," said Cavitt, ignoring Kindred's displeasure.

"I thought you were supposed to be looking for Creed for me," said Kindred.

"Marshal Kindred, I was questioning some people who had a confrontation with your fugitive last week down in Wrencoe," explained Cavitt calmly.

"Wrencoe?" queried Kindred. "Where's that? And who were these people he had this...this...this-"

"Confrontation, Marshal," said Cavitt. "I supposed you'd call it a run-in."

"Never mind what I'd call it," said Kindred, bitter that Cavitt was showing him up. "Just who were these people that he had this run-in with?"

"They aren't important," said Cavitt with a sigh, "but since you won't let me rest until I tell you, their names are Josiah Ewing and Mary Perkins."

"Never heard of them. Who the hell are they?"

"Mrs. Perkins is the mother-in-law of Marshall Quade, a man that your fugitive seems to be after."

"Marshall Quade? Who the hell is he?"

"He's one of the men who took part in the raid on that Army supply train down in Mississippi last year. You know; the crime that your fugitive is supposed to hang for."

Kindred almost asked the next question that came to his mind: Why does he want to find Quade? But he kept it to himself, thinking he might sound stupid if he asked it. He would have been right. Instead, he muttered, "Oh, one of them."

"Marshal, I believe this Creed has left Nashville for Kentucky," said Cavitt.

"Kentucky? He just came from there."

"Yes, sir, I know, but this time he's gone to Logan County just over the state line."

"How do you know this?" asked Kindred.

"Mr. Ewing and Mrs. Perkins told Creed that Quade and Mrs.

Perkins's daughter had gone there some time back and were planning to go to Colorado from there. It seems that Mr. Ewing and Mrs. Perkins have a cousin in Logan County that Quade hoped to find employment with. His name is George Washington Ewing, and he lives in a place called Adairville. I believe Creed has gone there to look for them."

"You believe? Don't you know for certain."

"No, I don't," said Cavitt, "but there are ways of finding out for certain whether he's left Nashville yet. Come with me, Marshal."

Cavitt led Kindred outside where the detective looked up and down the street as if he were looking for someone in particular. In a second, he saw the person that he wanted and started walking in his direction, finally stopping on the sidewalk near a manure cart where an old man, an ex-slave, was shoveling horse dung into the two-wheeled wagon.

"Ezra!" shouted Cavitt above the din of the city's horse and buggy traffic.

The streetcleaner threw another scoop of droppings into the cart, then turned to see who was addressing him. When he saw Cavitt, a wide, white-toothed grin spread across his sweaty chocolate face. He straightened up to his full height, which was a lean six feet and more, and stepped over to the walk to greet Cavitt. "Mr. Rance, how you doing today, sir?"

"I'm just fine, Ezra," said Cavitt. He offered his hand to the streetcleaner.

"No, sir, Mr. Rance. My hands ain't so clean this morning, but thank you for the honor, sir."

"Ezra, I'd like you to meet Marshal Kindred. He's here on some official business that I thought you could help us with. Marshal, this is Ezra Cheatham, the best pair of eyes and ears in the Nashville Police Department. If there's one of those gray Appaloosas that you told me about here in Nashville, Ezra would know about it. Ezra knows just about every horse in these parts. You might say they're clients of his."

Kindred was obviously affronted by the introduction, and he chose to express his displeasure with words as well as looks. "Who the hell do you think I am, Cavitt, that you think you can bring me out here to talk some shit-shoveling nigger?"

Cavitt had suspected Kindred would react this way, and he was prepared for it, "Marshal, Ezra is my friend," he said slowly and firmly, "and although he may not have the best job in the world, he is still my friend. And he may be a Negro, but he is still my friend. And while you may be a United States deputy marshal, you have no call to be abusive to an upstanding, law-abiding citizen of this community who happens to be my friend. Have I made myself clear, Marshal? Or do I have to explain further that you have insulted my friend and me and that an apology is very much in order?" To add emphasis to his words, Cavitt stretched himself as tall as he could and tried to look as menacing as he could.

"I don't owe you and this nigger any such thing," snarled Kindred like a rabid mongrel.

Cavitt lost his temper, grabbed Kindred by the lapels of his coat, and jerked him off the ground until they were nose to nose. "You little turd! Just who in the hell do you think you are? I've had my fill of you, you little sonofabitch." He shook Kindred violently, then threw him to the sidewalk. "I don't care that you're a U.S. deputy marshal, you little turd! You act and smell and look like dog shit, but you're lower than that, Kindred. You're white trash, that's what you are!"

Kindred wasn't going to bother with words this time. Having landed on his butt, he came to a sitting position quickly, reached for his Remington, cleared leather, cocked the piece, and prepared to kill Cavitt.

Seeing the gun in Kindred's hand put fear into Cavitt, but not Cheatham. The ex-slave swung his shovel at Kindred and struck his gun arm just below the elbow, smashing it downward. The six-gun discharged, but the ball ricocheted harmlessly off the brick street into the side of the manure cart.

Kindred screamed in pain and dropped the .44 on the sidewalk. He writhed in agony as he held his injured limb close to his body and whined like a small child looking for sympathy.

Cavitt picked up the revolver and thought of shooting Kindred dead, going so far as to cock the gun and take aim at the Texan's head.

Cheatham stopped him. "No, Mr. Rance, he ain't worth it," said the streetcleaner, as he cautiously took the revolver's smoking barrel into his massive hand and lifted it upward, away from its target.

"Yes, you're right, Ezra," said Cavitt, coming to his senses. "He's not worth killing, but he sure needs a good horse-whipping. Have you got one handy?"

Cheatham shook his head slowly as he took the gun from Cavitt's hand.

"Too bad," said the detective. "I guess this will have to do."

And with that, he kicked Kindred solidly in the side of the head, putting him out of his pain for the moment.

Cavitt grabbed his kicking foot and began dancing on the other one. "Dammit all to hell!" he swore. "That little sonofabitch broke my toe! You saw it, Ezra. He assaulted a police officer, didn't he?" He stopped hopping, dropped down on one knee, and bent over Kindred. "You're under arrest, you little sonofabitch, for assaulting an officer of the Nashville Police Department." Seeing that Kindred was unconscious, he turned to Cheatham. "Would you mind carrying him to jail for me, Ezra?"

"Why not?" said Cheatham with a big grin. "I shovel shit all day long. What's one turd more or less?"

19

Missouri suffered during the War Between the States. Both sides robbed, pillaged, burned, raped, and, above all, murdered. But worse, when the war ended for the rest of the country, it continued in Missouri, as vengeance still demanded its day.

Missouri was still in pain when Creed and his four new friends journeyed across the state in early February, 1866.

Creed, James, White, and the Shepherd brothers left Russellville within minutes after Creed's altercation with the Whittaker brothers, riding west to Hopkinsville where they spent their first night on the road. The next morning, they rode over to Canton; and caught a packet boat that was headed down the Cumberland River. The steamer's final destination was Cairo, Illinois, at the junction of the Ohio and Mississippi Rivers, where it would offload its cargo for shipment by rail to Chicago. This suited the travelers fine; they spent a night in Cairo, then rode out the next morning for the ferry that took them over the Mississippi to Cape Girardeau, Missouri. They had planned to make a connection there with the Cape Girardeau and Columbus Rail Road, which would take them to St. Louis, but they arrived late and missed the train.

"Instead of waiting around until tomorrow for the next train," suggested Alex James, "why don't we ride on up to Potosi where we can catch an earlier train in the morning."

"How far is that from here?" asked Creed.

"Oh, about a hundred miles," said James. "It's a fair piece of riding, but we've done it before in one day." He smiled at his compatriots and said, "Ain't we, boys?"

"Sure, we have," said Oil Shepherd, "and we was fighting Redlegs and Federal regulars all the way sometimes."

"A hundred miles shouldn't be nothing to you, Slate," said James, "what with you riding with Morgan and all. You must have rode a hundred miles and more on lots of days."

"And nights," said Creed, recollecting those dark days when his outfit was pursued relentlessly by Union cavalry that had blood in their eyes for every son-of-a-Butternut who got in their way. "But why should we push ourselves so hard? Tomorrow is Sunday, and I don't think the trains run on the Sabbath."

"You know," said James, "I believe you're right, Slate. Tomorrow is the Sabbath, and trains don't run on Sundays." He bowed his head. "I promised my ma that I wouldn't forget the Lord while I was away, and for the most part, I've kept that promise." He looked up at the faces of his friends and said, "You boys wouldn't mind if we layed over somewhere tomorrow and went to preaching, would you?"

The Shepherds exchanged questioning looks, each wondering if the other would object; and so did Creed and White. Oll was the first to clear his throat and speak up. "If nobody else minds, then I could go for a little hell-fire and brimstone from a good Baptist preacher. How about you, Jim? Feel like getting saved in the morning?"

"Sounds all right to me, Oll." said White. He turned to James and said, "Let's do 'er, Buck."

"My folks are Methodist," said Creed, "but I think I'd like listening to a good sermon on the evil in this world. I vote for preaching tomorrow."

"Then it's settled," said James. "We'll hole up someplace tonight where there's a Baptist church so we won't have to go far tomorrow to hear the Gospel."

The five of them headed out on the road to Jackson with the idea that they would push on toward dark, which would put them in the vicinity of Fredericktown. A nor' wester blew up early in the day, slowing their progress. When they reached Patton at midday, they were forced to decide whether to go through Fredericktown as originally planned or shave a dozen miles off the trip by taking the direct route to Farmington, the next town of any significance before Potosi. The deteriorating weather helped them to make up their minds. They opted to take the mountain road through Crossroads and Libertyville, hoping to make Locust Ridge by dark, which they did.

Throughout the day, Creed noticed that whenever they came across another traveler on the road they would receive one of two distinct greetings: either they would be hailed in a most friendly manner or the other fellow would give them a wide berth and hurry on his way as soon as they had passed him. At their campfire that night, Creed asked his companions about these opposite reactions and was given a trepidacious reply that put him on his guard for any and all possibilities.

"It's these long coats we're wearing," said James. "They're Yankee overcoats. Everybody thinks we're in the Militia or the Federal army." He smiled at Oll Shepherd before finishing his reply to Creed. "Those fellows that have been friendly must be Union men, and those that run scared are probably our people."

"Our people?" queried Creed.

"Sure, you know," said Oll Shepherd. "Folks who fought for the South or at least supported the South during the war. You know, our kind of people."

Creed hadn't ever thought of making divisions of people, of categorizing them as one kind of folks or another. He couldn't even see separating them by color or nationality or religion. To him, people were people, and each and every one of them was unique in his or her own way and, to his way of thinking, each should be treated that way. After all, that's how he wanted to be treated. "That's what the Golden Rule is all about," he often said with conviction whenever the conversation turned philosophical around a campfire.

"I still don't understand why anybody would be afraid of seeing Federals now," he said. "The war's been over for almost a year now."

"Not here in Missouri, it ain't," said James. "You see Slate, while you boys in the regular army were fighting battles back in Tennessee and Virginia, we guerrillas were fighting for our homes and our kinfolks right here in our own state against Kansas Jayhawkers and men who had been our neighbors before the war came. They called themselves Militia, and they called us Bushwhackers. Well, we had to take to the brush because the Militia had burned our homes, or they'd driven us off, like they did to my folks who were forced to move up to Nebraska until the war ended. Now it seems that lots of those men who fought in the Militia don't want to forgive and forget like the Good Book says we should do. They want what they couldn't get during the war. They want men like us dead. One way or another."

"There's even some Militia units still riding around doing the same sort of devil's work that they did during the war," said Oll Shepherd. "That's why we're wearing these coats. If we should come across any of them, they'll mistake us for being like them.

"But what about me?" asked Creed. "I'm not wearing one of those coats, and folks are treating me the same as you. How is that?"

"They must think you're an officer," said James with a grin. "Yankee officers don't wear these light-blue coats like we're wearing. They wear coats like you're wearing."

Creed looked down at his navy blue, knee-length, woolen cape-coat and recalled how he'd seen Union officers wearing something similar to it during winter campaigns. A thought suddenly struck him. "Is that why you boys have been letting me ride out front all the time he asked. "Because I look like an officer?"

All four of them smiled, and James said, "Well, you were an officer, weren't you?"

"I guess," said Creed, scratching his head. "I suppose I don't mind being out front as long as no one goes to shooting at us because we look like Union militia."

"Don't worry about that, Slate," said Oll Shepherd, "Our folks quit fighting the war."

For some reason, Creed had his doubts about that.

20

The next day the travelers found a Baptist church at Locust Ridge, a crossroads community of a half dozen houses, one store, and the church straddling the road between Libertyville and Farmington. The Stars and Stripes waved bravely over the front door of the house of worship, a sight that Creed found odd. It was. But this was Missouri.

It wasn't much of a building as churches go; clapboard painted white, two tall windows on each side with oak double doors for a main entrance and a small pine door for a rear exit, and it was built over a storm cellar. A grove of oaks shaded it on the south from a winter sun that fought valiantly to warm the morning, and a cemetery was located to the north of it. One hitching rail and several hitching posts were strategically planted out front for the convenience of the congregation.

When Creed and his companions rode up, the church looked more like a fortress under siege. On the graveyard side of the building were eight carriages of various types, each one with a man, a woman, and anywhere from one to seven children in it. A half dozen mounted men were scattered among them. On the wooded side of the church were nearly twice the number of conveyances, people, and horses. All of them were dressed in Sunday meeting clothes, and they seemed to be Waiting for something - or someone. Whatever or whoever it was, it wasn't Creed and his friends. Those on the north side of the church looked at the new arrivals with a mixture of fear and disgust, while those to the south seemed delighted that they had come along.

Creed surmised that this was a divided congregation, divided by politics instead of religion. He was only right.

Before anyone could approach the newcomers and either welcome them or warn them off, a buggy with a man and a woman in it came up the road from the direction of Farmington. The gentlemen's attire designated him as a minister of the Gospel, while the lady who sat so primly beside him was probably his wife or sister.

"We are all brothers in the Lord," said Hadlee, as if he were about to begin a sermon. He spread his arms wide, Bible in hand, to indicate the breadth of his statement.

Wilson stepped past Stubbs and said, "No, sir, we ain't. Not any more, we ain't. Not since you bushwhacking Secesh took up your guns against our flag." He pointed to the Stars and Stripes waving above them in the cool breeze. "The day you Rebs did, that was the day we quit being brothers, Mr. Hadlee."

"The war is over, Brother Wilson," said Hadlee, allowing his arms to relax against his body again. "Let us put the past behind us."

"How do you think we're agonna do that, Mr. Hadlee?" demanded Wilson who was growing angrier by the second.

"How do you think we're agonna do that when half the good men who were living peaceably in this country when you left are dead now? Killed by the Bushwhackers that you stirred up with your preaching against the Union like you did Sunday after Sunday. How do you think we're agonna live together in peace again when you'll be around to remind us of all the killing and suffering that you and your Secesh friends brought on us peaceable Union folk?"

"I never lifted a finger against the Union," said Hadlee in his own defense.

"How do we know what you was doing down there in Arkansas?" demanded Wilson.

"Not even during my exile," said Hadlee, "did I ever lift a finger against my fellow man. Not then, not ever."

"No, sir, you most likely didn't," said Stubbs, now joining Wilson in attacking the parson. "You didn't have to. All you had to do was preach treason every Sunday."

"Treason?" spat Hadlee, appalled by the word. "I never preached treason, Brother Stubbs. I only preached the Gospel, and you know it."

"The Gospel according to Jeff Davis," said Wilson, moving closer to Hadlee.

"The Gospel according to the Lord," said Hadlee.

"It don't make no difference what you call it, Reverend," said Stubbs, stepping between Wilson and Hadlee, "it don't change nothing. We ain't agonna let you into our church. We've been doing just fine without you these past four years, and we'll do just fine without you today. We don't need you to preach to us. Not today. Not ever again." He got nose to nose with Hadlee. "You hear me, Reverend?"

A strange feeling crept over Creed as he watched this real-life vignette unfold before him. He and the others remained mounted observers.

The pastor and his passenger drove right up to the front of the church where he climbed down from the seat and tied up the horse. As he went to help the woman alight from the buggy, several men from the group on the south side of the church got down from their horses and carriages and moved toward the front door of the building. Some of them took up positions on the steps, their arms folded across their chests and defiant expressions on their faces. The parson and the lady, both carrying Bibles, turned and started toward the door with what appeared to be brassy determination etched on their faces.

"Hold on, Reverend," said a sour-eyed fellow on the bottom step to the church. He held up a hand to emphasize his command. "We ain't agonna let you preach here no more."

"What's this you say, Brother Stubbs?" asked the preacher, halting a few feet from Stubbs. He seemed to be acting, pretending that he didn't expect this confrontation. "Are you barring Martha and me from worshipping in our church?"

"You heard him, Mr. Hadlee," said the man behind Stubbs. "We ain't agonna let you preach here no more. We don't want you here no more."

"That ain't so, Reverend Hadlee," said a skinny, emaciated fellow who had been standing near the gate to the cemetery. He came forward to join in the conversation. "We don't all feel that way. There's lots of us who want you to be our preacher again." He was quite sincere, so sincere that he removed his hat when he spoke to Hadlee.

"Thank you, Brother Maddux," said Hadlee with a benevolent smile that a patient parent would give a bashful child.

"But there's more of us who don't want you," said Stubbs, who shifted his view to Maddux, "or your kind in our church no more."

"Your church?" queried Hadlee. "I was under the impression that this was the Lord's house. Not yours, Brother Stubbs. Or mine. Or any other man's." He scanned the unfriendly faces before him and stopped when he came to the man behind Stubbs. "Or any group of men, Brother Wilson."

"I ain't your brother, Mr. Hadlee," said Wilson, "and leave us alone. That's all we want. To be left alone to live in peace the same as them."

Hadlee glared back at Stubbs and calmly said, "I was under the impression that this was still the United States of America where every man, woman, and child is free to worship the Lord as he pleases."

"You are free to worship the Lord as you please," said Wilson, "but you can just do it somewhere's else. We don't want you here, Reb."

The parson heard the flag flutter in the wind above them. Without warning, he pushed Stubbs into Wilson, sprawling the two men onto the steps at the feet of three more of their persuasion. In the next instant, he raced up the steps, grabbed the banner with his free hand, and ripped it from the staff sticking out from the wall. Before Stubbs, Wilson, and the other men could recover, he began rending the Stars and Stripes into tatters and shreds, standing on the field of blue while he pulled at the red and white stripes with his free hand. "Damn this flag," he said, "and damn this country that harbors such villains as these sinners who would defile the house of the Lord with their abominations! Be gone to Hell with all of ye!" He cast down the torn banner and hustled back to his wife's side. "Come, my dear. We will hold services elsewhere." He helped her into the buggy, then untied the horse and climbed up on the other side. Before seating himself, he announced, "I will be conducting services at my home for those of you who care to worship with Martha and me." He glared at Wilson and Stubbs who had now regained their feet. "That invite is extended to you," he said before jabbing a thumb over his shoulder at Creed and his traveling companions, "and your Militia friends, too, Brother Stubbs." He sat down, pulled on the reins to make the horse step back, then snapped them against the animal's back to command it to move ahead. They drove off at a trot.

"Those ain't our kind of folks," said Oll Shepherd, indicating the group on the south side of the church.

"Nope, they sure ain't," said White.

"That fellow sounds like a real good Baptist preacher to me," said White. "How about you, Buck?"

"I was thinking the same thing," said James. "Suppose we ride on after him and listen to him preach some. What do you say, Slate?"

"Might as well," said Creed. "It looks to me like there won't be any Baptist preaching here today."

The five of them fell in behind the other worshippers all those folks who had been on the north side of the church who decided to accept Hadlee's invitation to services at his home. They started down the road toward Farmington in a train that stretched out nearly a hundred yards from the preacher's buggy to the strangers at the rear. They had gone only a quarter of a mile when a lone rider came galloping up behind them. Those riding at the rear turned to see who was coming toward them at such a fast clip.

The man named Wilson reined in his mount as he closed in on Creed and the others. "Morning, gents," he said with a friendly grin. Then, tipping his hat to Creed, he added, "Captain." Before anyone could reply, he kicked his horse and sped off toward the vanguard of the procession.

"I don't know why," said Creed, looking after Wilson, "but something tells me that man is up to no good."

"I got the same feeling," said James, "but this ain't a place for us to go sticking our noses into business that ain't ours. Right, boys?"

"That's right," said White.

"It ain't our business, Buck," said Oll Shepherd, "but that man does look like he's up to no good, and that preacher just might be in for it."

"I say we ride up there and make sure he rides on by the preacher," said Creed.

"Can't hurt, I suppose," said James. "Let's go."

They put heels to their horses and began passing the carriages and the other mounted men, only to find themselves being harangued and cursed by many of the churchgoers as they moved forward. Mostly, they were called "damn Militia," "damn Yankees," or "damn Redlegs." It's these overcoats, thought Creed. They think we're Union men. Best to ignore them, I guess.

They rode on, keeping their eyes on Wilson, who was rapidly approaching the parson's buggy now. They were a good twenty yards behind Wilson when they saw him pull a revolver out of his coat, ride up beside Hadlee's buggy, lean over toward the unsuspecting preacher, put the muzzle up close behind the parson's left ear, squeeze the trigger, and blow the man's brains out the other side of his head, splattering them all over his wife's brand new, store-bought Sunday meeting dress.

Mrs. Hadlee screamed in horror as her husband's dead body fell into her lap.

The horse lurched into a dead run as the rems that controlled it went limp. The road was a little twisty and slightly declining, which allowed the animal to pick up speed quickly.

Wilson broke off for the woods, which lined both sides of the road, and he soon disappeared.

Those people in the caravan who had witnessed the murder were too shocked to do anything except stare in disbelief, while those who hadn't seen Wilson pull the trigger questioned the origin of the shot that seemed to echo through the hills like a death knell. "Oh, Lord!" whispered Alex James, unable to express any other sentiment at seeing Hadlee murdered in cold blood. James had killed a few men in similar fashion during the war, but that was war. This was different. Mrs. Hadlee's anguish rousted up a deep-rooted memory of the time when his mother had first heard the sorrowful news that his father, also a Baptist minister, had died in California. He was only a boy then and didn't quite understand anything except that his mother was experiencing deep-down hurt. How she wailed and carried on! It pained him to see her that way. Now he felt for Mrs. Hadlee, but like then, he could think of little in the way of offering comfort. He just rode on.

The terrible murder stirred Creed in much the same manner as James had been affected. His mother had cried for days after she had been told that his father had been killed by Comanches. Unlike James who didn't know what to do, Creed, the fatherless child, had a very definite reaction to the news: he wanted to get a gun and go shoot those bad Injuns for killing his father and making his mother cry. Now he wanted to shoot Wilson for his crime, and he had the gun to do it with, too. He drew his Colt's and would have ridden after the killer if not for the plight of Mrs. Hadlee. Seeing the buggy career down the road ahead of him, he chose to rescue her instead.

Meanwhile, Oll Shepherd took command of the others. "Come on, boys," he said, drawing his weapon. "Let's get that sonofabitch." He led them into the woods in pursuit of Wilson, but the killer's lead was too great for them to overtake. Besides that, Wilson had the advantage of knowing the terrain. Within minutes, it became evident to Shepherd that they would never catch the murderer, so they gave up and retraced their tracks to the road.

When they struck the two-track again, they saw that the church-goers were knotted up down the road. Cautiously, guns in hand, they moved at a walk toward the locals. As they drew closer, they could hear a mingle of voices, both male and female, children as well as adults, crying out for blood, and much to their surprise, it was Creed's blood that they wanted.

"String him up!" was the most frequent demand.

"Let's hang him!" was the second most popular phrase. Several men had Creed in their grasp. One of them, the man called Maddux, had Creed's six-shooter and was threatening him with it. "Militia bastard!" he swore at Creed. "We're agonna hang you for this!" He pointed at Reverend Hadlee's dead body lying on the ground beside the road, his mutilated head resting in the lap of his widow who stroked the blood-soaked hair with a caressing touch as she cried ever so softly.

Creed's companions came up at this moment, and the crowd fell silent and fearful of these four armed men. Many of them backed away from the riders, forming a half-circle behind Creed and the men who held him.

"You folks got this all wrong," said James. "He ain't Militia any more than we are."

"Who're you trying to fool, mister?" demanded Maddux. "I seen enough of them blue coats during the war to know Militia when I see them."

"We ain't Militia," reiterated James.

"Why don't you tell them who you are?" George Shepherd suggested to his brother.

"Can't hurt, I guess," said the brother. "Perhaps you folks have heard of me. I am Oll Shepherd."

This brought a few gasps from those folks in the crowd who had heard of Shepherd's exploits up in Clinton County. He had commanded a small group of guerrillas who had been known for their stealth and cunning as well as their murderous ways.

"You're a liar, mister!" said Maddux. "Oll Shepherd was killed with Quantrill up in Kentucky last spring."

"No, he wasn't." said James.

"How do you know that?" demanded Maddux.

"I know because I was with Colonel Quantrill when he was killed," said James, "and Oll here was nowhere around us then."

"I don't believe you neither," said Maddux.

"Mister, would you believe me if I was to put a ball between the eyes of that young'un there?" asked Shepherd, pointing at the boy who held the reins to Creed's horse.

Maddux blanched but didn't back down. "If you're who you say you are," he said, "why are you wearing those Yankee overcoats like you are?"

"Same reason we wore them during the war," said Shepherd. "To fool the real Militia into thinking we're part of them so as we can get up close enough to them to shoot enough of them sons-a-bitches before they know what's happening to them."

Maddux, having been a guerrilla in his part of this state, was acquainted with that tactic, having used it on occasion himself. "But the war's over Captain Shepherd," he said, the edge gone from his voice. "How come you boys are still wearing those coats?"

"Hell, man, it's cold out, don't you know?" said Shepherd with a smile. His mild attempt at humor brought a ripple of laughter from the locals, removing some of the tension from the moment.

"And these are the warmest coats we got. Besides, we got a long way to go to get home up to Clay County, and we don't want to be bothered by any Militia that might still be around."

"Enough of this talk," said James. "We got to be moving on before more of those murdering bastards like the one that killed that poor man over there come riding along here. This ain't our affair, folks. We're sorry about your parson, but it wasn't none of our doing or our friend there. Now if you'll just let him be and give him back his horse and gun, we'll be on our way."

Maddux hesitated for a second, then said, "Let him go, boys." He handed Creed the Colt's and said, "I should have knowed you wasn't Militia by the way you rode after Mrs. Hadlee and saved her the way you did. I apologize, mister, for all of us for treating you the way we did."

Creed took his gun and put it back inside his coat. A boy picked up his hat and gave it to him, while the youth holding his horse's reins brought Nimbus around to him. Creed donned the plainsman and mounted the Appaloosa. "This isn't the first time that I've been blamed for something that I didn't do," he said, "and it probably won't be the last. I only wish that I could have saved the parson as well." He urged Nimbus over to where Mrs. Hadlee sat cradling her dead husband's head. She looked up at him through her tears. He removed his hat again and said, "I'm sorry, ma'am. I wish I could have stopped it."

Mrs. Hadlee could only nod her head and begin sobbing all over again.

Creed felt like crying with her, but instead, he replaced his hat and rode off down the road toward Farmington, wondering how this tragedy could have been avoided and feeling impotent because he knew that this same thing would happen again and again, and he could nothing to prevent it as much as he wanted to stop all senseless killings.

21

Throughout the remainder of the day, the recollection of the man Wilson shooting Reverend Hadlee replayed vividly in Creed's mind, mingling with visions of boar hunts back home in Texas.

As a youth before the war and again after the great conflict, he and some friends would ride into the brush and flush out a wild pig or three. The first hunter to spot a boar would take out after it in order to get as close as possible to the frightened beast that could turn at any second and attack the legs of the horse. The rider would then lean over the pig with a six-gun in hand and shoot it in the head. This put sport into the chore of putting meat on the table. The sportsman was judged by his ability to make the kill with one ball in the animal's head. Any damn fool could take a rifle and plug a pig through the heart or the brain, but it took a real expert to shoot one with a pistol while riding at a gallop and not mess up any of the good eating parts like the hams or ribs.

But Reverend Hadlee's murder wasn't a pig hunt. It disturbed Creed's peace of mind. He couldn't see how anyone, no matter how deranged, how anyone could be so cold-blooded that they could ride up to a man and put a ball through his skull the way Wilson had done to Hadlee.

Creed reasoned that shooting an armed man in a fight was one thing; that was combat, in which the other fellow had the chance to defend himself. He'd killed many men during the war, and although he didn't enjoy it, he accepted it as his duty to kill or be killed. Executing a man for committing a capital crime was acceptable because the condemned bastard had forfeited his own existence by destroying another life. Creed accepted this, too, proving it by having hung some of the men who had murdered his brother Dent. But to take a life, a human life, for no apparent reason-and with no more feeling than that of a snake swallowing a toad-was totally incomprehensible to him. What had Hadlee done to deserve such a fate? What had been his capital crime that he should be executed so singularly? And what sort of man would kill in this manner? And in front of so many witnesses? In front of women and children? Every time these questions came to mind, a shudder of fear of the unknown would shake Creed's sensibilities and he would determine to come to grips with this fear.

None of Creed's companions could answer Creed's questions for him as they rode on to Potosi, arriving there well before dark without further incident. They checked into a hotel at Creed's expense. The others had money, but none budgeted for lodging. Creed knew this, but because he was tired of sleeping outdoors and he didn't feel it would be right for him to have a nice warm bed while James, White, and the Shepherds had to settle for a hay mow at a livery stable, he offered to pay for their rooms as well.

In spite of the comfort, Creed failed to sleep well. The murder of Reverend Hadlee continued to haunt him. Besides the actual episode, he was disturbed by the attitude of his friends.

"It wasn't none of our affair," Alex James had said.

When a man goes to spouting off like this Baptist minister must have done," said Oll Shepherd, "he's got to expect that someone's going to take offense and try to put a ball into him sooner or later."

And Jim White had offered the philosophy that "A man never knew when his time on this earth might be up, and maybe the parson had lived past his."

How could these Missourians be so apathetic to the blatant murder of man of God? Or any man, for that matter? More questions to interfere with Creed's rest that night.

By the next morning, word of Reverend Hadlee's murder had spread across county lines to Potosi. Although they had witnessed the killing, as James had said, it was none of their business, and he admonished Creed and the others to keep mum on the subject. This didn't prevent them from listening, however.

While the strangers ate breakfast at the hotel, they overheard varying conversations about the bloodletting at Locust Ridge the day before. No one seemed to know who had done it, although everybody knew that the killer was a Union man.

To those folks who had been States' Rights advocates during the recent war - which didn't necessarily mean that they had been Confederates or had sympathized with the Confederacy, but were merely opposed to Federal authority to those folks - Hadlee's assassination was one more example of the high-handed ways of those Unionists who were hell-bent on subjugating them and depriving them of their property, their rights as white people, and their constitutionally guaranteed right to the pursuit of happiness.

To those folks who had remained loyal to the Union during the war, Hadlee's death was justifiable homicide. Hadlee had preached secession before the war and had encouraged his congregation to take up arms against their nation, and after the war was begun and it had become obvious that the Federal forces would gain the upper hand in Missouri, he had advised his people to take to the brush and fight the blue-coated minions of the Devil with whatever means was at their disposal. Dozens of Hadlee's churchgoers had followed his advice and had joined the Confederate army, or they had become guerrillas or, worse, bushwhackers.

Speaking out for his rebellious beliefs wasn't reason enough for killing him, but the additional factor of cowardice was. The reverend, after calling for others to shed blood for the noble cause of States' Rights, had fled south to Arkansas at the first sign that his own safety was in jeopardy in Missouri. This pusillanimous act compounded his initial crimes, and thus, Unionists figured that he deserved to be shot down like any other cur dog.

After eating, the five travelers bought tickets on the St. Louis & Ironton Rail Road for St. Louis and paid for their horses to be transported in the express car.

The talk on the train was much the same as it had been in the hotel. Everybody was gossiping about Reverend Hadlee's murder. This didn't surprise Creed, but the way that the conversant spoke so casually about the killing did. They seemed to give it no more importance than they would the weather. Are these people that calloused to death? wondered Creed.

James tried to make Creed understand their attitude by relating why he'd become a guerrilla during the war and why his family stood for the South.

In the fall of 1861, when eighteen years of age, Alexander Franklin James volunteered for the Confederate States Army, becoming a member of Captain Minter's company, Hughes's regiment, Stein's division. He was present at the capture of Lexington and marched with General Price's army into southwest Missouri. At Springfield, he was taken with the measles, and on the retreat of Price's army before General Curtis in February 1862, he was left behind in the hospital. The Federals, when they captured Springfield, took him prisoner, paroled him, and allowed him to return home to his mother's farm in Clay County. Back home again, he was arrested by the Federals in the early summer, then released on a $1,000 bond that was supposed to guarantee his parole. He returned home and went to work farming.

From time to time, James was accused of having aided and abetted the Confederate cause in violation of his parole, and in the early spring of '63, he was again arrested, taken to Liberty, the seat of Clay County, and cast into jail. From there, he contrived to make his escape, and soon afterwards, while a fugitive, he determined to go to the brush and accordingly joined a small band of bushwhackers under the leadership of Fernando Scott. This was in May, and a few days later he took part in the raid on Missouri City. Thereafter, he was a guerrilla until the close of the war, winding up his quasi-military career with his surrender in Kentucky.

Soon after James went to the brush, a detachment of Clinton County militia accompanied a few Clay County militiamen to the home of Dr. Reuben and Mrs. Zerelda Samuel, James's stepfather and mother, who lived in Kearney township. The Federals were searching for James and his guerrilla companions. Failing to find them, they sought by threats and violence to force the members of the family to give them certain information that they desired.

Dr. Samuel was taken out to the Woods and tortured by being hung twice by the neck until nearly exhausted. He was hung a third time and left to die, but Mrs. Samuel and her daughter, Susie James, were able to reach him soon enough and cut him down in time to save his life.

James's younger brother, Jesse, then not quite sixteen, was plowing a field when the Militia came. They whipped him very severely in order to make him reveal his brother's whereabouts, but he told them nothing other than that he would make them pay for their abuse of him and his family someday. They only laughed at him and left the farm.

A few weeks later the Samuels were arrested by the Federals and taken to St. Joseph where they were accused of feeding and harboring bushwhackers. This charge was brought against Mrs. Samuel, but no charges were filed against the doctor. Jesse and Susie weren't arrested with their parents. Mrs. Samuel, who was pregnant and who gave birth to another daughter in three months, had her two small children with her when she was imprisoned in St. Joseph. After being imprisoned for two weeks, the Samuels were released upon taking the oath of loyalty to the Union.

Jesse James continued to live at home during this time, raising a crop of tobacco. The following summer he, too, took to the brush, joining Fletcher Taylor's small band of guerrillas first, then changing his allegiance to Bloody Bill Anderson. In August of '64, he was badly wounded by an old German Unionist named Heisinger who lived in the southern part of Ray County. With a couple other guerrillas, he went to Heisinger's to get something to eat, and while they were reconnoitering the premises, the old man fired on them from a sorghum patch, putting a bullet through Jesse's right lung and routing the party. This nearly ended the younger James's career as a bushwhacker. His companions hid him away because they expected him to die, but Nat Tigue nursed him for a considerable time until he recovered and resumed his activities with the guerrillas.

In January of '65, the Samuels were banished from Clay County, and they removed to Rulo, Nebraska where Dr. Samuel eked out a living for them with his medical practice.

That spring Jesse tried to surrender and was shot for his efforts. He escaped into some woods where he was found by a friendly farmer who dressed his wound and took him to a doctor. The Federals caught up to him, but when they saw his wound, they figured he would die soon and thus let him be. A kindly Union officer arranged for him to be taken to his family in Nebraska, where he recovered slowly. When Jesse could travel again, the family returned to their home in Clay County.

"When I was paroled in '62," James told Creed, "I would have stayed out of the war like I promised, but the Unionist governor put out an order that every Missouri man of fighting age had to join the militia and fight the Confederacy. I couldn't do that. I couldn't fight against my own kind. I refused to do it, so the Militia kept on hounding me, arresting me every so often, and giving me a hard time of it with abusive words and a whipping once in a while. I tried to keep my word, but they wouldn't leave me alone. I felt like I'd been double-crossed by the Unionists, so I took to the brush.

"Then they did all those things to my family when they hadn't done anything to deserve such treatment. That's why Jesse took to the brush, too, and look how they treated him when he tried to surrender. We knew that's how they'd treat us guerrillas in Missouri, so that's why I went with Colonel Quantrill to Kentucky to surrender."

"It was them damn Jayhawkers who started it all," said Oll Shepherd. "Our people were living peaceable in Missouri, minding our own affairs, when those Kansas Abolitionists started raiding in Missouri and stealing our slaves and killing our people and burning our homes. And when the war came, things just got worse. We fought back as best as we could, but every time we shot one of them, they'd shoot two of us, and it didn't make a damn bit of difference whether they shot a man, a boy, or a woman. They even killed a bunch of women in the St. Joe jail."

"That's when Colonel Quantrill decided we should teach those Jayhawkers a lesson that they'd not soon forget," said James. "We raided Lawrence, Kansas for what they did to our womenfolk in the St. Joe jail."

While he was serving in Tennessee in '63, Creed had heard about the slaughter of 150 men and boys at Lawrence. Colonel Morgan, his commander, had detested Quantrill's attack, calling it the act of a butcher, a barbarian, and a lunatic, and those sentiments were echoed in Richmond.

Creed had agreed then that the guerillas were nothing more than bloodthirsty animals, but now, after having made the acquaintance of Alex James, Jim White, and the Shepherds, he wondered if he'd been too hasty in his judgment. Especially now, after seeing and hearing how the Unionists of Missouri were no better than their Secessionist counterparts were reputed to be.

Then he considered his own past. When his brother Dent and his best friend, Jess Tate, were murdered, Creed had reacted with a cold heart toward the cowbirds who had committed those crimes and had tried to find and kill every one of the murderers. He had caught and hung three of them without a lick of remorse, and he had shot two others, but not until one of them, Champ Golihar, had tried to kill him first and the other, Harlan Detchen, had been a party to the murder of two more of his friends. He had regretted shooting Golihar because he was only a boy; he regretted shooting Detchen only because he had deserved a fate worse than death.

Creed noted a similarity in his situation with that of the Missourians. He had always been at odds with the Detchens back in Texas, and this feud with them had grown to include his friends and family and their friends and family. In his mind, the Detchens, two of the meanest little bastards in Lavaca County, had drawn the line between them when they tried to whip Dent. He had whipped the Detchens instead. Then later in life, they had murdered Jess Tate, had been among those who had killed Dent, and had killed Kent and Clark Reeves, two of his good friends. In turn, he had hung three of their friends, had shot another accomplice, and had shot Harlan on the pier at Indianola. Even with all this bloodshed, the score remained unsettled.

Missouri had always been a state divided by the slavery issue. That was enough to set brother against brother, let alone neighbor against neighbor. The argument over slavery was escalated into a fight when the Federal Congress decided to let the people of Kansas decide whether their state should be free or slave. The War Between the States had allowed that fight to come out into the open as uniforms and commissions from the state governments gave both sides licenses to kill. For four long years, Missouri had been torn by a war that was fought county to county, town to town, household to household, leaving everybody men, women, and every child who was old enough to understand death emotionally scarred and bitter and calloused and unforgiving, especially unforgiving, in one way or another. The score here also remained unsettled.

Creed considered himself to be like these Missourians in that he was emotionally scarred, bitter, and calloused. But was he unforgiving like them as well? As far as Farley Detchen was concerned, he was. What was next in their feud? Would he kill Farley Detchen? Or would Farley kill him? Given the chance, he knew Farley would shoot him in the back could he do the same? He did hate Farley, but did he hate him so much that he would simply kill him as coldly as Wilson had murdered Reverend Hadlee? Like his brother, Farley deserved a fate worse than death. Maybe shooting him down like a rabid hog would be the humane thing to do, Who knew for certain? Creed didn't. He'd face that decision the next time he saw Farley.

And what about Jim Kindred, the wild card in his feud with the Detchens? He was responsible for Dent's death, having led the raid on the cattle herd, Did Creed hate him as much as he hated Detchen? Kindred was as much of a coward as Detchen was, and he did deserve to die for his crime. But Creed hardly knew Kindred, had had very little contact with him, and even had a tough time trying to picture the little bastard in his mind. From what he could recall about Kindred, he felt a little sorry for the runt. He pitied Kindred more than he hated him. Would he kill Kindred the next time he saw him? Probably not, he told himself. Kindred was a pest, a heel-fly, for sure, to be shooed away until he forces you to squash him once and for all time. Since Kindred wasn't bothering him now, Creed decided to give him no further thought.

Putting both of those badmen out of his mind, Creed considered his present situation. He was in Missouri with men who were thoroughly dangerous, and although they were his friends, his mere association with them put him in jeopardy. Exactly how, he didn't know. He did know that violence could strike any one of them or him at any moment, just the same as it had struck the parson of the Locust Ridge Baptist Church the day before.

The vision of that cold-blooded murder passed through his mind, and he shuddered again with the thought that it could happen to him as well - at any time, at any place, by any hand - because he was a neutral here and that placed him at odds with both sides.

Damn! I hope Quade has gone on to Colorado! He prayed silently as the ravaged Missouri countryside passed by their train in the night.

22

From the River City, Creed and his traveling companions took the Missouri and Pacific Rail Road's late train to Warrensburg, which was as close to Lexington as any railroad came in February 1866. They boarded their mounts in a cattle car that was being returned to Kansas City where it would be loaded with beeves from western Missouri and eastern Kansas for the market in Chicago. They arrived in Johnson County the following day, offloaded their horses, and started the four-hour ride north to Lexington.

This was familiar territory to Alex James, Jim White, and the Shepherds. James was with the regular Confederate army in 1861 at the Battle of Lexington, and all of them had fought here under Bloody Bill Anderson and the infamous William Quantrill when General Price took the town again in 1864.

Lafayette County had been a house divided during the war, and it was still so. The Unionists continued to control the government, although their hold on it was precarious because the Democrats, most of whom were former Confederate sympathizers if not active participants in the rebellion, were very strong in numbers and voice. The latter was mostly due to the efforts of the editor of The Caucasian, James A. Berry, the very man that Creed had come to see in Lexington.

Colonel John Burch had given Creed a letter of introduction for George Washington Ewing in Kentucky, and Ewing had, in turn, given Creed a letter of introduction to Berry, his kinsman in Missouri. Creed didn't read Burch's missive to Ewing because it had been sealed and he figured that it contained some personal message for

Ewing. He didn't read Ewing's letter to Berry for the same reason, but he thought it was strange that Ewing had resealed Burch's letter before returning it to him with the instruction of presenting it to Berry with his own letter. What do these letters contain, he wondered, that they have to be sealed from my eyes? The thought never crossed his mind to open the letters and betray the trust both men had placed in him. Even so, he was still curious about the letters as he climbed the stairs to the offices of *The Caucasian* on the third floor of the Tevis building located on the corner of Pine and Main streets.

Jim Berry was a thin, little man with a receding hairline, spectacles, and a clean-shaven face. He was wearing ink-stained maroon sleeve garters over a white shirt that also had seen better days, and a black visor shaded his bright blue eyes that seemed to be marveling at everything that came into their view. A counter separated him from Creed when the two met for the first time that afternoon of February 6, 1866.

"I'm Jim Berry. May I help you, sir?"

"Slate Creed, sir," said the Texan, extending his hand to the newspaper editor.

Berry accepted the handshake and said, "Pleased to make your acquaintance, sir."

"Mr. Berry, I have two letters of introduction for you," said Creed. He produced the missives from inside his coat and handed them over to Berry. "The one is from a kinsman of yours, Mr. George Washington Ewing, and the other is to Mr. Ewing from Colonel John Burch of Nashville."

"Cousin George?" queried Berry, appearing to be impressed. He took the letters, opened them, and read each one in turn, beginning with Ewing's. As soon as he was finished with Burch's letter, he folded them up again and returned his attention to Creed. "Cousin George says you are a Texan and that you are looking for Marsh Quade."

"Yes, sir, that's correct on both accounts," said Creed. "I do hail from Texas, and I am looking for Marsh Quade."

"Well, he and Cousin Sal were here last month," said Berry, "but they've gone on to Colorado. Marsh came looking for work here at the newspaper, but unfortunately, we had nothing available for him. I couldn't even find steady work for him in town. The war was hard on us folks here in Lexington, but we'll come back soon enough." He offered a confident smile and a wink.

"Do you know where they went in Colorado?" asked Creed. "Yes, I do," said Berry. "Denver. At least, that's where they said they would try first. I told them not to go. It being winter and all. Too dangerous to travel at this time of the year. You never know when a storm will come roaring down from up north and cover everything with snow. I told him to try Kansas City or Independence or even St. Joe before he goes off to Colorado. I told him he might find some temporary work in one of those places, and who knows? He might even find something permanent. I understand the railroad will be starting up again real soon. I told him he ought to look into that. I don't know if he did, though. He said they were going to Colorado."

"Well, thank you, Mr. Berry," said Creed. He tipped his hat and started to leave.

"Captain Creed," Berry called after him, "are you staying over in Lexington tonight?"

Creed stopped at the door, turned, and said, "Yes, I'm traveling with some friends, and we're staying at the Virginia Hotel." Then he wondered why Berry had addressed him as Captain Creed.

Burch had called him Lieutenant Creed, but not the higher rank.

Had Burch mentioned his former station in the Confederate army in the letter to Ewing? Most likely. How else would Berry know that he had been an officer?

"Friends, you say? Texans like yourself?"

"Actually, no. They're from near here. Clay County, they said."

"Clay County men?" asked Berry, his curiosity growing. "How did you come to be with them?"

"We met at a horse race near Mammoth Cave, Kentucky, last month," explained Creed. 'Then we met again in Russellville, Kentucky, last week."

The phrase, "a horse race near Mammoth Cave, Kentucky" struck a chord in Berry's memory. He said, "One moment, Captain Creed. I'd like to look at something, then speak with you further. Would you mind waiting?"

He wasn't sure why he did it, but Creed returned to the counter and waited while Berry read an article in a newspaper. He watched the editor's face brighten with satisfaction at whatever it was that he was reading.

Berry finished the article, then returned to the counter. "Just as I thought," he said. "When you mentioned a horse race in Kentucky last month, I recalled a story that was in The Chicago Tribune about a horse race in Kentucky where a man was killed, a gambler, by the man who staged the event. I only wanted to confirm that you were that same man."

Creed felt a slight annoyance over being detained for this rather trivial reason. "Is that all you wanted from me, Mr. Berry?" he asked evenly in order to disguise his displeasure.

The editor sensed that not all was right with Creed. "I beg your pardon, Captain Creed," he said. "Please excuse my rudeness. I meant no offense, I assure you. Originally, I was intending to ask you if I might join you for supper at the Virginia this evening. I wanted to interview you for *The Caucasian*. If you don't mind, that is."

"I don't know that I would make interesting reading for your readers, Mr. Berry," said Creed, slightly taken aback by the editor's request.

"Would you let me make that decision, Captain Creed?" asked Berry. "Any man who has done What you have done should prove to be interesting enough for the people of this locality. At the very least, you could introduce me to your traveling companions. You say that they, too, were at the race in Kentucky? And that they hail from Clay County?"

"Yes, sir, that's what I said. Their names are Alex James, Jim White, George Shepherd, and Oll Shepherd."

"Did you say Oll Shepherd?" asked Berry, now quite excited. "The guerrilla leader from Clinton County?"

"I believe he said something about having ranged there during the war," said Creed.

"Would certainly like to meet Oll Shepherd," said Berry. "He served the cause greatly during the war."

"Well, I suppose it wouldn't do any harm for you to have supper with us, Mr. Berry."

"I'll get my coat and be with you in a moment," said Berry. He removed his sleeve garters and visor, grabbed a pocket notebook, took his hat, coat, and overcoat from the hat tree in the corner, donned the clothing, and joined Creed on the exit side of the counter. "Shall we go?" he asked.

They walked over to the Virginia Hotel where Creed made all the proper introductions in the lobby, then the six of them sat down to eat in the dining room.

"I take it that the man you're looking for isn't here in Lexington," said James as soon as they were seated.

"No, he's gone on to Colorado," said Creed, now a bit dejected that his quarry had taken flight again.

"I suppose you'll be wanting to go there now?" asked James.

"That was my thought," said Creed. "I wish Quade would light somewhere so I can meet up with him and get this thing settled once and for all. I'm getting a mite tired of all this traveling about the country."

"Well, you might as well ride on with us tomorrow," said James. "I'd be honored if you'd stop over at my folks' place for a night. It's only a four-hour ride from here. I know Ma would like to meet you."

"I thank you for the invitation, Alex," said Creed. "It'd be my pleasure to meet your family."

"Well, I'm certainly glad you boys stopped over here in Lexington," said Berry. "Folks around here will be real surprised to read about you in my newspaper." He took out his notebook and pencil and started making notes. "Imagine! Oll Shepherd! Right here in Lexington! And you, too, Captain Creed! This really is a red-letter day for Lexington, *The Caucasian*, and the Order."

"The Order, Mr. Berry?" asked Creed.

Berry stared at Creed, not understanding why Creed had questioned him on that point. "Well, you know," he said nervously, the smile twitching up and down on his face. "The Order." When he saw that Creed still didn't understand, he said, "Cousin George and Colonel Burch both wrote that you were one of us, Captain Creed."

Creed shook his head and said, "I don't believe I'm following you here, Mr. Berry."

"Slate, I believe Mr. Berry is referring to the Order of American Knights," said James.

The Texan looked at James, understood what he was saying, then turned to Berry and said, "I'm sorry, sir, but I believe Colonel Burch and Mr. Ewing have misinformed you. I am not a member of your order."

Berry reacted as if he had betrayed a confidence, which he had. He was at a loss for words.

"That's all right," said Oll Shepherd with a smile. "You can join up any time you want, Slate. We'd be proud to have you as a member. Wouldn't we, boys?" He looked around at his friends whose faces expressed their agreement, then at Berry. "Right, Mr. Berry?"

"Certainly," said Berry. "It would be an honor to have you join us, Captain Creed."

Creed shifted his view to James and said, "Are you boys in this order?"

"You might say that," said James.

Some rapid thoughts passed through Creed's mind along with some recollections of what Colonel Burch had said to him and what George Ewing had said. As much as he admired these men, he wasn't sure that he wanted to be a member of their organization, although he felt this without knowing exactly what it was that the Order represented. Something told him that, whatever it was, it went against his principles of equality among men and women, and that was a sacrifice that he was unwilling to make.

"Well, I'm sure you have your reasons for belonging to this order," said Creed, "and under any other circumstances, I would seriously consider becoming a member, too. But I can't do it right now. Not until I get my own life straightened out. I think you boys understand that, don't you?"

"Sure, we do, Slate," said James. "Don't we, boys?"

They all agreed, including Berry.

With that point settled, they ordered their suppers, and Berry interviewed them during the meal. After dinner, all but Creed retired to the hotel's saloon for a drink before calling it a night. The Texan went up to his room and wrote a letter to Texada, telling her of what had happened to him since he last wrote. Of course, he left out the parts that concerned Mattie Whittaker. He was still baffled about them himself.

23

The Samuel home was located three miles from the country villages of Greenville to the east and Centerville to the west on the road that connected the two tiny communities. The house's original structure was a log cabin built in 1822 by the man who sold the property back in '43 to Alex James's father, Reverend Robert James. When Reverend James died in California in 1850, his widow, Zerelda, inherited the place, and it remained hers through her one-year marriage to Benjamin Simms and was still under her sole ownership, although she was now married to Dr. Reuben Samuel.

During the '50s, the log cabin was covered with clapboard and a one-and-a-half story Chicago-style wing was added to accommodate Zerelda's growing family. Already with three children by her first husband, she and Dr. Samuel brought three more into the world and were expecting their fourth when the eldest son, Alexander Franklin James, returned home, bringing with him four friends.

Creed, Alex James, Jim White, and the Shepherd brothers rode up to the house in time for lunch on Wednesday, February 7, 1866.

A light snow was falling gently when they climbed down from their horses and tied them to the four posts that held up the porch roof on the south side of the one-story section. The Samuels and their three small children burst through the doors to greet them. Susan James, Alex's sixteen-year-old sister, waited at the door, cautiously eyeing the men with her brother.

"Mr. Frank," said Zerelda Samuel, smiling maternally and addressing her son by her own special appellation for him, "come here and kiss your old mama." She was a tall woman, taller than her son, and rather homely, although a light in her blue eyes claimed her to be a daring, vivacious woman who would take no grief from the Devil himself. Her brown hair was parted severely and combed into a tight bun on the back of her head. She wore a faded butternut-colored shift that announced her maternal condition.

James obeyed his mother and kissed her cheek as they hugged.

Then he shook Dr. Samuel's hand and patted young Sally, little Johnny, and even smaller Fanny on their heads. "Ma," he said, "I want you to meet some friends of mine. You might have heard of these fellows. Jim White, George Shepherd, and Oll Shepherd."

Zerelda acknowledged them with a smile and a nod, saying, "Yes, I've heard of them. How do, boys?"

Each one took his turn doffing his hat to Zerelda and greeting her with a "Pleasure to meet you, ma'am."

"And this is Captain Slate Creed, Ma" said Alex. "Captain Creed served under Colonel Morgan in Kentucky and General Forrest in Tennessee during the war."

"Captain Creed, I'm pleased to meet you," said Zerelda.

"The honor is mine, ma'am," said Creed, removing his hat and giving her a half-bow.

"My, my, Captain Creed," said Zerelda, "you are a man of breeding and manners, aren't you?"

"He's a Texan, Ma," said Alex as if that would explain everything to her.

"A fine state, I've heard," said Zerelda.

"Thank you, ma'am," said Creed.

"Boys," said Alex, "this gentleman is my stepfather, Dr. Reuben Samuel."

With the same regard that they had shown Zerelda, each of the young men paid their respects to the bearded Dr. Samuel, shaking hands with him and making polite greetings. The doctor was shorter than his wife by a few inches, and he was a bit on the stocky side. His passive blue eyes told the viewer that this was a man with a gentle nature.

"Well, don't just stand there," said Zerelda, as soon as the introductions were complete. "Come on inside and warm yourselves by the fire."

Susan held the door for all of them Zerelda, her husband and children, and the five newcomers as they entered the house in single file. Creed was the last to walk past the pretty teenage girl. Hat in hand, he smiled and nodded at her, half expecting her to blush and look away, but she did neither. Instead, she remained stolid, fixing her cobalt-blue eyes on Creed's, as if to challenge him to a stare-down. Recognizing the strength in her aspect, his red man's instincts took control and painted his face with the stoicism of his Choctaw ancestors as he halted just inside the door to confront her will with his own. He had enough confidence in his manhood to accept anyone, man or woman, as his equal, but he refused to allow anyone, man or woman, to back him down with a mere look.

Before Creed and Susan could settle their impromptu contest, Jesse Woodson James, the final member of the Samuel household, stepped into the room from a bedroom. All eyes turned to this emaciated young man who made no sudden moves, instead choosing to keep his distance, standing just inside the doorway with his left hand behind his back and his right hanging loosely at his side. He wasn't as tall as his mother, but he was so thin that he appeared to be something of a beanpole. However, it wasn't his height that drew attention to him. His eyes - icy blue, defiant, haughty, commanding, calculating - magnetized everyone as he stood in the doorway scanning the guests, recognizing all but Creed and staring hard at the Texan.

Zerelda was the first to act. "Jesse," she said, moving to his side, "look who's come home."

Alex offered a brief smile and held his hand out to Jesse. "You look downright skinny, Jesse," said Alex. "Skinnier than I remember. How're you doing?"

Jesse took his brother's hand, shook it firmly, and said, "Still breathing, Frank," while refusing to avert his eyes from Creed. "How about you?"

"Can't complain," said Alex. He noted that Jesse was still staring at Creed. "Jesse, I'd like you to meet Captain Slate Creed from Texas. He rode with Colonel Morgan in Kentucky and General Forrest in Tennessee during the war. Slate, this is my brother Jesse. You've heard us talk about him."

Creed crossed the room to shake Jesse's hand. "How do you do, Mr. James?" he said, being formal. "Pleased to make your acquaintance."

"Hello, Captain Creed?" said Jesse. "How do you come to be with this bunch of Missouri bushwhackers, sir?" he asked bluntly.

Releasing Jesse's hand, Creed smiled and said, "Please call me Slate. I haven't been a captain since the war ended."

"It hasn't ended for everybody, Slate." said Jesse.

Creed hesitated as he studied Jesse's countenance, for a hint of meaning behind his words. Discovering it, he said, "I know what you mean. We saw how some folks haven't been able to forgive and forget."

"Forgive and forget?" queried Jesse, still holding his left hand behind him. "Scripture, Slate? The only Scripture that makes any sense in Missouri is the one about an eye for an eye and a tooth for a tooth. Only here it means something a lot harder than that. A ball in the brain for a hanging." He touched his right breast. "A ball in the brain for one in the chest. That's all anyone understands around here, Slate. A killing for a killing."

A tension filled the room. It was so strong that it even held Zerelda in abeyance.

Jesse's eyes, the sound of his voice, his choice of words combined to cast a spell over everyone in his audience except Creed. Although he was impressed by the younger James brother's charisma, Creed was the only person in the room who didn't share Jesse's opinion on the remedy for the state of affairs in Missouri, and it was this difference that saved him from succumbing to Jesse's messianic hypnosis.

"Six months ago," said Creed, breaking the silence, "I would have agreed with you." The sad memory of his brother dying in his arms kept Creed from saying anything more on the subject. He cleared his throat, lowered his head, then stepped aside to let the others greet Jesse.

"Dingus," said Oll Shepherd jovially, "it's good to see you again." He shook Jesse's hand. "You all healed up yet?"

"Getting stronger every day, Oll," said Jesse. "Ma feeds me real good."

"It wasn't me that did it," said Zerelda. "It was his cousin Zee down to Harlem that nursed him back to health. That girl waited on him every single minute we were living with Cousin John's family."

George Shepherd and Jim White shook hands and exchanged pleasantries with Jesse, then Zerelda invited the travelers to join the family for lunch. They accepted graciously, then went to tend to their horses.

As he was leaving the house, Creed noticed Jesse turn and go back into the bedroom, a Remington .44 in his left hand. I guess the war isn't over for him yet, thought the Texan as he followed Alex through the door.

After putting their horses in the barn and feeding them, the travelers returned to the house for what smelled like a royal banquet. The table wasn't big enough to seat everyone, so the men ate first. Zerelda and Susan served them hot potato soup, slices of ham, fresh bread with lard butter, and cold sweet buttermilk.

During the meal, Alex related how they had first met Creed in Kentucky, then told of their adventures after meeting up with him again in Logan County, including the tragic incident at Locust Ridge. As an apparent afterthought but with a look that Creed noticed was directed at Jesse, Alex remarked that they had met with James Berry in Lexington, taking care to mention Berry's position as editor of *The Caucasian* and Berry's relationship to George Washington Ewing back in Kentucky. At the time, the Texan gave the moment little thought except that it was odd that Alex should look at Jesse as if the telling should mean something special to him.

After eating, the men relaxed around the fireplace, some smoking and all, including Creed, sampling Dr. Samuel's home-stilled corn liquor. The warmth of the hearth, the numbing effect of the alcohol, and the fatigue of their ride soon had the guests sleeping like little boys.

The last thing Creed saw before drifting off was the pretty face of Susan James. With her image firmly imprinted in his mind, he wondered what secrets lay behind those challenging eyes of hers. The white lightning told him that he ought to take the trouble to find out. But later. When he felt like moving again.

24

By the time Creed awakened that afternoon, several inches of snow had fallen, making the northwest Missouri countryside treacherous for travel. That and the late hour made it easy for Creed to accept Zerelda Samuel's invitation to stay over the night.

The Shepherds, White, and Creed were accommodated in the barn, each of them throwing a bedroll over a soft pallet of hay in the least drafty corner of the structure. Outside the wind howled and swirled the powdery snow into tall drifts against all the buildings of the Samuel farm.

"From the sounds of this storm," said on Shepherd from beneath his blanket, "you won't be going nowheres for a few days, Slate. It's gonna pile up snow all over the place and make it near impossible to get anywhere on a horse. Not even a tall stud like the one you ride can make it through some of the drifts we get in these parts."

"Of course," said White, who had covered his blanket with a thick layer of straw, "this storm could blow itself out quick, and tomorrow could be bright and shiny and warm and melt all this snow. I've seen that happen more than once."

"Yeah," said Oll, "and when it does warm up like that after a heavy snowstorm like this, the melting makes every road knee deep in mud, and every creek that's usually no bigger than a healthy stream of piss turns into the Missouri River. No matter which way you cut it, Slate, you're stuck here with us for the next few days."

This wasn't exactly what Creed wanted to hear. He'd hoped to be on his way in the morning, figuring he had a long way to go to Colorado in pursuit of Marshall Quade, who was at least a week ahead of him. Every minute spent dallying here was time wasted, time lost in his quest to clear his name and resume the life that he wanted to live in back in Texas. I can't do anything about the weather, he told himself, so I won't let it worry me. I'll just have to make the most of my stay here.

The image of Susan James intruded into Creed's pre-slumber thoughts. He saw her cobalt-blue eyes staring back at him when they met earlier that day at the door. The strength forged in them attracted him, aroused a desire in him to take her into his arms and show her that his will was equal to hers, that his passion was just as great as hers. He recalled catching her eyeing him during the evening meal. She didn't look away then either, not until her mother interrupted with an order to get the men more coffee. He considered her form. She was tall for a woman. Not as tall as her mother, but still tall. And lithe. With long limbs that could envelop a man with lust. He could almost feel their warmth surrounding him, urging him to respond, moving him, arousing him as he drifted off to sleep.

When he peeked out of his blanket-and-hay cocoon at the early light of morning, Creed was surprised to see a small boy, dressed in enough homespun clothes to withstand the cold, standing over him. He didn't know who the child was, but he knew what he was. He'd seen children like this one before. Hazel eyes; very curly, chocolate-brown hair; golden-brown complexion; narrow facial features: the offspring of a male master and a female slave. Creed gauged the lad's age to be about four years-old enough to talk.

Creed crooked an elbow and propped his head on the hand. "What's your name, son?" he asked with a smile.

"Perry," said the child, not showing any fear of this stranger in the hay.

"Do you live around here, Perry?" asked Creed.

"Yes, sir," said Perry. He turned and looked at the rear of the barn. "In the house out back."

Creed recalled seeing a little shack beyond the barn the day before, but he didn't think much about it then except that it was either some sort of storage place or a smokehouse. The possibility that it could be a home never entered his mind; the place was that small. "The house out back?" queried Creed.

"Yes, sir."

"Who lives out there with you, Perry?"

"Just Mammy," said the boy.

The barn door opened as if it had been cued. A dark, skinned woman, a red woolen scarf tied around her head and a red woolen shawl wrapped around her shoulders, peeked inside. From the way she squinted, she was finding it difficult to see in the dim light.

"Perry?" she called out. "You in here, boy?"

"That's Mammy," said Perry.

"Perry, is that you back there?" she called again.

"Yes, Mammy, I's in here."

"You come out of there right this minute, boy!" she snapped. "And stop bothering them gentlemens."

"Ain't but one of them left in here, Mammy," argued Perry.

Creed stood up and said, "It's all right. He wasn't bothering me." He noticed that the Shepherds and White had already risen and left the barn. "Besides, it was time I was getting up anyway."

Perry's mother came inside and walked up to her son. Seeing Creed, then averting her eyes as was the attitude forced on slaves, she said, "I's sorry my boy done bothered you, sir. I don't know what gets into him sometimes."

Creed smiled and said, "It's all right." He chuckled a bit. "I've seen lots worse things than him when I've first come awake in the morning." He patted the child on the head. "He's a fine looking boy."

Still looking away, the woman smiled bashfully and said, "Thank you kindly, sir." She reached down and took Perry's hand. "Well, we best be going, sir." She hesitated as if waiting for permission to leave.

For some reason, this woman aroused Creed's curiosity. She was pretty and young; he guessed her age to be around seventeen, maybe a little older, maybe not. She must have become a woman awfully early, thought Creed for her master to have taken her so young. Or maybe Dr. Samuel isn't the so-polite gentleman that he seems to be.

Dr. Samuel? Creed looked at the boy again. He had none of the features of the doctor, but he did look like a James. No, Dr. Samuel didn't sire this child, he thought. Alex then? He doesn't seem to be the type to sleep with slaves. Jesse. Most likely. He seems to have that same attitude toward slave women that Dent had.

Dent? Jesse? Yes, Creed did see some similarities between them. Although his experience with Jesse James was limited, he could tell that Jesse was as fiery, as excitable, as eager to act without thinking of the consequences first as Creed's brother Dent had been. Maybe that explained why he had felt that it was in his best interest to walk softly with Jesse the day before. And maybe even softer today, thought Creed.

"Your son said his name is Perry," said Creed. "He's about four, isn't he?"

"Yes, sir," said the woman. "He'll be four this spring."

Creed bent down to the child; smiled at him, and said, "Thank you for waking me up, Perry. You'd better go with your mama now." He stood up again, smiled at the boy's mother, and said, "It was nice to have met him. And you, too," Then he realized that he didn't know her name, "My, name is Slate Creed. What's yours?"

"Mine's Rachel."

"Perry said you lived in the house out back of the barn," said Creed.

"Yes, sir, Mr. Creed, we does. Perry and me. My folks lives over the hill from here now that we's all been freed."

"Why do you still live here?" asked Creed.

Rachel became agitated as if she didn't wish to reply to the question. Her eyes looked everywhere except at Creed. "Please, Mr. Creed, we gots to go," she said rapidly.

Creed understood. "Sure," he said, nodding.

In the next instant, she was headed for the door, dragging Perry behind her. The boy waved farewell to Creed, then he and his mother were gone.

Creed heaved a sigh as a wave of homesickness swept over him. Jesse reminded him of Dent; Rachel reminded him of Hannah, the house servant back home at Glengarry. All sorts of memories came to mind. One that disguised itself and hid in his subconscious was the comparison he made between Susan and Texada; they had little in common except that they were both women and both stimulated him. He was lonely for Texada, but she was a thousand miles away. Susan was here. Dammit I want to go home! was the thought that was cognizant to him.

But it wasn't to be today. The weather said so. So did a few people.

Suddenly, Creed realized that he needed to attend to three of the base needs of all humanity. He was hungry; he was cold; but most urgent of all, he had to piss-real bad. He opted for the outhouse first.

As soon as he had finished his business in the privy, Creed went to the house and joined the other men at the breakfast table. After all the morning pleasantries were out of the way, Susan James stepped up to him and asked, "Coffee, Captain Creed?"

"Yes, please," said Creed. He leaned sideways to give her more room to pour the brew into the tin cup on the table in front of him. "Thank you."

Their eyes met as she said without smiling, "It's my pleasure."

Each continued to stare into the other's soul for what seemed to them to be minutes but was actually only three brief seconds.

Even so, the look was long enough and longing enough that it didn't go unnoticed by any of the adults in the room, although none of them made mention of it at the time.

"I'll have some of that coffee, too," said Dr. Samuel, drawing Susan's attention away from Creed for the moment. Susan poured her stepfather's coffee, then went back to the stove to help her mother with the meal of biscuits and gravy and slices of fried ham. She picked up the platter of meat from its warming place on the stove and carried it back to the table where she placed it in front of Dr. Samuel, which was only right because he was the head of the household, or so Zerelda said for public consumption. As hard as she tried, Susan couldn't resist looking at Creed again.

The same was true of Creed. He couldn't resist looking at Susan again. She possessed something that commanded his constant attention. He didn't have a word for whatever it was that drew his eyes to her, but he did know that he liked it and hated it, that it made him feel good and bad at the same time.

"You aren't planning on leaving today, are you, Slate?" asked Alex James. "It snowed a terrible lot last night, and from the looks of the drifts around here, it must be piled pretty high on the roads. It could make traveling near to being impossible."

"That's what we told him last night," said Oll Shepherd. "We told him he ought to stick around for a few days. Leastways, until the weather clears and the roads ain't so bad."

Reluctantly, Creed shifted his eyes away from Susan to her oldest brother. "Well, I'd hoped to be on my way as soon as possible," he said, "but it looks like I'm not going too far in this weather."

Susan walked back over to the stove where Zerelda was listening to the conversation. She gave her mother a pleading look and nodded toward the table, toward Creed.

Zerelda was no fool, and she wasn't blind either. She knew perfectly well what Susan wanted. "You're welcome to stay with us until the weather clears, Captain Creed," she said. "We'd be real honored to have your company for a few more days." Creed's first thought was to turn down the invitation as politely as he could, but when he looked up and his eyes met Susan's instead of Zerelda's, he said to the mother, "I'd be delighted to stay, Mrs. Samuel."

The only person in the room who wasn't happy about his decision was Jesse, but the younger James brother said nothing. He ate in silence, brooding.

25

The morning had dawned clear and bright, although the wind continued to move the snow around. But as the hours ticked by, the weather improved; the temperature rose above the freezing mark, and the wind decreased, allowing the sun the chance to do some melting. By mid-afternoon, patches of brown grass began showing in the yard again.

Creed passed the time pleasantly by answering dozens of questions about his home and family back in Texas. The more he spoke of them, the more he longed for them. But realizing that they were out of his reach for the time being, he found solace for his anguish in the eyes of Susan James and the friendliness of her family.

"If this keeps up," said Zerelda, peeking through the kitchen window at the scene outside, "tomorrow ought to be a real nice day." She released the curtain and turned back to Creed and the other men who were sitting around the table. "I suppose you'll be wanting to move on then, won't you, Captain Creed?"

"Yes, ma'am, I suppose so," said Creed.

"Too bad," said Zerelda. "I've enjoyed hearing about Texas so much that I wish you'd consider staying over for another day. You've been right pleasant company."

"Thank you, Mrs. Samuel," said Creed, "but I wouldn't wish to wear out my welcome."

"Any man who fought for the South like you did, Captain Creed," said the woman of the house, "will always be welcome in my home. Isn't that right, Dr. Samuel?"

Sleepy-eyed, the doctor pulled himself out of his lethargy to say, "Yes, Missus, that's right. You'll always be welcome in our house,

Captain Creed."

"I certainly do appreciate that, folks," said Creed.

"So why don't you stick around for a few more days?" said Alex James. He glanced at Oll Shepherd, then added, "I'm sure we can find some way to entertain you around here."

"Of course, we can," said Oll, winking at Alex.

"I'm sure you could," said Creed, "but I'm not the kind to take advantage, Alex. I'd rather work for my keep."

Jesse burped a laugh and said, "Well, we can fix you up on that score, too. The barn needs shoveling out real bad. I'd do it, but I ain't exactly in the best of shape for shoveling horse dung. And I guess Frank wouldn't exactly relish doing it alone."

Much to Jesse's surprise, Creed said, "That sounds fair enough to me. I'd be pleased to help you shovel out the barn, Alex." He looked at Zerelda. "I hope I haven't insulted your most gracious hospitality, Mrs. Samuel, by offering to work for my keep."

"No, sir," she said, "you haven't." Then casting a steely glare in the direction of the Shepherds and Jim White, she added, "You set a fine example, Captain Creed."

Oll Shepherd could take a hint. "Yes, rna'am, he does," he said. "I believe I'll give you boys a hand with that shoveling." He nudged his brother's leg, prompting George to volunteer his labor, too.

"I guess we should all pitch in and help Buck with the barn," said George. "Right, Jim?"

"Sure," said White. "Work up a real appetite for supper. Sounds to me like the thing to do."

"Well, let's get to it then," said Jesse, "before all of you change your minds."

"What are you gonna do out there, Dingus?" asked Alex. "Someone's got to tell you boys how to do the job," said Jesse. "Now come on. The day's wasting."

The men rose almost in unison, excused themselves from the presence of the women and Dr. Samuel, then repaired to the barn where Jesse handed out tools and assignments. They doffed their coats and started the laborious, filthy task of removing the horse and cow manure from the stalls and pens. When they were finished an hour later, Oll Shepherd was the first to comment on the experience.

"You know, Buck," he said, "I don't mind shoveling shit like this, because your folks have been so hospitable and all, but I sure as hell don't intend to do it for a living like I've seen free niggers doing in some of the towns we've been through. No, sir, not me."

The others gathered around Shepherd, either leaning on their shovels or against a loft stanchion.

"What sort of work do you plan on doing?" asked Creed.

"I don't know for sure," said Oll. "I was thinking about opening me a store or maybe buy a farm and grow tobacco."

"Where are you going to get the money to open a store or buy a farm?" asked Jesse.

"I'll borrow it from a bank," said Oll.

Jesse laughed and said, "A bank? Ain't you heard, Oll? The Unionists own the banks, and they don't loan money to Confederates like us."

Creed thought about making some remark about the war being over but didn't bother once he remembered that he was still in Missouri; that thought conjured up the image of Reverend Hadlee's murder. No, the war isn't over here yet, he thought.

"There's lots of ways of getting money from a bank, Dingus," said Shepherd.

"Is that right?" smirked Jesse. "What are you going to do, Oll? Sneak in at night and help yourself to the cash drawer?"

Shepherd glanced at Alex James, then said, "Not exactly at night. Right, Buck?"

Consternation twisted Jesse's face as he looked from Shepherd to his own brother and back again. "What are you talking about, Oll?" he asked.

Creed knew exactly what Shepherd's allusion meant, and he was stunned by it. Rob a bank? he thought. The man must be crazy. Then he recalled that he had been asked to lead an expedition that did the exact same thing back in '64, but he had declined because he felt it was wrong to make war on civilians. Instead, Lieutenant Bennett H. Young accepted the assignment and led the raid on the banks of St. Albans, Vermont, on October 19, 1864, committing one of the first daylight bank robberies in the history of the United States. To Creed's way of thinking, Young could be excused for the deed because he was acting under orders and it was done as an act of war, but Oll Shepherd was proposing an out-and-out crime.

"Think about it, Dingus," said Shepherd. "You said it yourself. The Unionists own all the banks, and where did they get all that money they've got locked up in them? They stole it from folks like your Ma and Pa. They stole it from all of us. You remember what it was like around here before the war. And how about during the war? Didn't them Unionists steal everything they could get their hands on? And who did they steal it from? From your folks, my folks, you, me, Buck, Jim, George, Slate." He looked at Creed.

"Just look at what they did to Slate here down in Texas. And they're still doing it down there and up here, too. Hell, the war ain't over. It's just begun, boy, and it's our turn to win a battle or two." He turned to Alex. "Ain't that what Mr. Berry over to Lexington said, Buck?"

"That's the way I recollect it, Oll," said James. "He said it was our duty to the Order to keep up the fight, to strike back at the Federals at every turn because the bastards sure ain't about to give us no quarter."

"That's right," said White. "He said the black flag is still flying, and it's our duty to keep it flying."

Creed was incredulous. These men were talking about going to war all over again. Haven't these boys had enough of war? he wondered. Then another thought struck him. Maybe the war hasn't had enough of them yet. Maybe they were supposed to be killed in the war, but somehow they escaped retribution. Maybe. Maybe not.

Jesse's eyes were glassy.

Creed had seen the look before but not in a barn. He'd seen people in church get the Spirit and appear like the younger James brother was right then. Filled with zeal for the Lord, he thought. What was it the preacher had called it back in Hallettsville? Ecstasy? Something like that. They had the Spirit, or as the preacher had put it, the Spirit had them. Hallelujah, brother! Hallelujah, sister! The Spirit had never quite caught up with Creed, although he'd tried his best to let it catch him. Then puberty struck, and suddenly, he wasn't as eager to have the Spirit as he was before. Leastways, not all the time, like those times when Lucy May was within arm's reach and was more than willing to be in his arms for more than just a little hugging and kissing. But those were days gone by, irretrievable. This was now, and he had the chance to avoid sinning again.

"Yes, I see it now," said Jesse softly. "We can rob us a Unionist bank, and let those bastards know that they ain't quite won the war just yet."

"I was looking at it more like it was a raid," said the older James brother. "Stealing don't exactly seem right to me, but raiding Unionists is just fine. Like we did in the war."

"What are you talking about, Alexander Franklin James?" asked Susan James who was standing in the bam doorway. No one had heard or seen her come in.

"What are you doing in here?" demanded Jesse angrily. "You get back in the house where you belong."

"I heard what you said, Frank," said Susan, ignoring Jesse.

"You're talking about robbing a bank"

"No, Susie," said Alex, "we're talking about making a raid on the Unionists."

"No, you're not," argued Susan. "You're talking about robbing a bank. I heard you." She looked from one man to the next until her eyes came to Creed. "Are you in this with them?"

Looking her straight in the eyes, Creed shook his head slowly and said, "I don't believe so. The war's over for me."

"The hell you say!" said Jesse, mocking him. "You're still fighting to save your hide, the same as we are."

"No, Jesse, I'm not," said Creed, turning to face the younger James brother. "Leastways, not the same way as you are. You boys don't have a noose waiting for you back in Texas. You've got your homes and your families, and you can go just about anywhere you please and not have to worry about running into the law. Leastways, you won't have to worry about that as long as you don't cross the line."

"You still don't understand what's going on around here, do you, Slate?" asked Alex James. "Jesse tried to surrender, and they shot him. One practically sold his soul to guarantee they wouldn't hang him when he surrendered, and I was on the run until the end of July last year when I finally found a decent Yankee officer who gave me a parole and let me go in peace. We were guerrillas, Slate, and the Unionists won't let us forget that."

"That's right, Frank," said Jesse. "Bud and Donnie Pence were over here the other day, and they told me that the Militia were out to their folks' place the other night looking for them. Fortunately, they heard the Militia coming and had time to hide. If they hadn't, they would have been killed for sure."

"Didn't you learn nothing down to Locust Ridge, Slate?" asked

Alex James. "Don't you remember what those Unionists down there did to that poor parson?"

"Yes, I do remember that," said Creed, his head bowed. Then looking up at James, he said, "I recollect it all too well."

"Then you should understand by now," said one, "that the Unionists ain't letting the war end. They want to keep fighting, and as long as they want to fight, then we're gonna fight, too."

"Like I said the other day," said Jesse, "this is Missouri, Captain Creed. It ain't an eye for an eye here. It's a bullet in the brain for an eye. A killing for a killing." He looked at Susan," then added, "we stop short of making war on women and children. That's more than I can say for them Unionists."

Creed realized that he was wasting his time on these men. They were hell-bent for revenge, and that was that. Resigning himself to that fact, he said, "Well, you boys can do what you want, but don't count me in. I've got enough trouble with the law already." He leaned his shovel against a stall wall and headed for the doorway, stopping in front of Susan. "Maybe you can talk some sense into them, Miss Susie. They don't want to listen to me." When she made no reply, he turned back to the other men. "Like I said, boys. You can do what you want, but don't count me in." And with that he left the barn.

Susan scanned the faces before her, wondering if she should lecture them about the sin of thievery. She didn't get the chance.

"Well, baby sister," said Oll Shepherd with a mischievous grin, "are you gonna do what he said and try to talk some sense into us?"

"No, Oliver Shepherd, I'm not," said Susan. "I don't have enough breath for that. I can see that you're all crazy and that there's no stopping you once you've made up your minds."

"You're using good sense, Susie," said Jesse with a smile.

She shook her head with resignation, then said, "Since you're gonna do it anyway, you might as well do it right." She noted the surprise on their faces, then continued. "The fattest Unionist bank in these parts is the Clay County Savings Association down to Liberty. If you're gonna rob a bank, you might as well rob a good one."

26

Creed didn't go to the house immediately. He stopped in the yard to consider his situation. The thought crossed his mind to leave the Samuel farm that very minute, but he knew that he couldn't do that; he had already accepted Zerelda's hospitality, so it would be rude if he left now. I can ride out in the morning, he told himself, no matter what the weather is like.

Although he had made his decision, Creed still felt unsettled, that he was leaving something unfinished, that he wasn't tying up one last loose end. He was troubled even more by his inability to identify the problem. He knelt down and picked at the grass sticking up through the snow, as if that would help him find a solution. All he knew for certain was he had a pain that hurt bittersweetly deep inside him.

Susan exited the barn within a few minutes of Creed. She looked off to the southwest and noted that the sun had just set, leaving the horizon a vibrant orange that faded to pale shades of yellow then green and blue before growing to a deep azure overhead. The afternoon warmth was already gone. She pulled her shawl tighter around her shoulders to keep out the chill, then started for the house. She was only a few steps from the back door when she saw Creed squatting on the snow-covered grass and looking down the slope toward the creek. Curiosity brought her to a stop, and all sorts of machinations and fantasies blended wantonly within her as she studied him. He's like no other man that I've ever met, she told herself. He's tall and handsome to be sure, but he's more than that. He's strong inside, strong enough to be his own man, strong enough to bend but not break. Her heart gathered speed, and her breathing kept pace, oxidizing her emotions, warming her against the cold, and giving her the confidence to go to him.

Hearing Susan approach, Creed stood and met her steady gaze with one of his own. What is it about this girl? he asked himself. Another question that needed answering.

"I'm glad not every man around here has lost his good sense," she said, halting only a few feet from him.

Seeing her steamy breath in the frosty air stirred something within Creed. He felt an urge to take her hand, to touch her cheek, to pull her close to him and warm her with his own body; but he resisted the impulse. "I take it you weren't successful in talking some sense into them," he said, disregarding the turmoil beginning to bubble within him.

"I didn't even try," said Susan. "I know my brothers too well. You can't tell them anything. The only person they'd listen to is Ma, and I don't think she'd try to stop them, knowing how she feels about Unionists. No, Captain Creed, there's no stopping them once they've made up their minds to do something as foolish as what they're aiming to do."

"That's too bad," said Creed. "They seem like good men, but so did those boys who put the blame on me for their crime down in Mississippi. Part of me says that I should try to stop your brothers and the others, and another part says I ought to ride on and forget that I was ever here." He paused as he realized that he was trying to see into her soul. He felt his own loneliness, and it caused him to reverse his decision to leave in the morning. He said, "I don't think I can do either one. If I try to stop them, they're liable to turn on me, and someone's liable to get killed. Most likely me, but not before I took out one or two of them. Bloodshed like that just wouldn't do."

"What's stopping you from riding out of here and forgetting you were ever here?" asked Susan, ignoring his other remarks.

Creed wasn't sure how to answer her or whether he should even answer her. Was she the reason he couldn't leave and forget this place and these people? He had to admit that he felt something for her, but what was it? His emotions wrestled with his hormones as he couldn't decide whether he was attracted to Susan because She was a pretty girl or because she was a living, breathing, provocative woman within easy reach. Chemistry won out as he said, "You are."

"Me?" she queried, quite surprised by his response. "Why me? I mean, how am I stopping you from leaving here?"

"You aren't keeping me here," said Creed, stumbling in the dark of what was rather unfamiliar territory for him. "That's not exactly what I meant."

"Then what did you mean?" she asked.

"I meant, I won't ever be able to forget this place, your family, or you."

"Oh, is that it?" she said without disappointment flavoring her tone. "I thought you meant me in particular."

"I did," said Creed.

She moved closer to him and said, "I thought so. I was hoping so, too. I've seen how you've been looking at me, Captain Slate Creed. I like it."

Creed felt challenged all of a sudden. "And I've seen how you've been looking at me; Miss Susan James," he said.

"Then you know how I feel," she said.

"Don't you think you're being a bit forward?"

"I have to be forward if I'm going to get what I want," she said, closing the gap between them to mere inches. When Creed didn't respond instantly, she said, "Have you ever heard any of those stories about the preacher's daughter? "

"Some," said Creed.

"Well, there is some truth to them." she said, her face now so close to his that she could feel the heat of his breath. She liked that, too.

Creed was only a heartbeat away from taking her into his arms and kissing her with all the passion that he'd been keeping imprisoned inside him for far too long. Damn! I want this woman! He screamed in his head. And she was his for the taking, if not for that flash of memory-the image of Texada's tear-stained face begging him not to leave her-that made him clench his fists in restraint.

"Susie!"

The sound of her mother's voice backed Susan away from Creed and reminded her of the errand she had been sent to do. In a second, her aspect changed from desire to anger to disappointment to resignation to optimism. "The sun has barely gone down," she said, "and the whole evening is ahead of us. But we've got to have supper first. That's what I came out here to tell everybody, but it must have slipped my mind." She smiled coyly and added, "I wonder why." And with that, she broke off looking at Creed and headed for the house.

I wonder why, too, thought Creed as he watched her go.

27

The James brothers, the Shepherds, and Jim White remained in the barn after Creed left, and they began plotting the robbery of the Clay County Savings Association's bank.

"Susie's right about the Liberty bank being a fat one," said Alex James. "Those Unionists down there hardly lost a thing when the Redlegs came around here back in '61."

"Seems to me," said Oil Shepherd, "that the Unionists hardly felt the war at all around here."

"They didn't," said Jesse bitterly. "Leastways, not that I could ever tell. They're all still just as fat and sassy as they ever were before the war. They ought to have all sorts of money in that bank down there in Liberty, and I think it's our duty to see that some of that money gets back into the hands of its rightful owners."

"How do you propose that we go about robbing this bank, Oll?" asked White.

"First off, this is gonna be a raid," said Shepherd, "not a robbery. We ain't criminals. We're guerrillas fighting for the Cause, like Brother Berry down to Lexington said."

"That's right," said Alex. "It's gonna be a raid, not a robbery. Mr. Shakespeare wrote that someday the common folks would rise up in rebellion and the first thing they'd do was kill all the lawyers and bankers. Well, we don't have to kill all the lawyers and bankers, but we sure as hell can take from them what they stole from us. So we ain't doing this for ourselves, boys. We're doing this for the common folks. For our people. For Ma and Dr. Samuel. Folks like us." He eyed every man in the barn for any conflict. When he didn't see any, he said, "All right now, let's get down to business."

"First off," said Oil Shepherd, "we ain't got enough men for this raid. I say we need at least a dozen to do the job right. Maybe more."

"We'll do with what we can get," said Alex, "even if it's just the five of us. Hell, Oll, weren't we gonna rob the bank in Russellville with just the four of us."

"Sure, Buck, but that was Kentucky," said Shepherd, "and there wasn't no armed Militia night-riding in Logan County. We'll need more than the five of us, Buck."

"We can probably get Bud and Donnie Pence to join up with us," said Jesse.

"And some of the boys up to Clinton County might still be around," said Oll. "I can ride up there and have a look around for them."

"That might not be a good idea, Oll," said George. "Those folks up there probably ain't forgot about all what you did up there during the war. They're liable to take exception to you coming back there."

"George is right, Oll," said Alex. "Maybe we'd better look elsewhere for more men."

Oil bit his lip pensively, then said, "Yeah, I see what you mean." His head bobbed as if a new thought had come to him. "All right, why don't we go down to Lafayette County and ask Brother Berry about who we can enroll for this raid?" A wicked smile spread over his face. "After all, we're doing this for the Cause, ain't we?"

"All right," said Alex, "so we get us enough men for this raid. Don't you think we ought to scout out this bank first?"

"Good idea, Buck," said Oil. "You ride down to Liberty and scout this bank for us."

"Not a good idea," said Alex. "They had me in jail down there during the war. Someone's liable to recognize me and tell the Militia I'm back here in Clay County. Who knows what that might lead to?'

"Frank's right," said Jesse. "I'm the only who can ride into Liberty and not worry about being recognized." He burped a chuckle and added, "Hell, I'm so skinny now that no one will be able to see me anyway. I can ride into town, have a look around, pay a visit to the bank, and ride out without anybody knowing I was even there."

"You might be right about that, Dingus," said Oil. "I know I can't go in there without being recognized. George or Jim might be able to do it, but you're the best choice. No one's gonna suspect anything of a skinny kid riding into town. All right, you ride into Liberty and scout out the town and the bank. When do you think you'll be able to do it?"

"Tomorrow," said Jesse. "I was planning on riding down to Harlem to visit Zee on Saturday and stay over so I can go to church with her on Sunday. I'll just go a day earlier and be back here Sunday night."

"Good idea, Dingus," said Oll. "In the meantime, George and I will ride over to Lafayette County and confer with Brother Berry. Jim, you and Buck can visit with the Pence boys and see if they feel like going on a little raid. And you might ask around about some of the other men from this county who rode with us during the war. See if you can find Ning Letton or Jim and Alf Corum or Milt Dryden. They were with me when I surrendered last year. They might be interested in riding with us."

"Has anyone heard anything about Arch Clement?" asked Jesse.

"He might be a good one to have on this raid."

"Not a bad idea, Dingus," said Oll. "I'll ask around while we're down to Lexington."

"Why don't you go by way of Jackson County when you go down to Lexington?" asked Alex. "Arch might be biding out down there. He's still wanted in some parts of the state for what we did during the war, and Jackson County has got lots of places for a fellow to lose himself."

"I'll do that," said Oll.

The shrill urgency of Zerelda calling, "Susie!" broke up their impromptu meeting.

"That's Ma," said Jesse. "It must be time for supper. We'd better get cleaned up and head for the house."

"Not a word of this to Ma," said Alex, warning everybody. "Don't you think Susie's already told her?" asked Oll.

"Susie won't say a word," said Jesse over his shoulder as he led them toward the pump house at the edge of the barnyard. "You can bet on that."

"What about Slate?" asked White.

"He's your friend," said Jesse, as he and Alex washed their hands in the icy water. "You'd better tell him to keep his mouth shut about this to Ma."

"I'll have a word with Slate right away," said Alex, as he wiped his hands on a towel. He followed Jesse and the others into the house.

Creed was standing at the far end of the table when the James's, Shepherd's, and Jim White came inside. He anticipated receiving some sort of lecture about keeping mum on the subject of bank robberies, so when the older James brother came over to him, he made sure that Zerelda and Dr. Samuel were out of earshot before saying in a low voice, "Don't worry about me, Alex. What you boys do is your affair. As far as I'm concerned, I don't know a thing about anything, and I don't want to know anything about anything either. I'll stick around here another day or two because it pleases your mother, and then I'll be on my way. If that's all right with you, I mean."

"This is Ma's house, Slate," said Alex conspiratorially. "You're welcome here as long as she says so. As for me and the boys, we appreciate you keeping this to yourself. Right now, it's all talk, and that don't amount to a hill of beans yet. Even so, we do appreciate you keeping our confidence."

"I haven't forgotten how you boys saved my hide down there to Locust Ridge, Alex," said Creed. "Let's just say that this will even us up a bit on that score."

"Sounds fair enough to me," said Alex. Seeing that Jesse and the conspirators were watching him and Creed, he nodded toward them in such a way as to indicate that all was well as far as Creed was concerned.

"Well what's everybody waiting on?" asked Zerelda as she carried steaming bowls of boiled potatoes and rutabagas from the stove to the table. "Sit yourselves and get to eating before everything gets cold."

The men sat down, and Dr. Samuel said grace. With the last Amen, the women began serving them.

"I'm gonna go down to Harlem tomorrow to see Zee," said Jesse at the outset of the meal.

"I thought you weren't going until Saturday," said Zerelda.

"I changed my mind, Ma," said Jesse. "It's kind of crowded around here, so I thought I'd make a little more room for everybody else by leaving a day early."

"George and me were thinking the same thing, Mrs. Samuel," said Oll Shepherd. "We thought we'd be moving on tomorrow. We sure do thank you for your hospitality and all. It's been a right pleasant stay."

"We were glad to have you, Oll," said Zerelda. She glanced at Jim White and wondered whether he would be going with the Shepherds. Seeing his mother looking at White, Alex said, "Jim's gonna stick around for a few days, Ma. We thought we'd go visit some of the old crowd tomorrow. You know, the Pence boys and maybe the Wilkerson's."

"Will you be going with them, Captain Creed?" asked Zerelda.

"Now why would Captain Creed want to go visiting the Pence boys?" asked Susan. "I was thinking he might want to accompany Rachel and me down to Liberty tomorrow."

"What are you going to Liberty for?" asked Jesse uneasily.

"Don't you recollect that we'd planned to go to the stores on Saturday and that we were gonna ride along with you?" said Susan.

"But now you say you're going tomorrow. So why shouldn't we go tomorrow, too? I just thought Captain Creed might like to join us instead of sitting around here all day."

Before Creed could say yea or nay to Susan's proposal, Zerelda took a liking to the notion and said, "I know I'd feel a lot better about you and Rachel coming back safe from Liberty if Captain Creed was along with you, Susie." She turned to Creed and asked, "You wouldn't mind, would you, Captain Creed? I wouldn't worry about Susie and Rachel if you was to go along and see that they got home safe."

Creed wanted to look at Susan, but he thought better of that idea. Instead, he smiled at Zerelda and said, "No, ma'am, I wouldn't mind going along at all."

"Then that settles that," said Zerelda.

Creed glanced around the table and noticed that George Shepherd and Jim White were looking askance at Oll Shepherd who was giving the same look to Alex James whose attention was focused on his brother who was glaring at Creed. The Texan didn't like the expression on Jesse's face or the intent in his eyes, but instead of showing his displeasure, he let his Choctaw instincts wipe his features clean of any emotion. This seemed to anger Jesse even more, but it did make him shift his view to Alex who appeared to be annoyed by his brother's attitude.

What the hell's going on here? Creed asked himself. For some reason, he was beginning to feel like a marionette and that Susan and her family were taking turns being the puppeteer. He wondered which of them would be next to jerk on his strings and make him dance to a tune that was starting to sound a little tinny.

28

Susan was wrong about the whole evening being ahead of her and Creed. They never had a minute to themselves, and to make matters worse, Zerelda insisted that everybody turn in early for the sake of those who would be traveling the next day because they would need their rest, especially Jesse.

When the hour to retire arrived, Creed, feeling a bit wistful over not having had another moment with Susan, followed the Shepherds and Jim White to the barn for the night. Zerelda and Dr. Samuel put the small children in the loft above their room, then retired to their bed. Susan climbed up to the old loft in the log cabin section of the house above the room that Alex and Jesse shared. The brothers were the last to call it a night and turn in.

As soon as all was quiet, Jesse climbed up to Susan's bed and whispered, "Come on down here, Susie. Frank and I want to talk to you."

"What about?" she asked irritably.

"Just get down here," he insisted, then he descended the ladder and returned to his room to wait for her.

Susan was wearing a butternut nightshirt that hung to her stockinged feet. "What is it?" she demanded, squinting in the dim light from the single lamp in the Prothers' room.

"What's the big idea inviting yourself along tomorrow?" demanded Jesse, coming straight to the point.

"I told you at supper that we were gonna go on Saturday with you anyway," she said. "What's the difference whether Rachel and I go on Saturday or with you tomorrow?"

"It ain't so much that it's Friday or Saturday, Susie," said Alex.

"How come you invited Slate along?"

"Yeah, how about that?" demanded Jesse. "I don't need him along to get in my way."

Susan was a mite perplexed by the last statement. "Get in the way?" she queried. "Get in the way of what?"

"I got business in Liberty," said Jesse matter-of-factly.

"Business?" she asked. "What sort of business?"

"That's none of your concern," said Jesse.

Susan's curiosity now had control of her. "Is this business why you're really leaving a day early to go see Cousin Zee?"

"So what if it is?" said Jesse. "It's still none of your concern. Is it, Frank?"

'That's right, Susie," said Alex. "It's none of your concern what Jesse's business is in Liberty."

Susan perused her brothers' faces, then a thought struck her.

"Don't tell me you boys are really thinking about robbing that bank down to Liberty," she said. "I don't believe you're that foolish." When neither of them denied her accusation immediately, she said, "Omigod! You are thinking about robbing that bank! I don't believe it. I simply do not believe it." She shook her head and clucked her tongue. "I can believe those jugheads out in the barn are dumb enough to rob that bank, but you two? I thought you were smarter than that, Alexander Franklin James." She was lecturing them as if she were their mother, and she rather liked the role. "And how about you, Jesse Woodson James? Don't you at least have the smarts of a mule? For God's sake, Jesse, haven't you had enough of this foolishness that nearly got you killed twice?"

"That's the whole point, Susie," said Jesse. "I owe them Unionists for what they did to me and for what they did to Ma and the doctor during the war."

"No, you don't," argued Susan. "Not any more you don't. Didn't you kill enough Unionists during the war to last a lifetime and then some?"

Jesse looked her straight in the eye and said, "No, I didn't. Not for what they did to us."

Realizing that she was getting nowhere with Jesse, Susan turned on Alex. "And what about you, Frank? Didn't you kill enough during the war? Haven't you settled matters with the Unionists yet?"

"No, I haven't," said Alex. "Not as long as they continue to abuse us like they're still doing. Matters won't be settled until they let us alone and let us go on with our lives the same as they get to do. The legislature said that the Unionists were free from all the crimes that they committed during the war, but because we fought for the South, we're still liable for what we did, even when it was done during the heat of battle. That ain't fair, Susie, and as long as we're being treated unfairly, I'm gonna keep fighting the Unionists."

Susan had lost the argument, and although she felt that it would be senseless to continue lecturing them, she tried one more tactic. "What are you going to do in Liberty, Jesse?" she asked.

"I'm gonna scout the bank," he said.

"Now that makes good sense," said Susan with a touch of sarcasm. "You go into that bank and have a look around and let everybody in town see you do it. That's good. And when you go to rob this bank, do you think no one's gonna recognize you and recollect that you'd been in town before scouting out the bank? Is that what you think, Jesse?"

"No one knows me in Liberty," said Jesse. "I can ride in there and look around, and nobody will be the wiser,"

"That's not what I'm talking about, Jesse, said Susan, "Sure, nobody will know this time, but don't you think they might remember you when you come back to rob the place?"

"So what if they do?" said Jesse, "No one knows me by my name in Liberty, I tell you, Susie."

"But what if there's someone there who does know you by name and does recognize you and tells the law?" asked Susan. "Then what?" When he didn't answer immediately, she continued. "I'll tell you what. The law will be coming out here to the farm and things will be just the way they were during the war. They'll give us all hell until they find you and put you in jail or worse, until they hang you. The both of you. Because if they figure one James brother was in on it, then they're sure to believe the other one was there, too."

"That's the risk we'll have to take," said Alex.

"You ain't just risking your own necks with this business, Frank," said Susan. "You're fooling around with my neck and Ma's and Dr. Samuel's, too. Don't you remember what happened to him during the war, Frank? He protected you then, and this is how you're gonna repay him?"

"We're gonna rob the bank," said Jesse defiantly, "and there's nothing you can do or say, Susie, that's gonna stop us."

"That's right, Susie," said Frank. "We're gonna rob that bank, and there's nothing you can do to stop us. So why try?"

Susan studied her brothers, then surrendered. Jesse and Alex were right; nothing she could say or do would change their minds. They were determined men, bent on robbing the bank in Liberty. The set of their jaws said so.

"Yes," she said, nodding at them, "I can see that now, Frank." A new thought struck. "Well, since you've made up your minds to do this thing, then you might as well do it right. There's no sense in taking the chance that Jesse will be seen scouting the bank, so I'll scout the bank for you."

29

The distance between the Samuel farm and the city of Liberty, the seat of government for Clay County, was every inch of fifteen miles along roads that, although frozen at sunrise when Creed, Susan, Rachel, and Jesse James started out, thawed into muddy lanes by midmorning.

Wearing the black overcoat that he'd purchased two months earlier in Mississippi and had worn throughout that winter, Creed drove Susan and Rachel to town in the family wagon. Susan sat beside him on the seat, sharing a blanket that covered their laps and legs - against the wind from the ride - a situation that stirred Creed to joke to Susan that "in some countries, sharing a blanket means a man and woman have to get married."

To which, Susan smiled wickedly and replied, "That sounds like a reasonable proposal to me. I accept." Susan punctuated her statement by rubbing her leg against Creed's, which served its purpose of sparking his passion.

As much as he wanted to return the gesture, Creed let the subject drop because Jesse was watching them like a circling hawk and because Rachel was curled up under a comforter in the bed of the wagon.

Although the weather was warm, and the air was calm, Jesse rode alongside them with the collar of his cape-less tan overcoat turned up to cover his ears and cheeks and his hat pulled down so low that little could be seen of his face. The trip took a full four hours.

At the edge of town, Jesse suggested that they take the wagon team and his mount to a livery stable for water, feed, and a rubdown.

Creed agreed with the plan but with one amendment: he would let the women off at a restaurant or hotel where they could wait in warmth for him and Jesse.

The travelers entered Liberty along Lightburne Street and followed that street south to Kansas Street where they turned west and rode three blocks uphill to the town square that had Kansas Street on its south side, Franklin on the north, Main on the west, and Water on the east. Situated at the southeast comer of Kansas and Water streets was the Arthur House, a three-story brick hotel that was built in 1853 as a showcase for the burgeoning city. Creed stopped the wagon in front of the establishment and helped Susan and Rachel down to the boardwalk, instructing them to wait inside until he and Jesse returned from seeing to the animals.

"There's a livery one block that way," said Jesse, pointing south along Water Street. "Follow me."

Creed thought it was odd that Jesse should give him an order, but he could see that the younger James brother gave it with all the nonchalance of a natural-born leader. Instead of resenting Jesse for it, he simply shrugged and said, "I'm right behind you."

They rode the block to Mill Street and turned into the Wymore Livery Stable barn. A muscular man with a short brown beard came out of the office to greet them.

"Good morning," he said, eyeing them cautiously. "Something I can do for you, sir?" He was addressing Creed, which suited Jesse just fine.

"Yes. sir," said Creed. He climbed down from. the wagon and offered his hand to the man. "Slate Creed from Hallettsville, Texas, sir."

The man shook Creed's hand reluctantly and said, "George Wymore. sir. I'm the proprietor here."

"It's a pleasure to make your acquaintance, Mr. Wymore." "Texas, you say?" queried Wymore. "What brings you to Missouri, Mr. Creed?"

"I'm here visiting friends before going on to Colorado soon," said Creed, knowing that if he didn't volunteer the information then Wymore would pester him with questions until the man was either satisfied with the information obtained or he was more suspicious than before.

"Friends? Here in Clay County?" asked Wymore. "Yes, sir," said

Creed. "The Samuels."

Wymore paused for a second before saying, "Don't know them. They must not live around Liberty."

"No sir" said Creed. He looked to Jesse for help. "What's the name of that little town near where you live?"

"Centerville," said Jesse from atop his horse.   .

Wymore scanned Jesse, then returned his attention to Creed. "Well what brings you to Liberty today, Mr. Creed?"

"I drove some ladies down to visit some of your fine stores," said Creed politely. "It was a long ride, Mr. Wymore, and I was of a mind to leave my friend's horse and the wagon team here while we're in town." He unbuttoned his coat and dug into a jacket pocket for his last silver cartwheel. Presenting the coin to Wymore, he said, "Would a dollar cover feed, water, and a good brushing for all three animals?"

"Depends on how long you were planning on leaving them here," said Wymore.

Creed looked up at Jesse and said, "I suspect you'll be wanting your horse back before Susie and Rachel are ready to leave this afternoon."

Jesse nodded.

Creed turned back to Wymore and said, "No more than four of five hours for the team, and of course, my friend will want his horse back before that."

"Then a dollar ought to cover it nicely, Mr. Creed," said Wymore with the satisfaction that he'd come out the better on the bargain. "I'll have them fed and watered and brushed right away, and you can call for them at any time this afternoon."

"Thank you, Mr. Wymore," said Creed, handing the dollar to the liveryman. He tipped his hat, then turned to Jesse. "Good enough?"

Jesse nodded and dismounted. They walked the block back to the Arthur House, entered the hotel, and found Susan and Rachel waiting for them in the lobby.

"It's almost noon," said Creed, "Why don't we eat first, then you can visit the stores, Miss Susie, and Jesse can be on his way to Harlem?"

"That sounds like a good idea to me," said Susan. "I am powerful hungry." She turned to Rachel, dug a dime out of her purse, handed it to the servant girl, and said, "You go around back to the kitchen and get yourself something to eat, Rachel. Then wait for us out front when you're done."

Rachel curtsied politely and said, "Yes'm, Miss Susie," then did as Susan had told her to do.

Creed, Susan, and Jesse repaired to the dining room and ate a lunch of cold sliced beef, larded bread, and sweet buttermilk.

Their conversation was limited to Creed making complimentary remarks about the apparent prosperity of Liberty and the immediate countryside in comparison to the rest of Missouri that he had seen. As much as Jesse wanted to reflect on the collective condition of the Unionists as compared to those folks whose sympathies had gone in a southerly direction during the war, he held his tongue, eating voraciously, then asking to be excused because he still had three full hours of riding ahead of him and be wished to be on his way. Susan gave her permission, as if it were hers to give, and she and Creed wished Jesse a safe trip.

With Jesse now gone, Creed and Susan finished their meal and met Rachel in front of the hotel. "Where to first?" asked Creed.

"Mr. Denny's," said Susan. "We always go there first."

As they walked along the fairly busy boardwalk toward John Denny's General Merchandise Store, Jesse rode up to them and said, "Susie, don't forget to buy the kids some candy," he said.

"It wouldn't do to come to Liberty and forget the sweets for the kids." He noticed Rachel looking up at him and added, "And get a nice cinnamon stick for Perry, too. "

"Don't worry, Jesse," said Susan. "I won't forget the kids or Perry. Now get on with you."

"All right, I'm going" said Jesse. He continued up Water Street to the intersection with Franklin Street where he stopped and surveyed the area.

The Clay County Courthouse occupied the center square of the city, and in its basement was the county jail. The Clay County Savings Association's bank was located on the northeast comer of the intersection. Directly across Franklin Street from the bank was the old Green House, Liberty's first hotel. East on Franklin was William Jewel College, an institution of higher learning that Jesse's father, Reverend Robert James, had helped to found in 1849 before he departed for the goldfields of California.

While he was scanning the streets, Jesse was approached by a young man who had been loitering in front of the Green House. He appeared to be about Jesse's age, was clean-shaven, and rather cherubic in his facial features which gave him the aspect of being a happy, friendly sort. He held a book in his left hand. "Pardon me, sir," he said, tipping his hat to Jesse.

Jesse bad no wish to reply to the fellow, but not to do so would bring more attention to him than he desired. "What is it?" be asked cautiously.

"My name is George Wymore, sir," said the young man, "and I couldn't help noticing that you-"

Jesse interrupted, saying, "I just met another George Wymore over to the livery stable. Are you kin to him?"

"My uncle, sir," said the younger Wymore. "Our family came here from Fayette County, Kentucky in '43, and we own several businesses and farms within the county." He imparted this information with a pride that was meant to impress his listener more than it was to lord it over Jesse. When Jesse made no remark about the Wymore's' prosperity, young George continued. "As I was about to say, sir, I couldn't help noticing that you spoke to that lady who's coming this way in the company of an army officer and a colored woman. Would you happen to know her on a personal basis, sir?"

"She's my sister," said Jesse.

Wymore smiled broadly and said, "Then, sir, might I request an introduction to the lady?"

Jesse glared down at Wymore, then looked back at Susan, Creed and Rachel coming toward them. "She's already got a beau, Mr. Wymore," he said. He returned his gaze on Wymore. "You're tough out of luck, friend."

Wymore looked wistfully in Susan's direction, noted how she was talking animatedly with Creed, and said, "Yes, I suppose I am." Then back to Jesse, he tipped his hat politely and said, "Thank you all the same, sir."

"Don't mention it," said Jesse, and he spurred his horse and rode off to the west along Franklin Street.

When Susan, Creed, and Rachel came abreast of the Green House, Wymore tipped his hat to the lady and addressed the Texan with a casual passing greeting. Susan ignored Wymore, but Creed returned the salutation in kind before assisting Susan and Rachel across the street to the bank's comer. Creed noted the name of the establishment painted in gilt-edged letters on the front windows and wondered if this was the bank that the boys back at the Samuel farm were thinking of robbing. Probably not, he thought. They wouldn't be so foolish as to rob a bank this close to their own home.

"Slate, Ma only gave me two silver dollars to spend," said Susan, "but Frank gave me a twenty-dollar gold piece. That might be too much for any of the stores to change, so I think I'd better exchange it in the bank for silver dollars."

"That's probably a good idea," said Creed. "You know I saw a bootmaker's shop on the way to the livery, and it got me to thinking that I could use a new pair of boots. I think I'll go in with you and exchange a double eagle for smaller money, then see about those boots."

The three of them entered the bank through its Franklin Street entrance. Another door from outside was in the west wall. Inside, the bank was divided roughly into quadrants. The lobby made up one quarter of the room, and it had a desk for customers in the comer where the two outer walls met, and a pot-bellied stove stood in the middle of the area. A railing separated the lobby from a desk and work area in the northwest quarter. The southeast section was the cashier's working space behind a long counter that ran north and south for more than half of the room. Behind this bar were a fireplace in the east wall and two desks, one on each side of the vault door which occupied the final fourth of the bank.

Two men worked at the desks behind the counter. One was much older than the other, but the younger man resembled the elder so greatly that they had to be father and son or at least brothers. The former was true. Each had brown hair cut short, dull blue eyes, and sallow complexions that said the sun saw little of them.

Susan approached the counter with Creed, while Rachel warmed herself at the pot-bellied stove.

Seeing that he had customers, the younger banker left his desk to wait on them. "Good day, miss," he said in a cool but polite tone. He nodded at Creed and said, "Sir, may I help you folks?"

"We'd like to make some change please," said Susan. She took the twenty-dollar gold piece from her purse and placed it on the countertop.

"Could I get this exchanged for silver dollars?"

"Certainly," said the clerk. He picked up the coin and went into the vault where he placed the double eagle in the- cash box, then counted out twenty silver dollars. He returned to Susan and one-by-one counted out the cartwheels as he put them on the counter in front of her.

"Thank you," she said as she gathered up the money.

Then Creed took his turn. While waiting for the clerk to serve Creed, Susan scanned the interior of the bank, making mental notes of where everything was located, including the rear door which led to adjoining office that had its own entrance on Water Street. She looked out the front windows at the Green House across the street and noted the staircase that went up the side of that building. A good place for a rifleman to watch the street, she thought. Through the side windows across Water Street. she saw the blank wall of the business that faced the courthouse.

The clerk returned with Creed's money and said, "Is there anything else that I can do for you folks?"

"What hours does this establishment keep?" asked Susan.
Now that's an odd question, thought Creed as he scooped up his money and put it away inside his overcoat. Why would she want to know that?

"We open our doors to the public at nine o'clock everyday except Sunday and holidays," said the clerk, "and we close for business at three each afternoon."

"You don't seem to be very busy right now," said Susan. "Don't you have many customers?"

"Most of our customers do their banking with us during the morning hours, miss," said the clerk, "and that leaves my father and me plenty of time to keep the accounts in the afternoon."

"Your father?" queried Susan.

"Yes, miss. I am William Bird, and that gentleman is my father, Mr. Greenup Bird. Father is the bank cashier."

"I see," said Susan. "And you are the only two men who work here? Is that correct?"

"Yes, miss, that is correct," said Bird.

Susan took one more look around the bank, then smiled and said, "Thank you kindly, Mr. Bird. You've been most helpful." For the first time, the clerk smiled and said, "I hope you will call on us again, miss."

"Yes, of course," said Susan. Then turning to Creed, she said, "Shall we go, Slate?"

Creed didn't bother to bid adieu to Bird. His mind was too busy pondering the conversation that he had just heard. Why does Susie want to know all about this bank? He kept asking himself. He knew the answer, though he wished that he didn't. He held the door for Susan and Rachel, then followed them outside. On the street comer, he said, "Rachel, would you mind crossing the street and waiting for us on the other side, while I have a word with Miss Susie?"

"No sir, I don't mind," said Rachel. She looked at Susan and asked, "Is it all right, Miss Susie?"

Susan ignored Creed and said, "Go on, Rachel. We'll be along in a minute."

Rachel crossed the street and waited.

"Now what's this all about, Slate?" asked Susan.

"You tell me," said Creed.

"Whatever are you going on about?"

"Why are you so interested in this bank?" he asked in a voice that he hoped and prayed only she could hear.

"I might want to put my money in this bank someday," said Susan as nonchalantly as if she were telling someone what day it was or that the sun was shining.

'That's so much horse shit," said Creed angrily, "and you know it. You're helping your brothers and those muleheads, aren't you?"

"Helping them what?" she asked innocently.

"Don't play dumb with me, Susie," said Creed. "I know what they're up to, remember?"

Susan stared into Creed's eyes and liked what she saw. This was a man who was a match for her. This was a man who didn't fear honesty, who had the integrity to take a stand. Hot damn! I love this man! she told herself. To Creed, she said, "All right, I'll tell you. But not here. Later. When we can really be alone and no one else can hear."

Creed took his turn looking deep into Susan's eyes, and he liked what he saw. She had the fire, the verve, the sensuality that could drive him insane with passion. Damn! she makes my blood hot! he told himself. To Susan he said, "All right. Later. When we're alone."

30

By the time Creed, Susan, and Rachel reached the Samuel farm that evening, Alex James and Jim White had returned from visiting old guerrilla friends in their part of the country, and it was past supper time. Susan handed out the candy that she'd bought for the children, and Creed showed off the new boots that he'd purchased at Philip and James Fraher's Shoe and Boot Store on Kansas Street. As soon as the late arrivals had eaten, Zerelda shooed everybody to bed; it was that late already.

With fewer people around, the sleeping arrangements were changed. White and Creed were allowed to sleep in the house. White with Alex in Jesse's room, and the Texan on a pallet of extra quilts on the kitchen floor. This was Susan's doing, of course. She said it was no longer necessary for their guests to sleep in the barn when they had enough room in the house for them now. Zerelda concurred, and that was that.

As soon as all was quiet, Susan slipped down from her loft and went to her brother's room. "Frank, are you awake yet?" she whispered in the dimly lit room.

"Yes, I am," he replied. "Jim, you awake, too?"

"Sure am," said White. "What's doing?"

"I want to tell you about the bank while it's fresh on my mind," said Susan.

Alex sat up and turned up the flame on the lamp on the stand beside the bed. "What about it?" he asked.

White rolled over and propped himself up on one elbow, but he was careful to keep the rest of him under the covers, being a bit shy about letting a girl see him in his longjohns.

Susan sat on the foot of the bed and said, "There's not a whole lot to tell, Frank, but what there is to tell is important. Like the hours the bank is open. The clerk's name is William Bird. He told me that the bank opens at nine in the morning and closes at three in the afternoon and it's open for business every day except Sunday and holidays. He also told me that only he and his father work there. He said business is usually quiet in the afternoon. There're two entrances to the bank. One on Franklin Street and the other on Water Street. And there's another door in the back that goes into some office, and that office has an outside entrance on Water Street. The vault was wide open when I was there, and I'd say the money was easy to get to because the clerk was real fast at getting me change from inside the vault."

"Did you see any guns in the place?" asked Alex.

"No, I didn't, but I did notice that there's a staircase on the Green House across the street where you could put a man with a rifle to watch the street."

"We'll keep that in mind," said Alex. "What else did you see that might help?"

"That's about it, Frank. There's a business across Water Street, but all you can see of it is a blank wall. And catty-comer to the bank is the courthouse. You might be concerned about that because the sheriff is there, you know."

"Don't I know, though?" remarked Alex sardonically. "Don't forget that I spent a little time in that sheriff's jail not too long ago."

"And you're liable to spend more time there in the future if you boys go ahead with this business," said Susan. "I'm telling you, Frank, I don't think this is the smartest thing that you and Jesse have ever done. I still think you're all being foolish with this business."

"Save your breath, Susie," said Alex. "Like we said last night, we're gonna do it, and that's all there is to it."

She stood up and said, "Well, if it all goes wrong, don't say I didn't tell you so. Good night, Frank." She left the room.

"What do you think, Buck?" asked White.

Alex turned down the flame of the lamp again, slid back under the covers, and said, "I think I'm awful tired and this business can wait until Oll and George get back from seeing Mr. Berry down to Lafayette County." And that was that.

Susan didn't return to her loft. Instead, she tiptoed to the kitchen where Creed was already asleep near the cookstove. She bent low over him until her lips were nearly touching his ear. "Slate honey," she whispered sweetly. When he didn't respond immediately, she kissed his cheek, then repeated his name. "Wake up, Slate honey," she said, laying down beside him.

Creed stirred in his slumber, his mind filled with fuzzy dreams of another dark-haired girl and another winter night long past. The girl in his dreams was so real that he could not only see her, but he could smell her, touch her, and feel her in his arms. The sweet scent of clover seemed to be everywhere around them as they lay in the hay making love. He rolled onto his hack, eyes closed, unsure of whether he was still dreaming or waking to find that he wasn't dreaming after all.

"Slate honey," whispered Susan again.

Creed awakened to discover that the face before his wasn't the same as had been in his dream. He was still in Missouri, and the woman that he could see; smell, and touch was Susan James; she was in his arms, atop him. "Susie, what are you doing here?" he whispered angrily, rolling to one side and pushing her away. Then he realized how aroused he was.

So did Susan. She threw her arms around him and began kissing him rapidly and as passionately as she knew how to kiss a man, which wasn't all that exciting considering her very limited experience in such affairs.

Creed fought back. He pushed her away again and rolled on top of her. "Stop it," he said.

"I don't want to stop," she said huskily. Then she squirmed in such a way that he was forced to straddle her thigh. "And from the feel of that, you don't want me to stop either."

You're so right, he thought, but he said, "Yes, I do want you to stop. We can't be doing this."

"Why not?" she asked. "We both want it"

"Good Lord, Susie! We're on your mother's kitchen floor!"

"Then get your boots on, and we'll go out to the barn."

Creed hesitated, then thought, The cold air ought to cool her down. It won't hurt me none either. "All right," he said, "we'll go out to the barn. Just give me a minute to get my boots on, and you get dressed, too."

"What for?" she asked wickedly.

Creed knew what she meant. "Just get a coat on and some shoes, too," he said. "It's winter, remember?"

As they dressed, the thought crossed Creed's mind that some other member of the household might hear them leave the house, but he passed on that notion. If someone did hear them going out to the barn, most likely that person would dismiss the noise as someone taking an unwelcome emergency stroll to the out-house.

Susan had already figured out that much as she returned to the kitchen, wearing shoes and with a blanket wrapped around her. She took Creed by the arm and pulled him toward the back door. It creaked when she opened it, but the sound didn't slow her down. She tugged harder on Creed, leading him through the doorway, barely giving him the chance to close the door behind them. He stumbled once on the path to the barn, but she kept him from falling.

The night air felt good to Creed, doing the job that he thought it would do on him, cooling down his sweaty body. He had a flash of Deja vu, more real than phantasmal, like he really had done this before but with someone else. He started to search his memory for the name of that other girl, but before he could come up with anything, his thoughts were interrupted.

"Look, Slate honey," said Susan, pointing skyward. "Look how bright the moon is."

Creed looked up and saw the quarter moon. It was bright, but it wasn't affecting him in the same manner that it was her. He regained control of his emotions, his morals, and the situation. By the time they were inside the barn, his common sense had taken charge of him.

Susan knew the barn well enough to find the softest pile of hay in the dark. She flopped down on it, then pulled Creed down on top of her. "Oh, Slate honey," she said heavily as she squeezed him hard against her willing body, "I love you so. I want to do it with you."

Creed stiffened as he recalled the episode from his past that was haunting him this night. It happened in a barn very much like this one, and the girl was Mattie Whittaker back in Russellville, Kentucky. They had made love because they were in love and he was leaving to do battle with the Federals. He might never return to her, so this would be their one time, no matter how severe the consequences might be. How severe could they be? he remembered asking Mattie, but she made no reply, simply kissing him instead. Now, four years later, he wondered about those consequences again. How severe could they have been?

"Are you sure, Susie?" he asked, allowing his genitals to think for him again.

"Yes, I'm sure," she said. "I love you, and I want to do it with you and have your baby."

Oh God! he thought. That's it! How stupid could I be? No wonder Ginny Rapp spoke to me the way she did! And the Whittaker boys! They should have shot me instead of just trying to whip me. I gave Mattie my child. That must be it. Oh God! What do I do now?

Before he considered that problem with any depth of thought, Susan kissed him and reminded him that he had an immediate situation that demanded his attention. He moved his mouth away from Susan's, unsure of how to handle her exactly, but he had to do or say something. "No, Susie," he said slowly, "you don't."

This wasn't the response that she wanted to hear. "Yes, I do, Slate honey," she said anxiously. "Honest, I do." She tried to kiss him again.

He stopped her, and more firmly this time, he said, "No, Susie, you don't."

"Yes, I do love you, Slate Creed," she insisted with much more self-control than she had displayed a few seconds earlier. "I really do love you, Slate, and I do want to do it with you and have your baby."

"Why?" he asked simply. When she hesitated to answer, he said, "Is it because you think that's what you have to do to keep me here?"

Susan gave a quick thought to what he said and replied, "Yes, that's it. I love you so much that I'll do anything to keep you here."

"You'd just be wasting it." said Creed. "There's nothing that you can do to keep me here, Susie." He thought about telling her about Mattie, but that was too far in the past for her to believe that he still loved her and had made a commitment to her. He would have to take another tack. "I've got a sweetheart back in Texas," he said, "and I intend to marry her as soon as I get my name cleared and I can go home a free man. '

If he'd slapped her in the face, he couldn't have gotten her attention any better. "A sweetheart in Texas?" she queried. "What's her name?"

"Texada."

"Texada? What kind of name is that?" she asked sarcastically. The pain of rejection was beginning, and she had to fight it, not let him see it.

"It's her name," said Creed, "and that's all that matters."

"No, that's not all that matters, Slate." I matter. Me. Susan James. I matter. I love you, Slate Creed, and that means something, too. I love you, and I believe that you love me, too, but you're afraid to admit it."

"No, Susie, that's not it," he said. "That's not it at all. It's Texada. I love her, and I promised her that I'd come back to her."

"But she's not here, Slate, and I am. Doesn't that mean anything at all?"

Creed rolled away from her and sat up. "Susie, believe me. If I didn't know that Texada was waiting for me back in Texas-"

"How do you know she's waiting for you back in Texas?" Susan interjected. "Tell me that. How do you know?"

"I know. I know she's waiting for me because of everything that's ever happened between her and me in the past. I know because she tried to kill a Yankee colonel because she wanted to get back at those that she thought had killed me. She risked her life more than once to save my hide." He chuckled softly, then added, "She loved me when I only thought of her as a little nuisance who was always pestering me and my friends." He indulged himself with recollections of Texada in boys clothes, barefoot, and pigtailed. "Looking back now," he continued, "I realize how she was always there, close to me, and all I had to do was reach out and take her. Just like you are now, Susie. She would have done anything to have me love her in return, but I hardly knew her for what she really was. A girl. A warm, soft, loving girl." He laughed out loud. "You know, she was such a tomboy that when I saw her in a dress for the first time in years I didn't even recognize her. And she said to me, 'I'm trying to be a lady, Clete. Honest, I am. I'm not sure I like it much, but I am trying.' "

He chuckled at the memory of that moment. Then serious again, he said, "I think that's when I first realized that I was in love with her, too, and that maybe I'd been in love with her for years and had been too dumb to know it." He laughed again and continued with the tale. "We were riding along the lane in the moonlight when she said she was trying to be a lady. I leaned over and kissed her and told her that I loved her for the first time. She tried to hug and kiss me back and fell off her horse."

"You do have that effect on girls," said Susan.

"I don't mean to," said Creed.

"Why did she call you Clete?" asked Susan.

"That's my real name," said Creed, remembering the quest that he was on. "Cletus Slater, that's the name that I'm trying to clear so I can go home again."

"I see," said Susan.

"Do you really, Susie?"

"Yes, I do," she said softly, surrendering to reality, "and I love you all the more for telling me all this about your Texada. I envy her, Slate."

Tears welled up in Creed's eyes. "I'm glad to hear you say that, Susie," he said. "I get so lonely sometimes." He had to swallow hard before continuing. "I get so lonely sometimes that I want to take the first woman I see and hold her in my arms and pretend that she's Texada and share everything that's inside me with her."

Susan sat up and scooted over beside Creed. She touched his hand and said, "I'll be that woman for you. If you want me to."

"You don't know how tempted I am, Susie. The other day. This afternoon. Maybe I would have taken you up on that offer then. But not now. I've had too much time to think about it, and I know now that it would be wrong. Wrong for me. Wrong for you. Wrong for Texada. And I don't know which one of us would be hurt the most if you and I…" He wiped his eyes on his upper arm.

"She would never know," said Susan, caressing the back of Creed's hand.

"Maybe not," he said. He sniffled, then said, "But you'd know, and I'd know. That would be enough. I'd always feel guilty about it because I'd betrayed her love."

"But I wouldn't feel guilty about it, Slate. I love you."

"You might not feel that way right off, but you would sooner or later. Most likely when you meet the man you'll marry and settle down with. You'll rue the day that I ever came into your life and spoiled you."

"No, I wouldn't, Slate."

"Trust me, Susie. I know about that feeling." His mind filled up with thoughts of Mattie, but he suppressed the urge to tell Susan about them. Instead, he said. "There's a lewd woman down in New Orleans that makes me feel that way to this day. She didn't exactly spoil me in the same sense that a man spoils a woman, but she did things to me all the same that I will always regret."

"What terrible things could a woman do to you?"

"I'll just let that rest there, if you don't mind."

"All right, if that's the way you want it," she said.

A silence separated them for the next few moments. Finally, Susan leaned against him, crooked her arm inside his, and said, "Slate, would you please stay for a few more days? Stay and let me pretend a little that we're in love and that we're gonna live happily ever after like it says in the storybooks. Would you do that for me? Please?"

Creed put his hand to her chin, lifted her face close to his, and said, half-jokingly, "Can I pretend you're Texada?"

"Yes," she said a heartbeat before she put her free hand behind his head and pulled his mouth to hers.

His loneliness coerced him into cooperating but only long enough for her to have that one kiss.

31

Although he had a notion to leave the Samuel farm and head west first thing Saturday morning, Creed gave in to Susan's plea that he stay until Monday, but not until she explained why she was scouting the Liberty bank for her brothers and the other would-be bank robbers. Her explanation that she was trying to discourage them from raiding the bank by showing them how difficult and dangerous it would be for them satisfied him, although he knew that she was probably wasting her time.

Besides Susan's request that he stay, Zerelda asked him to join the family for Sunday meeting. Creed could hardly turn down a gracious invitation to hear their preacher fulminate on the sins of the world. He accompanied the Samuels to the Clear Creek Baptist Church on Sunday.

Late Sunday afternoon George and Oll Shepherd returned from their trip to Jackson and Lafayette counties, and within an hour of their arrival, Jesse came home from his visit to Harlem. After supper, the James brothers, the Shepherds, and Jim White met in the barn to discuss the raid on the Liberty bank.

"We found Arch Clement," said Oll Shepherd. "Brother Berry told us where he was hiding out in the Sui Hills. He's been surviving by riding into Johnson County and holding up anybody he thinks was Unionist during the war. He's got Ben Cooper, Frank Gregg, and Joab Perry riding with him. They're all willing to join up. How did you boys do around here?"

"The Pence's and the Wilkerson's said they'd ride with us," said Alex James. "Ning Letton said he was through with riding and hiding. He just wants to be left alone now. Milt Dryden and the Corum's said the same thing."

"Well, that makes us thirteen," said Oll. "Do you think that's enough, Buck?"

"I'd feel better if we had a few more men," said Alex.

"So would I," said George. "Thirteen is unlucky."

"We don't need luck," said Jesse.

"Did Arch say anything about rounding up a few more boys?" asked Alex, ignoring Jesse and George.

"He said he thought he might be able to find us a couple more," said Oll.

"We got enough," said Jesse. "We don't need no more than thirteen. Not from what I saw in Liberty the other day."

"What about the bank?" asked Oll. "Did you get inside and have a look around?"

"Susie scouted the bank for us," said Alex James. "From what she said, this bank ought to be easy to rob. The vault was open when she was there, and she got the idea that the money was just laying there waiting for us to come take it away."

"That sounds good to me," said Oll. "What else did she find out? What sort of hours does this place keep? How many men inside, and do they have guns?"

"No guns," said Alex, "and only two men. An old man and his son. Their name is Bird. The bank opens in the morning, but she said that's when the bank does most of its business. She said the clerk told her that things were usually quiet in the afternoon. I'd have to say the best time of day for making this raid would be in the middle of the afternoon."

"That makes sense to me," said White. "The closer to dark, the better our chances of getting away."

"All right," said Oll Shepherd. "We'll do it in the afternoon. We'll ride in as fast as we can, rob the bank, and ride out as fast as we can."

"I think we'd do better if we rode in separately," said Jesse. "And from different directions. In small groups. I think we should try to slip into town as quietly as possible, rob the bank with as little fuss as possible, then ride out slowly as long as no one knows we've robbed the bank."

"Dingus might be right there," said White. "We could rob the bank and be miles away before anybody knows we've done it."

"How are going to stop the men in the bank from spreading the alarm?" asked Oll. "Shoot them? The sound of gunshots would bring the whole town down on us before we could get back to our horses on the street."

"We can lock them in the vault," said Jesse. "After we've removed the money, we can put the clerk and cashier inside the vault and lock the door. It'd be hours before anyone missed them and came looking for them. In the meantime, we'll have ridden miles away, and no one will even know that we've robbed the bank."

"Sounds to me like you've thought this out pretty good, Dingus," said Oll. "Start at the beginning and tell us how you'd make this raid."

As Jesse outlined his plan for them, Creed was saying goodnight to the Samuels in the house before retiring to the barn. Susan said she would walk out to the barn with him and tell her brothers that it was time for bed. Zerelda had noticed her daughter's behavior toward the handsome Texan and was worried by it. She called Susan back into the house to ask her one question before she turned in: "Have I got anything to fret about between you and Captain Creed?"

Susan was never one to lie to her mother, having learned at an early age that the consequences for prevarication could be quite severe. She looked Zerelda straight in the eye and said, "No, Ma, you've got nothing to fret about as far as Slate and I are concerned."

"I don't mean to pry, Susie, but a mothers got to know these things."

Susan smiled and said, "I know, Ma." She shrugged and looked wistful on purpose. "I suppose I'll have to wait to get lucky with the next fellow that comes along."

Zerelda gasped and said, "Susan James! Shame on you!"

Susan laughed and said, "I was only fooling, Ma." She kissed Zerelda's cheek and added, "Slate's been a perfect gentleman that way. Now you go on to bed and don't fret about us. We're not doing anything that would cause anybody any shame. Now or later."

"All right, Sugar," said Zerelda. She kissed her daughter's cheek and went to bed.

Susan rejoined Creed on the path to the barn. "What was that all about?" he asked.

"Just Ma being a mother, Slate," said Susan. "She was worried that you might be thinking of something more than holding hands." She giggled a bit. "If she only knew the whole truth, boy, would she be in for a surprise!"

"No, I don't think so," said Creed. "Sometimes we forget that our folks were young once and that they've done most of the things we're doing now."

Susan stopped, gave Creed a quizzical stare, then said, "Are you trying to tell me my mama...?"

"All I'm saying is that she was a young woman once," said Creed, "and she's not stupid or blind. That's all."

"Yes, I suppose she was. I guess that might explain how she came to have all these kids."

"I think we'd be wise to change the subject," said Creed.

The sound of several voices coming from the barn supported Creed's supposition. Jesse had just concluded outlining his plan, and the others were agreeing that it sounded like a viable strategy to them.

"Now the question is," said Oll, "when do we make this raid on the Liberty bank?"

Susan and Creed heard that much of the conversation, and it aggravated both of them. They hurried inside.

"The sooner, the better," said Jesse. He would have expounded on his statement, but seeing his sister and the Texan come among them, he held his tongue.

"Don't let us interrupt you boys," said Creed. "You go right ahead and make your plans to rob the Liberty bank. It doesn't mean a thing to me. I'm riding out of here tomorrow for Colorado, and tomorrow night I hope to be bedding down somewhere in Kansas. I just hope that I don't read about you boys being shot down by the people of Liberty while you were trying to steal their money."

Alex, White, and the Shepherds had spent too much time with Creed to take umbrage with him over this matter, but not so Jesse. He didn't care much for Creed's attitude about the raid or Creed's relationship with Susan, and although he would never admit it, he was jealous of Creed's easy manner with his mother and the rest of the family. Everybody, even down to little Perry, seemed to be enamored with this Texan, and he hated Creed for it.

"You're right about one thing," said Jesse. He had the cold, cruel look of a cat that was sitting by a mouse hole and was already tasting its intended victim. "It doesn't mean a thing to you. This raid is none of your business, and I think we ought to do something about making that situation permanent." He reached over to the saddlebag hanging on a peg protruding from a loft stanchion.

Creed recognized the specter of bloodlust in Jesse's eyes, and he saw the butt of a revolver inside the saddlebag as soon as Jesse lifted the flap. He knew exactly what Jesse planned to do with it, and he didn't hesitate to react once he saw the pistol's grip inside the saddlebag.

Susan saw the gun at the same time and gasped.

The Shepherds and White saw the weapon, but they did nothing and said nothing.

When Alex saw the Remington, he shouted, "No, Jesse!" but he failed to act.

Jesse pulled the .44 from the saddlebag, cocking the hammer in the same motion, and started to level it at Creed. He wasn't fast enough.

The distance between them was too great for Creed to leap and stop Jesse from shooting him, but it wasn't so great that the Texan couldn't grab a horse bridle down from its peg, fling it at Jesse, and strike his gun hand, throwing his aim off long enough for Creed to take the three strides and a jump at his would-be killer. He collided with Jesse, knocking him down and landing atop him. The revolver discharged, its ball flying harmlessly into the loft. Sitting up on his knees and straddling Jesse, Creed took hold of Jesse's right wrist and slammed the hand against the stanchion, forcing Jesse to drop the gun and wince with the pain. He released Jesse's arm, got a fistful of coat, and prepared to punch the youth senseless, but he didn't strike him.

"No, I'm not gonna hit you, Jesse," said Creed. "Not this time. You're in no condition for a fight with me." He pushed himself erect without using his hands and stood over Jesse, glaring down at him. "But I'll tell you this much, Mr. James. If I'd been armed just now, I guarantee you'd be breathing your last breath this very minute."

Alex picked up the Remington and put it back in the saddlebag. "I'm sorry about this," he said to Creed.

Jesse slid out from under Creed and stood up, facing the Texan.

"You don't have to go apologizing for me, Frank," he said, his eyes fixed on Creed's. "I'm just sorry I wasn't quicker with my aim."

"That's enough, Jesse," said Alex angrily. "Now get yourself up to the house while you've still got the health to make the walk."

Jesse knew that Frank was usually very passive, but he also knew that his older brother was as unpredictable and as deadly as a rattler when he was riled up like he was now. Using what little good sense he possessed, Jesse said nothing more and made tracks for the house.

"I don't know what got into him, Slate," said Alex. "I do know he's got a powerful lot of hate built up in him. I guess he needs to let some of it out now and then, and you sort of got in the way of it."

"It's all right, Alex," said Creed, brushing debris from the barn floor off his pants. "No harm was done, I guess. I don't think I hurt him any."

"He'll be fine," said Alex. "I'll have a talk with him."

"Do you think it'll do any good?" asked Creed.

"I don't know," said Alex. "I can't make any promises when it comes to Jesse."

No, I suspect not, thought Creed.

32

When he awoke the next morning, Creed felt feverish, his nose was runny, and his throat was sore. Damn! he thought. I'm coming down with the catarrh. He coughed, as if to punctuate his thoughts, then forced himself to get up. His whole body ached. Damn! What a great time to get sick!

"You don't look so good, Slate," said Oil Shepherd who had just pulled himself out of the hay. "Do you feel all right?"

Creed tried to speak, but his throat hurt too much. He swallowed hard, and when he did, he had the sensation of someone poking him in the ear drums with needles. The sudden, piercing pain was so great that ·his face twisted involuntarily with agony. Once the torturous moment had passed, he managed to rasp, "I've felt better, Oll."

"We'd better get you up to the house and let Miz Samuel have a look at you," said Shepherd. "Come on, George. Let's give him a hand."

"No, it's all right," said Creed. "I can get by." He managed to slip into his new boots, but when he stood to walk, vertigo sent him reeling sideways. He grabbed the closest stanchion and held on until his head quit spinning, which seemed to take forever.

"I'm telling you, Slate," said Oll, "you ain't looking so good. You'd better let us help you."

"No, it's all right," insisted Creed, "I'll be fine as soon as I get some coffee into me." He wobbled off toward the outhouse to take care of his morning business.

George and Oll followed Creed and waited for him to come out of the privy. When he did exit, he stumbled and fell to the frozen ground. The Shepherds didn't hesitate. They flanked him and took him under his arms and practically carried him to the house where they helped him into Dr. Samuel's easy chair.

Susan and Zerelda came over from the cookstove to have a look at him. "You feeling poorly this morning, Captain Creed?" asked Zerelda. She didn't wait for him to answer, feeling his forehead, then his cheek with the back of her hand. "Why, you're burning up." She turned to Susan and said, "Fetch Dr. Samuel in here right now."

"Yes, Ma," said Susan as she hurried toward the back door.

Jesse and Frank came out of the bedroom. "What's wrong with him?" asked Jesse bitterly.

"Captain Creed's sick," said Zerelda. "Come and help me get him into bed."

"Bed?" queried Jesse. "Whose bed?"

"Yours," said Zerelda in a tone that indicated she would entertain no argument at this time. "You, too, Mr. Frank. Come and help me."

Frank, Jesse, and Zerelda helped Creed into the bedroom and into Jesse's bed.

"Get his boots off," said Zerelda. When Jesse made no move to obey her, she glared at him but said nothing. Instead, she looked at Alex who removed Creed's boots for him. Zerelda covered Creed with the quilt, then said, "You just sit tight, Captain Creed. Dr. Samuel will have a look at you, and we'll get to making you well right soon."

Creed nodded his understanding and gratitude because speech was too painful.

In a minute, Susan returned with Dr. Samuel. Zerelda met them at the back door. "Captain Creed looks mighty sick, Pa," she said. "You'd better take a look at him."

"Now you know I can't do that, Ma," said Dr. Samuel. "The law says so now. I'm not allowed to practice my profession here in Missouri anymore."

"Who's gonna know any different, Pa?" asked Zerelda. "You're only gonna look at a sick friend and see what's wrong with him. Nothing more than that."

"I suppose it won't hurt none," said Samuel reluctantly. "Where is he?"

With Susan following them, Zerelda led him to Jesse's room where Creed was sitting up in bed. The doctor felt Creed's fore- head, then confirmed that he had a fever. He looked down Creed's throat and saw how red it was. "Throat sore, son?" he asked.

Creed nodded.

"Do you hurt all over, too?" asked Samuel.

Creed nodded again.

"Catarrh," announced the doctor. "He needs lots of rest, plenty of water to drink, and soup to eat. Clear soup, like chicken broth."

"Jesse, go kill a couple of roosters," said Zerelda. "I'll make some broth, and we'll have fried chicken for supper."

Jesse thought about making a fuss, but he held his tongue and obeyed his mother.

"He needs medicine, too," said Dr. Samuel.

"Medicine?" queried Zerelda. "What kind of medicine?"

"The kind only a doctor can make up and give out," said Samuel. "He needs another doctor to tend to him, Ma. I can't do for him."

"Then I guess we'll have to send for one,"-said Zerelda. "Mr. Frank, you'll have to ride down to Liberty and fetch back a doctor for Captain Creed."

This wasn't an idea that appealed to Alex James. "I'd like to, Ma," he said, "but I don't think it would be wise if I was to ride into Liberty just yet. Bud and Donnie Pence told me that there's some folks there who would still like to see me dead for what I did during the war. I'd just as soon not let them get the chance to settle their grudges against me."

"I see what you mean," said Zerelda. She looked for Jesse, but he'd already gone out to kill the roosters for his mother. Her eyes fell on Susan.

"I'll go, Ma," said Susan without being asked.

"I ain't so sure that's such a good idea, Sugar," said Zerelda. "It's a long ways to Liberty, and the weather don't look too promising this morning."

"It's all right, Ma," said Susan. "I'll be just fine. I can ride Jesse's mare."

"All right, go then," said Zerelda.

Creed listened to this conversation, and his first inclination was to tell them not to bother, that he'd be fine after a little rest and some hot food. But his body said differently. He was really sick and needed medical attention, and he was absolutely unable to tend to himself. He simply sat there and let Zerelda do with him as she pleased.

"Mr. Frank, get Captain Creed's clothes off him," she said.

Alex obeyed her without question, and a few minutes later he had Creed propped up in bed.

Jesse opened the back door but didn't come inside. He stood at the doorway, holding the two roosters - both headless, dripping blood from their necks - that his mother had told him to kill. "Ma, do you want to dry-pluck these birds out here?" he asked. "Or do you want to dip them first?"

"It'll take too long to get the big pot boiling," said Zerelda. She took the tea kettle from the cookstove and grabbed a cooking pot. "Come on," she said, walking through the doorway. "We'll just have to do it the hard way." She led Jesse to the chopping block where the chickens' blood was so fresh that it was still steaming in the cold air. She placed the pot on the wooden block and said, "Put one of them roosters in there, Jesse."

Jesse did, and Zerelda poured boiling hot water over it. As soon as the bird was soaked, she said, "Take that one out and put the other one in." Jesse did, and Zerelda soaked it, too. "Now pluck them," she said, and she went back into the house.

Jesse watched her go. His first thought had been to argue about plucking the feathers from the birds, but he knew better than to have words with" his mother, especially when she was in one of her take-charge moods, like now. Instead, he started removing the feathers by the handful, all the time wishing that he'd been a shade quicker with his six-gun the night before.

He didn't have much time to brood on his situation-because Susan came outside and approached him. "Come help me saddle up your mare, Jesse," she said.

"Where are you going on my horse?" he demanded to know.

"I'm going for a doctor in Liberty," she said, "Ma said I could take your horse."

"But I didn't say you could."

Susan glared at her brother with fire and determination in her eyes. "I'm taking her, Jesse," she said, and that's all there is to it. Slate needs a doctor, and I'm going to get him one right now."

"You're too damn thick with that Texan, Susie, and I don't like it."

"I don't care what you like, Jesse Woodson James. If you won't help me saddle the mare, then I'll just do it myself."

"Sonofabitch!" swore Jesse as he slammed the dead rooster on the chopping block. "That Texan has been a thorn in my side ever since he arrived here. I've just about had my fill of him. I've been put out just a little too much because of him. Sick or not, I think it's time I settled his hash for him."

Susan stepped between him and the back door to the house. "Don't you dare go near him, Jesse," she said. "He's real sick and needs a doctor. Now you remember that you're a Christian and leave him be. He needs his rest."

"That's right," said Jesse. "He needs his rest. And in my bed, too. What if I get to feeling poorly from my wound again? I won't have my own bed to lay in."

"I don't think the bed will know the difference between you and Slate," said Susan.

Jesse stared at his sister as be considered what she bad just said. Then an idea struck him. All at once, he had a change of heart, and he said, "You know, Susie, you're right. I'm not being very Christian about Creed, am I? Of course, he can have my bed, and you go ahead and take my mare and fetch back a doctor for him. Come on. I'll help you saddle her right now."

Susan was suspicious of Jesse, but she said nothing about this sudden transformation in him. But why should she? This was nothing out of the ordinary for Jesse. He was known for his mood swings. She followed him to the barn not knowing that Jesse had found a way to turn the situation to his advantage and that he planned to use it for his own selfish purposes.

33

As soon as Zerelda had Creed situated in bed and everybody had been fed their breakfasts, Jesse motioned to his coconspirators to follow him outside where they could talk freely. They went to the barn.

"What's up, Dingus?" asked Oll, just a tiny bit annoyed by Jesse calling this conference.

"Susie gave me an idea about when we should raid the Liberty bank," said Jesse, coming straight to the point. He had a glint of danger in his eyes that his brother had seen before and had been fearful of.

"Is that so?" queried Oll, slightly amused by this sudden announcement, as if it were a command decision that was Jesse's alone to make.

"How's that?" asked Alex, knowing that Jesse was serious.

"Susie said that my bed wouldn't know the difference between me and Creed," said Jesse excitedly.

"Now what the hell does that mean?" asked Oll, still not taking Jesse seriously.

"It means that maybe a doctor might not know the difference between me and Creed either," he explained.

"What on earth are you talking about, Jesse?" asked Alex.

Jesse laughed and said, "I'm talking about having a witness who says I was here when the bank was raided." He looked at the faces around him and saw that they didn't understand. Anxiously, he continued. "Don't you see what I'm talking about? If someone in Liberty was to see me during the raid and point me out later to the law, then I could say that I was home sick in bed, recovering from my wound, and the doctor that Susie went to fetch would swear to it."

"Are you saying we ought to pass Creed off as you?" asked George, confused but trying desperately to sort out Jesse's words.

"That's exactly what I'm saying," said Jesse, glad that someone was finally catching on.

"Now how the hell are we gonna do that, Dingus?" chortled Oll. "You don't look nothing like Creed, and Creed sure as hell won't go along with it."

"Creed's delirious with the fever," said Jesse. "He won't know much of anything until lie starts getting well or he's dead and gone to Hell, and then it won't make no difference."

"But Creed's got the catarrh," said Alex. "He doesn't have a chest wound like you had."

"What's the difference?" asked Jesse. "So, I'll say I had a bad case of the catarrh. It won't make any difference. The important thing is that we make the doctor believe that Creed is me." He scanned their faces for support for his plan, but he didn't see any yet. His anxiety stepped up a notch as he added, "Don't you see it? No one around here knows you boys are here except folks we can trust. Everybody thinks Frank is still in Kentucky, and the same with George and you, Oil. As for Jim, hell, nobody even knows him around here. If anybody saw any of us in town and said it was us that robbed the bank, I can say that I was home in bed, and you boys can say you were in Kentucky, and our families and this doctor that Susie's gonna bring back can back us up on that."

"How are we gonna make this doctor believe that Creed is you," asked Alex, "when we're not even supposed to be around here? And what about Ma and Dr. Samuel and Susie? How are they gonna go along with this plan of yours?"

"Susie's already agreed to do it," said Jesse. "I told her about it before she left, and she thought it was a good idea."

"But what about Ma and Dr. Samuel?" asked Alex.

"We'll just tell them that it would be better for you and me if they told the doctor that Creed is me," said Jesse. "We can say that we're worried about the Militia finding out that you're home and that I'm well because they might want to start trouble with us again. And we wouldn't be lying about that, Frank."

"No, I guess not," said Alex. He paused, then added, "So then what?"

"We raid the bank right away," said Jesse. "Today's too late, but we can do it tomorrow."

"That's awful soon, Jesse," said Alex, shaking his head. "I'm not so sure we're ready to ride just yet."

"How much time do we need to prepare for a raid?" asked Jesse, pshawing his brother's negative attitude. Then with the zeal of a preacher caught up in the Spirit, he added, "We were guerrillas, weren't we? Weren't we always ready to ride at a moment's notice? Why do we need to take so much time now?"

"Dingus is right, Buck," said Oll eagerly. His eyes were full of fire, desirous for daring action, fast riding, and gunplay. "Why don't we do it tomorrow like he says?"

"That's right, Frank," said Jesse. "Let's do it tomorrow. Oll and George and Jim can ride back to Jackson County tonight and alert Arch and the boys down there, and we can ride over to the Pence's and Wilkerson's and tell them. We'll ride out tomorrow morning- separate so nobody suspects that anything's up - and we'll meet in that thicket along Rush Creek north of Liberty. Then we'll split up again after everybody's there, and we'll ride into town tomorrow afternoon - separate, like I said last night - and be there at two o'clock. Frank, you and Oll will go into the bank. Arch and I will wait for you out front. The Pence's, Wilkerson's, and a few more of Arch's boys will guard the street and make sure nobody interferes. George and some of Arch's boys will set up an ambush on the road out of town in case some of those Unionists in Liberty take a notion to chase after us, and Jim will make sure the ferry is waiting for us when we reach the crossing."

The five of them exchanged looks, searching for any sign of dissension. When they saw none, Oll said, "Then we'll do it tomorrow. Just like Dingus said. Agreed?"

"Agreed," they said in unison.

"One more thing, Jesse," said Alex. "When we ride out of here tomorrow, what do we tell Ma?"

"We tell her we're gonna go look for work," said Jesse.

"All right" said Alex. "That sounds good, but what kind of work and where?"

"Hell, I don't know," complained Jesse. "I can't think of everything, Frank. You think up the answer to that one."

"I know," said Oll. "I saw a story in Brother Berry's newspaper about the Union Pacific Railroad hiring men for this year's work. All a feller has to do is get himself to Omaha to get a job. You can tell your Ma that you're gonna go up to Nebraska and get a job on the railroad."

"That'd be lying," said Alex. "I've never lied to Ma before. I'd just as soon not start now."

"I don't see that we have much other choice," said Jesse.

"Unless you can come up with something better by the time we have to ride out of here tomorrow morning, then I say we go with what Oll said about getting jobs on the railroad."

Alex looked at Jesse, then the others in turn. He nodded said, "I guess that's the way it'll have to be. All right, boys guess we're gonna raid the Liberty bank tomorrow."

34

Susan brought Dr. John Allen back to the Samuel farm late that Monday afternoon. When Susan told Dr. Allen that her brother was quite sick and needed a doctor right away, he asked her the name of the patient, and she told him without hesitation. Dr. Allen, a veteran surgeon of the Confederate States Army, had heard of young Jesse James.

"You've got another brother named Alex, don't you?" inquired the doctor.

"Yes, I do," said Susan.

"I treated him for the measles down in Springfield," said Dr. Allen. "Back in '61 or '62. It seems so long ago that I forget exactly when it was. He was one of those that we had to leave behind to get captured by the Federals. I heard that he took to the brush after he was paroled. Is that true?"

"Yes, sir."

"I've never met your other brother, but I've heard that he took to the brush, too."

"Yes, sir, he did."

"Isn't he being treated by Dr. Lankford from Kansas City for a chest wound that he received in the war?" asked Dr. Allen.

"Yes, sir, he is," said Susan, "but Kansas City is too far for me to ride to and get Dr. Lankford back to our farm in time to save Jesse. Ma said I was to bring a doctor from Liberty. Oh, please, Dr. Allen, come and see about him. He's powerful sick with a fever and all."

Dr. Allen couldn't say no. He tied Jesse's mare to the back of his buckboard, and he and Susan rode in the buggy to the Samuel farm.

Jesse and Alex convinced Zerelda and Dr. Samuel that it would be best if the doctor that Susan was bringing home thought Creed was Jesse, then they rode over to visit the Pence's until they were positive that it was safe for them to return home.

As for Creed, Jesse was right. He was too delirious to know that Dr. Allen was even there, no matter that the physician called him Jesse.

Dr. Allen examined Creed, fully believing the Texan to be Jesse James. He diagnosed Creed's illness as catarrh, the same as Dr. Samuel had done, and just as Dr. Samuel had said the outside physician would do, he gave creed a medicine of his own concoction to relieve some of the symptoms. His patient was to be given the medication every four hours or so, when he was awake.

Satisfied that his orders would be carried out, Allen said that he would send word to Dr. Lankford that Jesse was ill, that he bad tended to him, and that the Kansas City physician should look in on Jesse as soon as possible. The doctor from Liberty then left the farm without seeing the real Jesse James or his brother.

Like most medicines of the day, the primary ingredient in Allen's catarrh remedy was whiskey, and adding a knockout punch was a pinch of opium. The alcohol dulled Creed's senses, and the narcotic allowed him to sleep, which in turn permitted his natural defenses to combat the virus infecting his body more effectively than the medicine ever could. He slept comfortably through the night. Tuesday dawned cloudy with a hint of snow in the air. It was cold enough for it, that much was certain.

Except for a few moments to tend to her personal needs, Susan remained at Creed's side from the moment that she returned the previous afternoon from Liberty with Dr. Allen, even choosing to sleep in a chair in Jesse's bedroom instead of climbing up to her- loft which was just above. She would see to his every need, just like the doctor had prescribed.

Sleeping through the night was a good sign that Creed's illness wasn't serious, and that Dr. Allen's medicine was doing its job. The Texan was awakened by the crowing of the cock-o-the-walk, which started a regular barnyard serenade. He wanted to get up and go about his morning business, but Susan wouldn't let him. Zerelda came into the bedroom and said, "You'll just have to keep using the chamber pot, Captain Creed. Susie, you go see about the kids while Captain Creed tends to his business."

The James brothers had slept on the kitchen floor. They were slow to rise, needing a nudge from Zerelda's foot to make them get up and make room for her to work at the cookstove. Alex and Jesse dressed, performed their morning ablutions, then came inside to eat breakfast, as if this would be just another ordinary day in their lives.

Dr. Samuel went about his usual routine of farm chores before breakfast, living by the old adage that a farmer feeds his stock before he fills his own gizzard.

While Zerelda fed her menfolk, Susan tended to Creed, prop- ping him up in bed so he could eat a hot breakfast of chicken broth and grits flavored with molasses. He ate slowly, without enthusiasm, his hunger not being as great as the discomfort in his throat and head. As soon as he finished the meal, he asked for Dr. Allen's medicine, and Susan administered it to him. He was asleep again within minutes.

Jesse and Alex told their mother that the Pence's had told them that the Union Pacific Rail Road was already hiring men to work on the transcontinental line that spring. Thinking that they might have a better chance of gaining employment in Nebraska than they would in their own neighborhood, they said that they would be riding out that morning for Omaha and that they expected to be gone for the better part of a week, maybe longer.

This news saddened Zerelda, but she knew it was necessary. Until the Unionists could do the Christian thing by forgiving and forgetting what her sons had done during the recent war, neither of them would be safe in her house. She packed them some vittles, gave them extra blankets against the cold, kissed them farewell, then watched them ride off toward the west.

When they came to the crossroads north of Centerville, Jesse and Alex met up with Bud and Donnie Pence. As planned, they split up into new pairs, Bud and Alex turning south toward Liberty, while Jesse and Donnie continued to ride west toward the Mt. Gilead Christian Church where they met up with the Wilkerson brothers, Don and Billy. The four of them then rode due south for Liberty. Having had an earlier start than Jesse's bunch, Alex and Bud stopped off at Bob Minter's place to water and feed their horses. Thinking that they might need something for carrying off the bank's money, Alex took the grain sack that Minter gave them.

At one o'clock that afternoon, the six riders came together again in a thicket along Rush Creek. Joining them within the hour were Oll

Shepherd, Arch Clement, Ben Cooper, Frank Gregg, Red Monkus, Jim Couch, Joab Perry, Aaron Book, Jim Easter, and George Shepherd. They exchanged brief greetings, then Oll took command.

"George will take Aaron and Jim Easter and Jim Couch with him and set up an ambush on the Missouri City road," said Oll.

"You boys can go ahead and leave now. Next time we meet we'll have the bank's money with us." He winked at them, then said, "Now get on out of here." He watched them leave, then continued. "Everybody else will pair up. Buck and I will be one pair. Dingus and Arch will be another. Ben and Frank. Red and Joab. Donnie and Billy. Bud and Jim. We'll ride into town separately. Red and Joab will take up places across the street from the bank at the Green House. Arch and Dingus will stay with the horses out front of the bank. Bud and Jim will be down the street toward the college. Not too far, though. Ben and Frank, Donnie and Billy will take up places on the corner of the courthouse square in case the sheriff gets curious about what we're doing in town. Buck and I will go into the bank and get the money. I don't want no shooting unless someone else starts it. Is that clear, boys?" Seeing that everybody understood, he said, "All right, let's get our coats on and get on with it."

The twelve men donned the long blue overcoats of Federal soldiers, paired up as Oll had said, then rode off for town one twosome at a time. The weather was cold and growing colder as the wind started to gust. Flurries of snow began falling fr.om ever-threatening skies. By two o'clock, all but four of raiders were in place around the intersection of Franklin and Water streets in Liberty.

Alex James and Oll Shepherd rode casually eastward along Franklin Street, noting that few people were out that afternoon and those who were walking along the boardwalks were paying the strangers little attention. This was a good sign. Coming toward them from the direction of William Jewell College were Arch Clement and Jesse James. The four men reached the bank within seconds of each oilier, and they dismounted together. Alex and Oil took one last look around before entering the bank.

Coming up the street from the college were two students. Jesse recognized one of them as George Wymore, the fellow who had asked him about Susan the previous Friday. Damn! thought Jesse.

It had to be him. He turned away and said quietly to Arch Clement, "See those boys walking up the hill on the other side of the street?"

A short man with a huge thirst for blood, Arch Clement stood on tiptoes and peered over his horse's back in order to get a look at Wymore and his companion. "Yeah, I see them," he said. "What about it?"

"I met up with them the other day when I was here looking over the bank," said Jesse. "I'm thinking that if I can recollect them, then they might remember me."

"I wouldn't worry about it none," said Clement, "They might just walk on by and never even notice what's going on here. Just keep your back to them, and don't let them see your face."

Jesse did as Clement said.

Inside the bank, Alex James and Oll Shepherd warmed their hands at the Franklin stove, while the clerk and cashier worked at their desks. Shepherd approached the counter.

Young William Bird left his chair to wait on Shepherd. "May I help you, sir?" he asked.

"Can I get this bill changed?" asked Shepherd. He put a ten dollar note on the counter.

Bird smiled and said, "As long as it's not Confederate." He picked up the bill to examine it. Shepherd reached inside his coat, pulled out a six-gun, and leveled it at the clerk. "I'd like all the money in the bank," he said. Bird saw the revolver, smiled, and looked up at Shepherd, thinking this was a joke of some sort. When he saw the steel in the robber's eyes, he knew differently and backed away.

Alex James reached inside his coat, pulled out his own weapon and the feed sack he'd received from Bob Minter, then joined Shepherd at the counter. He thrust the bag at Bird and said, "Put the money in here."

When the clerk hesitated, the gunmen leaped the counter. Finally, aware that not all was right in the bank, Greenup Bird looked up and asked, "What's this all about?" Then he saw the guns.

"Get up, you," said Shepherd, waving his Remington at the elder Bird. "You," he said to the son, "get over there." He motioned toward the area beside the cashier.

The younger Bird turned slowly, but he wasn't moving fast enough to suit the outlaw. Shepherd slammed the clerk in the back with the side of his pistol, rocking him forward.

Instead of waiting for the Birds to get the money for them, James entered the vault and made a major withdrawal of the bank's assets, filling the feed sack with all the cash and bonds that he could find. As soon as he was done, he exited the vault and said, "That's it. Let's get the hell out of here."

"Get in there," said Shepherd, motioning for the bankers to enter the vault.

"I won't do it," said the senior Bird.

"Get in there or I'll blow your brains out," said Shepherd, cocking his revolver and putting the muzzle up close to Bird's pointy nose.

The Birds argued no more. They stepped into the vault.

Just before closing the door on the bankers, Shepherd laughed and said, "Don't you know that all Birds ought to be caged?" He laughed raucously at his own joke, then closed them inside the vault. He moved the bolt into position, but failed to lock the door. He and James jumped back over the counter and left the bank.

Just as Shepherd and James came out of the bank, George Wymore and his companion came abreast of Red Monkus and Joab Perry. They noticed the long blue overcoats on the strangers and supposed them to be soldiers. Then they saw Shepherd and James exit the bank with the feed sack bulging with loot. They watched the robbers step into the street and start to mount up. The two college men traded looks.

Monkus had been watching the students carefully for any sign that they might "raise the alarm." "Just mind your own business here," said Monkus to them, "and nothing will come of this." He opened his coat to show them that he was armed.

Wymore's eyes grew wide with fright. His friend backed away. "Let's go," said Joab Perry, tapping Monkus on the arm. He jumped into the saddle, and Monkus followed suit.

All of the other raiders were mounted now except Jesse. His mare was suddenly skittish. As he tried to gain control of her, his hat blew back on his head, revealing his face.

The expression on young Wymore's face said that he recognized Jesse. Clement saw the look, drew his six-gun, and fired a single shot at the student. The ball hit Wymore in the chest and sprawled him on the boardwalk. He was dead; shot through the heart. His companion ran off to spread the alarm. Clement fired twice at him but missed both times.

The Birds discovered that the vault door was unlocked. They

opened it and cautiously stepped out. Not seeing anyone, they went to the Franklin Street door, opened it, and went outside in time to see the robbers fleeing toward William Jewell College, all of them now shouting their guerrilla yells and shooting their guns wildly into the air.

"The bank's been robbed!" shouted Greenup Bird. "The bank's been robbed!"

Shepherd led his band of robbers down Franklin Street toward the college, and at Lightburne Street they turned left, went one block north, then turned east again. In another minute, they were speeding past the city cemetery and into the countryside. When they struck on Rush Creek, they broke up into smaller groups, each one going a different direction, and each man knowing that they were to rendezvous at Blue Mills Landing on the Missouri River at sundown in order to make their escape complete.

In the next few minutes, nearly all the people of Liberty became aware that something terrible had just happened in their town, but it was nearly an hour before Sheriff Joe Rickards could muster a posse to pursue the raiders.

35

Sheriff Rickards and his posse pursued the bandits into the bottoms of Rush Creek, where the outlaws seemed to have joined with more men, then split up into smaller groups. The lawmen followed the tracks of what appeared to be the largest bunch of desperados toward Missouri City, until a heavy snowstorm blew down from the north and obliterated the trail with a blanket of swirling white fluff. With darkness closing in, Rickards was forced to abandon the chase for the time being.

News of the robbery spread across the countryside like a wildfire. By the next morning, the Liberty Tribune had printed up one thousand handbills ordered by Mr. James Love, president of the Clay County Savings Association, and riders scattered to the four points of the compass to post them throughout that county and the neighboring counties. The message was plain and simple:

$5000
REWARD!

The Clay County Savings Association, at Liberty, Mo., was robbed on the 13th inst. of SIXTY THOUSAND DOLLARS, by a band of Bushwhackers, who reside chiefly in Clay county, and have. their rendezvous on or near the Missouri river, above Sibley in Jackson county. The sum of

5000.00 DOLLARS

will be paid by the Association for the recovery of the stolen money, or in that proportion for the sum recovered. Every citizen, who values his life

or property, will be expected to give his aid in
capturing the thieves, as they are thoroughly
organized and will no doubt continue to depredate
on life and property, as they did here yesterday.
Done by order of the Board of Directors.
JAMES LOVE, Prest.
February 14th, 1866.

As for the thieves, they had dispersed into the Sni Hills of Jackson County in a further effort to. elude pursuit and detection. Only a few of them remained in the area for more than twenty-four hours. When night fell on St. Valentine's Day, some of them rode out for distant parts, each man taking his share of the loot with him. The Shepherds, Alex James, and Jim White decided that they would be better off back in Kentucky. The Wilkerson's, Pence's, and Jesse James returned to their homes in Clay County; the two pairs of brothers splitting up and taking circuitous routes homeward, while Jesse rode to Kansas City, crossed over to Harlem, and spent a day with Zee before returning home on Friday, audaciously passing through Liberty.

When Zerelda saw Jesse coming up the lane toward the house, she wondered why her son was alone and why he was come home so soon from Omaha. She met him at the door with a warm hug and both of the loaded questions that were on her mind. "After being on the road for a day," said Jesse, "I decided that working on a railroad wasn't exactly the kind of work I really wanted to do, so I left Frank at St. Joe and went down to Harlem to visit with Zee."

"So Mr. Frank went on up to Omaha by himself?"

"I guess so, Ma." He looked beyond her at Susan standing in the doorway to his bedroom. "How's Creed doing? Is he feeling better yet?"

"He's doing much better," said Zerelda. "I suspect he'll be up and around later. He ate noon meal with us at the table, but it tuckered him out, so he went back to bed."

"He's sleeping now," said Susan. "He's getting stronger now, and he'll probably be wanting to leave here soon."

"Well, I'm in no hurry to get my bed back," said Jesse. "He's welcome to it as long as he needs it."

"Did you hear the news about the robbery when you came through Liberty on your way home?" asked Zerelda.

Jesse froze at first mention of the holdup, but he regained control of his senses quickly and said, "Not much, Ma. I was still with Frank when it happened, and Zee and Uncle John and Aunt Mary were the first to tell me about it when I got to their house yesterday." So far, Jesse hadn't told a lie, although he wasn't exactly telling his mother the whole truth. "They said some college boy was killed by the robbers."

"That's what the post rider told us," said Susan, glaring at her brother. "He said his name was George Wymore, and that he wasn't doing nothing except standing on the sidewalk minding his own business when one of the robbers shot him dead."

Jesse gave his sister as good as he got and said, "That's the way I heard it, too."

"The post rider told us that the robbers were all wearing Federal army overcoats," said Zerelda, "but the sheriff suspects that they were bushwhackers. He said that the sheriff and some men tracked the robbers down to the Missouri but lost them in the storm the other night. He said the sheriff thinks they crossed over to Jackson County and they're hiding out in the Sni Hills over there like Captain Quantrill did during the war."

"That's what I heard, too," said Jesse.

"But no one seems to know who the robbers were," said Susan.

"It seems they were all strangers in Liberty. Leastways, nobody recognized any of them."

"Well, they'll be caught and punished before too long," said Zerelda. "You can put your faith in that."

"What if they were some of our boys from the war?" asked Jesse. "How would you feel then, Ma?"

Zerelda gave him a queer look that betrayed what she had been fearing since she had first heard about the robbery of the Liberty bank. Even so, she said, "I'm not sure what I'd feel if they were some of our boys. I do know that I wish the killing would stop once and for all. The war is supposed to be over, but I guess some of our boys are still fighting for their freedom because the Unionists won't let them be." She set her eyes on Jesse's and added, "I'm just glad that you and Mr. Frank weren't mixed up in that business."

Jesse never flinched. He smiled and said, "What's for supper, Ma? I'm powerful hungry after riding all day."

Before she could reply, Creed coughed, drawing her attention to him for the moment. "You'd best see to Captain Creed, Susie," said Zerelda, "while I get supper started."

Jesse followed Susan to the bedroom where they found Creed sitting up in bed. He was quite surprised to see Jesse again. "Susie tells me the Liberty bank was robbed the other day," he said hoarsely. "I won't bother asking whether you and Alex had anything to do with it."

"That's good," said Jesse as he leaned casually against the doorjamb, "because a man shouldn't go sticking his nose in where it ain't wanted."

"Did you have to kill that poor Wymore boy?" demanded Susan. "I didn't kill anybody," said Jesse, suddenly angry with his sister for bringing up that subject. "Then who did it?" she asked.

Jesse glanced over his shoulder to make certain that their mother wasn't close enough to hear him. "It doesn't make any difference who did it," he said. "It was done, and that's all there is to it."

"But why, Jesse?" she insisted.

He lowered his head, averting his eyes, and said, "He saw me. Leastways, I think he did, so one of the other boys shot him." He looked up. "I swear I didn't do it, Susie." Then he anticipated her next question. "Frank didn't do it either. I swear on our father's grave that it was one of the others."

Susan knew her brother well enough to know that he wouldn't make such an oath unless he was telling the truth. "Well, as long as you and Frank didn't do it," she said. "That's all I was concerned about."

Creed shook his head with disbelief and said, "That's all you're concerned about? An innocent boy is dead, Susie, and your brothers are just as responsible for it as the man who pulled the trigger. Don't you see that?"

"He wouldn't be dead if he'd minded his own business like he was told," said Jesse.

This was too much for Creed to take. He put up a hand and said, "Save your breath, Jesse. I don't want to talk about this. Like I said before you fools rode out of here the other day, I don't want anything to do with this business. You people have got your problems, and I've got mine. And the sooner I can get back to taking care of my own affairs, the happier I'll be."

"That makes two of us," said Jesse.

36

By Monday, Creed was feeling well enough to travel, but Susan and Zerelda pleaded with him to stay one more night. He acquiesced to their supplications, but he insisted on vacating Jesse's room and spending his last night in the Samuel's house sleeping on the kitchen floor. This suited Jesse just fine, although Zerelda was disappointed that her son didn't have the good manners to offer up his bed one more time to their guest.

Creed and Jesse hadn't gotten along with each other since the Texan first entered the Samuel home, and Jesse saw no reason for him to be hospitable at this late date. As far as he was concerned, Creed had been a thorn in his paw from the start, and the sooner that he could be rid of this interloper, the happier he would be. It was with that singular thought in mind that made Jesse offer to saddle Creed's horse for him on the morning of his departure.

Creed accepted the gesture, although he reserved suspicions about Jesse's motives.

Jesse went out to the barn before breakfast to saddle up Nimbus for the Texan. Picking up the horse's blanket, he thought it was a bit on the heavy side. He examined it and felt the coins sewn in the folded edges. So that's where he keeps his money, thought Jesse. Pretty smart. I'll have to remember that one.

The discovery of Creed's hiding place for his money gave Jesse an idea. He went to the grain box, opened it, and dug deep into the mixture of oats and corn to retrieve a burlap sack that held his share of the loot from the bank robbery. He took out the U.S. treasury bonds, thumbed them, then peeled two off the top. This ought to do it, he thought. He replaced the other 7:30s in the sack, then buried the sack in the grain again. He stuffed the two bonds inside his shirt, went back to the house, and waited for the opportunity to conceal them in Creed's saddlebags. That moment came right after breakfast.

Creed said good-bye to Zerelda and Dr. Samuel in the house, but Susan chose to accompany him out to the barn for a private farewell. Jesse followed them outside.

"I'll get your horse for you," said Jesse. "Here, let me take those for you." He reached out for the saddlebags that Creed was carrying. "I'll put them on your horse for you."

Jesse's sudden rash of courtesy seemed out of character to Creed, but the Texan reasoned that Jesse was probably just glad to see him go and wanted to hasten the moment.

"I really wish you would stay," said Susan. "I really do love you, Slate."

Creed sighed and said, "We've been over this ground before, Susie. I'd just as soon not go over it again, if you don't mind."

"Then at least write to me once in a while," she pleaded, "just so I'll know that you're all right and that no harm has come to you."

"That's not a good idea either, Susie. It's best that you forget that you ever knew me, and you find yourself a beau who will give you the love that you're looking for."

Susan wasn't quite sure what to say or do next. Tears were welling in her eyes. She sniffled. Then she reacted, leaning forward suddenly and raising herself on tiptoe to kiss him firmly on the mouth. She wanted the kiss to last forever but knew that it wouldn't. She would have to be satisfied that he didn't pull away immediately, that he held the kiss for as long as she wanted it. The sound of Jesse leading Nimbus out of the barn caused her to break away from Creed and run for the house. She stopped just outside the door, turned around, and stood there, all forlorn and limp as she gazed at him through blurry eyes.

Jesse handed the reins to the Texan and said, "So long, Creed. I can't say that I'm real sad to see you leave."

Creed swung up into the saddle, situated himself, then looked down at Jesse and said, "If we meet again, Jesse James, it'll be too soon." He nudged Nimbus in the ribs and rode off without looking back.

Jesse joined Susan at the doorway. He glanced back at Creed, then burst out laughing.

"What's so funny?" blubbered Susan through her tears. "Are you making fun of me, Jesse Woodson James?"

Not totally without feelings, Jesse realized just at that instant that his sister was hurting. "No," he said softly, taking hold of Susan by her arms, "I'm not making fun of you. I'd never do that. You know that."

"Then what were you laughing about?" she demanded.

"Him," he said, jerking a thumb over his shoulder in Creed's direction. "I gave him a little going-away present."

Susan blinked the tears from her eyes and said, "What did you do now, Jesse?"

"Nothing much," he said. "I just put a couple of the bonds from the bank in his saddlebags, that's all."

Susan scrunched up her face and said, "Why'd you do that?"

"Because he's so high and mighty, that's why. He didn't want anything to do with us raiding the bank, but I made sure that he had something to do with it. What do you think he's gonna do when he finds those bonds? Throw them away? Hell, no, he won't do that. He'll take them to the nearest bank and cash them, that's what he'll do. He won't think twice about it neither. He'll cash them and spend the money without blinking an eye. And then, his hands won't be so clean, will they?"

"Jesse, you ought not to have done that," she said. "Suppose someone gets to nosing around about why he's got those bonds and starts thinking that maybe he got them from the bank in Liberty. Then what, Jesse?"

Jesse burped a laugh, then said, "I hadn't thought about that, Susie, but I wish I had. It'd serve him right if he was caught with them and someone told the law about it and he got himself arrested for what we did down to Liberty. Then he'd really find out what it's been like for us around here, wouldn't he?" He chortled again, then said, "Yep, it'd serve him just right, wouldn't it?"

"No, it wouldn't," said Susan. "Now you go after him and get those bonds back right now."

"Nope, not me," said Jesse. "He's on his own now. Besides, why should you be so concerned about him now? Didn't he just walk out on you and leave you crying? Seems to me that you ought to be madder than a wet hen about that instead of still feeling something good about the sonofabitch. I know that's how I'd feel, if I was you."

"But you aren't me, Jesse," said Susan. Then she thought, but he did snub me, didn't he? Maybe Jesse's right. Maybe I should be angered with him.

"Have it your way," said Jesse. "As far as I see it, Creed made a fool out of you, and you let him do it like you were some nigger bitch like Rachel or something. If that's the way you want to be treated, then that's up to you, but I wouldn't let anybody treat me like that. Not him. Not anybody."

Jesse's remarks confused Susan, threw all her thoughts and feelings into disarray. She didn't know what to think now. Had Creed really treated her so poorly? She didn't know for sure, but Jesse thinking and saying so was enough to make her doubt that he hadn't. Maybe Jesse's right, she wondered again. Damn him, if he is. And in the next instant, she was angry. But not with Creed; with Jesse instead. She flattened her hand and gave the back of it to her brother's cheek. "Damn you, Jesse James!" she swore at him as he backed away. "Damn you all to Hell!" And with that, she turned and stormed into the house, bypassing her mother and making straight for her loft where she would sort out her thoughts and feelings about Creed, about her brother, about love, about sin, about everything. But first, she would have a good cry.

37

Platte City was the seat for Platte County. The road between it and the Samuel farm was twenty-five miles long, and it took Creed nearly the whole day to make the uneventful journey.

Exhausted from the long ride, Creed checked into the Green Hotel, the first hotel that he saw in Platte City, and paid to have Nimbus boarded at a nearby stable for the night. He inquired about the evening meal at the inn and was told that it wouldn't be served for nearly two hours yet. He'd hoped to eat sooner, but he could wait; he could rest a bit before supper. He asked the clerk, Mr. Blair, to come to his room and wake him for supper, then he went up to his room on the second floor.

The clerk tended to his duties and knocked at Creed's door ten minutes before supper was to be served in the dining room. "Mr. Creed?" he called. "Suppertime, sir."

Creed sat up on the edge of the bed, rubbed the sleep from his face, then said, "Thank you. I'll be right down."

"Yes, sir," said Blair on the other side of the door.

Creed heard the clerk walk down the hall and descend the stairs to the small lobby, then he stood up, stretched, and realized that he was famished. But first he washed up and used the chamber pot. He pulled on his boots, then wondered whether he should wear his hat and coat downstairs. The coat, yes; the hat wasn't really necessary - since he didn't plan to go outside after eating. He donned the coat and started for the door only to stop when he grasped the handle. Something was missing from his costume, he thought. But what? He was fully clothed. So, what could it be? He glanced around the room until his view fell on the Colt's resting quietly on the chair at the foot of the bed. That's ridiculous, he told himself. I don't need a gun to eat with. It was a logical argument, 'but for some inexplicable reason, it sounded as hollow as his stomach was feeling right then. Something phantasmal deep in the back of his mind was telling him that he would need the weapon before the night was through. He picked up the six-gun, checked the loads and caps, then tucked it into the left front side of his pants. The haunting voice seemed soothed, placated. He could leave now.

The dining room wasn't much on appearance: a single long table covered with a white cloth, four chairs on each side, and one at each end; a sideboard and a hutch for the dishes; walls papered with a flowery yellow pattern on a white background; a doorway to the kitchen and another to the lobby; a tall window curtained with- gauzy fabric that hadn't been dusted in months; and a homemade square chandelier of iron and wood construction that had a kerosene lamp mounted on each of its four comers. Four place settings, each consisting of a pewter plate, knife, fork, soup spoon, and coffee cup, adorned the table, one each at the first and third seats on one side and at the second and fourth seats on the other side. The only odd piece on the table was a porcelain call bell at the third setting.

A man of medium height, reddish-brown hair and the pretense of a mustache, green eyes, and appearing to be in Iris early twenties at the most was standing behind the first chair when Creed entered the room. "You may sit there, Mr. Creed," Howard Blair said, motioning toward the second chair on the opposite side. As Creed took his place, Blair explained, "It's the custom of the house to wait until everybody is ready to sit down before we seat ourselves. You understand, of course?"

"It sounds like a very polite custom and a worthy tradition, Mr. Blair," said Creed. "I am honored to be a part of it."

Blair smiled graciously and said, "Thank you, sir, for your kind remarks. We are delighted to have you with us this evening."

Before Creed could make another reply, a short man in a brown suit and an older lady entered the room and stepped lightly to their chairs; his the fourth seat on Creed's side and hers the third seat on Blair's side.

"Mr. Creed, allow me to introduce my mother," said Blair, "and Mr. Wilson. Mother, this is Mr. Slate Creed, a traveler on his way to Colorado."

"How nice to meet you, Mr. Creed," said Mrs. Blair, nodding and offering a hint of a smile.

"It's an honor to meet you, Mrs. Blair," said Creed. He did a half-bow in her direction, then straightened up to greet Wilson, offering his hand to him. "Mr. Wilson, how do you do?"

"I do quite well, thank you," said Wilson, accepting Creed's handshake. Releasing the grip with Creed, he dug into a coat pocket and removed a business card. He handed it to Creed. "Robert Wilson at your service, sir. I am an attorney-at-law."

Creed read the card, then returned it, saying, "From the look of you, Mr. Wilson, the law business around here must be fairly decent."

"Yes, it is," said Wilson, "thanks mostly to our recent difficulties between the North and South. Hundreds of disputes have arisen due to that trouble."

"From what I've seen here in Missouri," said Creed, "I have no doubt about that."

"Shall we eat, gentlemen?" asked Mrs. Blair. She was a petite woman with auburn hair tied in a bun, rosy cheeks, green eyes, triangular face, attired modestly in a gray dress trimmed with white lace.

Blair held his mother's chair for her, then he sat down. The guests followed his lead. Mrs. Blair picked up the porcelain call bell, rang it twice, then replaced it.

The door to the kitchen opened, and a tall, dark-skinned waiter came into the room carrying a soup tureen, a ladle, and four bowls on a tray. He placed the tray on the sideboard, dished up a thick, creamy soup that was diced with white potatoes, orange carrots, and red ham, and served the diners, starting with Mrs. Blair. Wilson was the last to receive a bowl.

"Thank you, Silas," said Mrs. Blair.

The waiter bowed and averted his eyes in the same manner that slaves had been taught to do in times gone by. "Yes'm," he said as he backed away from the table and took up a station next to the sideboard.

As the other men followed Mrs. Blair's example and started to eat their soup, Creed made no move to join them, instead allowing his eyes to observe the waiter.

Mrs. Blair noted his interest in the man and said, "You look as if you've never seen a darky before, Mr. Creed. I would have thought by your manners that you were a Southern gentleman and, therefore, had seen darkies before now."

"It isn't his color that surprises me, Mrs. Blair," said Creed.

"It's just that in these new times I find it odd to see an ex-slave still working as a servant."

Mrs. Blair gave Creed a patronizing smile and said, "Silas."

Silas stepped forward instantly and said, "Yes'm?"

"Silas, what else have you done in your life besides be a house nigger?" asked Mrs. Blair.

Silas didn't hesitate to answer. "Nothing, ma'am," he said.

"Are you a free nigger, Silas?" asked Mrs. Blair. "Yes'm."

"Do you want to leave here?" she asked. "No, ma'am."

"If you did leave here, what would you do, Silas?"

'I'd most likely starve, ma'am," said Silas.

"Thank you, Silas," said Mrs. Blair. As the waiter stepped back to his post, she said smugly, "There you have it, Mr. Creed. Silas was freed with all the other niggers of Missouri when that hateful new constitution was forced on us last year, but he chose to remain in our service because he doesn't know any other kind of work. If we should discharge him, he would starve unless he could find employment elsewhere as a house servant, which isn't very likely in these parts, sir."

"No, I suspect not, ma'am," said Creed.

"It would be un-Christian to turn Silas and his wife out in the cold, cruel world in his present state of ignorance," said Mrs. Blair. "Therefore, we have allowed them to continue working for us here in the hotel."

Only because they'll work cheaper than white people, thought Creed. But he said, "Yes, ma'am, I see your point."

"But you don't agree with it, Mr. Creed?" she queried.

Of course, he didn't, but he wasn't about to tell her that. He smiled and said, "Ma'am, I believe our Savior once said, 'He who hath no sin, let him cast the first stone.' "

"Meaning, sir?"

"Meaning, I am in no position to pass judgment on you or any other person on this earth, Mrs. Blair, but if I have given offense, then I offer a most sincere apology."

"Well put, Mr. Creed," said Mrs. Blair, smiling and feeling like she had won the debate. "No offense taken, I assure you."

"Thank you, ma'am." He lifted his spoon and began to eat his soup, hoping that the silence that had fallen over the room would continue for the remainder of the meal and that he could escape to his room after eating without having to converse with this bigoted woman again. The first part of his wish was granted with the exceptions of Mrs. Blair giving orders to Silas at various points during the supper, and so was the second - somewhat.

The four diners had nearly finished their repast when the din from a disturbance outside reached their ears. Before any of them could remark or react to it, the clamor burst inside the hotel lobby. Instinctively, Creed allowed his right hand to drop into his lap and grasp the butt of his Colts.

Blair came to his feet, as did Wilson; both of them were quite agitated by the intrusion.

Mrs. Blair remained seated and outwardly calm.

Silas moved to the doorway to the lobby and stationed himself in the path of whatever it was causing the ruckus.

Eight men, all armed with handguns, forced their way past Silas, the leader of them growling, "Out of the way, nigger! We got business with your master." They pushed Silas aside and surrounded the dinner table.

"What's the meaning of this, Peacock?" demanded Wilson of the leader.

"Lawyer Wilson," said Peacock, a stout fellow with a heavy brown beard that hid his jowls and mouth. "When did you take to eating with Secesh?"

"The war is over, Peacock," said Wilson. "There is no more North and South."

"Bullshit!" grunted the intruder.

"Peacock, you and your men would be well advised to leave this place peaceably," said Wilson.

"We would, would we?" mocked Peacock. "Well, maybe we will, but not until we've had a few words with Mr. Blair and his mama here." Aiming ill words at the hotelkeeper, he said, "We don't like you or your kind, Blair, and we don't want you around here anymore. If I was you, I'd sell this place and move on as soon as possible."

"You are not a Blair, Clarence Peacock," said Mrs. Blair, "and I thank the Lord for that."

"I will ask you politely to leave," said Blair.

"Go ahead and ask," said Peacock. "It won't do you no good."

He pushed Blair who stumbled backward into his chair, sitting down directly on the seat. "You puny little shit! We ought to run you out of town right this minute."

"Why bother with that?" said another ruffian. He drew his six-shooter, a Remington, and pointed it at Blair's head. "A ball in the brain will be a good lesson to all the other Secesh around here to get the Hell out of our county. Just say the word, Clarence, and I'll send him to Hell."

"Put that weapon away, Jim Clark!" shouted Wilson.

"This is my house," said Mrs. Blair, raising her voice angrily, "and I demand that you leave it this very minute."

Peacock ignored Mrs. Blair and addressed Wilson. "Since when did you side with Secesh in these matters, Bob Wilson?"

"I told you before," said Wilson, "the war is over."

"No, it ain't," said Peacock. "It ain't over until every one of these goddamned Secesh are either dead or moved out of Platte County."

"Silas, go fetch the marshal back here at once," said Mrs. Blair. "He'll make you leave my house, Clarence Peacock."

Silas moved toward the doorway only to have one of the intruders block his path, saying, "No, you don't, nigger." Then he knocked Silas down and kicked him.

The assault on Silas angered Creed, and for a second he let his ire show, making a slight movement toward the fallen man but catching himself before actually coming to his feet. Silas curled into a ball in order to protect his ribs from any more kicks.

Peacock saw Creed move and acted as if he'd seen the Texan for the first time that very second. "What business is this of yours, stranger?" he demanded.

Creed's face took on the stoic appearance of the Choctaw warrior confronted by a dangerous enemy. "None," he said, "except that I don't like seeing a man abused like that."

"What are you?" demanded the man who had attacked Silas, "Some sort of nigger-lover or something?"

"That's right," said Peacock. "Who are you, stranger?"

"My name is Creed," He brought his gun hand up slowly and placed it palm down on the table.

"You ain't from around here, are you?" asked Peacock.

"No, sir, I'm not," Creed gently pushed his feet against the floor, moving his chair an inch farther from the table.

Irritated that Creed didn't volunteer any information, Clark leveled his gun at the Texan and said, "Then where are you from?"

"Texas," said Creed. He moved back another inch.

Just the mere mention of the state took all eight ruffians aback for a few seconds until Clark said, "Another goddamned Reb, I'll bet." He cocked the hammer on the Remington.

"Put that gun away, Jim Clark," said Wilson, "and leave this man alone. He's only passing through town."

"Is that right?" asked Peacock.

"Yes, sir, it is," said Creed. He moved another inch away from the table.

"Leave him be, Jim," said Peacock. "He ain't our problem here. Blair and his kind are our problem."

"That's right," said Clark as he shifted his aim toward Blair again. "Get up, Blair. You're going outside with us."

Seeing that the intruders had focused their attention on Blair again, Creed let his right-hand slide back to his lap, while his left clandestinely unbuttoned his coat.

"You stay right where you are, Howard," said Mrs. Blair. "Shut up, bitch!" snapped Clark. He pulled his gun back and with his free hand reached out to slap Mrs. Blair.

That was all the opening Creed needed. In one motion, he drew his Colt's, popped to his feet, cocked the gun, and brought it to bear only inches from Clark's nose before he could strike Mrs. Blair.

"I am from Texas, sir," said Creed evenly, "I can kill you in the wink of a cat's eye, and I will, too, if you or any of your friends make one wrong move."

Nobody moved. Nobody drew a breath. Everybody believed him. They'd heard about Texans before.

Confident that he was in control of the situation, Creed said, "Now, sir, you can uncock that revolver and slowly put it back in your trousers."

Seeing that Clark was too scared to act, Peacock said softly, "Put it away, Jim. He means business."

"You are quite correct, Mr. Peacock," said Creed without looking away from Clark. "Because if I have to kill your friend here, I will certainly kill you, too. And three of your other friends after that. The question you must ask yourselves is which three."

"I don't think I want to find out the answer to that one, Mister," said Peacock. "Put your gun away, Jim. Just like the man says."

Clark did as Creed had said.

"Now," said Creed, still keeping his eye on Clark, "I want you gentlemen to remove yourselves from this lady's house muy pronto."

"Mooey what?" asked Peacock, not understanding the Spanish words.

"That's Mexican for pretty damn quick," said Creed. "Pardon my language, ma'am."

"You are excused, Mr. Creed," said Mrs. Blair.

"Come on, boys," said Peacock. "We'd best be doing what the man says."

Silas rolled out of their way and came to his feet, grateful that Creed had interceded on his behalf.

Cautiously the ruffians moved toward the doorway, although all of them kept an eye on Creed as they did.

Creed was just as cautious as he watched them go, keeping his Colt's leveled at Clark all the time. He followed them into the lobby and made certain that they left the hotel going so far as to step outside behind them.

Silas followed Creed.

"Goddamned nigger lover!" one of them grumbled as they walked away.

"A nigger-lovin' Reb," said another. "Can you imagine that?"

"I should have shot the sonofabitch when I had the chance," said Clark. He glanced back at the hotel doorway and saw Creed standing there silhouetted by the light from the lobby with his revolver pointing upward now. "Goddamned sonofabitch! I ought to kill him anyway." Clark drew his Remington again, spun, and fired wildly at Creed. "Goddamn you! I'm gonna kill you, you sonofabitch!" He started running toward Creed, firing a second shot that was as equally off-target as the first had been.

His companions followed his lead, drew their weapon and turned around to join him in the fight. Before any of them could draw a bead on the Texan, Clark fired again.

Silas retreated to the dining room.

Creed dropped calmly to one knee, and although Clark was difficult to see in the dark, he was able to distinguish enough of the lout to take deadly aim, squeeze off a round, and hit the man in the chest, knocking him backward into the street.

Clark screamed in pain and slapped a hand over the wound as he rolled in the thick, cold mud of the street.

The other ruffians now began a general fire in Creed's direction, although none of them was sure where the Texan was exactly because he had moved away from the light in the open doorway to the shadow of the low porch.

The report of Clark's first shot was heard all over town, putting every man who owned a gun on alert.

"Run and get the marshal, Silas," said Mrs. Blair when she heard the gunfire outside.

Silas obeyed, slipping out the kitchen door and disappearing down the alley.

The gunfight was in earnest now as Creed's eyes became better adjusted to the dim light in the street and he began to make out the silhouettes of the intruders who stood in the open firing at him. He took aim at one, fired, then rolled to one side in order to keep the enemy guessing about his position. The ball he'd fired struck flesh and bone, and another man screamed in pain and fell backward clutching his breast.

Marshal H.T. Callahan was already in the street and running toward the sound of the shooting when Silas came up to him. "Hurry, Marshal!" shouted Silas. "It's Clarence Peacock and that bunch of outlaws of his. They's shootin' up Miz Blair's hotel."

This news brought Callahan and every other man who had heard Silas to an abrupt halt. Peacock and his outlaws had been terrorizing Platte City for months, usually entering the business of some former Confederate or Southern sympathizer and roosting the owner and his patrons until the assailed were provoked into a fight, which gave the outlaws an excuse to shoot down the man that they had come to kill in the first place. No one, not even Callahan, had had the courage to arrest them and bring them to trial for their crimes. Not so much that they feared Peacock and his gang but because they feared retribution from one of the pseudo-military units that were still roaming the state carrying out reprisals against anybody who might have had sympathies lying south of the Mason-Dixon Line.

"Do you mean to tell me that Howard Blair had the backbone to get into a fight with Peacock and his boys?" asked Callahan. "No, sir, Marshal," said Silas. "They's a Mr. Creed from Texas at the hotel who done got the drop on them outlaws and made them leave the hotel. That's when the shootin' started up. I thinks Mr. Creed is shootin' it out with them badmen."

Several citizens had joined Callahan in the street by now. He noted that all of them were armed with rifles and shotguns. If he were ever to stop Peacock, then now was as good a time as any to try. "How many men with Peacock, Silas?" he asked.

"I only counted seven of them, Marshal," said Silas. "Eight, includin' Peacock."

"Did you hear that, boys?" Callahan asked the men around him.

"There's only eight of them. I say it's time we put an end to these outlaws once and for all. Who's willing to stand with me?"

Before anybody could answer him, Lawyer Wilson came among them. "What are you waiting for, Harry?" he asked the marshal.

"I'm getting up a posse right now," said Callahan.

"Well, you'd better hurry it up," said Wilson, "because if you don't, that Texan's gonna have your job. He's already killed two of Peacock's men."

"Did you hear that, boys?" said Callahan. "The Texan's already killed two of them. That means there's only six left for us to handle. So what do you say?"

A general round of approval erupted from the men.

"All right now," said Callahan. "You're all sworn in as deputies. Let's go."

Callahan couldn't be certain, but he estimated that he had twenty men in all to fight Peacock and his gang. He divided his force into three groups, sending one with Wilson and Silas to the rear of the hotel where they were to go through the building and join Creed in front of it, while he led another group to the far side of the outlaws' position in the street, and the third portion of his posse blocked the other side of the street.

Creed had fired his gun judiciously, using up only four rounds by the time Wilson and the posse members came to his support, and with each ball, he had managed to wound an outlaw, killing one outright. He was just as surprised as Peacock and his gang when Callahan and the posse opened fire.

Undaunted, the outlaws shot back at the hastily assembled lawmen. The battle continued for the next several minutes until every one of Peacock's gang had taken lead. Seeing that it was senseless to fight on, Peacock surrendered.

38

Peacock and his gang had been Unionists during the war. So had Bob Wilson, but unlike the outlaws he wanted to put the war behind him and get on with living. Thus, he was glad that Creed had taken a stand against the villains.

"Let me shake your hand, Mr. Creed," said Wilson as Callahan and the posse took Peacock and his surviving gang members into custody. "You're the first man in these parts to show any backbone to these ruffians." He pumped Creed's hand vigorously.

"I would like to thank you also, Mr. Creed," said Mrs. Blair as she and Silas stepped outside onto the porch. Her son was conspicuously absent. "I can't begin to tell you how much we've dreaded these badmen these past several months. They've done nothing except terrorize this community, since they came home from the war. They've done everything that they could possibly do to drive us away from our homes and businesses because we supported the Confederacy during the war. Maybe now we will finally have peace around here."

"That's right, Mr. Creed," said Silas who was still caught up in the excitement of the affray. "They's real badmen. They sure is."

"It was the Texan who started it!" Peacock was shouting in the street. "He shot first! He killed Jim Clark and Jake Kenny! We was only firing back to protect ourselves!"

"You can tell it to the judge," said Callahan, as he pushed Peacock ahead of him toward the jail.

"Any of our people hurt, Callahan?" asked Wilson, as the lawman and his prisoner passed by them.

"Hold up there, Peacock," said Callahan. The marshal and the

214

outlaw stopped at the hotel's porch. "Just my cousin Bill," said Callahan sadly. "One of these bastards shot him dead right off. I don't know which one did it, but I know someone's gonna hang for it"

"That's him!" said Peacock, pointing a finger at Creed. "He's the sonofabitch that started it, Callahan. The Texan. He started it."

"Shut up, Peacock," said Callahan. "You've got nothing to say that I want to hear."

"You can't arrest us without arresting him, too," said Peacock. "He's a Reb, I tell you, and he started it. He killed Jim Clark and Jake Kenny. He's probably a bushwhacker, too."

"I told you to shut up, Peacock," said Callahan.

"If you don't arrest him, too," said Peacock, in a last stand effort to convince Callahan of his innocence in the affray, "there'll be Hell to pay. You can bet on that, Callahan. Every good Union man in the county will ride down on this town and set things right if you don't."

Peacock was speaking the threat that Callahan and most of the people of Platte City had feared all along. This was something that the marshal didn't wish to consider right then, but he knew he would have to think about it sooner or later. Worse, he would have to take some sort of stand, then live with the consequences of his action-or lack of it.

Lawyer Wilson knew that Peacock was speaking truth about former Union men riding down on Platte City to set matters right - that is, right as they thought should be. He stroked his chin as he gave the moment some quick thought, then said, "Callahan, I'd like a word with you. In private."

"You tell him, Bob," said Peacock. "You tell him there'll be Hell to pay if he don't do the right thing here. You tell him, Bob."

"I told you to shut your mouth," said Callahan. Without another word, he jammed the butt of his shotgun into Peacock's gut, driving the wind from his lungs and doubling him up with pain. "There! That ought to keep you quiet for a while."

Wilson and Callahan stepped away from the porch to converse out of earshot of the others.

"The sonofabitch just might be right about what he's saying there, Callahan," said Wilson. "This is gonna stir up every Union man in the county, and who knows how far it will spread? If you don't arrest Mr. Creed for something, they're gonna see it as one former Confederate helping another against some good Union men. You got to make it look like you aren't playing any favorites here, Callahan. You see what I'm getting at?"

"I sure do," said the marshal. "I don't like it, but I see it. I suppose I should arrest this fellow and let the county attorney and the judge sort it all out."

"Sounds like a good plan to me," said Wilson.

They returned to the porch.

"Don't you worry none about this, Mr. Creed," said Wilson.

"The marshal's just doing his duty here. I'll have you out in no time at all, and we'll get this matter finished once and for all. Just trust me. I know Judge King to be a fair and honest man who doesn't put up with lawlessness. He'll give you justice. You can rely on that much."

Creed wasn't sure of what Wilson was trying to tell him, but something said he had two choices here. He could either cooperate and hope that everything turned out for the best, or he could put up a fight and try to ride out of town right now. Cooperating felt risky, but fighting his way out seemed downright fatal.

"Mister, I'm sorry about this," said Callahan, "but I have to arrest you."

"Could you at least tell me what the charge is, Marshal?" asked Creed.

Callahan scratched his head and thought for a second or two. He looked at Wilson for help but got none. Finally, he said, "How about shooting off a gun in town and disturbing the peace?"

"Disturbing the peace?" grunted Peacock. "Hell, Callahan! He murdered Jim Clark and Jake Kenny. I call that a little more serious than disturbing the peace."

"I've had just about enough out of you, Peacock," said Callahan. He slammed the stock of his shotgun across the outlaw's cheek and knocked him senseless. Looking down at Peacock's crumpled form, the marshal shook his head and said, "Danm! Now I'll have to carry the sonofabitch to jail."

Creed stepped down to the sidewalk, held out his gun grip first to Callahan, and said, "Permit me to do it for you, Marshal." After the lawman took the Colt's from him, Creed bent down, picked up the outlaw, and slung him over his shoulder. "Lead the way, Marshal."

39

Sometimes Creed wished that he hadn't been brought up with the notion that women were the weaker sex and that protecting them was the chivalrous thing to do. Just maybe if he'd been raised to think of women as chattel and that men had the right to treat them any way they pleased, just maybe then he wouldn't have defended Mrs. Blair, shot it out with Peacock and his outlaw gang, and landed in the Platte County jail-and subsequently in the Clay County jail. Just maybe. Lawyer Wilson volunteered to represent Creed after he was arrested by Marshal Callahan and taken to jail. He told the Texan that he would find Judge King immediately and get him to release Creed that very evening, so he wouldn't have to spend the night in a cold, damp cell. Then he'd request an immediate hearing before the court and get the charges dropped so Creed could be on his way to Colorado. It was a good plan, but one that went awry from the start.

Judge King wasn't in town that February night. He was in Kansas City and wouldn't be returning to Platte City until the next afternoon. "Sorry, Mr. Creed," said Wilson, "but there's nothing that I can do until he gets back. You'll have to spend the night in jail."

Creed shrugged it off; he'd slept in worse places than the Platte County jail. "Could you have someone bring my things over from the hotel?" he asked the attorney.

"Certainly," said Wilson. That was the second flaw.

Wilson retrieved Creed's belongings from the hotel and took them to the jail. He would have given them directly to Creed, but Callahan couldn't permit that. "Prisoners aren't allowed to have their personal stuff in the cell with them," he explained to Wilson. "You can just give them to me, and I'll check them over and make a list of what he's got in those saddlebags. Then I'll see that he gets everything back when he's released."

Seeing nothing wrong with that, Wilson explained the policy to Creed, then left the jail and returned to the hotel.

Callahan opened Creed's saddlebags and started the inventory of the Texan's personal effects. He'd hardly begun when he discovered the two 7:30s that Jesse James had hidden there. His first thought was innocent enough: the man had money. Then he was struck with the thought that the robbers of the Liberty bank had taken nearly $45,000 in bonds. Could these be some of those same stolen bonds? He'd better ask.

"Where'd you get these?" he asked, holding up the fifty-dollar bank notes so Creed could see them through the cell bars.

Creed recognized them as bearer bonds, which meant they smelled of trouble. Beyond that, they were totally foreign to him. "I didn't get them anywhere," he said evenly.

"I found them in your saddlebags," said Callahan. "So, where'd you get them?"

The marshal's disclosure put Creed's thought processes into high gear. Bank notes in my saddlebags? Who's been near my saddlebags besides me? The marshal. Mr. Wilson. Mr. Blair? Mrs. Blair? Silas maybe? Why would any one of them put one hundred dollars in bank notes in my saddlebags? No answer.

"They aren't mine, Marshal," said Creed.

"I said that I found them in your saddlebags, Mr. Creed. They must be yours."

"No, sir, I'm sorry, but they're not mine. I've never seen them before in my life."

Callahan studied Creed for a moment. He wanted to believe the Texan, and his intuition said that Creed was telling the truth. Even so, how'd those bonds get in his saddlebags if he didn't put them there? Maybe I'd better talk to somebody who knows more about these things than I do.

"All right, have it your way, Mr. Creed," said the marshal. "For now, anyway. We'll talk some more about these tomorrow."

Callahan left the jail and sought out Lawyer Wilson at the Green Hotel for his opinion on the bank notes.

"Sure, they could've come from the Liberty bank robbery," said

Wilson, "but you don't have any proof that they did."

"Then why is he denying that they're his?" countered Callahan.

"He says he's never seen them before in his life. If that's so, how'd they get in his saddlebags?"

That was a question that Wilson couldn't answer either. "That doesn't make any difference," said the attorney. "The first thing you have to do is prove that they're part of the loot stolen from the Liberty bank. And if you do that, then Mr. Creed will no longer be your problem."

"How's that?" asked Callahan, puzzled by Wilson's remark.

"If those bonds are part of the loot from the Liberty robbery," Wilson explained, "then just maybe Creed was one of the robbers, and if he was, then he's wanted over to Clay County for murder and robbing the Liberty bank."

Callahan smiled and said, "And I'll have to turn him over to Sheriff Rickards, won't I?"

"That's right, Callahan," said Wilson. "Then we won't have to worry about Peacock and his gang either, because Creed will be out of our hands. They can take their revenge out on Clay County if they don't do anything about Creed over there."

"I see what you mean." And with that, Callahan sent word to Liberty that he had apprehended one of the robbers of the Clay County Savings Association bank and that Sheriff Rickards was to send someone to fetch the desperado. The Clay County sheriff did just that, and Creed found himself cooling his heels in the Clay County jail on George Washington's birthday.

40

Sheriff Rickards inspected the two bonds that had been discovered in Creed's saddlebags, but he couldn't determine whether they were part of the loot stolen from the Liberty bank. He showed the 7:30s to Greenup and William Bird, and neither the cashier nor the clerk could definitely declare that the fifty-dollar notes had been among those taken from the vault that dark day. Discouraged, Rickards came within seconds of deciding to release Creed for a lack of evidence, but his suspicions were aroused all over again when William Bird identified Creed as having been in the bank only a few days before the robbery. "He was in the company of a young white woman and a young Negress," said Bird. And that was sufficient reason to hold Creed in jail, especially since Creed admitted being in the bank like Bird said but he refused to reveal the identities of the two women who had been with him on that occasion.

By now, Creed had figured out how the bonds had gotten into his saddlebags, but he continued to deny any knowledge of how they came to be in his possession. As much as he despised Jesse James and felt no loyalty to him whatsoever, he couldn't betray Alex James or Susan James or their mother and stepfather, four people who had befriended him and cared for him when he had been in dire need of their aid: Alex when the people of Locust Ridge had turned on him; Susan and the Samuels when he'd been sick with the catarrh and they had nursed him back to health. No, if it was only Jesse James that he would have to implicate, then he wouldn't hesitate to turn him over to the law. Since he couldn't do that without hurting Jesse's family, he'd just have to keep his mouth shut and hope for the best.

News that Creed had been captured and had been charged with

robbing the Liberty bank spread across the country as fast as the telegraph wires could carry it from one newspaper to the next. After all, the robbery had been sensational news, considering the incredible amount of money stolen and the fact that the crime had been committed in broad daylight. Such a thing was hardly heard of before now. Of course, some banks had been robbed during the war, but those incidents had been lost in the greater context of the strife between North and South. The Liberty bank had been raided during peacetime, and that alone made it all the more newsworthy for the nation's tabloids, giving them a very desirable boost in circulation. Now that somebody had been captured and charged with the robbery and a trial was pending, the newspapers could milk the story for several more issues.

Nashville Police Detective Ransome Cavitt read the story of Creed's capture in the Nashville Daily Dispatch. He found it amusing that the man U.S. Deputy Marshal James Kindred was pursuing had gotten that far away from Nashville in such a short time. The humor of the episode struck him as being so ironic that he wondered if Kindred would find it equally funny.

Cavitt took the newspaper down to the jail in the basement of the Davidson County courthouse where Kindred was serving a thirty-day sentence for assaulting a Nashville police officer, namely Cavitt. The jailer took him to Kindred's cell and let him inside to visit with the imprisoned lawman.

"What brings you down here?" asked Kindred. "Come to gloat again, you bastard?"

"It's talk like that that got you thrown in here in the first place; Marshal Kindred," said Cavitt. "You should learn to keep your mouth shut when you're in the presence of your betters, don't you think?"

"Is that what you came down here for?" groused Kindred. "To give me a lecture on manners?"

"No, actually I came down here to let you read the newspaper," said Cavitt. "You can read, can't you?"

"I went to school," said Kindred defensively.

"Then have a look at this," said Cavitt as he thrust the newspaper at the prisoner.

Kindred took the paper and read the article that Cavitt had circled in red pencil. With each word, his eyes grew bigger and bigger. He couldn't believe his good luck: Creed was in jail in Missouri.

Unfortunately, he was in jail in Tennessee. Creed might as well have been stuck on the moon.

"Cavitt, you've got to get me out of here," said Kindred excitedly. "I've got to get to this place in Missouri before anything happens to Creed."

"I wouldn't worry too much about Mr. Creed, Marshal," said Cavitt. "It says in there that he's being held for trial, and that won't happen for nearly a month yet. You'll have plenty of time after you're released from our jail to go visit him in his."

"I don't want to visit the sonofabitch, Cavitt," said Kindred. "I want to take him back to Texas to hang."

"Well, you won't have to worry about that either," said Cavitt, laughing. "The Missouri authorities will probably hang him for you."

"It isn't the law in Missouri that I'm worried about, Cavitt," said Kindred. "It's a lynch mob that concerns me most. Didn't you read the whole article? It said that the people of Clay County are very agitated about Creed being given a trial. Don't you know what that means, Cavitt?"

"It means that he might not make it to the courthouse on time," said Cavitt, still laughing.

"This is no joke, Cavitt. The story also said that he was only one of a dozen or so men. His friends might try to free him from jail, and that would be worse than a lynch mob, Cavitt. I've got to get out of here and get to Missouri and take custody of Creed before something happens to him."

"Well, you can do that soon enough, Marshal. You've only got ten days left on your sentence. I'm sure that nothing will happen to Creed in that time."

"Get me out of here, Cavitt!" screamed Kindred.

"Calm down, you little piece of shit!" snapped Cavitt. "You aren't going anywhere until your sentence is completed. Do you understand that, Marshal Kindred?"

"The least you could do is let me send a message, a telegram or something, to this sheriff in Missouri who's holding Creed," said Kindred, "so I can tell him that Creed is wanted on a Federal warrant and to hold him until I can get there to take custody of him. You could do that for me, couldn't you, Cavitt?"

Cavitt thought about Kindred's request, then said, "I'll see what I can do about that, but you'd better start showing a little more respect,

Marshal, if you want things to go your way. You hear now?"

"Sure, sure, I hear you. Now how about it?"

"Like I said, I'll see."

The jailer came and let Cavitt out of the cell as Kindred continued to plead with the detective to get him released or at least send the message.

"That little sonofabitch!" swore the jailer. "He's been carrying on like that ever since we locked him up three weeks ago. The day that he gets out of here can't come too soon to suit me."

"He's been a real troublesome prisoner, has he?" asked Cavitt as they walked toward the stairs.

"Troublesome is being polite, Mr. Cavitt," said the jailer. "He's been a real pain in my ass from the first moment you brought him down here. I've never had a prisoner like him. I've tried everything I can think of - short of cutting the little bastard's throat-to make him behave like the other prisoners, but nothing's worked. He just keeps on causing trouble. Day in and day out."

"I'm real sorry to hear that, Horace."

"You know, Mr. Cavitt, I wish there was something that you could do to get him out of here early."

"He's that bad, Horace?"

"He's that bad."

"I'll see what I can do."

Cavitt went straight upstairs to City Marshal James Brantley's office and showed him the article in the newspaper.

"So this Creed fellow is out of our jurisdiction now," said Brantley. "That's good."

"It would be better if we could get rid of Marshal Kindred as well, sir," said Cavitt.

"What do you mean, Ranse?"

Cavitt explained about Kindred's troublesome ways in the jail, then said, "We'd be doing our people down there a real favor if we could get him released and out of town real quick like, sir."

"I see what you mean. I'll see what I can do about it right away, Ranse."

Brantley didn't waste any time before calling on Colonel John Burch at the Nashville Union and American first Burch had read the article in the newspaper, and he was quite disturbed by it. Creed was his client, and he had received word from General Canby's headquarters in New Orleans that the trial of Cletus Slater would be reviewed by the provost marshal for the whole military district. If Slater, alias Creed, was involved in this bank robbery in Missouri and the military authorities heard of it and realized that Creed and Slater were one and the same man, then obtaining a favorable review by the provost marshal would be nearly impossible. Besides all that legal foofaraw, Burch liked Creed and sincerely hoped that the young Texan hadn't gotten himself mixed up in this bad business in Missouri.

"Your friend has certainly found himself a peck of trouble in Missouri, hasn't he, Colonel?" said Brantley.

"Yes, he has," said Burch. 'I'm wondering what we can do to help him."

"I can't see that there's anything that we can do, Colonel. He's in Missouri, and we're here."

"Yes, but we have friends over there," said Burch. "Maybe they can help him."

"Well, I guess that's up to you, sir," said Brantley. "As far as matters go here, that Marshal Kindred is making himself a real problem in our jail. Detective Cavitt tells me that Kindred wants out of jail, so he can go to Missouri and arrest Creed before the Missouri authorities hang him or his friends free him from jail." An idea struck Burch. He said, "Kindred wants out of jail to arrest Creed before the Missouri authorities hang him. That's not a bad idea, Jim. Can you get him released? Kindred, I mean. Can you get him released?"

"Why, of course, I can," said Brantley, "but why would you want him released? Do you want him to go to Missouri to arrest Creed?"

Burch smiled and said, "Yes."

41

Of course, the Nashville newspapers weren't the only tabloids in the country to carry the story about the Liberty bank robbery and Creed's subsequent arrest.

The Advocate in far-off Victoria, Texas, picked up the story from the Houston papers and circulated it in the surrounding counties, which included Creed's home county of Lavaca. It was a sensational story there because all of Clete Slater's friends and enemies now knew that he was using the name of Slate Creed.

Colonel Lucas Markham, the military commander for Lavaca County, delighted in the story, although he kept his joy to himself because he was married to Creed's sister Malinda. It would do him no good to let his wife see that he was happy that her brother was once again behind bars and would probably be convicted of yet another crime and eventually hung. He could have brought the story about Creed to the attention of the provost marshal in

New Orleans, but he figured that was unnecessary because U.S. Deputy Marshal James Kindred was on Creed's trail and would catch up to him now. Why muddle things?

For her part, Malinda was distressed that her brother was again behind bars and possibly facing a hangman's noose. She wished that she could do something to help him, but she realized that she could do no more for him than she could do for their mother and stepfather, Howard Loving, who lived near Weatherford, Texas. Like most Texans that winter, the Loving's were having their financial difficulties, and Mrs. Loving had written her daughter to ask for help. Malinda could offer her mother no more aid than she could offer her brother; she wrote both to tell them that her thoughts and prayers were with them. Nothing more, nothing less.

Texada Ballard and the hands at the Double Star Ranch read the story with great concern, too. As much as Jake Flewellyn and the boys wanted to write to their friend and tell him all that had happened on the ranch and in the county- since his departure the previous autumn, they were forbidden to do so by Texada. She had sworn them to secrecy about matters involving the ranch and her to everybody, not just Creed, because she feared that one of them might accidentally reveal something in a letter that would give Creed cause to forego his quest to clear his name and return to Lavaca County where his life would be forfeit. Therefore, Texada was the only one who wrote to him.

Farley Detchen read the story about Creed being in jail in Missouri, and it angered him. He had wanted the privilege of killing Creed for the murder of his brother Harlan. At least, he and his foster mother, Sophia Campbell, considered Harlan's death to be murder, but, Creed shot Harlan in retribution for the Detchen twins' cold-blooded murders of three of his best friends and his brother Dent. Farley didn't know how lucky he was that Creed had left Texas to prove his innocence. Had he stayed behind, Farley would most likely be moldering in a grave beside his brother now.

Besides the Texas papers, the Kentucky tabloids carried the story, and among their readers were four men who were most interested in reading about the Liberty bank robbery. After the raid on the bank, Oll and George Shepherd, Jim White, and Alex James hid out for a night and a day in the Sni Hills, then rode back to Logan County as fast they could, avoiding contact with people as much as possible and arriving at James's Uncle George Rite's farm on the same day that Creed was arrested in Platte City. They planned to lay low there until they were certain that it was safe for them to return to Missouri. That was all well and good until the newspaper carrying the story about Creed's arrest and incarceration in the Clay County jail was delivered to the Hite farm.

"It says here," said James who was reading the newspaper article to his friends, "that Creed refuses to identify the two women who were with him at the bank before it was robbed."

"Sounds to me like he knows how to keep his mouth shut," said Oll Shepherd. "Of course, he never struck me as the kind who would shit on a friend anyway."

"No, he's not that kind," said James. "But there's more to this than what it says here, Oll. Creed has to know that we were the ones who raided the Liberty bank, and he's not telling the law that we did it. He could, you know, just to save his own hide."

"Who's to say he still won't tell to save his own hide?" asked White. "What if it comes down to him hanging or telling the law it was us that raided the bank? Don't you think he'll spill his guts then to save his neck?"

"I don't think it'll come down to that," said James. "It says here that he had two fifty-dollar bonds on him, but the Birds can't swear that the bonds are part of the loot taken from the bank. The only thing they know for sure is that Creed and two young women were in the bank a few days before we raided it. Beyond that, they don't know anything. They don't have anything more than that to hold against Creed. The thing I'm wondering about is how he came to have. those two bonds."

"He probably had them all the time," suggested Oll.

"I don't think so," said James. "When he was traveling with us, he always used hard cash. He never had any folding money on him.

"You know," said George, "you're right. I can't recall him ever having any folding money."

"So, what are you thinking, Buck?" asked Oll.

"I'm thinking that brother of mine gave them to Creed," said James. "Either that or he hid them on him. Knowing Dingus like I do, I'd have to say he hid them on Creed. Besides, it says in here that Creed denies knowing anything about the bonds. Why would he say that unless he was trying to hide something?"

"Hide what?" asked Oll.

"Everything," said James. "After all he does know just about everything about the raid, doesn't he?"

Shepherd scratched his head and said, "So what are you getting at, Buck?"

"I'm saying that I don't think Creed deserves to rot in that jail for something we did," said James. He scanned the faces of his three companions, then said, "I think we ought to ride back to Missouri as fast as we can and get Creed out of that jail."

42

Dr. and Zerelda Samuel and Susan and Jesse James didn't read about Creed in any newspaper. They heard the story in the same manner in which they usually received news of events outside their immediate area: from Mr. McCray, the post rider, who came by their place with the mail on his weekly rounds.

As was the custom when the postman had more to deliver than the mail, Zerelda invited the weary rider into the house for a cup of hot coffee, a piece of carrot cake, and some juicy gossip. The family sat or stood around the kitchen table to listen to McCray relate the tale of Creed's arrest in Platte City for killing two Unionist ruffians in a shootout, how the sheriff over to Platte County found some of the money stolen from the Liberty bank on Creed, how Creed was brought down to Liberty so the Birds could identify the money as part of the stolen loot, and how William Bird had pointed a finger at Creed as one of the robbers.

"Now, the Birds couldn't say positively that the money was part of the money stolen from the bank," said McCray. "And William Bird didn't come right out and say that this Creed fellow was one of them that robbed the bank, but he did say that Creed was in the bank with a white girl and a young nigger woman just a few days before the bank was robbed. Creed don't deny young Bird's claim, but he won't tell who the women were that were with him. If you ask me, this Creed fellow is one of them that robbed the bank and killed poor Jolly Wymore, God rest his soul, and he ought to hang for what he did."

Jesse, Susan, and the Samuels listened politely, but none of them let on that they even knew Creed, let alone that he'd been a guest at their home for several days before and after the robbery of the Liberty bank, a fact that had eluded the postman when he came by their place twice during Creed's visit. As soon as McCray was finished with his story, they thanked him for the news, then waved farewell to him as he rode off to the next farm for another cup of coffee and maybe a piece of pie while he repeated the tale.

"Now we all know that Captain Creed had nothing to do with that robbery," said Zerelda as soon as the postman was gone. "He was sick in bed right here on the day it happened."

"That's right, Ma," said Susan, "but we told Dr. Allen that he was Jesse, remember?"

"That's right, we did," said Zerelda, exasperated.

"Ma, I know what you're thinking," said Jesse. "You're thinking that we told a lie to Dr. Allen that day, and now it's gone and caught up with us. Isn't that right?"

"That's right, son," said Zerelda. "Haven't I always told you young'uns that lying only leads to more trouble than you're already in?"

"Yes, Ma, you have told us that," said Jesse. "A hundred times, if you've told us once."

Zerelda glared at Jesse and said, "And now you see a perfect example of what I've been saying all these years. Our good friend is in serious trouble, and we're the only ones who can get him out of it, and tile only way we can do that is to tell the truth that he was here sick in bed on the day the bank was robbed. First thing tomorrow we're riding into Liberty--to tell the sheriff the truth."

Susan and Jesse exchanged looks, each knowing that their mother's proposal was out of the question. If they were to approach the sheriff with the truth, then Dr. Allen would have to be called in to verify their story. Of course, he would, but that wasn't the problem. They knew that Rickards would ask the inevitable question: Why did they want to pass off Creed as Jesse? They had convinced Zerelda and Dr. Samuel that it would be best if Dr. Allen thought Creed as Jesse because then he could tell folks that Jesse James, the former guerrilla, was still hurting from his war wound and therefore was no threat to anybody in the county. But would this excuse hold up with Rickards? Wouldn't he then ask: Why should the people of this county have anything to fear from Jesse James anyway? They worried that one question would lead to another and eventually Rickards would get around to asking about Frank James, and sooner or later, the sheriff would begin to suspect that the James boys were involved in the robbery of the Liberty bank. This would never do. Susan and Jesse had to discourage their mother from the course she had chosen to follow.

"Ma," said Susan, "that might not be such a good idea."

"The truth is always a good idea," said Zerelda flatly and firmly with finality.

"I know, Ma," said Susan, "but riding into Liberty and seeing the sheriff might not be a wise thing to do. What's the sheriff gonna say when we tell him that we wanted Dr. Allen to think Captain Creed was Jesse? Don't you think he's gonna start asking a whole bunch of questions about Jesse and Frank then?"

"So, what if he does?" queried Zerelda. "We'll just tell him the truth and be done with it. We don't have anything to be ashamed of. We haven't done anything wrong."

Susan glanced at Jesse, her eyes pleading for help.

"Ma," said Jesse, "we can't tell them Frank and the rest of them was here."

"And why not?" demanded Zerelda.

"Because we were all guerrillas," said Jesse, and the Unionists are blaming everything on us these days. Uncle John told me that things are so bad down to Harlem that if someone breaks wind in church all the Unionists hold their noses and point the finger at the Confederates."

Dr. Samuel laughed at Jesse's tale, but Zerelda saw nothing funny about it. "But you boys haven't done anything wrong," she argued. "You've got no reason to fear the law."

"It ain't the law, Ma," said Jesse. "It's the Unionists. Didn't you hear what Mr. McCray said about Creed killing a couple of Unionists over to Platte City? They're bound to be stirred up over it, and I just know that they're gonna do something about it. Those bastards don't know when to quit."

Zerelda knew Jesse had made his point, but she was adamant about helping Creed. "There must be something we can do to help him," she said.

"Yes, we have to help him," said Dr. Samuel.

"We've got to get him out of that jail," said Zerelda, suddenly looking all forlorn and discouraged. "Every time I think about that place, I see Mr. Frank in there like he was during the war."

"I've got an idea, Ma," said Jesse. "Why don't I get up a crowd from the boys around here who fought for the South during the war and see what we can do about getting Creed out of jail?"

"Are you thinking about breaking him out?" asked Susan.

"Something like that," said Jesse. "If we have to. I was thinking more like paying a call on the sheriff and asking him to let Creed go, and if he don't listen to reason, then we'll break Creed out of jail."

"I sure wish Mr. Frank was here to help," said Zerelda, fret lines turning the comers of her mouth downward. "I'd feel a whole lot better about it if he was."

"I don't need Frank's help in this," said Jesse, resentful that his mother would say such a thing. "If I have to have help, I'll ride down to Jackson County and find Arch Clement and get him to help me."

"That's a good idea, Jesse,' said Zerelda, perking up. "You get."

Jesse didn't say so, but getting Creed out of jail wasn't exactly what he had in mind.

43

After gaining an early release from the Davidson County Jail, U.S. Deputy Marshal James Kindred couldn't get to Liberty too soon to suit him. He was fortunate that Nashville was a major railroad center, which made it easy for him to book a trip to Kansas City, where he caught the stagecoach for the final leg of his journey. He arrived in Liberty late on the twenty-seventh of February and marched straight to the county jail in the basement of the Clay County Courthouse.

Creed was still there, wishing he wasn't. It was his birthday, his twenty-fourth, and he would have much preferred to spend the day at home in Texas with his sweetheart and friends. But that wasn't yet to be.

After presenting his credentials to Sheriff Rickards in his office on the first floor, Kindred was led downstairs; to the jail. As far as cells went, Creed's accommodations weren't all that bad. He had a bed with a real mattress, a clean sheet, a soft blanket, and a down pillow; a window with a southern exposure; a little table for writing and eating on; a caned straight-back chair; and a small Franklin stove for heat. Creed had slept in hotel rooms that had fewer comforts.

Creed felt a twinge of nostalgia when Kindred entered the cellblock. In a bizarre, somewhat morbid way, Creed was glad to see the marshal. Although Kindred was a reminder of sad times and tragic events, he was also a link to Texas, to home, to the people and places that Creed loved. Creed stood in front of the cell door and watched Kindred and the sheriff come down the corridor and stop directly in front of him.

"Is this your man, Marshal?" asked Sheriff Rickards, a thin man with a droopy black mustache and placid blue eyes.

Kindred stood there with his hands on his hips, looking like a boar hog that had just finished swallowing the last morsel of swill from the trough. His head bobbed up and down as he said, "That's him all right. Cletus Slater. Convicted thief and killer who's got a noose waiting for him down in Texas."

"How are you, Kindred?" asked Creed. He glanced at the badge on Kindred's chest. "I'd heard that some fool got you a deputy marshal's job, but I didn't believe it. I didn't think there was anybody stupid enough in the Federal government to hire a fox to watch the chickens. I guess I was wrong."

Kindred's Cheshire cat smile disappeared, replaced by a frown and a glare. "You'd better watch that smart-ass mouth of yours, Slater," he said. "You've got a long trip back to Texas with me, and I can make that trip easy or I can make it damn hard on you."

"Well, he's not going anywhere just yet," said Rickards.

"Of course he is," said Kindred, turning on the sheriff. "I'm taking him to Texas to hang."

"Not if we hang him first," said Rickards.

"You can't do that," said Kindred. "He's my prisoner, and I'm taking him back to Texas."

"No, sir," said Rickards. "He's my prisoner, and he's staying right here in Clay County until he's been tried for the robbery of the Clay County Savings Association's bank and the murder of young George Wymore. And if he's found guilty of those crimes, he'll either hang or he'll go to prison here in Missouri. You can have him after he's served his sentence or if he's found innocent of the robbery and murder. But not until one or the other happens, Marshal."

"That's where you're wrong, Sheriff," said Kindred. "I'm a Federal officer, and I have first rights to him. He's already been convicted of a crime against the United States Army, and he's been sentenced to hang for that crime. It's my duty to take him back to Texas so that sentence can be carried out."

"I have no doubt about what you're saying, Marshal," said Rickards, "but like I just told you, he's not going anywhere until we've tried him here in Clay County."

Kindred studied Rickards's stern jaw and realized that he was doing no better than a blue tick hound barking into one end of a hollow log after the coon had long since scooted out the other end.

"Well, we'll just see about that, Sheriff," he said. His head bobbed up and down again. "Yep. We'll just see about that." And with that, he brushed past Rickards and stormed out of the jail.

"Annoying little bastard, isn't he?" said Creed as he watched Kindred leave.

"You got that right," said Rickards. "Do you know him well?"

"Well enough, I suppose," said Creed. He briefed the sheriff about Kindred's sordid past. "So you see why I said what I did about him getting an appointment to a deputy marshal's job. He's more of an outlaw than those boys who robbed your bank."

A quizzical expression spread over Rickards's face as he noted a curiosity in Creed's statement. "You say that like you know who it was that robbed the bank," he said. "Why don't you make my job a little easier and tell me who they were?"

Creed smiled and said, "I don't know who it was that robbed your bank, Sheriff. I wasn't there when it happened."

Rickards smiled back and said, "That's right. I forgot." He scratched at the nape of his neck and added, "I must be getting old. I can't recall whether or not you told me who those women were that were with you on the day you were in the bank."

"I didn't say, Sheriff."

"That's right, you didn't." Rickards turned serious. "Why won't you tell me who they were, son? It'd sure make things go easier for you if you were to tell us what we want to know."

Creed sighed and took his turn at being serious. "I've thought about that, Sheriff. I've thought about it a lot, but the answer keeps coming out the same. I can't do it. I can't tell you anything. I wish I could because I don't hold with thieving and killing like the way that Wymore boy was killed. And you've treated me so decently, but I just can't do it. It's a matter of honor, Sheriff. If I tell you everything I know for a fact, I'd be betraying a trust and I'd be dishonoring some good deeds that were done for me. I'm sorry, Sheriff, but if I told you anything, I wouldn't be able to look at myself in a mirror again."

Rickards nodded his understanding and said, "These friends of yours must really be something special to command so much loyalty, Creed."

"Let's just say that I owe it to them, Sheriff."

"You don't owe them so much that you're willing to hang for it, do you?" asked Rickards.

"Something tells me that I won't hang, Sheriff," said Creed. He glanced at the stairway at the end of the hall, then looked back at the lawman. "Leastways, it tells me that I won't be hanging here in Missouri. Maybe that little bastard who just left here will get me hung in Texas, but I won't hang here." He smiled and added, "I'd stake my life on that, Sheriff."

44

In a cave in the Sni Hills of Jackson County, the hideout that Quantrill and his guerrilla band had used during the war, James Berry, the Lexington newspaper editor, was meeting with Arch Clement and several of the other outlaws who had taken part in the raid on the Liberty bank.

"I've received word from friends in high places concerning this fellow Slate Creed," said Berry. "They want him freed as soon as possible."

"Who are they, these friends of yours in high places?" asked Clement, suspicious of Berry. "And what's their concern with this fellow Creed?"

'Well, for your information, Captain Clement," said Berry, "they are two gentlemen who rank high in the Order."

"The Order?" queried Clement. "Do you mean the Order of American Knights?"

"Of course, I do," said Berry, slightly exasperated. "So who are these two men you're referring to?"

Berry knew that it was against the rules of the Order to reveal the names of other members, especially superiors; but he could think of no directive concerning a member's occupation. "One," he said, "is a former Kentucky congressman, and the other is a former colonel in the Confederate Army."

The former guerrilla leader shook his head slowly and said, "You ain't said one name to me that I know yet."

Berry sighed with greater exasperation as he fenced with the decision of whether to reveal the names of higher-ups. Realizing that Clement and his gang wouldn't listen to him and take action until he gave them some names, he said, "All right, since you insist. One is the Honorable George Washington Ewing of Kentucky, and the other is Colonel John Burch of Tennessee."

"Ewing?" queried Clement. "Is he any relation to that Ewing who fought for the Unionists around here during the war?"

"Distant cousins, I believe," said Berry, "but that doesn't mean anything. Lots of families were divided in their loyalties during the war."

"That's true enough," said Clement. "But who is this Colonel Burch? Where did he serve?"

"I believe Colonel Burch served on General Nathan Bedford Forrest's staff," said Berry, hoping the mention of such a notable Southern hero would impress the outlaws.

It did.

"All right," said Clement, nodding, "what do these friends of yours want us to do?"

Berry was incredulous. For the last fifteen minutes, he'd been telling Clement the purpose of his mission, and now the man asked him what the Order wanted him to do. Incredible! "They want you to free Creed," said the editor.

Before Clement could respond to that statement, the lookout announced, "Riders coming in!"

"How many?" asked Clement, drawing his sidearms as did the other men.

"Five," said the sentinel.

"Know any of them?" asked Clement.

"Looks like Dingus James is leading them," said the lookout.

Clement heaved a sigh and said, "Lucky for you it's only Dingus, Mr. Berry. If it had been the law, then you'd be dead right now. Dingus is one of us."

In the next minute, Jesse James, the Pence brothers, and the Wilkerson brothers rode into the cave. They dismounted and approached Clement and Berry.

"What brings you back here so soon, Dingus?" asked Clement, his face beaming with a friendliness that totally disguised the soul of the bloodthirsty maniac lying deep within him. "You got another raid you want us to go on?"

"Sort of," said Jesse. He glared at Berry and asked, "Who are you?"

"This is Mr. Berry, come over from Lexington," said Clement. "He's one of us."

"One of us?" queried Jesse. "I don't recollect seeing you before, Mr. Berry. Who'd you ride with during the war?"

"He worked for the Confederacy in other ways," said Clement. "Mr. Berry is the editor of the Lexington newspaper."

"That's right, young sir," said Berry, offering his hand in friendship. "I am the editor of The Caucasian, and I'm a member of the Order."

This was terminology that Jesse understood. "Is that so?" he inquired in a friendlier tone, while shaking Berry's hand. "Well' we are, too," he said as he indicated the Pence's and the Wilkerson's with a sweeping motion of his left arm. Then he introduced the five of them, finishing with, "We all rode for the South during the war."

"I've heard of you," said Berry. "Your brother is Frank James, right?"

Jesse looked at Clement as if to ask whether it was all right to admit to being Frank's brother. When he didn't see any negative reaction in Clements aspect, he looked back at Berry and said, "Yes, he's my brother. What of it?"

"That's good," said Berry, "because I've come out here on a matter of importance to the Order."

"You don't say," said Jesse. "And what might that be?"

"You know that fellow that's locked up in the Clay County jail?" queried Clement.

Instant concern painted Jesse's face. "What about him?" he asked nervously.

"Some friends of mine would like to see Creed set free," said Berry.

Jesse smiled and said, "You don't say." Then he burst out laughing. "Did you hear that, boys?" he asked the Pence's and Wilkerson's. "He wants Creed out of jail."

The two sets of brothers began laughing, too, but Clement, Berry, and the other outlaws didn't get the joke. Finally, Jesse stopped laughing long enough to explain. "I'm sorry, Arch, Mr. Berry," he said. "You see, we came down here to get you boys to help us break Creed out of jail."

Now it was Clements, Berry's, and the other outlaws' turn to laugh. "No fooling, Dingus?" queried Clement.

"No fooling, Arch," said Jesse.

"This is perfect," said Berry. "Now you'll have enough men to do the job right."

"Hold on now, Mr. Berry," said Jesse. "You ain't heard all of it yet."

"What do you mean, Dingus?" asked Clement.

"I mean after we get him out of jail," said Jesse, "I plan to kill him." He broke into laughter again, but nobody shared this bit of gallows humor with him.

"That's not what my friends want," said Berry, as if he were in charge of the situation.

Jesse turned serious instantly and said, "I don't give a shit what your friends want, Mr. Berry. Creed needs to be dead, and that's that."

"But why?" asked Clement.

"To keep him from talking," said Jesse simply. "He knows all about us, Arch, and what we did, and he's gonna tell the law sooner or later just to save his miserable hide from hanging. So, I figure we should get him out of jail and put a ball in his brain, so he can't ever tell anybody about us and what we did."

"What you did?" queried Berry. "What are you talking about, Mr. James?"

Jesse looked at Clement and asked, "Don't he know?"

Clement shook his head negatively.

Jesse turned back to Berry and said, "Well, if you don't know now, then you don't need to be told, Mr. Berry. Let's just say we did something that could get us all hung."

Berry squinted at Jesse, then it came to him that he was in the company of the men who had raided the Liberty bank. "Yes," he mumbled. "Yes, of course. I mean, no, I don't need to be told, do I? No, of course not."

"No, sir, you don't," said Jesse. He turned back to Clement.

"Now how about riding into Liberty with us and breaking Creed out of jail?"

"You don't have to break him out of jail," said Berry without thinking.

"Why not?" asked Jesse.

Realizing that he revealed information that he should have kept to himself but that it was now too late to reverse himself, Berry said,

"Because he won't be there for long."

"How do you know this?" asked Jesse, now growing suspicious of Berry.

"There's a U.S. marshal in Liberty right now," said Berry, "who will be taking Creed out of jail in order to take him back to Texas to be hung by the Army."

"Are you sure about this?" asked Jesse.

"It was all arranged before I heard about it," said Berry. "The idea was to let this marshal take Creed out of jail, then to let him get some distance away from Liberty before we move in and set Creed free."

"This marshal?" queried Jesse. "Is he one of us, too?"

"No, I don't think so," said Berry. "As far as I know, he's just a Federal doing his job. He doesn't know about the plan to free Creed."

Jesse turned away and thought about the strategy for a second. Then, as if he'd just received the Holy Spirit at a revival meeting, he said, "That's not a bad plan, Mr. Berry." He smiled and added, "Yep. That's a first-class plan, Mr. Berry. Don't you think so, Arch? All we have to do is follow this marshal and Creed for a ways, then ambush them on some lonesome piece of road and we'll be done with him and a Federal marshal all in one swoop. Easier than making apple pie, right?"

"But you aren't supposed to kill Creed," argued Berry. "My friends only want him set free."

"Mr. Berry, I've already told you that I don't give a shit about what your friends want," said Jesse. "I'm gonna kill Creed, and that's all there is to that." He drew his Remington and pointed it at the editor's nose. "Now have I made that perfectly clear to you, Mr. Berry?"

Berry could do ·nothing more than nod nervously.

45

Just as Marshal Jim Kindred had done, Alex James, the Shepherds, and Jim White took advantage of the railroad service - now that they could afford it - to reach their destination in Missouri. Unlike Kindred, however, their final stop wasn't Kansas City because they didn't need to go that far. They left the train at the new railroad town of Lee's Summit, the closest station to the Sni Hills, which was their ultimate goal. They arrived there early on the second day of March.

As the four men rode toward the cave that had been one of their hideouts during the war, they were surprised that nobody was guarding the approach. "I don't like this," said Oll Shepherd.

"It don't look right."

"I know what you mean," said James. He reined in his mount, and the others followed suit. "Maybe we'd best hold up right here and talk about this for a minute."

"Good idea, Buck," said White.

"Could be that the cave is deserted," said James, "and that's why nobody's standing guard. Also, could be that the law's in there waiting to ambush us. I'd like to find out which it is without being shot up."

"Me, too," said White.

"Let's dismount here," said James, "and go in on foot." "Good idea," said White.

Just as James suggested, they climbed down from their horses, tied them to nearby trees, drew their weapons, then split up into pairs - James and White as one and the Shepherds as the other - and proceeded to sneak up on the cave. With winter still on the land, they didn't have as much cover as they would have liked in the bright midday sun, but they made do, slipping from one tree to the next boulder until they were pressed against the rock facing on either side of the cave's entrance. No sound came from within. James motioned to the Shepherds that he would go into the cave first and that they should follow. They nodded their agreement to the plan, then watched him cock his revolver and burst into the hollow, staying low and close to the wall. In the next second, he was all the way inside, his eyes darting back and forth, scanning the area, and trying to adjust to the dimmer light of the cave.

Only one man sat by the campfire, staring vacantly at the flames, and only one horse was tied to the corral rail.

James recognized the cave's sole occupant, straightened up, and said, "Mr. Berry, what are you doing here?"

Not having heard James sneak up on him, Berry jumped sideways, startled by the newcomer whose face he didn't recall at first, but he did know the gun and the death it could cause in an instant.

"Don't shoot!" he cried out. "I'm a friend!" He crunched up into a fetal position, as if that would save him from a fatal bullet.

James was taken aback. His face pinched up with confusion as he tried to figure out why Berry had reacted so.

The Shepherds and White carne running in behind James, each holding his six-shooter at arm's length, ready to fire at the first target that presented itself.

"Hold on, boys," said James. "It's only Mr. Berry."

"Mr. Berry?" queried White.

"The newspaper editor from Lexington?" asked Oll Shepherd.

"Mr. James," said Berry, looking ghostly one second and excited the next as his view shifted from James to George Shepherd to White to Oll Shepherd. "Mr. Shepherd. It's good to see you boys." He scrambled to his feet and rushed over to them with his hand stretched out in greeting. "I'm really glad to see all of you."

"Are you here alone, Mr. Berry?" asked James, his eyes still scanning the cave for anybody or anything unusual.

"Yes, I am," said Berry. "I figured on spending the night and riding back to Lexington tomorrow. Now I'm glad I stayed."

The four men put their guns away.

"What are you doing here, Mr. Berry?" asked Oll Shepherd. "I came looking for you boys," said Berry.

"For us?" queried Oll.

"Well, not you four specifically," said Berry, "but men like you. You know, former guerrillas who are members of the Order."

"And nobody was here when you came?" asked James cautiously.

"Oh, yes, there were several men here," said Berry, "including Arch Clement. And your brother Jesse and four of his friends joined them soon after I arrived. If we don't catch up with them before they get across, then we'll catch up with them on the other side. How about it, boys? Do we give it a go or not?"

"I'm with you, Ruck," said White. "Me, too," said Oll.

"I'm in," said George.

"Thank you, Mr. Berry," said James. "Don't you worry about a thing now. We'll catch up to them and put a stop to their plan and see that Creed goes on his way, just like the Order wants him to. You can bet on it."

"I certainly hope so," said Berry. He had done his duty, although he didn't know why. But that wasn't a question that he should be asking himself anyway because the Order didn't make such allowances; anything less than blind obedience was unacceptable. A wave of relief swept over him as he watched the four men rush out of the cave. He followed them as far as the entrance, at which he saw them run down the gentle slope to their horses, mount up, and ride off at a gallop. Such bold and fearless warriors! he thought. Lord, how I wish I were one of their number!

"Dingus was here?" asked Oll.

"That's right," said Berry. "I believe Arch called him that, but he was introduced to me as Jesse James."

"We call him Dingus," said White.

"Well, where are they now?" asked James.

"They've gone up to Clay County to murder your friend Slate Creed," said Berry.

This wasn't exactly what James had expected to hear. "Gone up to Clay County to murder Creed?" he asked. "Are you sure of that, Mr. Berry?"

"As sure as I'm standing here this very moment," said the editor. "They rode out of here first thing this morning. They plan to ambush Creed and the marshal somewhere between Liberty and Harlem, assuming, of course, that's the route the marshal chooses to take."

"How do you know all this?" asked Oll.

The editor bit his lip nervously, then explained everything that he knew: that a marshal would be arriving any day now in Liberty - he might even be there already - to take Creed back to Texas to hang, that higher-ups in the Order had charged him with rounding up some men to free Creed from the marshal after they left Liberty, that he had come to this cave for that very purpose, and that Jesse James and Arch Clement had ridden out to carry out his plan, but that they were planning to murder Creed and the marshal.

"That sure sounds like Dingus," said Oll "He's still having a fit about Creed, ain't he?"

"We've got to stop them, Oll," said James. "Creed's our friend, and we owe it to him. I say we ride after Arch and Jesse and the boys and stop them from killing Creed."

"But how will you find them?" asked Berry.

"A bunch of men on horseback leave a real nice trail, Mr. Berry," said James. "We won't have any trouble finding them."

"But they're half a day ahead of you," said Berry. "You'll never catch them."

"They can't get there as fast as we can," said James. "That many men riding together will have to stay off the main roads to keep from raising suspicion about what they're up to. Besides that, I don't think they want to cross the Missouri at Kansas City, which means they'll have to cross down river somewhere, like Liberty Landing or Blue Mills. There's only four of us. Once we figure out which landing they're heading for, we can ride straight for it."

46

Kindred wasted little time looking for a federal judge. He found one in Kansas City the next day, and he was able to obtain a writ of habeas corpus that ordered Sheriff Rickards to bring Creed before the court in Kansas City and show cause for detaining him in the Clay County jail.

Rickards was reluctant to remove Creed from the jail, feeling that too many people in town wished him harm and if they were to see Creed in the open they might get the wrong idea and do something rash, like lynch him. To prevent such an incident from happening, Richards asked Elijah Esteb, the county's prosecuting attorney, to appear for the county in the federal court and brief the judge on the county's case against Creed. Esteb wasn't sure that he approved of disobeying the court's order to produce Creed in per- son, but he went along with the sheriff's plan because he figured it was the lesser of two evils. Besides, if the judge did order Creed's release, then Creed would become Kindred's responsibility, and if anything happened to Creed after that, then they could no longer be held accountable.

The judge listened politely to Esteb, then he said very succinctly, "You don't have a case against this man, Mr. Esteb. I hereby order you to release the prisoner into the custody of Marshal Kindred for the sole and specific purpose of returning him to Hallettsville, Texas, where he is to be turned over to the military commander for further disposition, which I believe he is to be hung for killing Federal soldiers in Mississippi last year after he was paroled." He banged his gavel, and that was that.

Triumphantly, Kindred returned to Liberty and served the court order on Sheriff Rickards. "Have him ready to ride first thing tomorrow morning," said Kindred. "I'll be here to get him at first light."

Rickards reluctantly accepted the paper. "All right, Marshal," he said, "he'll be ready when you get here."

Word spread quickly that Creed was being released into Kindred's custody, and within the hour, some men in Liberty were already talking about being robbed a second time and that they should do something to stop it. They had two choices as they saw the situation: they could either keep Creed locked up in their jail, meaning they would have to defy the federal court and stop Kindred from taking him into custody and let the local court try him for the Liberty bank robbery and the killing of George Wymore; or they could simply try Creed right then and there, find him guilty, then give him the maximum sentence for his crime.

Lynchings were nothing new in Clay County. Back in 1850, a Liberty man named McClintock and a slave woman were hung by a mob for trying to murder the slave's mistress. Sam Shackelford, Bill Shackelford, and Jack Callaway were strung up for killing two citizens of Smithville in 1854. Early during the following year, a slave named Peter was lynched by a mob in Liberty because he had murdered William Russell. And, of course, several men had been taken out of their homes during the war and had their necks stretched by Kansas Redlegs or Bushwhackers, or Missouri Militia. Putting a rope around Creed's neck would be easy enough to do, if not for the fact that several prominent citizens raised serious doubt regarding his guilt. Among those gathered in the Arthur House's saloon were Esteb and the other George Wymore, the proprietor of the livery stable on Mill Street.

Wymore said that he had seen Creed in town a few days before the robbery in the company of a young man whose name he didn't know or couldn't recollect but who said he was from up by Centerville. When Esteb asked him why he hadn't come forward with this information before, Wymore said simply that he didn't want any trouble.

"You can do better than that, George," said Esteb.

"All right, I will," said Wymore. "It's like this, most of those boys up that way around Centerville, I mean. Well, they were Bushwhackers who rode with Quantrill during the war. I figure they might have something to do with this bank robbing and the murder of my nephew, and if that's true, they're liable to bring us a whole peck of trouble if-we do something to this fellow Creed. That's why I say we'd be better off if we let the laws handle this the way they see fit to handle it."

The majority of the drinkers fell in step with Wymore, but a very vociferous minority comprised of men who had been staunch Unionists during the war disagreed and demanded that some sort of action should be taken before Kindred rode out of town with his prisoner in tow.

"I don't want nothing to do with any plan that will bring trouble down on us here in Liberty," said Wymore adamantly. "We had enough of that during the war."

Nobody argued with that point, but one of the Union men said that they had to take a stand on lawlessness sometime, somewhere. To that, Esteb suggested that those who were so fired up to take a stand could take it elsewhere, and he left them to plot Creed's demise. Unknowingly, he gave them the key to the solution to their problem.

General agreement had it that Creed was involved in some fashion or another with the outlaws who robbed the Clay County Savings Association's bank and killed young Jolly Wymore, and that because of his connection to them, he was as guilty of the two crimes as they were, and he should pay with his life for the dastardly deeds. It was further conceded that he should suffer his punishment at the hands of the citizens that he had helped to victimize. Only two questions remained to be answered: Where? and, When? Nobody argued with the proposal that justice had to be served outside Clay County, and that gave rise to another question: How far outside the county? Not too far. Maybe just across the Missouri River in Jackson County. But what if the marshal took Creed through Kansas City, which he was most likely to do? Then they could be waylaid on the other side of Kansas City. But what if the marshal decided to take Creed back to Texas by train? After all, he could catch the train in Kansas City, take it to St. Louis, then get on a riverboat for New Orleans where he could catch an ocean-going vessel for Texas.

That last started the scratching of heads in search of an answer until one man said, "We can follow the marshal and Creed to Kansas City and see if they go to the train depot. It's not likely that they'll get on a train right off, so we'll have time to ride out of town and find a spot where we can stop the train and take Creed off and hang him. If they don't go to the train depot when they get to Kansas City and they just ride on through, then we can waylay them south of the city and hang Creed then."

That made sense to everybody, and the plan was adopted by most of those who were still present. They drank up and adjourned for the night, promising to reassemble at Wymore's stables at dawn.

Of course, this idea of lynching Creed wasn't a well-kept secret. Sheriff Rickards heard about it that same evening, and he repeated it to Kindred in his hotel room at the Green House.

"Sheriff, I expect you to provide an escort for me and Creed," said Kindred.

"I don't think so, Marshal," said Rickards. "I'm not risking my neck for you, and I know that there isn't another man in this town who's willing to risk his neck to protect Creed. If you want my advice-"

"That's just it, Sheriff," interrupted Kindred. "I don't want your advice. If you won't help me, then I'll handle this business my way, and my way is this. If any of your local yokels interfere with me while I'm trying to do my duty, I'll bring the United States Army in here and deal with them. Is that understood, Sheriff?"

Rickards glared at Kindred and said, "Who do you think you're fooling with here, Marshal? Do you think I was born yesterday or something? You don't have that kind of power, and I know it. You can just try bluffing somebody else. You ain't bluffing me with that sort of bullshit. Now if you want to avoid any trouble with folks around here, then I suggest you either take Creed out of my jail right now and hit the road tonight or leave him here until we've had a chance to try him."

Kindred perused Rickards's face and came to the quick decision that the sheriff was offering him the best possible advice that he could give and that he would be wise to take him up on it. "How do I go about getting Creed out of here tonight?" he asked.

Rickards nodded and said, "Now you're catching on, Marshal."

47

Sheriff Rickards had Creed ready to leave his jail two hours before daylight on the morning of March 3, 1866, and Kindred showed up a few minutes later to take him into custody.

"If you want my advice, Marshal," said Rickards, "you'd be wise to get Creed across the Missouri River and out of my county as soon as possible. The closest ferry landing is just three and a half miles due south of here at Liberty Landing. You take him down there and wake up Jim Baxter. His house is the last one before you get to the landing. He'll take you across. There's only one road on the other side. It'll take you to Independence or Kansas City, depending on which fork you choose down the road a piece. That's up to you, of course. However, if I was you, I'd go to Independence and try to catch the morning eastbound train. If you don't get there too early, that is. Or too late. I wouldn't stay around there too long if I was too early. Waste too much time."

"Anyway, you can take the train all the way to St. Louis, if you want, or you can get off anywhere along the line and ride south on horseback. If it was my choice, I'd take the train as far south as Pleasant Hill. That will put you a good fifty miles away from here by noon. I doubt whether a lynch mob from here would bother to follow you that fat. From Pleasant Hill, you can go about your business without any trouble. The decision is yours, of course."

After tying Creed's wrists together, then securing them to the horn of Creed's saddle, Kindred left Liberty with his prisoner. He took the sheriff's advice and headed due south for Liberty Landing.

First light was just caressing the horizon when Kindred knocked on Jim Baxter's door, and it was dawn an hour later when the ferryman deposited the marshal and his prisoner on the south bank of the Missouri River. With the road visible now, Kindred and Creed were able to ride at a fair pace for Independence, arriving at the depot before seven o'clock. The train wasn't due from Kansas City until almost nine. That was too long to wait. They continued southward toward Lee's Summit, some fifteen miles distant from Independence.

Formerly known as Big Cedar, the town of Lee's Summit was platted by William B. Howard only five months earlier, and thus far, it consisted of but few buildings: the railroad depot, some houses, a store, a Baptist Church that was already in place at the time the town was laid out, and a hotel owned by Christopher Mounts, a descendant and namesake of the colonial Indian fighter who had saved hundreds of Maryland and Virginia colonists from being massacred through his foresight, bravery, and leadership. Howard named the town in honor of the late Dr. P. J. G. Lee, an early settler whose farm lay a half mile north of the town. The doctor's sons served the Confederacy during the war, and for this reason, he was taken from his home by a band of Unionist raiders and murdered near the place where the railroad depot now stood. Also, the land chosen for the town was the highest point in Prairie Township.

Before the war, Prairie Township was populated by peaceful, law-abiding citizens whose sympathies leaned toward the Union, but this was all changed when radical Abolitionist raiders from Kansas rode through the area under the guise of serving the Stars and Stripes, taking what they could carry or drive off and destroying what they couldn't. Their depredations only served to push dozens of Missourians into the ranks of the Confederacy, and from that first summer of the conflict until the present, lawlessness had reigned supreme in the vicinity. So much so that Lee's Summit had become a haven for men who were still considered to be living outside the law, although their only transgression had been to serve the South during the war.

Of course, Kindred and Creed were totally unaware of the town's circumstances that Saturday morning when the marshal chose to stop at the Mounts Hotel to have a meal and to rest the horses before moving on to Pleasant Hill that afternoon. He and Creed ate in relative silence and peace, but instead of leaving thereafter, Kindred let his full belly and tired body dictate to him. He rented a room and opted to catch up on the sleep that he had missed the night before.

"What about me?" asked Creed. "Where do I sleep?"

This was something Kindred hadn't considered. He stroked his chin, then said, "You sleep on the floor like a dog, Slater. Mr. Mounts, would you mind guarding him while I tie him up some more?" The hotelkeeper took Kindred's shotgun and held it on Creed, while the lawman used more rope to truss up Creed's feet, then tie the bindings around his ankles and wrists together. "That ought to hold you." He pushed Creed, and the Texan lost his balance and fell heavily to the floor. "Throw a blanket over him, would you, Mr. Mounts? It wouldn't do for him to come down with the catarrh and die on me before I can get him back to Texas to hang." He laughed morbidly, then took the shotgun from Mounts and stood it in a corner where it would be handy if he should need it later.

As he put a blanket over Creed, Mounts asked, "What did he do, Marshal?"

Kindred didn't hesitate to relate the tale of the raid on the Federal supply wagons down in Mississippi the year before. "And this sonofabitch led it," he concluded. "Now go on and let me sleep. And see that I'm not disturbed." He rolled over and covered himself with a blanket.

Mounts looked down at Creed with sympathetic eyes, then backed out of the room.

Kindred was asleep within seconds of the hotelkeeper's departure, but Creed had trouble drifting off. The ropes were so tight around his wrists and ankles that they hurt every time he moved, and he couldn't get into a comfortable position anyway. He thought about trying to escape, but he was too tired now. Maybe later, thought Creed, when we're on the road again. It's a long way to Texas, and with Kindred being on the stupid side, he's bound to give me a chance to get away sooner or later. Damn! I just hope it's sooner.

48

Twilight was settling over Missouri when Creed awakened to the voices of several men outside the hotel room. He opened his eyes to the dim light, and it took him a few seconds to realize where he was and the predicament that he was in. He was still bound hand and foot, and he hurt all over, worse than ever, from the tight bindings.

"What the hell is that?" groused Kindred as he came awake.

He sat up in bed to get his bearings.

Before the marshal had time to think, the door burst open and a half dozen hooded men poured into the room. "Who the hell are you?" demanded Kindred.

"Shut up, Marshal," said the first man, his voice muffled by the grain sack over his head, "and don't get in the way. We don't want you. We're after him." He pointed toward Creed on the floor.

"He's all tied up," said another intruder.

Creed was more alert now, and he thought that he recognized something familiar in the voices of the two men. He listened closer and decided that he should go along with them.

"What are you doing there?" demanded Kindred. He tried to stand but was pushed back onto the bed by the first man.

"I told you, Marshal," said the gent. "Just shut up and don't get in the way and you won't get hurt."

"Who are you?" demanded Kindred again.

"Get him up, boys," said the second man. He grabbed Creed's coat off the floor.

"Never you mind who we are," said the leader. "Just be grateful that we're only gonna hang him."

The other four men got Creed into a standing position.

"That man's my prisoner," said Kindred, "and I'm taking him back to Texas to hang."

"Well, we're gonna save you the trouble," said the leader. "You got him, boys?"

"Wait a minute," said the second, "His feet are tied." He knelt down and untied the rope around Creed's ankles. "There. He can walk now."

"All right, let's go," said the leader.

"You can't do this!" shouted Kindred, "He's my prisoner! You can't do this!"

"We're gonna do it, Marshal," said the leader, "and there's nothing you can do to stop us."

Kindred recalled setting his shotgun in the comer. He lunged for it, but before he could get a hand on it, the leader caught him in the gut with a well-aimed boot. Oof! The wind exploded from his lungs, leaving his best burning for air as he collapsed and writhed on the floor.

The leader picked up the shotgun, examined it, then took it with him as he left the room.

In less than a minute, Kindred regained his breath, then collected his senses. Those bastards took my prisoner, he told himself. I've got to stop them. He slipped into his boots, grabbed his coat off the hook on the back of the door, then raced after the mob that had taken Creed. He caught up with them in the street. Instead of the six that had invaded his room, they were now more than a dozen; fifteen to be exact. They had Creed sitting atop Nimbus, and they were just beginning to mount up.

"Hold on there!" shouted Kindred. "You can't do this!"

"We're doing it, Marshal," said the leader. "Now stand clear and let us get this over with." He kicked his horse and headed west out of town. The others followed suit, taking Creed with them.

Kindred was speechless as he watched them go. Frustrated but not deterred, he looked around him and discovered that he was the only man on the street. "Damn!" he swore aloud. "Where is everybody?" he shouted. "I need help here!" Nobody responded.

"Sonsabitches!" he swore again. "I'll bring the Army down on you! That's what I'll do! Sonsabitches! You'll pay for this! I swear it!"

Thinking that he had to save Creed from the mob, Kindred ran for the stable at the rear of the hotel, found his horse, threw the saddle on the mare, and cinched it up as quickly as he could. He climbed on, kicked the animal in the ribs, and rode off after the lynch mob as fast as the horse could run. He caught up with them a mile out of town.

"Hold up there!" he shouted at the nightriders as he bore down on them.

They had come to a creek bottom that had several large oaks and cottonwoods growing in it, any one of which had a strong limb that would be suitable for hanging a man. The leader held up his right hand as a signal for them to halt.

Kindred thought that they were obeying him, and this gave him undue confidence. He charged the leader, thinking that he would grab the horse's reins from the man's hand and bring the animal and its rider down on the ground. The dark caused him to miscalculate, and he crashed his mount into the leader's. Both riders were thrown clear, but the horses went down in a heap of legs thrashing crazily as they tried to right their bodies.

"Crazy bastard!" swore the leader as he regained his feet. He saw Kindred struggling to get up on his hands and knees, ran over to him, and kicked him solidly in the ribs. "Little bastard!" he swore again. "I ought to kill you for that."

The second man from the hotel room jumped down from his horse and stopped the leader from kicking Kindred again. "Let him be," he said. "We've got other business here."

"Just let me kick him once more," said the leader.

"No, let him be," said the second. He pulled his friend away from the writhing marshal.

Kindred was hurt bad. His side throbbed: Broken ribs, he thought. He could do nothing except lay on his side, holding his injured body, and watch.

The mob took Creed to a good-sized tree, where the second man threw a rope over a strong limb. Then he slipped a noose around the Texan's neck and fussed with it for a minute that seemed like an eternity to Kindred. When he was done with his handiwork, the leader slapped Nimbus on the rump, scaring the horse from under his master. Creed swung back and forth, his feet kicking violently at the air.

Damn! thought Kindred. The sonsabitches hung him. He dropped his head in defeat.

49

Two days later Kindred stormed into Sheriff Rickards's office in the Clay County Courthouse, looking like a bantam rooster who'd been in a cockfight and lost. "I'm holding you personally responsible, Rickards," he announced as bold as could be without even greeting the sheriff first.

Rickards was surprised by the sudden intrusion. He looked up from where he sat at his desk and asked in complete innocence, "Marshal Kindred, what are you doing back here?"

"You know perfectly well why I'm here," said Kindred, his tone filled with venom.

Rickards took exception to Kindred's tone, lowered his voice, and said, "If I already knew the answer to my own question, Marshal, I wouldn't have asked it."

"Don't try fooling with me, Rickards," said Kindred. "You know perfectly well what I'm doing back here. Your lynch mob hung Creed!"

Rickards jumped to his feet and said, "What the hell are you talking about?"

"You know what I'm talking about, Rickards," said Kindred.

"A bunch of your good citizens followed me the other day and took Creed and hung him."

"I don't know anything about it, Marshal," said the sheriff. "I figured you and Creed would be half way to Texas by now."

"Well, we're not," said Kindred. "I'm here, and Creed's in Hell, and your people put him there."

"When did this happen, Marshal?" asked Rickards.

"You know when it happened," said Kindred.

The sheriff had had about all he wanted to take from Kindred. He leaned heavily on his desk and said slowly, "No, sir, I do not know when it happened. If I did, I wouldn't be asking. Now you can either tell me about it, or you can get your puny little ass out of my office. The choice is yours."

Kindred stared at Rickards for a moment, and he finally came to the conclusion that the sheriff was telling him true - he didn't know anything about the lynching. Even so, Kindred wasn't about to give in so easy. "All right, Sheriff," he said, "I'll tell you about it." He proceeded to relate the events of the past Saturday from the moment that he left Liberty until he witnessed Creed's hanging. "Then they put me on my horse and led me back to the hotel in Lee's Summit. The innkeeper got me a doctor, and he bandaged my ribs for me. He told me not to ride, but I rode up to Independence and spent Sunday night there. Now I'm here, and you're telling me that you don't know anything about Slater being lynched."

"That's right, Marshal," said Rickards. "That's exactly what I'm telling you. I'm also gonna tell you that I don't think it was any of our folks from around here that lynched Creed. Hell, nobody even knew he was gone until Saturday night."

"How do you know that?" asked Kindred.

"George Wymore came by to warn me that a bunch of Unionist boys were getting tanked up over at the Arthur House," said Rickards, "and they were planning to come take Creed out of jail. I went over and told them that they were wasting their breaths because Creed was long gone with you. Hell, I figured you were a hundred miles away from here by then. What were you doing in Lee's Summit that late? That's only a good half day's ride from here."

"I was tired and needed some rest," said Kindred lamely.

"I see," said Rickards. "So you stopped over in Lee's Summit, and a lynch mob took Creed out and hung him."

"That's about the size of it, Sheriff. Rickards nodded, then asked, "What did you do with Creed's body and his belongings?"

"The lynch mob took his horse and his trappings, I guess," said Kindred.

"All right," said Rickards. "But what about his body? What did you do about that?"

"What did I do with it?" queried Kindred. "I didn't do anything with it."

"You don't mean to tell me that you left him hanging in that tree, do you?"

"I told you that the lynch mob took me back to Lee's Summit," said Kindred. "I told the innkeeper what happened, just like I told you. I supposed that he sent somebody out to bring Creed's body in."

"You suppose, but you didn't bother to ask him if he'd done that, did you?"

"Well, no, I didn't," said Kindred. "But what difference does it make if I did or didn't?"

"Not much I suppose," said Rickards. "But seeing that his body was taken care of would have been the decent thing to do. Creed got a letter from his sister the other day while you were getting your writ to have him released to you. I was just thinking that it would only be right to let her know that he's dead and maybe ask what she wants done with the body."

"I don't care anything about that business," said Kindred. "All I'm interested in is finding the bunch that hung Slater, and when I find out who did it, I'll arrest the whole lot of them and see that they get what they've got coming to them."

"Well, you can start looking down in Jackson County," said Rickards. "There's all sorts of bad men down there who hang folks for sport."

"Is that so?"

"Yes, that's so," said Rickards, glaring at Kindred. "But that's your problem. Right now, I think I'll see what I can do about getting Creed a decent burial, and since he was your prisoner, I think you ought to pay for it."

"That's a laugh, Sheriff," said Kindred.

"Is it? Well, maybe you'd better come along with me and see that I don't spend too much money on his funeral."

Kindred gave that some thought and said, "All right, I will." The two lawmen rented a wagon from George Wymore, then headed south to Lee's Summit, arriving in the little community late that day. They went to the Mounts Hotel to see about a room for the night because it would be dark by the time they returned from the grove where Creed was hung.

"Afternoon, Mr. Mounts," said Kindred as he stepped up to the desk. "This is Sheriff Rickards from Clay County. We'd like rooms for the night."

"Yes, sir, Marshal Kindred," said Mounts. He pushed the registry book toward them and asked, "Would you gents mind signing your names in the book for me?" While Rickards signed his name, the hotelkeeper asked, "How are you feeling today, Marshal? Your ribs aren't giving you too much trouble, I hope."

"I'm feeling better, Mr. Mounts," said Kindred, as he took his turn signing in "Thank you for asking."

"Mr. Mounts, I take it you know what happened here the other night," said Rickards.

"If you mean the lynching," said Mounts, "sure, I know about it. Why?"

"I was just wondering if anyone went out and cut down Creed's body?" asked the sheriff.

"I don't know that anybody did that, Sheriff," said Mounts. "As far as I know, he's still hanging out there."

Rickards nodded grimly, then said, "Well, we'll just take a ride out there and have a look. Could you have some supper ready for us when we return?"

"Sure will, Sheriff," said Mounts.

The lawmen drove the wagon out to the creek bottom where Creed was hung. Rickards let the horses drink from the stream, while Kindred climbed down and started looking for the tree that had been Creed's gallows. Certain that he'd found it, he called out, "Here it is! This is the one!"

Rickards tied the reins around the brake handle, then jumped down and joined Kindred beneath a giant cottonwood. "Are you sure?" he asked.

"This is the one all right," said Kindred. He pointed to a dusty area beside the road. "I was laying on the ground over there when they strung him up."

"Well, somebody cut him down," said Rickards, He scanned the area, saying, "I wonder if they gave him a decent burial."

"He didn't deserve a decent burial," said Kindred.

"I beg to differ, Marshal," said Rickards.

Then he saw a grave marker: a pile of rocks with a piece of paper sticking out between two stones. He went to it, lifted the top stone, and removed the paper. He read it aloud:

HERE LIES CREED

OUTLAW
HUNG MARCH 3, 1866

"I guess somebody did have the decency to bury him," said Rickards. He stared down at the grave marker for a moment. "I can't help but think that he didn't deserve this kind of an end. He seemed to be a more honorable man than the kind that would rob a bank and shoot down an innocent boy. No, sir. I don't think he deserved this."

"Well, I do," said Kindred. "I only wish I could have gotten him back to Texas to hang instead of watching him get hung here by a lynch mob."

Rickards glared at Kindred and said, "Dead is dead, Marshal. It doesn't make any difference now where he died. Creed is dead, and that's that."

"Yes, I suppose it is," said Kindred, although he couldn't help feeling that he'd been robbed, violated, deprived of the pleasure of seeing Creed, the man who had wanted to kill him so badly just a few short months earlier, hang in Hallettsville in front of all his friends, all those righteous bastards who looked down their noses at him, U.S. Deputy Marshal James Kindred. Being deprived of that satisfaction depressed him and made him hate Creed all the more because even in death Creed had come out the victor.

"Sonofabitch!" he swore aloud, then he kicked the pile of rocks repeatedly until the pain in his broken foot became as great as that in his black soul.

50

Colonel John Burch sat down at his office desk and picked up his mail for the day. Among the few envelopes was a copy of *The Caucasian*, James Berry's newspaper in Lexington, Missouri. He removed the brown paper wrapper, unrolled the sheet, and turned the first page to find the letter he expected to be there. He took the missive and read it with great expectation:

Dear Sir:

You will be heartened to learn that the mission which you charged me with has been completed successfully.

Captain Creed is now free to be about his business without interference, but let me say that it was no mean accomplishment as the following will attest.

As you requested, I contacted certain parties to obtain their services for the Order, but these men were reluctant to consider my proposition. In fact, they were opposed to freeing Captain Creed and allowing him to go his own way. One of them, a young hothead named Jesse James, actually wished to assassinate the captain, and he would have done so if not for his brother, Frank James, and three others whose names you may already know.

Jesse James led a group of men who were of a like ilk. They left the place where we met and went off with the sole purpose of intercepting Captain Creed and the marshal who had the captain in custody. At that point, they intended to murder the captain and the marshal.

I feared failure at this time, but that thought was quickly dispelled when Frank James and three others met with me and took it upon themselves to save Captain Creed. I have enclosed Frank James's detailed account of what transpired after he and his friends left me until the then they returned to inform me of their success.

Since there is no need for me to comment further, I will close here. If I can perform any further service for you or the Order, please do not hesitate to contact me.

Yours sincerely,
James Berry

Burch read Frank James's letter to Berry:

Dear Sir,

This letter is written to inform you that we were successful in preventing the assassination of Captain Creed and the marshal.

After leaving you at the cave, we caught up with my brother Jesse and three other men as they were waiting to cross the Missouri River to Harlem Friday evening.

We tried to convince them to leave Captain Creed and the marshal alone, but they were bound and determined to see them both dead. So were the other men that you met with that day in the cave. My three friends and I discussed the matter between us, and we made a plan to save Captain Creed's life.

We crossed the river with Jesse that evening. The next morning Arch Clement and the rest of the men joined us with the news that the marshal had taken Captain Creed from the Liberty jail during the night and was right then riding south through Jackson County. We wasted no time in crossing the river again and riding toward the road that we thought the marshal would be taking. We caught up with them at Lee's Summit where they were staying at the hotel. Jesse and Arch were all for going into the hotel and killing both of them as they slept, but we opposed them. I said we would be asking for real trouble from the Federals if we killed a marshal. This was something that they understood. I then said that we should cover our faces, so nobody would recognize us, and they agreed to this. Then I said we should hang Captain Creed ·so it would look like a lynch mob from Liberty had done the deed. They agreed to do this, too.

We stole grain sacks from the livery stable in back of the hotel, made holes in them for our eyes, then entered the hotel and took Captain Creed from the marshal. It was our idea that we would hang him by a rope that we would put around his chest but make it look like we were hanging him by his neck. We wanted to do this so as to fool Jesse and Arch and the others into thinking that we were really hanging him, and they would not shoot him then. We took Captain Creed to a grove about a mile away from town, and we were just *beginning to fix the ropes on Captain Creed when the marshal rode up and knocked Jesse from his horse. It was all that I could do to stop Jesse from killing the marshal, and while I was holding him off the marshal, my friends fixed the rope on Captain Creed. I put the noose around his neck, and while I was doing that, I whispered to him to pretend to be hung. He must have seen a few hangings before because he knew exactly how to act once Jesse chased his horse from under him.*

I convinced Jesse and Arch to take the marshal back to town, while we buried Captain Creed. We pleaded that it was our duty to a friend. They agreed to this. Jesse wanted to take Captain Creed's horse, but I wouldn't allow this, saying that he had taken his life, so he had no right to take his horse, too.

As soon as they rode away, we cut Captain Creed down from the tree. We dug a shallow grave, filled it with brush, shoveled the dirt into the hole again, and stacked some stones on it as a marker. Then I wrote an epitaph on a page from a book that I had, and I put it between two rocks on the grave.

Captain Creed thanked us for saving his life, then we pointed him west and watched him ride away safely.

We rejoined Jesse and Arch at the cave, and we all went our separate ways again. As far as Jesse, Arch, and the others are concerned, Captain Creed is dead and buried in that creek bottom west of Lee's Summit. From what they told me, the marshal thinks the same thing.

Now our friend is free to go about his business, and he will not have to worry about Jesse or Arch or the marshal coming after him. That is what we all wanted in the first place, is it not?

If there is anything that I can do for you in the future, please call on me and I will do whatever is within my power to accommodate you.

Your friend,
Frank James

Burch let the letter fall gently to the desktop as he considered its message. Captain Creed is free again, he thought. Good for him!

ABOUT THE AUTHOR

Larry Names is a prolific author of both fiction and non-fiction books. He is a recognized authority on the Chicago Cubs, Chicago White Sox, and Green Bay Packers. Names has had 43 titles published to date, 26 of them novels, and the remainder non-fiction all dealing with sports teams or sports figures. He resides in central Wisconsin with his wife Peg on a family farm that has been in his wife's family since 1854. They have two children: Torry and Tegan; four children from his first marriage: Sigrid, Paul, Kristin, and Sonje plus a football team of grandchildren; cats: Teti and Cleo; and are caretakers to their daughter and son-in-law's horses: an escape-artist horse Lucky Moondancer, Amerrah, Dazzle, Windy and Mae. The author was born in Mishawaka, Indiana in the shadow of the Golden Dome, the University of Notre Dame. He is an avid researcher and traveler. Besides being a passionate history buff, he is also an informed and enthusiastic sports fan and memorabilia collector.

Names researches his novels and non-fiction extensively. As he puts it, "I can't write about a place I haven't seen or touched." He and his family have averaged two months of travel a year since he took up writing full-time in 1976; often logging 30,000 miles annually. The settings for his books range from Mexico to New York to California and almost every place in between.

For more information about Larry Names and his books, go to www.larrynames.com

"Like" Larry Names on his Facebook Fan page at: https://www.facebook.com/LarryNames

§§§

AFTERWORD

If you've enjoyed this book you might like to leave a review on Amazon. Reviews help authors like me and also help readers like you find books they'll like. If you live in the **US: REVIEW ON AMAZON US.**

265

LARRY NAMES BOOK LIST

NON-FICTION
LAMBEAU YEARS, THE, PART ONE, THE HISTORY OF THE GREEN BAY PACKERS, VOL. 1
LAMBEAU YEARS, THE, PART TWO, THE HISTORY OF THE GREEN BAY PACKERS, VOL. 2
LAMBEAU YEARS THE, PART THREE, THE HISTORY OF THE GREEN BAY PACKERS, VOL. 3
SHAMEFUL YEARS, THE, THE HISTORY OF THE GREEN BAY PACKERS, VOL. 4
LOMBARDI'S DESTINY, PART ONE, THE HISTORY OF THE GREEN BAY PACKERS, VOL. 5
BURY MY HEART AT WRIGLEY FIELD: THE HISTORY OF THE CHICAGO CUBS
 -WHEN THE CUBS WERE THE WHITE STOCKINGS, PART ONE
GREEN BAY PACKERS FACTS & TRIVIA, 1ST EDITION
GREEN BAY PACKERS FACTS & TRIVIA, 2ND EDITION
GREEN BAY PACKERS FACTS & TRIVIA, 3RD EDITION
GREEN BAY PACKERS FACTS & TRIVIA, 4TH EDITION
CHICAGO WHITE SOX FACTS & TRIVIA
OUT AT HOME BY MILT PAPPAS, WAYNE MAUSSER AND LARRY NAMES
HOME PLATE BY STEVE TROUT, DAVE CAMPBELL, AND LARRY NAMES
DEAR PETE: THE LIFE OF PETE ROSE
LEAP OF FAITH STEVE ROSE AND LARRY NAMES

FICTION
SHAMAN'S SECRET, THE
LEGEND OF EAGLE CLAW, THE
BOSE
BOOMTOWN
COWBOY CONSPIRACY
PROSPECTING FOR MURDER
TWICE DEAD
THE OSWALD REFLECTION
IRONCLADS: MAN-OF-WAR
IRONCLADS: TIDES-OF-WAR
TEGAN O'MALLEY – THE TRAVELER IN TIME
TEGAN O'MALLEY – STOWAWAY ON TITANIC
A TWO REEL MURDER – STARRING MACK SENNETT & MABEL NORMAND – A MAISY
MALONE MYSTERY
With others
HUNTER'S ORANGE
PK FACTOR, THE
As Bryce Harte/Larry Names
CREED #1: CREED/A TEXAS CREED
CREED #2: WANTED/TEXAS PAYBACK
CREED #3: POWDERKEG/TEXAS POWDERKEG
CREED #4: CREED'S WAR/KENTUCKY PRIDE
CREED #5: MISSOURI GUNS
CREED #6: TEXAN'S HONOR
CREED #7: BETRAYED/TEXAS FREEDOM
CREED #8: COLORADO PREY
CREED #9: CHEYENNE JUSTICE
CREED #10: ARKANSAS RAIDERS
CREED #11: BOSTON MOUNTAIN RENEGADES

AUDIOBOOKS
CREED #1: SLATER CREED, THE
CREED #2: TEXAS PAYBACK
CREED #3: POWDERKEG
CREED #4: KENTUCKY PRIDE
CREED #5: MISSOURI GUNS

CREED #6: TEXAN'S HONOR
CREED #7: TEXAS FREEDOM
CREED #8: COLORADO PREY
CREED #9: CHEYENNE JUSTICE
CREED #10: ARKANSAS RAIDERS
CREED #11: BOSTON MOUNTAIN RENEGADES
IRONCLADS: THE TIDES OF WAR
A TWO REEL MURDER – STARRING MACK SENNETT & MABEL NORMAND – A MAISY
MALONE MYSTERY
OSWALD REFLECTION, THE
PROSPECTING FOR MURDER
SHAMAN'S SECRET, THE
BOSE
BOOMTOWN

KINDLE EDITIONS
THE OSWALD REFLECTION
BURY MY HEART AT WRIGLEY FIELD: THE HISTORY OF THE CHICAGO CUBS
 -WHEN THE CUBS WERE THE WHITE STOCKINGS, PART ONE
PROSPECTING FOR MURDER
A TWO REEL MURDER–STARRING MACK SENNETT & MABEL NORMAND – A MAISY
MALONE MYSTERY
TEGAN O'MALLEY – THE TRAVELER IN TIME
TEGAN O'MALLEY – STOWAWAY ON TITANIC
IRONCLADS: TIDES OF WAR
CREED #1: A TEXAS CREED
CREED #2: TEXAS PAYBACK
CREED #3: TEXAS POWDERKEG
CREED #4: KENTUCKY PRIDE
CREED #5: MISSOURI GUNS
CREED #6: TEXAN'S HONOR
CREED #7: TEXAS FREEDOM
CREED #8: COLORADO PREY
CREED #9: CHEYENNE JUSTICE
CREED #10: ARKANSAS RAIDERS
CREED #11: BOSTON MOUNTAIN RENEGADES
LAMBEAU YEARS, THE, PART ONE, THE HISTORY OF THE GREEN BAY PACKERS, VOL. 1
LAMBEAU YEARS, THE, PART TWO, THE HISTORY OF THE GREEN BAY PACKERS, VOL. 2
LAMBEAU YEARS THE, PART THREE, THE HISTORY OF THE GREEN BAY PACKERS, VOL. 3
SHAMEFUL YEARS. THE, THE HISTORY OF THE GREEN BAY PACKERS, VOL. 4
LOMBARDI'S DESTINY, PART ONE, THE HISTORY OF THE GREEN BAY PACKERS, VOL. 5
COMING SOON!
LOMBARDI'S DESTINY, PART TWO, THE HISTORY OF THE GREEN BAY PACKERS, VOL. 6

www.ingramcontent.com/pod-product-compliance
Lightning Source LLC
Chambersburg PA
CBHW071127170626
46809CB00002B/521